DIANA GABALDON

Lord John and the Brotherhood of the Blade

arrow books

Published by Arrow Books in 2008

1 3 5 7 9 10 8 6 4 2

First published in Great Britain in 2007

First published in the United Kingdom in 2003 by Century

Arrow Books
Random House, 20 Vauxhall Bridge Road,
London, SW1V 2SA

Addresses for companies within The Random House Group Limited can
be found at: www.randomhouse.co.uk/offices.htm

The Random House Group Limited Reg. No. 954009

www.randomhouse.co.uk

A CIP catalogue record for this book
is available from the British Library

ISBN 9780099463337

The Random House Group Limited supports The Forest Stewardship
Council (FSC), the leading international forest certification organisation.
All our titles that are printed on Greenpeace approved FSC certified
paper carry the FSC logo. Our paper procurement policy can be
found at: www.rbooks.co.uk/environment

Mixed Sources
Product group from well-managed
forests and other controlled sources
www.fsc.org Cert no. TF-COC-2139
© 1996 Forest Stewardship Council

Typeset by SX Composing DTP, Rayleigh, Essex
Printed and bound in Great Britain by
CPI Cox & Wyman, Reading, RG1 8EX

This book is for Barbara Schnell,
my dear friend and German voice

Acknowledgments

The author would like to thank all the kind people who have given me information and help in the course of this novel, particularly –

. . . Mr. Richard Jacobs, Krefeld local historian, and his wife Monika, who walked the battlefield at Krefeld ('Crefeld' is the older, eighteenth-century spelling) and the *Landwehr* with me, explaining the local geography.

. . . the staff of the small museum at Hückelsmay – where cannonballs from the battle of Crefeld are still embedded in the walls of the house – for their kind reception and useful information.

. . . Barbara Schnell and her family, without whom I would probably never have heard of Crefeld.

. . . Mr. Howarth Penney for his kind interest, and his most useful gift of *Titles and Forms of Address* (published by A&C Black, London), which was of great help in negotiating the perilous straits of British aristocratic nomenclature. Any error in such matters is either the author's mistake – or the author's exercise of fictional license. While we do strive for the greatest degree of historical accuracy possible, we are not above making things up now and then. (That is not, by the way, a Royal 'we'; I just mean me and the people who live inside my head.) A Duke, however, *is* addressed as 'Your Grace,' and a Duke's younger son(s) addressed as 'Lord ___ .'

... Mr. Horace Walpole, that inveterate correspondent whose witty and detailed letters provided me with a vivid window into eighteenth-century society.

... Project Gutenberg, for providing me with excellent access to the complete correspondence of Mr. Walpole.

... Gus the dachshund, and Otis Stout the pug (aka 'Hercules'), who generously allowed the use of their personae. (Yes, I do know that dachshunds were not an official breed in the eighteenth century, but I'm sure that some inventive German dog-fancier had the idea prior to their establishment with the AKC. Badgers have been around for a long time.)

... Christine Reynolds, Assistant Keeper of the Muniments of the Parish Church of St. Margaret's, for extremely useful information regarding the history and structures of the church, including a very useful organ loft under which to give birth, and Catherine MacGregor for suggesting St. Margaret's and for finding Ms. Reynolds.

... Patricia Fuller, Paulette Langguth, Pamela Patchet, pamelalass, and doubtless several other people *not* beginning with 'P,' for information regarding eighteenth-century public exhibitions of art, and the history of specific artists and paintings.

... Philip Larkin, whose remarkably revealing

portrait of the first Duke of Buckingham (presently displayed in the Royal Portrait Gallery in London) provided one of the first seeds of inspiration for this book. (And neither I nor Mr. Larkin are maligning the first Duke of Buckingham, either.)

. . . Laura Watkins, late of the Stanford Polo Club, for expert opinion as to the mechanics of a horse jumping ditches.

. . . 'oorjanie' of the Ladies of Lallybroch for graciously allowing the star employee of an up-and-coming brothel to share her name.

. . . Karen Watson, our London correspondent, of Her Majesty's Customs and Excise, for her generous sleuthing through the history and byways of her beloved city, to lend a reasonable verisimilitude to Lord John's geographical excursions.

. . . Laura Bailey, for insight and advice regarding eighteenth-century clothing and custom.

. . . David Niven, for his very entertaining and honest autobiographies, *The Moon's a Balloon*, and *Bring on the Empty Horses*, which included a useful look at the social workings of a British regiment (as well as helpful information regarding how to survive a long formal dinner). Also, George MacDonald Fraser, for his *McAuslan in the Rough*, a collection of stories about life in a WWII Highland Regiment.

. . . Isaac Trion, whose hand-drawn watercolor map of the battle of Crefeld, drawn in 1758, adorns my wall, and whose painstaking details adorn the story.

. . . The assorted gentlemen (and ladies) who were

kind enough to read and comment on sex scenes. (As a matter of public interest, a poll regarding one such scene came back with the following results: 'Positive: I want to know more – 82%; Negative: This makes me uncomfortable – 4%; Slightly shocked, but not put off – 10%; Neutral – 4%.)

SECTION I

As Kinsmen Met

Chapter 1

🍂

All in the Family

London, January 1758
The Society for Appreciation of
the English Beefsteak, A Gentlemen's Club

To the best of Lord John Grey's knowledge, step-mothers as depicted in fiction tended to be venal, evil, cunning, homicidal, and occasionally cannibalistic. Stepfathers, by contrast, seemed negligible, if not completely innocuous.

'Squire Allworthy, do you think?' he said to his brother. 'Or Claudius?'

Hal stood restlessly twirling the club's terrestrial globe, looking elegant, urbane, and thoroughly indigestible. He left off performing this activity, and gave Grey a look of incomprehension.

'What?'

'Stepfathers,' Grey explained. 'There seem remarkably few of them among the pages of novels, by contrast to the maternal variety. I merely wondered where Mother's new acquisition might fall, along the spectrum of character.'

Hal's nostrils flared. His own reading tended to be confined to Tacitus and the more detailed Greek and Roman histories of military endeavor.

The practice of reading novels he regarded as a form of moral weakness; forgivable, and in fact, quite understandable in their mother, who was, after all, a woman. That his younger brother should share in this vice was somewhat less acceptable.

However, he merely said, 'Claudius? From *Hamlet*? Surely not, John, unless you happen to know something about Mother that I do not.'

Grey was reasonably sure that he knew a number of things about their mother that Hal did not, but this was neither the time nor place to mention them.

'Can you think of any other examples? Notable stepfathers of history, perhaps?'

Hal pursed his lips, frowning a bit in thought. Absently, he touched the watch pocket at his waist.

Grey touched his own watch pocket, where the gold and crystal of his chiming timepiece – the twin of Hal's – made a reassuring weight.

'He's not late yet.'

Hal gave him a sideways look, not a smile – Hal was not in a mood that would permit such an expression – but tinged with humor, nonetheless.

'He is at least a soldier.'

In Grey's experience, membership in the brotherhood of the blade did not necessarily impute punctuality – their friend Harry Quarry was a colonel and habitually late – but he nodded equably. Hal was sufficiently on edge already. Grey didn't want to start a foolish argument that might color the imminent meeting with their mother's intended third husband.

'It could be worse, I suppose,' Hal said, returning to his moody examination of the globe. 'At least he's not a bloody merchant. Or a tradesman.' His voice dripped loathing at the thought.

In fact, General Sir George Stanley was a knight, granted that distinction by reason of service of arms, rather than birth. His family had dealt in trade, though in the reasonably respectable venues of banking and shipping. Benedicta Grey, however, was a duchess. Or had been.

So far reasonably calm in the face of his mother's impending nuptials, Grey felt a sudden drop of the stomach, a visceral reaction to the realization that his mother would no longer be a Grey, but would become Lady Stanley – someone quite foreign. This was, of course, ridiculous. At the same time, he found himself suddenly in greater sympathy with Hal.

The watch in his pocket began to chime noon. Hal's timepiece sounded no more than half a second later, and the brothers smiled at each other, hands on their pockets, suddenly united.

The watches were identical, gifts from their father upon the occasion of each son's twelfth birthday. The duke had died the day after Grey's twelfth birthday, endowing this small recognition of manhood with a particular poignancy. Grey drew breath to say something, but the sound of voices came from the corridor.

'There he is.' Hal lifted his head, evidently undecided whether to go out to meet Sir George or remain in the library to receive him.

'Saint Joseph,' Grey said suddenly. 'There's another notable stepfather.'

'Quite,' said his brother, with a sidelong glance. 'And which of us are you suggesting . . . ?'

A shadow fell across the Turkey carpet, cast by the form of a bowing servant who stood in the doorway.

'Sir George Stanley, my lord. And party.'

General Sir George Stanley was a surprise. While Grey had consciously expected neither Claudius nor Saint Joseph, the reality was a trifle . . . rounder than anticipated.

His mother's first husband had been tall and dashing, by report, while her second, his own father, had been possessed of the same slight stature, fairness, and tidy muscularity which he had bequeathed to both his sons. Sir George rather restored one's faith in the law of averages, Grey thought, amused.

A bit taller than himself or Hal, and quite stout, the general had a face that was round, cheerful, and rosily guileless beneath a rather shabby wig. His features were nondescript in the extreme, bar a pair of wide brown eyes that gave him an air of pleasant expectation, as though he could think of nothing so delightful as a meeting with the person he addressed.

He bowed in greeting, but then shook hands firmly with both Greys, leaving Lord John with an impression of warmth and sincerity.

'It is kind of you to invite me to luncheon,' he said, smiling from one brother to the other. 'I cannot say how greatly I appreciate your welcome. I feel most awkward, then, to begin at once with an apology – but I am afraid I have imposed upon you by bringing my stepson. He arrived unexpectedly this morning from the country, just as I was setting out. Seeing that you will in some sense be brothers . . . I, er, thought perhaps you would pardon my liberty in bringing him along to be introduced.' He laughed, a little awkwardly, and blushed; an odd mannerism in a man of his age and rank, but rather endearing, Grey thought, smiling back despite himself.

'Of course,' Hal said, managing to sound cordial.

'Most certainly,' Grey echoed. He was standing closest to Sir George, and now turned to the general's companion, hand extended in greeting, and found himself face to face with a tall, slender, dark-eyed young man.

'My Lord Melton, Lord John,' the general was saying, a hand on the young man's shoulder. 'May I present Mr. Percival Wainwright?'

Hal was a trifle put out; Grey could feel the vibrations of annoyance from his direction – Hal hated surprises, particularly those of a social nature – but he himself had little attention to spare for his brother's quirks at the moment.

'Your servant, sir,' he said, taking Mr. Wainwright's hand, with an odd sense of previous meeting.

The other felt it, too; Grey could see the faint expression of puzzlement on the young man's face, a faint inturning of fine dark brows, as though wondering where . . .

Realization struck them simultaneously. His hand tightened involuntarily on the other's, just as Wainwright's grip clutched his.

'Yours, sir,' murmured Wainwright, and stepped back with a slight cough. He reached to shake Hal's hand, but glanced briefly back at Grey. His eyes were also brown, but not at all like his stepfather's, Grey thought, the momentary shock of recognition fading.

They were a soft, vivid brown, like sherry sack, and most expressive. At the moment, they were dancing with mirth at the situation – and filled with the same intensely personal interest Grey had seen in them once before, at their first meeting . . . in the library of Lavender House.

Percy Wainwright had given him his name – and his hand – upon that occasion, too. But Grey had been an anonymous stranger then, and the encounter had been necessarily brief.

Hal was expressing polite welcome to the newcomer, though giving him the sort of coolly professional appraisal he would use to sum up an officer new to the regiment.

Grey thought Wainwright stood up well to such

scrutiny; he was well built, dressed neatly and with taste, clear-skinned and clean-featured, with an attitude that spoke of both humor and imagination. Both traits could be dangerous in an officer, but on a personal level . . .

Wainwright seemed to be discreetly exercising his own curiosity with regard to Grey, flicking brief glances his way – and little wonder. Grey smiled at him, now rather enjoying the surprise of this new 'brother.'

'I thank you,' Wainwright said, as Hal concluded his welcome. He pulled his lingering attention away from Grey, and bowed to Hal. 'Your Grace is most . . . gracious.'

There was an instant of stricken silence following that last, half-strangled word, spoken as Wainwright realized, a moment too late, what he had said.

Hal froze, for the briefest instant, before recovering himself and bowing in return.

'Not at all,' he said, with impeccable politeness. 'Shall we dine, gentlemen?'

Hal turned at once for the door, not looking back. And just as well, Grey thought, seeing the hasty exchange of gestures and glances between the general and his stepson – horrified annoyance from the former, exemplified by rolling of the eyes and a brief clutching of the shabby wig; agonized apology by the latter – an apology extended wordlessly to Grey, as Percy Wainwright turned to him with a grimace.

Grey lifted one shoulder in dismissal. Hal was used to it – and it was his own fault, after all.

'We are fortunate in our timing,' he said, and smiled at Percy. He touched Wainwright's back, lightly encouraging him toward the door. 'It's Thursday. The Beefsteak's cook does an excellent ragout of beef on Thursdays. With oysters.'

Sir George was wise enough to make no apology for his stepson's gaffe, instead engaging both the Greys in conversation regarding the campaigns of the previous autumn. Percy Wainwright appeared a trifle flustered, but quickly regained his composure, listening with every evidence of absorption.

'You were in Prussia?' he asked, hearing Grey's mention of maneuvers near the Oder. 'But surely the Forty-sixth has been stationed in France recently – or am I mistaken?'

'No, not at all,' Grey replied. 'I was temporarily seconded to a Prussian regiment, as liaison with British troops there, after Kloster-Zeven.' He raised a brow at Wainwright. 'You seem well informed.'

Wainwright smiled.

'My stepfather thinks of buying me a commission,' he admitted frankly. 'I have heard a great deal of military conversation of late.'

'I daresay you have. And have you formed any notions, any preferences?'

'I had not,' Wainwright said, his vivid eyes intent on Grey's face. He smiled. 'Until today.'

Grey's heart gave a small hop. He had been trying to forget the last time he had seen Percy Wainwright, soft dark curls disheveled and his stock undone. Today, his hair was brushed smooth, bound and powdered like Grey's own; he wore a sober blue, and they met as proper gentlemen. But the scent of Lavender House seemed to linger in the air between them – a smell of wine and leather, and the sharp, deep musk of masculine desire.

'Now then, Percy,' the general said, slightly reproving. 'Not so hasty, my boy! We have still to speak with Colonel Bonham, and Pickering, too, you know.'

'Indeed,' Grey said lightly. 'Well, you must allow me to give you a tour of the Forty-sixth's quarters, near Cavendish Square. If we are to compete with some other regiment for the honor of your company, we must be allowed to exhibit our finer points.'

Percy's smile deepened.

'I should be most obliged to you, my lord,' he said. And with that, some small, indefinable shift occurred in the air between them.

The conversation continued, but now as a minuet of manners, precise and delicate. And just as a courting couple might exchange worlds of meaning with a touch, so they did the same, with no touch at all, their unspoken conversation flowing unhindered beneath the disguise of routine courtesies.

'Are you fond of dogs, Lord John?'

'Very much so, though I am afraid I have none myself at present. I am seldom at home, you see.'

'Ah. You make your home with your brother, when in England?' Percy glanced in Hal's direction, then brought his eyes back to Grey's, the question plain in them.

Does your brother know?

Grey shook his head, attention ostensibly on the bread roll he was tearing. The question of what Hal knew was a good deal too complex to deal with here. Leave it that Hal did not know about Lavender House, nor his brother's association with it. That was enough for now.

'No,' he said casually. 'I stay at my mother's house in Jermyn Street.' He looked up, meeting Percy's eyes directly. 'Though perhaps I shall seek lodgings elsewhere, now that her domestic arrangements will be altered.'

Percy's mouth lifted in a slight smile, but Sir George, pausing in his own conversation to chew a morsel of beef, had caught this remark, and now leaned across the table, his round face reflecting earnest goodwill.

'My dear Lord John! You certainly must not alter your arrangements on my account! Benedicta desires to keep her house in Jermyn Street, and I should be most distressed to feel that my presence had deprived her of her son's company.'

Grey noticed his brother's lips press thin at the notion of Sir George's occupation of Jermyn Street.

Hal glanced sharply at his brother, admonition plain in his face.

Oh, no, you don't! I want you there, keeping an eye on this fellow.

'You are too kind, sir,' Grey replied to Sir George. 'But the matter is not pressing. I shall rejoin the regiment shortly, after all.'

'Ah, yes.' Sir George looked interested at that, and turned to Hal. 'Have you fresh orders for the spring, my lord?'

Hal nodded, a plump oyster poised on his fork. 'Back to France as soon as the weather permits. And your troops . . .'

'Oh, it's the West Indies for us,' Sir George replied, beckoning for more wine. 'Seasickness, mosquitoes, and malaria. Though I will say that at my age, that prospect is somewhat less daunting than mud and frostbite. And the rations are less difficult to manage, of course.'

Hal relaxed a bit at the revelation that Sir George would not be remaining long in England. Benedicta's money was her own, and safe, for the most part – or as safe as law and Hal could make it. It was his mother's physical welfare with which he was mostly concerned at the moment. That was, presumably, the point of this luncheon: to indicate firmly to Sir George that Benedicta Grey's sons took a close interest in her affairs, and intended to continue doing so after her marriage.

Surely you don't suppose he would beat her? Grey

inquired silently of his brother, brows raised. *Or install a mistress at Jermyn Street?*

Hal adopted a po-faced expression, indicating that Grey was an innocent in the wicked ways of men. Fortunately, Hal himself was not so trusting!

Grey rolled his eyes briefly and averted his gaze from his brother as the steward brought in a dish of hot prunes to accompany the mutton.

Sir George and Hal went off into an intense discussion of the problems of recruitment and supply, leaving Grey and Percy Wainwright once more to their own devices.

'Lord John?' Wainwright spoke low-voiced, brows raised. 'It *is* Lord John?'

'Lord John,' Grey agreed, with a brief sigh.

'But –' Percy glanced again at Hal, who had put down his fork and was drawing up a complicated pattern of troop movements upon the linen table-cloth, using the silver pencil he always kept to hand. The steward was observing this, looking rather bleak.

Is he not a duke, then? 'Lord John' was the proper address for the younger son of a duke, while the younger son of an earl would be simply 'the Honorable John Grey.' But if Grey's father had been a duke, then . . .

'Yes,' Grey said, casting his own eyes up toward the ceiling in token of helplessness.

Apparently, Sir George had not had time to brief his stepson on the matter, beyond warning him not to address Hal as 'Your Grace' – the proper address for a duke.

Grey made a slight gesture, not quite a shrug, indicating that he would explain the intricacies of the situation later. The simple fact of the matter, he reflected, was that he was quite as stubborn as his brother. The thought gave him an obscure feeling of pleasure.

'So you think of purchasing a commission in the Forty-sixth?' Grey asked, using his bread to soak up the juices on his plate.

'Perhaps. If that should be agreeable to . . . all parties,' Wainwright said, glancing at his stepfather and Hal, then back at Grey.

And would it be agreeable to you?

'I should think it an ideal arrangement,' Grey replied. He smiled at Wainwright, a slow smile. 'We should be brothers-in-arms, then, as well as brothers by marriage.' He picked up his wineglass in toast to the idea, then took a sip of wine, which he rolled round his mouth, enjoying the feeling of Percy's eyes fixed on his face.

Percy drank, too, and licked his lips. They were soft and full, stained red with wine.

'Lord John – tell me, please, how did you find our Prussian allies? Was it an artillery regiment with which you were placed, or foot? I confess, I am not so familiar as I should be with arrangements on the eastern front.'

Sir George's question pulled Grey's attention momentarily away from Percy, and the conversation became general again. Hal was relaxing by degrees, though Grey could see that he was still a long way from succumbing entirely to Sir George's charm.

You are a suspicious bastard, you know, he said with a glance at his brother after one particularly probing question.

Yes, and a good thing, too, Hal's dark look at him replied, before turning to Percy Wainwright with a courteous renewal of Grey's invitation to visit the regimental quarters.

By the time the pudding arrived, though, cordial relations appeared to have been established on all fronts. Sir George had replied satisfactorily to all Hal's questions, seeming quite untroubled by the intrusive nature of some of them. In fact, Grey had the feeling that Sir George was privately rather amused by his brother, though taking great care to ensure that Hal was not aware of it.

Meanwhile, he and Percy Wainwright had discovered a mutual enthusiasm for horse-racing, the theater, and French novelists – a discussion of this last subject causing his brother to mutter, 'Oh, God!' beneath his breath and order a fresh round of brandy.

Snow had begun to fall outside; in a momentary lull in the conversation, Grey heard the whisper of it against the window, though the heavy drapes were closed against the winter's chill, and candles lit the room. A pleasant shiver ran down his back at the sound.

'Do you find the room cold, Lord John?' Wainwright asked, noticing.

He did not; there was an excellent fire, roaring away in the hearth and constantly kept up by the ministrations of the Beefsteak's servants. Beyond that, a plentitude of hot food, wine, and brandy ensured sufficient warmth. Even now, the steward was bringing in cups of mulled wine, and a Caribbean hint of cinnamon spiced the air.

'No,' he replied, taking his cup from the proffered tray. 'But there is nothing so pleasant as being inside, warm and well fed, when the elements are hostile without. Do you not agree?'

'Oh, yes.' Wainwright's eyelids had gone heavy, and he leaned back in his chair, his clear skin flushed in the candlelight. 'Most . . . pleasant.' Long fingers touched his neckcloth briefly, as though finding it a little tight.

Awareness floated warm in the air between them, heady as the scents of cinnamon and wine. Hal and Sir George were beginning to make noises indicative of leave-taking, with many expressions of mutual regard.

Percy's long dark lashes rested for a moment on his cheek, and then swept up, so that his eyes met Grey's.

'Perhaps you would be interested to come with me to Lady Jonas's salon – Diderot will be there. Saturday afternoon, if you are at liberty?'

So, shall we be lovers, then?

'Oh, yes,' said Grey, and touched the linen napkin to his mouth. His pulse throbbed in his fingertips. 'I think so.'

Well, he thought, *I don't suppose it's really incest,* and pushed his chair back to arise.

Tom Byrd, Grey's valet, was rubbing at the gold lace on Grey's dress uniform with a lump of bread to brighten it, and listening with a lively interest to Grey's account of the luncheon with General Stanley and his stepson.

'So the general means to make his home here, me lord?' Grey could see Tom calculating what this change might mean to his own world; the general would doubtless bring some of his own servants, including a valet or orderly. 'Will the son come, too, this Mr. Wainwright?'

'Oh, I shouldn't think so.' In fact, the notion had not occurred to Grey, and he took a moment to examine it. Wainwright had said he had his own rooms, somewhere in Westminster. Having seen the cordial relations that appeared to exist between Sir George and his stepson, though, he had assumed that this state of things was either to do with the cramped nature of the general's present lodgings – or with Wainwright's desire for privacy.

'I don't know. Perhaps he would.' It was an unsettling thought, though not necessarily unpleasant. Grey smiled at Tom, and pulled his banyan close for warmth; despite the fire, the room was cold. 'I shouldn't think he will bring a valet with him if he does come, though.'

'Ho,' Byrd said thoughtfully. 'Would you want

me to do for him as well, me lord? I wouldn't mind,' he added quickly. 'Is he a dandy, though, would you say?'

There was such a hopeful tone to this last question that Grey laughed.

'Very kind of you, Tom. He dresses decently, but is no macaroni. I believe he means to take up a commission, though. Nothing but more uniforms for you, I'm afraid.'

Byrd made no audible reply to this, but his glance at Grey's boots, standing caked with mud, straw, and manure by the hearth, was eloquent. He shook his head, squinted at the coat he was holding, decided it would do, and stood up, brushing bread crumbs into the fire.

'Very good, me lord,' he said, resigned. 'You'll look decent for the wedding, though, if I die for it. Come to that, if we're a-going back to France in March, you'd best be calling on your tailor this week.'

'Oh? All right. Make me a list, then, of what's needed. Small-clothes, certainly.' Both of them grimaced, in joint memory of what passed for drawers on the Continent.

'Yes, me lord.' Tom bent to shovel embers into the warming pan. 'And a pair of doeskin breeches.'

'Don't I have a pair?' Grey asked, surprised.

'You do,' Byrd said, straightening, 'and Lord only knows what you sat on whilst wearing 'em.' He gave Grey a disapproving look; Tom was eighteen, and round-faced as a pie, but his disapproving looks would have done credit to an old gaffer of eighty.

'I've done me best, me lord, but bear in mind, if you go out in those breeches, don't be taking your coat off, or folk will be sure you've beshit yourself.'

Grey laughed, and stood aside for Tom to warm the bed. He shucked his banyan and slippers and slid between the sheets, the heat grateful on his chilly feet.

'You have several brothers, don't you, Tom?'

'Five, me lord. I'd never had a bed to meself until I came to work for you.' Tom shook his head, marveling at his luck, then grinned at Grey. 'Don't suppose you'll need to share your bed with this Mr. Wainwright, though, will you?'

Grey had a sudden vision of Percy Wainwright, stretched solid beside him in the bed, and an extraordinary sense of warmth pulsed through him, quite incommensurate with the heat provided by the warming pan.

'I doubt it,' he said, remembering to smile. 'You can put out the candle, Tom, thank you.'

'Good night, me lord.'

The door closed behind Tom Byrd, and Grey lay watching the firelight play over the furnishings of the room. He was not particularly attached to places – a soldier couldn't be – nor was this house a great part of his past; the countess had bought it only a few years before. And yet he felt a sudden peculiar nostalgia – for what, he couldn't have said.

The night was still and cold, and yet seemed full

of restless movement. The flicker of the fire; the flicker of arousal that burned in his flesh. He felt things shift and stir, unseen, and had the odd feeling that nothing would ever again be the same. This was nonsense, of course; it never was.

Still, he lay a long time sleepless, wishing time to stay; the night, the house, and himself to remain as they were, just a little longer. And yet the fire died, and he slept, conscious in his dreams of the rising wind outside.

Chapter 2

Not a Betting Man

Grey spent the next morning in a drafty room in Whitehall, enduring the necessary tedium of a colonels' meeting with the Ordnance Office, featuring a long-winded address by Mr. Adams, First Secretary of the Ministry of Ordnance. Hal, pleading press of business, had dispatched Grey in his place – meaning, Grey thought, manfully swallowing a yawn, that Hal was likely either still at home enjoying breakfast, or at White's Chocolate House, wallowing in sugared buns and gossip, whilst Grey sat through bum-numbing hours of argument over powder allocations. Well, rank had its privileges.

He found his situation not unpleasant, though. The 46th was fortunately provided for with regards to gunpowder; his half brother Edgar owned one of the largest powder mills in the country. And as Grey was junior to most of the other officers present, he was seldom required to say anything, and thus free to allow his thoughts to drift into speculation regarding Percy Wainwright.

Had he mistaken the attraction? No. He could

still feel the extraordinary warmth of Wainwright's eyes – and the warmth of his touch, when they had shaken hands in farewell.

The notion of Percy Wainwright's joining the regiment was intriguing. Considered in the sober light of day, it might also be dangerous.

He knew nothing of the man. True, the fact that he was General Stanley's stepson argued that he must be at least discreet – but Grey knew several discreet villains. And he must not forget that his first meeting with Wainwright had been at Lavender House, a place whose polished surfaces hid many secrets.

Had Wainwright been with anyone on that occasion? Grey frowned, trying to recall the scene, but in fact, his attention had been so distracted at the time that he had noticed only a few faces. He *thought* that Percy had been alone, but . . . yes. He must have been, for he had not only introduced himself – he had kissed Grey's hand.

He'd forgotten that, and his hand closed involuntarily, a small jolt running up his arm as though he had touched something hot.

'Yes, I'd like to throttle him, too,' muttered the man beside him. 'Bloody windbag.' Startled, Grey glanced at the officer, an infantry colonel named Jones-Osborn, who nodded, glowering, at Mr. Adams, whose rather high-pitched voice had been going on for some time.

Grey had no idea what Adams had been saying, but grunted agreement and glowered in sympathy.

This provoked the man on his other side, who, encouraged by this show of support, shouted a contradiction at Adams, liberally laced with epithet.

The secretary, Irish by birth and no mean hand at confrontation, replied in kind with spirit, and within moments, the meeting had degenerated into something more resembling a session of Parliament than the sober deliberations of military strategists.

Drawn perforce into the ensuing melee, this followed by a cordial luncheon with Jones-Osborn and the rest of the anti-Adams faction, Grey thought no more of Percy Wainwright until he found himself at mid-afternoon in his brother's office at regimental headquarters.

'Jesus,' Hal said, laughing over Grey's account of the morning's events. 'Better you than me. Was Twelvetrees there?'

'Don't know him.'

'Then he wasn't there.' Hal flipped a hand in dismissal. 'You'd have noticed him slipping a dagger in Jones-Osborn's back. Adams's lap-wolf. What did you think of the new brother? Shall we have him?'

Familiar as he was with Hal's quick-change methods of conversation, it took Grey only an instant to catch his brother's meaning.

'Wainwright? Seems a decent fellow,' he said, affecting casualness. 'Have you heard anything of him?'

'No more than we learned yesterday. I asked Quarry, but neither he nor Joffrey knew anything of the man.'

That said much; between them, Harry Quarry, one of the two regimental colonels, and his half brother, Lord Joffrey, knew everyone of note in both military and political circles.

'You liked him?' Grey asked. Hal frowned a little, considering.

'Yes,' he said slowly. 'And it would be awkward to refuse him, should he desire to take a commission with us.'

'No experience, of course,' Grey observed. This was not a stumbling block, but it was a consideration. Commissions were normally purchased, and many officers had never seen a soldier nor held a weapon prior to taking up their office. On the other hand, most of the 46th's senior officers were veterans of considerable battlefield experience, and Hal chose new additions carefully.

'True. I should suggest his beginning at second lieutenant, perhaps – or even ensign. To learn his business before moving higher.'

Grey considered this, then nodded.

'Second lieutenant,' he said. 'Or even first. There will be the family connexion. It wouldn't be fitting, I think, that he should be an ensign.' Ensigns were the lowliest of the commissioned officers, at everyone's beck and call.

'Perhaps you're right,' Hal conceded. 'We'd put him under Harry, of course, at least to start. You would be willing to guide him?'

'Certainly.' Grey felt his heart beat faster, and forced himself to caution. 'That is, should he wish to join us. The general did say they had not decided. And Bonham would take him at once as a captain in the Fifty-first, you know.'

Hal huffed and looked down his nose at the thought that anyone might prefer to reign in hell rather than serve in heaven, as it were, but reluctantly conceded the point.

'Yes, I should like to make him captain eventually, if he proves able. But we leave for France in less than three months; I doubt that is time to try him adequately. Can he even handle a sword, do you think?' Wainwright had not been wearing one; still, most nonmilitary gentlemen did not.

Grey shrugged.

'I can find out. Do you wish me to broach the matter of commission with Wainwright directly, or shall you open negotiations with the general?'

Hal drummed his fingers on the desk for a moment, then made up his mind.

'Ask him directly. If he is to be a member of both the family and the regiment, I think we must treat him as such from the beginning. And he is much nearer to you in age. I think he is somewhat afraid of me.' Hal's brows knitted briefly in puzzlement, and Grey smiled. His brother liked to think himself modest and inoffensive, and affected not to know that while his troops idolized him, they were also terrified of him.

'I'll talk to him, then.'

Grey made to rise, but Hal waved him back, still frowning.

'Wait. There is – another matter.'

Grey looked sharply at his brother, hearing the note of strain in Hal's voice. Distracted by thoughts of Percy Wainwright, he hadn't really looked at Hal; now he saw the tightness around his brother's mouth and eyes. Trouble, then.

'What is it?'

Hal grimaced, but before he could reply, footsteps came down the corridor, and someone knocked diffidently at the jamb of the open door. Grey turned to see a young hussar, his face flushed from the cold wind outside.

'My lord? A message, sir, from the ministry. I was told to wait upon an answer,' he added awkwardly.

Hal turned a dark countenance on the messenger, but then beckoned impatiently and snatched the message.

'Wait downstairs,' he said, waving the hussar away. He broke the seal and read the note quickly, muttered something blasphemous under his breath, and seized a quill to scribble a reply at the bottom of the page.

Grey rocked back in his chair, waiting. He glanced round the office, wondering what could have happened since yesterday. Hal had shown no signs of worry during their luncheon with the general and Percy.

He could not have said what drew his eye to the scrap of paper. Hal's office resembled nothing so much as the den of some large beast of untidy habit, and while both Hal and his elderly clerk, Mr.

Beasley, could lay their hands on anything wanted within an instant, no one else could find so much as a pin in the general chaos.

The paper itself lay among a quantity of others scattered on the desk, distinguished only by a ragged edge, as though it had been torn from a book. Grey picked it up, glanced at it casually, then stiffened, eyes glued to the page.

'Do let my papers alone, John,' Hal said, finishing his reply with a viciously scrawled signature. 'You'll muddle everything. What's that you have?' He tossed his quill on the desk and snatched the paper impatiently from Grey. He made to put it back on the desk, then caught sight of the words and froze.

'It *is*, is it not?' Grey asked, feeling queer. 'Father's writing?' It was a rhetorical question; he had recognized both the hand and the style of writing at once. Hal hadn't heard in any case; the blood had drained from his face, and he was reading the journal page – for that is what it clearly was – as though it were notice of his own execution.

'He burnt it,' Hal whispered, and swallowed. 'She said he'd burnt it.'

'Who?' Grey asked, startled. 'Mother?'

Hal glanced up at him sharply, but ignored his question.

'Where did this come from?' he demanded, barely waiting for Grey's shrug before shouting, 'Mr. Beasley! I want you!'

Mr. Beasley, promptly emergent from his own pristine sanctuary, denied any knowledge of the sheet of paper and confessed complete ignorance of its means of arrival in Hal's office. He was, though, able to supply the helpful information that the paper had definitely not been upon the desk earlier in the day.

'How on earth would you know?' Grey inquired, giving the desk and its contents a disparaging look. Two beady-eyed stares turned upon him. They'd know. Grey coughed.

'Yes. In that case . . .' He trailed off. He had been about to inquire who had come into the office during the day, but realized at once the difficulty of the question. Dozens of people visited the office every day: clerks, sutlers, officers, royal messengers, gunnery sergeants, weaponers. . . . He'd come in once and found a man with a dancing bear on a chain and a monkey on his shoulder, come to collect payment for performing at a jollification for the troops in honor of the queen's birthday.

Still, surely some effort should be made.

'How long had you been here before I came in?' he asked. Hal rubbed a hand over his face.

'I came in just before you. Otherwise, I should have seen it at once.'

'Ought we call in the door guard, and the men in the building?' Grey suggested. 'Query each of them as to anyone who might have entered the office whilst it was unoccupied?'

Hal's lips compressed. He'd got control of himself; Grey could see his mind working again, and rapidly.

'No,' he said, and consciously relaxed his shoulders. 'No, it's not important.' He crumpled the sheet of paper into a ball, and threw it with apparent casualness into the fire. 'That will be all, Mr. Beasley.'

Mr. Beasley bowed and went out. The paper glowed and burst into flame. Grey's hands clenched involuntarily, wanting to seize it from destruction, but it was already gone, ink stark for an instant on the charring paper before it fell to ash. The unexpected sense of loss made him speak more sharply than his wont.

'Why did you do that?'

'It doesn't matter.' Hal glanced at the door, to be sure that Beasley was out of earshot, then took the poker and thrust it into the fire, stirring it so that sparks flew up the chimney like a swarm of fiery bees, making sure no trace of the paper remained. 'Forget it.'

'I am not inclined to forget it. What did you mean, "He burnt it"?'

Hal put the poker back in its stand with a careful precision.

'That was not a suggestion,' he said softly. 'It was an order – Major.'

Grey's jaw tightened.

'I do not choose to obey you – sir.'

Hal turned, startled.

'What the hell do you mean, you bloody don't *choose* to –'

'I mean I won't,' Grey snapped, 'and you frigging

well know it. What do you propose to do about it? Clap me in irons? Have me locked up for a week on bread and water?'

'Don't bloody tempt me.' Hal glared at him, but it was clear to both of them that he had given in. Partly.

'Keep your voice down, at least.' Hal went to the door, looked out into the hallway, but didn't shut it. That was interesting, Grey thought. Did Hal suppose that Mr. Beasley might creep up to listen outside the door, if it were closed?

'Yes, it was a page from one of the journals,' Hal said, very quietly. 'The last one.'

Grey nodded briefly; the date on the page had been two weeks prior to the date of their father's death. The duke had been a meticulous diarist; there was a small bookcase in the library in Jermyn Street, filled with row upon row of his journals, kept over more than thirty years. Grey was familiar with them, and grateful to his father for having kept them; they had enabled him to know at least a little of his father as a man, once he reached his own manhood. The last journal in the bookshelf ended three months prior to the duke's death; there must have been another, but Grey had never seen it.

'Mother told you Father had burnt it? Did she say why?'

'No, she didn't,' Hal said briefly. 'I didn't inquire, under the circumstances.'

Hal was still watching the open door. Grey couldn't tell whether he was merely on the alert, or avoiding meeting Grey's eyes. Hal was a good liar when he needed to be, but Grey knew his brother extremely well – and Hal knew him. He took a deep breath, ordering his thoughts. The smell of burnt paper was sharp in his nose.

'Clearly it wasn't burnt,' Grey said slowly. 'So we must assume, first, that it was stolen, and then that whoever took it has kept it until now. Who, and why? And why does he – whoever he is – inform you now that he has it? And why did Mother—'

'Damned if I know.' Hal did look at him then, and Grey's anger faded as he saw that his brother was indeed telling the truth. He saw something else that disquieted him extremely – his brother was afraid.

'It is a threat of some sort?' he asked, lowering his voice still further. There had been nothing on the page he had read to suggest such a thing; it had been part of an account of a meeting his father had had with a longtime friend and their discussion of astronomy, quite innocuous. Therefore, the page had plainly been meant only to inform Hal of the existence of the journal itself – and whatever else it might contain.

'God knows,' Hal said. 'What the devil could it – well.' He rubbed a knuckle hard across his lips, and glanced at Grey. '*Don't* speak to Mother about it. I'll do it,' he added, seeing Grey about to protest.

The sound of boots and voices along the passage prevented further conversation. Captain Wilmot, with his sergeant and a company clerk. Hal reached out and quietly closed the door; they waited in silence as the noise died away.

'Do you know a man named Melchior Ffoulkes?' Hal asked abruptly.

'No,' Grey replied, wondering whether this had to do with the matter at hand, or was a change of subject. 'I am reasonably sure I'd recall him, if I did.'

That provoked the ghost of a smile from Hal.

'Yes, you would. Or a private soldier named Harrison Otway? From the Eleventh Foot.'

'What a ridiculous name. No, who is he?'

'Captain Michael Bates?'

'Well, I've heard of him, at least. Horse Guards, is he not? Flash cove, as Tom Byrd puts it. What, may I ask, is the purpose of this catechism? Do sit down, Hal.' He sat himself, and after a moment's hesitation, Hal slowly followed suit.

'Have you ever met Captain Bates?'

Grey was becoming annoyed, but answered flippantly.

'Not to remember, certainly. I couldn't swear that I've never shared a bed with him in an inn, of course –'

Hal's hand gripped his forearm, so hard that he gasped.

'Don't,' Hal said, very softly. 'Don't make jokes.'

Grey stared into his brother's eyes, seeing the lines of his face cut deep. The journal page had shocked him, but he had already been disturbed.

'Let go,' Grey said quietly. 'What's wrong?'

Hal slowly withdrew his hand.

'I don't know. Not yet.'

'Who are these men? Have they anything to do with—' He glanced at the fireplace, but Hal shook his head.

'I don't know. I don't think so – but it's possible.' The sound of footsteps echoed in the hallway, and Hal stopped speaking abruptly. The footsteps were distinctive, the sound of a heavy man with a decided limp. Ewart Symington, the second regimental colonel, Harry Quarry's opposite number.

Hal grimaced and John nodded understanding. Neither one of them desired to speak with Symington at the moment. They stood silent, waiting. Sure enough, the steps came to a halt, and a fist thundered on the panels of the door. Symington was as brutal of manner as of appearance, resembling nothing so much as a dyspeptic boar.

Another thunderous assault on the door, a moment's pause, and Symington uttered a muffled oath and limped off.

'He'll be back,' Hal said, under his breath, and took his cloak from its peg by the door. 'Come with me to White's; we'll talk on the way.'

Grey thrust his arms into his greatcoat and a moment later they had escaped into the street, Hal having instructed Mr. Beasley to tell Colonel Symington that Lord Melton had gone to Bath.

'Bath?' Grey asked, as they exited. 'At this time of year?' It was no more than half-past three, yet twilight was louring. The pavement was dark with wet and the air thick with the scent of oncoming snow.

Hal waved off his waiting carriage, and turned the corner.

'Anywhere closer, and he'd follow me there. Say what you will of the man, he's damned persistent.' That was said with grudging respect; persistence was Symington's chief military virtue, and not a mean one. In more social situations, it was somewhat trying.

'What does he want?'

Grey asked only for the sake of delaying discussion, and was not surprised to receive only a moody shrug from Hal. His brother appeared no more eager to resume their conversation than he was, and they walked for half a mile or so in silence, each alone with his thoughts.

Grey's own thoughts were a jumble, veering from anticipation and curiosity at the thought of Percy Wainwright to concern at his brother's obvious agitation. Over all of it, though, was the image of the page he had held so briefly in his hands.

He forced all other thought from his mind, concentrating on remembering, committing the words he had read to memory. He still felt the shock of Hal's throwing the paper into the fire, and could not bear the thought that those words of his father's, pedestrian as they might be, should be lost to him. The duke's journals were no secret, and yet he had read them secretly, abstracting one at a time and smuggling each volume to his room, returning them to their shelf, careful that no one should see.

He could not have said why it seemed important to keep this postmortem relationship with his father private. Only that it had been.

He had more or less succeeded in fixing at least the substance of the vanished page in memory, when Hal finally hunched his shoulders and spoke abruptly.

'There has been talk. Regarding conspiracies.'

'When is there not? Which particular conspiracy concerns you?'

'Not me, so much.' Hal settled his hat more firmly, bending his head into the wind. 'And it has not yet blown up into open scandal, but it almost certainly will – and soon.'

'I don't doubt it,' Grey observed caustically. 'There hasn't been a decent scandal since Christmas. Who does this one involve?'

'A sodomite conspiracy to undermine the government by assassination of selected ministers.'

Grey felt a tightening of the belly, but replied casually. It was not the first time he had heard of such a notion; sodomitical associations and conspiracies were a standby of street criers and Fleet Street hacks whenever news became too slow.

'And why does this concern you?'

Hal fixed his eyes on the slimy cobbles.

'Us. It is a thing that was said. Of – of Father.' The word struck Grey in the pit of the stomach, like a pebble from a sling. He was not sure he had ever heard Hal use the word 'Father' any time in the last fifteen years.

'That he was a sodomite?' Grey said, incredulous. Hal drew a deep breath, but seemed to relax a bit.

'No. Not in so many words. Nor was it – thank God – a popular rumor. Only random accusations at the time of his death, made by members of the Society – such accusations were common, thrown at almost every man of any visibility connected with the South Sea Bubble. The scandal was blamed on "companies of sodomites" – though God knows it was blamed on every other group, interest, or person anyone could think of, as well. But the Society was prominent at the time, and sodomitical conspiracies were their particular obsession.'

'The Society?' Grey said blankly. 'Which Society is this?'

'I forgot. You would not have been old enough to hear much at the time—'

'Damned little, in Aberdeen.' Grey made no attempt to keep an edge of bitterness from his voice, and his brother glanced sharply at him.

'Which is precisely why you were sent there,' Hal said, his voice level. 'In any case, it is the Society for the Reformation of Manners to which I refer; you *have* heard of them?'

'I have, yes.' Angry and unsettled, Grey was making no effort to hide his feelings, and let distaste and contempt show in his voice. 'Prigs and puritans, who will not acknowledge their own base urges, but find delight – and release, no doubt – in accusations of corruption, in blackening the characters of innocent men. They are—'

Hal put a restraining hand on his arm again – no more than a touch, this time – to keep him from speaking further, as two chairmen went by at the trot, their heads wreathed in white smoke from their panting breath.

The cold and twilight kept many folk indoors, but there were those whose livelihoods compelled them to the streets, and as they approached St. James's Street, there began to be more of them. A balladeer, chestnut sellers, apple-women crying the virtues of their wizened fruit. Grey saw his brother scrutinize each person they passed, as though he suspected them of something.

'Captain Michael Bates is thought to be deeply involved,' Hal said at last. 'The general told me of the matter after you and Wainwright had left yesterday; Bates's father is General Ezekial Bates – long retired, but an intimate of General Stanley's.'

'Ah,' Grey said. 'I see.' He felt unsettled still, vaguely alarmed, pointlessly angry – but this intelligence relieved his mind a little. At least now he knew why the matter had come to Hal's attention. 'And the other men you mentioned – Otway and Ffoulkes?'

'Otway is a private soldier in the Eleventh Infantry, a nobody. Ffoulkes is a reasonably well-known solicitor in Lincoln's Inn.'

'How are these men connected?'

'Through Bates.'

Captain Bates and Ffoulkes had met, according to General Stanley, when Ffoulkes had handled a minor matter of business for the captain's family. Otway had evidently met Bates in a tavern near Temple Stairs, formed an unwholesome connexion with him, and then later been introduced to Ffoulkes, though the general did not know the circumstances.

'Indeed,' said Grey, thinking of the bog-houses near Lincoln's Inn, a spot much patronized by both lawyers and mollies. 'This . . . association is what they refer to as a "company of sodomites"? It seems lacking in both membership and organizing principles, I think.'

Hal snorted a little; his breath purled white in the winter air.

'Oh, there's more. Our friend Ffoulkes, it seems, has a French wife. Who in turn has two brothers. One of these brothers is a notorious pederast – notorious even by French standards – while the other is a colonel in the French army.'

Grey grunted in surprise.

'And is there any evidence of – I suppose it must be treason?'

'It is. And there is. The War Office got wind of something, and has been quietly pursuing the matter for some months. Bates – he was General Stanley's chief aide-de-camp for some time before joining the Horse Guards, by the way—'

'Christ.'

'Precisely. He apparently had been passing secret

materials to Otway, who in turn delivered these to Ffoulkes in the course of their assignations. And from there, of course . . .'

Grey drew the evening air deep into his lungs. The last of his defensive anger chilled, leaving him cold. It *was* a personal matter – but not directly personal. Hal's concern was for the general, of course – and for their family, lest the old rumors be resurrected in light of fresh scandal, stimulated by their mother's new marriage.

'What has been done?' he asked. 'I have heard nothing of it in the streets, read nothing in the periodicals.'

Hal's shoulders hunched a little; they were passing a gate where torches burned, and Grey saw his brother's shadow, foreshortened and shrunk, the image of an old man.

'It has been kept as quiet as possible. Bates and Otway were both arrested yesterday, though.'

'And Ffoulkes?'

Hal's head lifted, and he blew out a long white breath.

'Ffoulkes shot himself this morning.'

Grey walked on, mechanically, no longer feeling chill or cobble.

'May God have mercy on his soul,' he said at last.

'And ours,' Hal said, without humor.

Hal could not or would not say more, and they walked the rest of the way in silence. Disturbed in mind though he was, Grey was jerked out of his thoughts as they turned into St. James's Street.

Candlelight streamed welcomingly through the windows of White's, illuminating what appeared to be the body of a man lying on the pavement by the door. As they approached the building, Grey saw a head pop out of the club's open door, survey the body, then pop back in, only to be succeeded by a different head, which repeated this procedure.

'Do you know him?' Grey asked his brother, as they came up to the body. 'Is he a member?' Grey was of course a member of White's, as well, but seldom patronized the club, finding the cozy shabbiness and excellent food of the Beefsteak more appealing.

Hal squinted at the body, and shook his head.

'No one I know.'

The body lay prone, legs sprawled apart beneath a greatcoat of decent quality. The man's hat was also a good one; it had fallen off and rolled against the wall, resting on edge there like a tipsy beggar.

'Is he dead, do you think?'

The man's wig had slipped askew, half covering his face. It had begun to snow lightly, and between the flickering light and the swirling flakes, it was impossible to perceive whether he was breathing.

'Let me look; perhaps—' Hal stooped to touch the man, but was prevented by a shout from the doorway.

'Don't touch him! Not yet!' An excited young

41

man issued from the club and seized Hal's arm. 'We haven't put it in the book yet!'

'What, the betting book?' Hal demanded.

'Yes – Rogers says he's dead, and I say he's not. Two guineas on it! Will you join the wager with me, Melton?'

'He's dead as a doornail, Melton!' came a shout from the open door, presumably from Rogers. 'Whitbread and Gallagher are with me!'

'He ain't, I say!' The young man slapped his palm on the doorjamb. 'You lot couldn't tell a corpse from a tailor's ham!'

'Hoy!' Grey caught a glimmer of movement from the corner of his eye and whirled round, hand on his sword – but not in time to grab the ragged boy who had darted in to snatch the body's hat. A hoot of triumph drifted back through the thickening snow.

'Call the Watch, for God's sake. We can't let him lie here, dead or not,' Hal said impatiently. 'He'll be picked clean.'

Grey obligingly belted down the street to the Fount of Wisdom, where he found two members of the Watch fortifying themselves against the weather. Reluctantly gulping their mulled cider, they huddled themselves grumbling into coats and hats and came back with him to White's, where he found his brother standing guard over the body, leaning on his sword.

'About time,' Hal said, sheathing it. 'They're here!' he shouted, turning toward the open door, where Mr. Holmes, the club's steward, hovered in anticipation.

Holmes promptly vanished, and the call of, 'The book is closed, gentlemen!' rang through the house.

In moments, the body was surrounded by a crowd of eager bettors, who poured out into the snow, still arguing amongst themselves.

'What do you say?' Grey muttered to Hal. He sniffed the air, but was unable to detect any telltale scent of death, above the waft of smoke, coffee, and food drifting from the club. 'Ten to one he's alive,' he said, on impulse.

'You know I never bet on anything but cards,' Hal muttered back. Still, he held his position at the front of the group, curious as any of the bettors, as one of the Watchmen gingerly lifted the wig away from the man's face.

There was a moment's silence as the face was revealed, gray and slack as potter's clay, eyes closed. The Watchman bent close, cupping the fallen jaw, then jerked upright.

'He's alive! I felt his breath on me 'and!'

The group exploded into voice and action then, several men hastening to lift the victim and carry him inside, others calling out for hot coffee, a doctor, brandy, had the man a pocketbook, papers? Where was the doctor, for God's sake?

A tall, gray-haired man came out of the cardroom glaring at the interruption.

'Who wants a doctor?'

'Oh, there you are, Longstreet. Your patient, sir.'

Hal greeted the doctor, whom he evidently knew, and gestured toward the man in the greatcoat, who had been laid out on a settee and was being tenderly ministered to by the same men who had been wagering on his demise moments earlier.

Doctor Longstreet grimaced, shed his coat, and began to roll up his sleeves.

'All right. I'll see. You lot, get out of it. Holmes – fetch me a bowl from the kitchen, if you would be so good.' He pulled a collapsible fleam from his pocket and flicked it open with a practiced air.

Mr. Holmes hesitated.

'You aren't going to do anything . . . messy, are you? We've only just had that settee reupholstered.'

Longstreet gave the steward a humorless grin.

'I'm going to bleed him, yes – but I'll endeavor not to stain your damask. Bowl!'

Grey, being nearest and not given to squeamishness, helped to lift the man – who was both tall and stout – and remove his outer clothes. The man's eyelids flickered for a moment, and his lips moved, but he relapsed back into unconsciousness, not stirring even when Longstreet took hold of his bared arm and cut into the flesh below the elbow.

Blood pattered into the bowl, and one of the onlookers went quickly outside, whence the sound of vomiting was heard through the still-open door. Mr. Holmes cast a look of despair at the blood spattering the carpet, and went out to render aid.

'I don't suppose you carry ammoniac salts on your person, do you?' Longstreet asked Grey, frowning at the unconscious man. 'I hoped the flow of blood might revive him, but . . .'

'My brother does. A moment.' Hal had disappeared into the cardroom with most of the other members, who had ceased to be interested in the subject of their wager, now that it was won or lost. Grey went in and returned almost at once with Hal's enameled snuffbox, which, when opened, proved to contain not snuff but a small corked vial containing sal volatile.

Dr. Longstreet accepted this with a nod of thanks, pulled the cork, and passed the bottle closely beneath the man's nostrils.

'Why does your brother – Melton *is* your brother, I perceive? The resemblance is marked – why does he carry salts?'

'I believe his wife is subject to fits of fainting,' Grey said casually. In fact, Hal himself now and then suffered odd spells of dizziness. Having fainted once on the parade ground on a hot day, he had resolved never to appear at such a disadvantage again, and had taken to carrying salts – though to the best of Grey's knowledge, his brother had never actually resorted to them. He was reasonably sure that Hal would prefer this precaution not to be public knowledge, however.

'Ah!' The doctor made a sound of satisfaction; the patient's face had suddenly convulsed.

Matters thereafter were so intent as to allow no further conversation. With continued application of salts, cloths wrung out in warm water and applied to the limbs, and – as returning consciousness allowed – judicious infusions of brandy, the gentleman was gradually returned to a state of consciousness, though he remained unable to speak, and merely frowned in a puzzled way when spoken to.

'I believe he has suffered an apoplexy,' Longstreet remarked, surveying his patient with interest. 'Common in subjects of a choleric disposition. Observe the burst small vessels in the cheeks – and most particularly the nose.'

'Indeed.' Grey peered at the man. 'Will he recover his powers of speech, do you suppose?'

Longstreet shrugged, but appeared in good humor. The man had survived, after all. What more could be asked of a doctor?

'With good nursing, it's possible. Do we know who he is?'

Grey had gone through the pockets of the man's greatcoat and discovered among the contents an open letter, addressed to a Dr. Henryk van Humperdinck, at 44 Great Ormond Street.

The gentleman gave some signs of response when addressed by this name, and so a message was sent to Great Ormond Street, and the patient carried off to one of the bedrooms upstairs, under the direction of the long-suffering Mr. Holmes, until his connexions should be located and informed.

'Did he have any money on him?' the doctor asked jovially, wiping his hands on a towel. 'I hope I have not beggared you by saving his life. Or your brother, for that matter.'

'No,' Grey assured him. 'I should have won, had I been in time to place a bet. And my brother is not a betting man.'

'No?' Longstreet sounded surprised.

'No. He wagers at whist, but only, he says, because he has faith in his skill, not his luck.'

Longstreet gave him a queer look.

'Not a betting man?' he repeated, and laughed in cynic fashion. Seeing Grey's look of incomprehension, his own face changed, and he pursed his lips, as though considering whether to say something.

'You've never seen it?' he said at last, looking sideways at Grey beneath gray brows. 'Truly?'

Receiving no reply, he strode across the room and picked up the betting book, which had been left on a side table, following Mr. Holmes's careful record of the settling of the wager on Dr. Humperdinck's state of animation.

Longstreet flipped back through the pages, long-fingered and swift, finally discovering what he wanted with a small grunt of satisfaction.

'Here.' He handed the book to Grey, pointing out an entry that stood alone at the head of a page, otherwise blank, save the signatures of witnesses to the wager in the margin.

The Earl of Melton states that the Duke of Pardloe was not a traitor. He stakes twenty thousand pounds on the truth of this. All comers welcome.

Below this was Hal's formal signature, big and black. Grey felt as though he had suddenly forgot how to breathe.

On the opposite page were three entries, the first written in small, evenly controlled letters, as though in deliberate contrast to the passion of Hal's wager:

Done. Nathaniel Twelvetrees, Captain, 32nd Foot

Below this were two more names, carelessly scrawled.

Accepted. Arthur Wilbraham, MP
Accepted. George Longstreet

Grey worked his tongue in an effort to regain enough saliva to speak, and mechanically noted the date of the wager. 8 July, 1741. A month after his father's death. There was no indication that the wager had ever been settled.

'You really didn't know?' Longstreet was regarding him with something like sympathy, mixed with curiosity.

'No,' Grey said, achieving speech. With some effort, he closed the book and set it down. 'George Longstreet. You?'

Doctor Longstreet shook his head.

'My cousin. I witnessed the wager, though.' The doctor's mouth, long and mobile, quirked at one side. 'It was a memorable night. Your brother came very close to calling Twelvetrees out and was dissuaded only by Colonel Quarry – he was only a lieutenant at the time, of course – who pointed out that he could not honorably risk leaving his mother and younger brother defenseless, were he killed. You must have been no more than a child at the time?'

Blood burned in Grey's cheeks at that. He had had nothing to drink, but felt a rushing in his ears, together with that peculiar sense of detachment that sometimes came upon him after too much wine, as though he were not responsible for the actions of his body.

'Mr. Holmes!' he called, his voice surprisingly calm. 'A quill and ink, if you please.'

He opened the book, and taking the quill hastily supplied by Holmes, who stood by anxious-faced and silent, he wrote neatly beneath his brother's entry:

Lord John Grey joins this wager, upon the same terms.

He hadn't got twenty thousand pounds, but it didn't seem to matter.

'If you gentlemen will be so kind as to witness my hand?' He held out the ink-stained quill to Longstreet, who took it, looking amused. Holmes coughed, low in his throat, and Grey turned round to see his brother standing in the doorway, watching, expressionless. The sound of laughter and shouts of dismay came from the cardroom behind him.

'What in God's name is the matter with you?' Hal asked, very quietly.

'The same thing that's the matter with you,' Grey said. He took his hat and coat from the hallstand and bowed. 'Good night,' he said politely. 'Your Grace.'

Chapter 3

Pet Criminal

Once home, he could not sleep, and after a restless hour spent churning the bedclothes into knots, he got up, poked the fire into life, and sat by the window with a blanket round his shoulders, watching the snow come down.

Ice crystals coated the glass like clouded lace, but Grey barely noticed the cold; he was burning. And not with the fires of sudden lust this time – rather, with the desire to walk across town to his brother's house, drag Hal from his bed, and assault him.

He could – he supposed – understand why Hal had never mentioned the wager to him. In the wake of the scandal following the duke's death, Grey had been shipped off promptly to some of his mother's distant relatives in Aberdeen. He had spent two grim years in that gray stone city, during which time he had seen his brother only once.

And when he had come back to England, Hal had been virtually a stranger, so preoccupied with the business of reconstituting the regiment that he had no time to spare for either friends or family. And then . . . well, then he himself had met Hector, and in the cataclysms of personal discovery that followed that event had had no attention to spare for anyone else, either.

The brothers had only come to know each other again when Grey took up his commission with the regiment, and discovered that he shared the family taste and talent for soldiering. Certainly Hal had not forgotten the wager, but as it had plainly never been settled, it was conceivable that it might not have occurred to him to speak of it, years after the fact.

No, what was galling him was not that Hal had never mentioned the wager, but the fact that his brother had never told *him* openly that he believed their father had not been a traitor. Grey had lived on the tacit assumption that this was the case, but the matter had never been mentioned between them – and a casual observer would have drawn quite a different impression from Hal's actions, taking these as the efforts of a man to live down shame and scandal, repudiating his patrimony in the process.

In fact, Grey admitted to himself, he had only assumed that Hal shared his faith in their father because he could not bear to think otherwise. If he were honest with himself, he must admit now that if Hal had not spoken to him of the matter, it was as much because he had never brought it up as because Hal had avoided discussion. He had been afraid to hear what he feared was the truth: that Hal knew something unpleasant and certain about the duke that he did not, but had spared him that knowledge out of kindness.

While it was good to discover the truth of Hal's feelings now, any sense of relief he might have felt in the discovery was obscured by outrage. The fact that he knew the outrage to be largely unjustified only made it worse.

Worst of all was a sense of self-disgust, a feeling that he had wronged Hal – if only in his thoughts – and anger at the sense that he had been betrayed into committing injustice.

He got up, restless, and strode round the room, careful to step softly. His mother's room lay below his.

He couldn't even have it out with Hal, as that would involve his admitting to doubts that he preferred to keep buried, particularly now that they had been disproved. At least, his doubts regarding Hal had been disproved. As to his father . . . what the devil did that page from the missing journal mean? Who had left it? And why had his mother told Hal the duke had burnt the journal, when clearly he had not?

He glanced at the floor beneath his feet, debating the wisdom of going down and rousing his mother in order to ask her. But Hal had wished to speak to her alone; Grey supposed that was his right. Still, if either one of them thought he would be fobbed off now with further evasions or easy reassurances . . . He realized that he was clenching his fists, and opened them.

'You are grossly mistaken,' he said softly, and rubbed his palm against his leg. 'Both of you.'

He had left his watch open on the desk. It chimed softly now, and he picked it up, holding it toward the fire to see the time – half two. He set it down again, next to the journal that also lay there, one of his father's. He'd taken the volume at random from the library and brought it upstairs with him, for no good reason. Only feeling the need to touch it.

He laid a hand gently on the cover. Rough-tanned leather, the pages sewn in. It was like all the duke's journals, made to withstand travel and the vicissitudes of campaign.

. . . watched the Perseids fall before the dawn twilight this morning, with V. and John. We lay upon the lawn, and counted more than sixty meteors within the space of an hour, at least a dozen very bright, with a visible tinge of blue or green.

He repeated the sentence to himself, making sure he had it word for word. That was the only sentence on the page Hal had burned that mentioned himself by name; a nugget of gold.

He hadn't remembered that night at all, until the casual record brought it back: cool damp from the lawn seeping through his clothes, excitement overcoming the pull of sleep and the longing for his warm bed. Then the 'Ah!' from his father and Victor – yes, 'V.' was Victor Arbuthnot, one of his father's astronomical friends. Was Arbuthnot still alive? he wondered. The sudden jerk of his heart at sight of the first shooting star – a brief and silent streak of light, startling as though a star had indeed fallen suddenly from its place.

That was what he most remembered – the silence. The men had talked at first, chatting casually; he had paid no attention, half-dreaming as he was. But then their conversation had faded, and the three of them lay flat on their backs, faces turned upward to the heavens, waiting together. Silent.

Poets spoke of the song of the heavens, the music of the spheres – and God knew, it was true. The silence of the stars chimed in the heart.

He paused by the window, looking up into a lavender sky, fingers pressed against the icy glass. No stars tonight; the snowflakes came down out of the dark, rushing toward him, endless, uncountable. Silent, too, but not like the stars. Falling snow whispered secrets to itself.

'And you are a fanciful idiot,' he said out loud, and turned away from the window. 'Be writing poetry, next thing.'

He made himself lie down, and lay staring up at the plastered ceiling. Remembering the stargazing had quieted him, though he thought he would not sleep. Too many thoughts swirled through his brain, endless and confusing as the snowflakes. Missing journals, reappearing pages, ancient wagers – was that wager at the root of the animus between his brother and Colonel Twelvetrees? And the so-called sodomite conspiracy – had that anything to do with his family's affairs? He might as well try to fit the falling snowflakes together in a way that made sense.

It was only as his eyes closed that he realized that while snowflakes cannot fit, they do accumulate. One upon another, until the sheer mass of them forms a crust that a man might walk upon – or fall through.

He would wait and see how deep the drifts lay, come morning.

In the morning, though, a letter came.

'Geneva Dunsany is dead.' Benedicta, Dowager Countess of Melton, set down the black-bordered letter very gently by her plate, her face pale. The footman froze in the act of presenting more toast.

For an instant, the words had no meaning. The hot tea in Grey's cup warmed his fingers through the china, fragrant steam in his nostrils mingling with the scents of fried kippers, hot bread, and marmalade. Then he heard what his mother had said, and set down his cup.

'God rest her soul,' he said. His lips felt numb, in spite of the tea. 'How?'

The countess closed her eyes for an instant, looking suddenly her age.

'In childbirth,' she said, drawing a long breath, and opening her eyes. 'The child has survived, so far. A son, Lady Dunsany says.' The color was beginning to seep back into the countess's face, and she picked up the letter again.

'Here is something remarkable, though terribly sad,' she said. 'She says that the child's father – that would be Ellesmere, old Ludovic, you know – died on the same day as his wife.'

'Oh, dear!' His cousin Olivia looked at her aunt, tears beginning to well up in her eyes. Olivia was a tenderhearted girl to begin with, and her inclination to be affected by sentiment had grown more pronounced with her own advancing pregnancy. Though Grey supposed that the news that Geneva Dunsany had perished in giving birth was bound to have a morbid effect on a young woman in similar condition.

Grey coughed, wishing to distract his cousin – and to keep his own feelings at bay for the moment.

'I do not suppose the earl died of a broken heart,' he said. 'The shock, perhaps?'

'How do you know it was not a broken heart?' Olivia asked reproachfully, dabbing at her eyes with her napkin. 'Were anything to happen to my darling Malcolm, I am sure I should not survive the news!' Her eyes overflowed at thought of her new husband, presently serving in the wilds of America.

The countess gave her son a jaundiced look; Olivia had come back to live with her aunt after Malcolm Stubbs's departure for Albany, and Grey supposed that his cousin's vivid imagination and outspoken emotions were perhaps beginning to wear upon his mother, who was kind but not particularly patient.

'I believe Ellesmere was a good fifty years his wife's senior,' Grey said, in an attempt to make amends. 'And while I am sure he was fond of her, I think his death much more likely to have been due to an apoplexy or seizure at the shock than to an excess of sorrow.'

'Oh.' Olivia sniffed and wiped her nose with the napkin. 'Oh, but the poor little mite, left an orphan on the very day of his birth! Is that not terrible?'

'Terrible,' the countess agreed absently, continuing to read. 'It was not an apoplexy, though, nor yet a surfeit of emotion. Lady Dunsany says that the earl perished through some tragic accident.'

Olivia looked blank.

'An accident?' she repeated, and wiped absently at her nose before replacing the napkin in her lap. 'What happened?'

'Lady Dunsany does not say,' the countess reported, frowning at the letter. 'How peculiar. They are very much distressed, of course.'

'Had Ellesmere any family,' Grey inquired, 'or will the Dunsanys take the child?'

'They have taken him. Her chief concern, beyond the immediacies of the situation, is Isobel. She was so close to her sister, and her grief . . .' The countess laid down the letter, shaking her head, then pursed her lips and focused a thoughtful look on Grey.

'She asks whether you might see fit to visit them soon, John. Isobel is so fond of you; Lady Dunsany thinks perhaps you might be able to distract her somewhat from the burden of her grief. The funeral – or perhaps funerals; do you suppose they will be buried together? – are set for Thursday next. I suppose that you would go to Helwater fairly soon in any case, to assure yourself of the welfare of your pet criminal before the regiment departs, but—'

'Your pet criminal?' Olivia, who had resumed buttering her toast, paused openmouthed, knife in midair. 'What—?'

'Really, Mother,' Grey said mildly, hoping that the sudden lurch of his heart did not show. 'Mr. Fraser is –'

'A Jacobite, a convicted traitor, and a murderer,' his mother interrupted crisply. 'Really, John, I cannot see *why* you should have gone to such lengths to keep such a man in England, when by rights, he should have been transported. Indeed, I am surprised he was not hanged outright!'

'I had reasons,' Grey replied, keeping voice and eyes both level. 'And I am afraid you must trust my judgment in the matter, Mother.'

A sudden flush burned in his mother's cheeks, though she held his gaze, lips pressed tight. Then something moved in her eyes, some thought.

'Of course,' she said, her voice suddenly as colorless as her cheeks. 'To be sure.' Her eyes were still fixed on Grey, but she was no longer looking at him, rather at something far beyond him. She drew a long breath, then pushed back from the table in sudden decision.

'You will excuse me, my dears. I have a good many things to do this morning.'

'But you've barely touched a thing, Aunt Bennie!'

Olivia protested. 'Won't you have a kipper, a bit of porridge perhaps . . .' But the countess had already gone, in a whisk of skirts.

Olivia turned a suspicious gaze on Grey.

'What was *that* about?'

'I have no idea,' Grey replied honestly.

'Something about this wretched Mr. Fraser of yours disturbed her,' Olivia said, frowning at the doorway through which the countess had vanished. 'Who *is* he?'

Christ, how was he to answer such a question? He chose the only possible avenue, that of strict factuality.

'He is, as my mother remarked, a Jacobite officer, a Scot. He was amongst the prisoners at Ardsmuir; I came to know him there.'

'But he is at Helwater? How comes he to be there?' Olivia asked, baffled.

'Ardsmuir was closed, the prisoners removed,' he replied, paying careful attention to his kipper. He lifted the bones and set them neatly aside, shrugging one shoulder. 'Fraser was paroled, but not allowed to return to Scotland. He labors as a groom at Helwater.'

'Hmm!' Olivia seemed satisfied with that. 'Well, and serve him right, no doubt, horrid creature. But why does Aunt Bennie call him your pet?'

'Only her little jest,' Grey replied casually, forking up a bite of kipper. 'As I am a longtime friend to the Dunsany family, I visit Helwater regularly – and as the erstwhile governor of Ardsmuir, it behooves me to see that Mr. Fraser is well behaved and in good health.'

Olivia nodded, chewing. She swallowed her toast, then, with a covert glance at the footman, leaned toward Grey, lowering her voice.

'Is he really a *murderer*?' she whispered.

That took Grey off guard, and he was obliged to simulate a minor coughing fit.

'I do not believe so,' he said at last, clearing his throat. 'I imagine my mother spoke rhetorically. She has the lowest opinion of Jacobites in general, you see.'

Olivia nodded wisely, eyes round. She had been no more than five or six at the time of the Rising, but must have heard some echoes of the public hysteria as the forces of Charles Stuart made what had seemed for a time their inexorable advance on London. Even the king had prepared to flee, and the streets were flooded with broadsheets painting the Highlanders as vicious savages who skewered children, pillaged and raped without mercy, and put whole villages to the torch.

As for his mother's personal animus toward the Jacobites . . . he did not know whether Olivia had ever been told anything; probably not. It had all happened long before she was born, and neither his mother nor Hal ever spoke of it, he knew from experience. Well, it was no business of Grey's to inform Olivia of the gory details of the family scandal. His mother and brother were both determined to let the past bury its dead, and surely . . .

He stopped eating, an extraordinary apprehension making the hair prickle on his nape.

No. Surely not. But it had been the mention of Fraser and the word 'Jacobite' that had made the countess blench and pale. Yet she had known about Fraser – Grey had gone several times to Helwater since Fraser had been paroled there. He had never made much of the matter himself, though, never mentioned Fraser's presence as the principal reason for his visits. No, some thought had occurred to his mother, something that had not struck her before. Could it be that she had suddenly thought his reasons for keeping James Fraser in England had to do with . . .

Something small and cold slid wormlike through his entrails.

Olivia had lost interest in the Scottish prisoner, and was happily outlining her plans for the suit he would wear for the wedding.

'Yellow velvet, I think,' she said, squinting consideringly at him over the tea cozy. 'It will be lovely against Aunt Bennie's blue, it will set off your own coloring, and I *think* it will be good for the general's stepson. Your mother says he is dark – have you met him?'

'I have, and yes, he is dark,' Grey said, his innards performing an immediate *volte-face* and growing noticeably warm. 'You intend that we should be dressed alike? In yellow? Olivia, we shall look like nothing so much as a pair of singing canaries.' He'd spoken in all seriousness, but the observation sent her off into giggles, and made her snort tea through her nose. Which absurd sight made Grey himself laugh.

'Well,' Olivia said, recovering first, 'if you *do* mean to go up to the Lake District, I suppose you'd best go quickly, in order to be back in good time for the wedding. Whether it is yellow or not, you *will* have a new suit, and the fittings . . .'

Grey was no longer attending, though. Christ, he *would* have to go at once, if he meant to go at all. The funeral and Isobel Dunsany's need quite aside, the wedding was in late February; were he to delay, he would have no chance to go and return before the regiment set sail for France in March.

For the first time, his anticipation at the prospect of visiting Helwater was tinged with slight dismay. Percy Wainwright . . . but after all, there was no hurry in that quarter, was there? Particularly not if Wainwright should indeed join the regiment. And he was meant to meet the man this afternoon; he would be able to explain. Perhaps even to . . .

A movement in the doorway drew his eye, and he glanced up to see his mother standing there, hand braced against the jamb.

'Go if you must,' she said abruptly. 'But for God's sake, John, be careful.'

Then she turned and was gone again. Thoroughly unsettled, he picked up his cup, found the tea had gone cold, and drank it just the same.

Chapter 4

Chisping

It was chisping, that ambiguous sort of precipitation, half snow, not quite drizzle. Misshapen flakes fell slow and scattered, spiraled through gray air and brushed his face, tiny cold touches so fleeting as not even to leave a sense of wetness in their wake. Dry tears, he thought. Appropriate to his sense of distant mourning.

He paused at the edge of Haymarket, waiting his chance to dodge through the traffic of cabs, carriages, horses, and handcarts. It was a long walk; he might have ridden, called for a chair, or taken his mother's carriage, but he had felt restless, wanting air and movement and the proximity of people with whom he need not talk. Needing time to prepare, before he met Percy Wainwright again.

He was shocked, of course. He had known Geneva since her birth. A lovely girl, with great charm of manner and a light in her eyes. Somewhat spoilt, though attractively so, and reckless to a degree. Superb on a horse. He would not have been surprised in the slightest to hear that she had broken her neck in some hunting accident, or died in leaping a horse across some dangerous chasm. The sheer *ordinariness* of death in childbirth . . . that seemed somehow wrong, obscurely unworthy of her.

He still remembered the occasion when she had gone riding with him, challenged him to a race, and when he declined, had calmly unpinned her hat, leaned over, and smacked his horse on the rump with it, then kicked her own mount and galloped off, leaving him to subdue a panicked sixteen-hand gelding, then to pursue her at breakneck pace over the rocky fells above Helwater. He was a good horseman – but he'd never caught her.

As though still challenged by the memory, he plunged into the street and dashed across the cobbles, ducking under the startled nose of a hurtling cab horse, and arrived at the other side, heart pounding and the cabbie's curses ringing in his ears.

He turned down St. Martin's Lane, feeling the blood thrum in his ears and fingers, with that half-shameful sense of pleasure in being alive that was sometimes the response to news of death, or the sight of it.

He could not yet think of her as dead. Perhaps he would not until he reached Helwater, and found himself amongst her family, walking through the places that had known her. He tried to envision her, but found that her face had faded from his memory, though he kept a strong sense of her form, lithe in a brown habit, chestnut-haired and quick as a fox.

Quite suddenly, he wondered whether he could

recall Percy Wainwright's face. He had spent all of a two-hour luncheon the day before yesterday in gazing at it, but was suddenly unsure. And much of the second hour in imagining the form that lay beneath the neat blue suit; he was more sure of *that*, and his heart sped up in anticipation.

What he saw in his mind's eye, though, was another face, another form, vivid as flame among the damp greens and grays of the fells. He *saw* it, the long, suspicious nose, the narrowed eyes hostile as a leopard's, as though the man himself stood before him, and the pleasant thrum of his blood changed at once to something deeper and more visceral.

He realized now that the vision had sprung up in him at once, the moment his mother had spoken the words, 'Geneva Dunsany is dead' – though he had instinctively been suppressing it. Geneva Dunsany meant Helwater. And Helwater meant not only his memories of Geneva, nor the griefs of her parents and sister. It meant Jamie Fraser.

'God damn it,' he said to the vision, under his breath. 'Not *now*. Go away!'

And walked on to his engagement, heedless of the chisping snow, his heated blood in ferment.

They had agreed to meet beforehand, and go together to Lady Jonas's salon. Not sure either of Wainwright's means or his style, Grey had chosen the Balboa, a modest coffeehouse chiefly patronized by sea traders and brokers.

The place was always cheerful and bustling, with men huddled intently in small groups, plotting strategy, wrangling over contracts, absorbed in the details of business in a fragrant, invigorating atmosphere of roasting coffee. Now and then a clerk or 'prentice rushed in in panic to fetch out one of the patrons to deal with some emergency of business – but in the postluncheon lull, most of the merchants had returned to their offices and warehouses; it would be possible at least to have a conversation.

Grey was punctual by habit and arrived just as his pocket watch chimed three, but Percy Wainwright was already there, seated at a table near the back.

He did recognize the man; indeed, his putative stepbrother's face seemed to spring smiling out of the dimness, vivid as though he sat by a candle flame, and the disquieting wraith of Jamie Fraser disappeared at once from Grey's mind.

'You are very prompt,' he remarked, waving Wainwright back onto his stool and taking one opposite. 'I hope you did not have too far to come?'

'Oh, no; I have rooms quite near – in Audley Street.' Wainwright nodded, indicating the direction, though his eyes stayed fixed on Grey, friendly, but intensely curious.

Grey was equally curious, but took care not to seem to examine his companion too closely. He ordered coffee for himself, and took the opportunity of Wainwright's speaking to the waiter to look, covertly. Good style, an elegant but quiet cut, the cloth a little worn, but originally of good quality. Linen very fine, and immaculate – as were the long, knob-jointed fingers that took up the sugar tongs, Wainwright's dark brows lifting in inquiry.

Grey shook his head.

'I am not fond of sugar, but I do like cream.'

'As do I.' Wainwright set down the tongs at once, and they smiled unexpectedly at finding that they shared this trifling preference – then smiled wider, finally laughing at the absurdity, for lack of anything sensible to say.

Grey picked up his coffee and spilled some into the saucer to cool, wondering quite what to say next. He was intensely curious to learn more of Percy Wainwright, but not sure how closely he might inquire without giving offense.

He had already learned a little from his mother: Percy Wainwright was the son of an impoverished clergyman who had died young, leaving the boy and his mother a small annuity. They had lived in genteel poverty for some years, but Mrs. Wainwright had been quite beautiful, and eventually had met and married General Stanley – himself a widower of many years' standing.

'I believe they were quite happy,' his mother had said, dispassionate. 'But she died only a few months after the wedding – of the consumption, I believe.'

She had been looking thoughtfully into her looking glass as they talked, turning her head this way and that, eyes half-closing in quizzical evaluation.

'You are very beautiful, too, Mother,' he'd said,

both amused and rather touched by what he took as this unusual evidence of doubt.

'Well, yes,' she said frankly, laying down the glass. 'For my age, I am remarkably handsome. Though I do think the general values me more for my rude good health than for the fact that I have all my teeth and good skin. He has buried two sickly wives, and found it distressing.'

His mother, of course, had buried two husbands – but she didn't mention that, and neither did he.

He asked the usual social questions now – did Wainwright go often to Lady Jonas's salons? Grey had not yet had the pleasure. How did Mr. Wainwright find the company there, by comparison with other such gatherings? – meanwhile thinking that the late Lady Stanley must have been very beautiful indeed, judging by her son.

And I doubt extremely that I am the first man to have noticed that, he thought. *Is there anyone . . . ?*

While he hesitated, Percy gave him a direct look and put the question that was in the forefront of his own mind.

'Do you go often? To Lavender House?'

He felt a slight easing, for the asking of the question answered it, so far as he was himself concerned; if Wainwright were in the habit of frequenting Lavender House, he would know that Grey was not.

'No,' he said, and smiled again. 'I had not visited the place in many years, prior to the occasion when I met you there.'

'That was my first – and only – visit,' Percy confessed. He looked down into his dish of coffee. 'A . . . friend sought to introduce me to the company, thinking that I might find some congeniality of persons there.'

'And did you?'

Percy Wainwright had long, dark lashes. These lifted slowly, giving Grey the benefit of those warm-sherry eyes, further warmed by a look of amusement.

'Oh, yes,' Percy said. 'Did you?'

Grey felt blood rise in his face, and lifted his coffee to his mouth, so that the warmth of the liquid might disguise it.

'The pursuit of . . . congeniality was not my purpose,' he said carefully, lowering the cup. 'I had gone there in order to question the proprietor about a private matter. Still,' he added, offhanded, 'it would be a foolish man who disregards a pound discovered lying by his foot in the road, only because he was not looking for it.' He darted a look at Percy, who laughed in delight.

Suddenly, Grey felt a rush of exhilaration, and could not bear to remain indoors, sitting.

'Shall we go?'

Percy drank off his coffee in a gulp and rose, reaching for his cloak with one hand, even as he set down his cup with the other.

The walls of the Balboa were plastered with trivia for the edification of patrons – the entire series of Mr. Hogarth's 'Marriage à la Mode' etchings

70

encircled the room, but were surrounded – and in some cases obscured – by thick flutterings of newspaper broadsheets, personal communiqués, and *Wanted* notices, these advertising a need for everything from six tonnes of pig lead or a shipload of Negroes, to a company director of good name and solid finances who might assume the leadership of a fledgling firm engaging in the sale of gentlemen's necessaries – whether these might include snuff-boxes, stockings, or condoms was not made clear.

Glancing casually at the new crop of postings as they made their way to the door, though, Grey's eye caught a familiar name in the headline of a fresh broadsheet. DEATH DISCOVERED, read the large type.

He stopped short, the name *Ffoulkes* leaping out of the smaller newsprint at him.

'What?' Percy had perforce halted, too, and was looking curiously from Grey to the newspaper.

'Nothing. A name I recognized.' Grey's elation dimmed a little, though he was too excited to be quelled completely. 'Are you familiar with a barrister named Ffoulkes? Melchior Ffoulkes?' he asked Percy.

The latter looked blank and shook his head.

'I am afraid I know no one, much,' he said apologetically. 'Should I have heard of Mr. Ffoulkes?'

'Not at all.' Grey would just as soon have dismissed Ffoulkes from his own mind, but felt obliged to see whether anything of what Hal had told him had made it into the public press. He tossed a silver ha'penny to the proprietor and took the broadsheet, folding it and stuffing it into his pocket. Time enough for such things later.

Outside, the chisping had stopped, but the sky hung low and heavy, and there was a sense of stillness in the air, the earth awaiting more snow. Alone, away from the buzz of the coffeehouse, there was a sudden small sense of intimacy between them.

'I must apologize,' Percy said, as they turned toward Hyde Park.

'For what?'

'For my unfortunate gaffe yesterday, in regard to your brother. The general *had* told me that I must not under any circumstance address him as "Your Grace," but he had not time to explain why – at the time.'

Grey snorted.

'Has he told you since?'

'Not in great detail.' Percy glanced at him, curious. 'Only that there was a scandal of some sort, and that your brother in consequence has renounced his title.'

Grey sighed. Unavoidable, he'd known that. Still, he would have preferred to keep this first meeting for themselves, with no intrusions from either past or present.

'Not exactly,' he said. 'But something like it.'

'Your father *was* a duke, though?' Wainwright cast him a wary glance.

'He was. Duke of Pardloe.' The title felt strange on his tongue; he hadn't spoken it in . . . fifteen years? More. So long. He felt an accustomed hollowness of the bone at thought of his father. But if there was to be anything between himself and Percy Wainwright . . .

'But your brother is *not* now Duke of Pardloe?'

Despite himself, Grey smiled, albeit wryly.

'He is. But he will not use the title, nor have it used. Hence the occasional awkwardness.' He made a small gesture of apology. 'My brother is a very stubborn man.'

Wainwright raised one brow, as though to suggest that he thought Melton might not be the only one in the Grey family to display such a trait.

'You need not tell me,' he said, though, touching Grey's arm briefly. 'I'm sure the matter is a painful one.'

'You will hear it sooner or later, and you have some right to know, as you are becoming allied with our family. My father shot himself,' Grey said abruptly. Percy blinked, shocked.

'Oh,' he said, low-voiced, and touched his arm again, very gently. 'I am so sorry.'

'So am I.' Grey cleared his throat. 'Cold, isn't it?' He pulled on his gloves, and rubbed a hand beneath his nose. 'It – you have heard of the Jacobites? And the South Sea Bubble?'

'I have, yes. But what have they to do with each other?' Percy asked, bewildered. Grey felt his lips twitch, not quite a smile.

'Nothing, so far as I know. But they had both to do with the – the scandal.'

Gerard Grey, Earl of Melton, had been a clever man. Of an ancient and honorable family, well educated, handsome, wealthy – and of a restless, curious turn of mind. He had also been a very fine soldier.

'My father came to the title as quite a young man, and was not content to potter about on the family estates. He had a good deal of money – my mother brought him more – and when the Old Pretender launched his first invasion in 1715, he raised a regiment, and went to fight for king and country.'

The Jacobites were ill-organized and badly equipped; the Old Pretender, James Stuart, had not even made it ashore to lead his troops, but had been left fuming impotently off the coast, stranded by bad weather. The invasion, such as it was, had been easily quashed. The dashing young earl, however, had distinguished himself at Sheriffmuir, emerging a hero.

German George, feeling uneasy on his new throne despite the victory, and wishing to demonstrate to the peers of his realm the advantages of supporting him in military terms, elevated Gerard Grey to the newly created dukedom of Pardloe.

'No money with it, mind, and only a scant village or two in terms of land, but it sounded well,' Grey said.

'What – whatever happened?' Percy asked, curiosity overcoming his impeccable manners.

'Well.' Grey took a deep breath, thinking where

best to begin. He did not want to speak at once about his father, and so began from the other end of the affair.

'My mother's mother was Scottish, you see. Not from the Highlands,' he added quickly. 'From the Borders, which is quite a different thing.'

'Yes, they speak English there, do they not?' Wainwright nodded, a small frown of concentration between his brows.

'I expect that is a matter of opinion,' Grey said. It had taken him weeks to become sufficiently accustomed to the hideous accents of his Scottish cousins as to easily understand what they were saying.

'But at least they are not barbarians, such as the Highland Scots. Nor did the Borderers join in the Catholic Rising – most being strongly Protestant, and having no particular sympathy or common interest with either the Stuarts or the Highland clans.'

'I suppose, though, that many Englishmen do not make distinctions between one Scot and another?' Percy said, with some delicacy.

Grey gave a small grimace of acknowledgment.

'It did not help that one of my mother's uncles and his sons *did* openly support the Stuart cause. For the sake of profit,' he added, with slight distaste, 'not religion.'

'Is that better or worse?' Percy asked, a half smile taking any sting from the words.

'Not much to choose,' Grey admitted. 'And

before the thing was finished, a good many more of my mother's family were embroiled. If not actually known Jacobites, certainly tainted by the association.'

'I see.' Wainwright's brows were high with interest. 'You mentioned your father's involvement with the South Sea Bubble. Do we assume that this had something to do with your profit-minded great-uncle?'

Grey glanced at him, surprised at the quickness of his mind.

'Yes,' he said. 'Great-Uncle Nicodemus. Nicodemus Patricius Marcus Armstrong.'

Percy made a small, muffled noise.

'There is a reason why I was christened "John," and that my brothers have such relatively common names as Paul, Edgar, and Harold,' Grey said wryly. 'The names on my mother's side of the family . . .' He shook his head, and resumed his account.

'My father invested a substantial sum with a certain company – the South Sea – upon the urgings of Uncle Nick, after Sheriffmuir. Mind you, this was some years before the collapse; at the time, it seemed no more than a somewhat risky venture. And it appealed, I think, to my father's sense of adventure, which was acute.' He couldn't help a brief smile at thought of some of those adventures.

'It was a substantial sum, but by no means a significant part of my father's property. He was therefore content to leave it, depending upon Uncle Nick to watch the business, whilst he devoted himself to other, more interesting ventures. But then the Jacobite threat—' He paused, glancing at Percy.

'How old are you, if you will pardon my asking?'

Percy blinked at that, but smiled.

'Twenty-six. Why?'

'Ah. You may be old enough, then, to recall the atmosphere of suspicion and hysteria regarding Jacobites during the '45?'

Percy shook his head.

'No,' he said ruefully. 'My father was a clergyman, who viewed the world and its affairs as nothing more than a threat to the souls of the godly. We heard little news, and would have taken no heed of political rumors in any case – the only king of any importance being the Lord, so far as my father was concerned. But that's of no consequence,' he added hastily. 'Go on, please.'

'I was going to say that that hysteria, great as it was, was no more than an echo of what happened earlier. Are you content to walk, by the way? We could easily take a carriage.' The weather had grown sharply colder, and a bone-cutting breeze swept through the alleyways. Percy was lightly dressed for the temperature, but he shook his head.

'No, I prefer to walk. It's much easier to talk – if you wish to do that,' he added, a little shyly.

Grey wasn't at all sure that he wished to do that – his offer of a carriage had been based as much on a sudden desire to abandon the conversation for the moment as on a desire to save Mr. Wainwright from a chilled liver. But he'd meant it; Wainwright had a right to know, and might better hear the details from him than from someone who held the late duke in less esteem.

'Well. You will know, I suppose, that raising, equipping, and maintaining a regiment is an expensive business. My father had money, as I said, but in order to expand the regiment when the Jacobite threat recurred in 1719, he sold his South Sea shares – quite against the advice of Great-Uncle Nicodemus, I might add.'

Within the previous five years, the price of South Sea shares had risen, from ten pounds to a hundred, then dizzyingly, from a hundred to a thousand within a year, driven up by rumor, greed – and not a little calculated chicanery on the part of the company's directors. The duke sold his shares at this pinnacle.

'And a week – one week – later, the slide began.' It had taken most of a year for the full devastation of the great crash to become evident. Several great families had been ruined; many lesser folk all but obliterated. And the public outcry toward those seen to be responsible . . .

'I can imagine.' Percy glanced at him. He wore no hat, and the tips of his ears were red with cold. 'But your father was *not* responsible, was he?'

Grey shook his head.

'He was seen to profit immensely, while others went bankrupt,' he said simply. 'Nothing else was needed to convict him in the popular mind.' And the House of Commons, that voice of the popular mind, had been vociferous in their denunciations.

'But he was a duke.' Grey watched the words purl out, his breath like smoke. 'He could not be tried, save by his peers. And the House of Lords declined to proceed.' Not from any sense of justice – many noble families had suffered in the crash and were quite as irrationally bloodthirsty as the commoners. But the Duke of Pardloe chose his friends carefully, and the ravenings of the mob moved on to easier prey.

'Such things leave a mark, though. Enemies were made, enmities lingered. And it was the more unfortunate that my father should have been a good friend of Francis Atterbury's. The Bishop of Rochester,' he added, seeing Percy's puzzled look. 'Convicted of being the focus of a Jacobite plot to exploit public feeling about the South Sea Bubble by staging a Stuart invasion and dethroning the king, in '22. Banished, though, not executed.'

Their path had led them to Hyde Park, for the most direct way to Lady Jonas's house lay straight across it. They were now well within the park, and Grey gestured to the wide spaces all around them, empty and desolate.

'When word got out of the plot in '22, His Majesty in panic ordered ten thousand troops to London, to safeguard the city. They were quartered here – in the park. My father told me of it; he said the smoke of their fires was thicker than the morning fog, and the stench was indescribable. Convenient, though; the family house stands on the edge of the park – just beyond those trees.' He gestured toward it, with a brief smile at the memory, then went on.

'My father merely played chess with the bishop; he had no Jacobite leanings whatever. But again—'

'The popular mind.' Percy nodded. '*And* your mother's family. So he was perceived as a Jacobite sympathizer? The notion being that he had somehow engineered the crash in order to facilitate the invasion – though it never happened?'

Grey nodded, a sense of hollowness growing beneath his breastbone. He had never told the story to anyone before, and was both surprised and disturbed that the words came so easily to him. He was coming now to the most difficult part of the history, though, and so hesitated.

'There was another Jacobite scare, a decade later – this one no more, really, than talk. Lord Cornbury it was, who was the instigator. No one would have noticed, really, save he was the Earl of Clarendon's heir. And it came to nothing in the end; Cornbury was not even imprisoned – merely left off meddling in politics.' He smiled again, though without humor.

Percy's lower teeth were fixed in his upper lip. He shook his head slowly.

'Don't tell me. Cornbury was also an intimate of your father's?'

'Ah – no. My mother.' He gave Percy a wry glance. 'Or rather, Cornbury had been a close friend to her first husband. Thus Cornbury is my eldest half brother's godfather. Not a close connexion, by any means – but it *was* a connexion, and it didn't help when the rumors about another Stuart Rising began in 1740.'

He took a breath and released it slowly, watching the steam of it.

'There were . . . other Jacobite influences. My mother's family, as you say. And then – one of my father's nearest friends was exposed as a Jacobite plotter, and arrested. The man was taken to the Tower and questioned closely – I do not know whether that is a euphemism for torture; it was not said – but under the pressure of such questioning, he revealed a number of names. Persons, it was claimed, who were involved in a direct plot to assassinate the king and his family.'

Speaking these words now, from the far side of Culloden, the idea seemed preposterous. He thought it had perhaps seemed equally ludicrous to his parents – at first.

'He – this Jacobite plotter – incriminated your father?'

Grey nodded, somewhat comforted to see that Percy looked both aghast and incredulous at this.

'Yes. There was no direct evidence – or at least none was ever produced. But the matter did not come to trial. A warrant was issued for my father's arrest. He . . . died – the night before it was to be executed.'

'Oh, dear God,' Percy said, very quietly. He did not touch Grey again, but drew closer, walking slowly, so that their shoulders nearly brushed.

'Of course,' Percy said after a moment, 'your father's death was taken as an admission of guilt?' He put the question delicately, but remembered bitterness filled Grey's throat with the taste of bile.

'It was. A Bill of Attainder was brought against my father's title, but did not pass.' He smiled wryly.

'My father had many enemies, but just as many friends. And a much better instinct in choosing godfathers for his sons than my mother's first husband. Hal's godfather was Robert Walpole.'

'What, the prime minister?' Percy looked gratifyingly agog.

'Well, he wasn't at the time of Hal's birth, of course. And when the scandal broke, twenty-some years later, Walpole was very near his own death – but still an immensely powerful man.

'And,' Grey added judiciously, 'whatever his personal feelings in the matter, it wouldn't have done Walpole's own reputation any good to have his godson's father publicly denounced as a traitor. Not at such a delicate point in his own affairs.

'So,' he concluded, 'the Bill of Attainder was quashed. My father had not, after all, been proved a traitor. There was sufficient public – and private – outcry, though, that Hal declared he would not bear a tainted title, and has ever since refused to use it. He did wish to renounce it completely, but could not by law.'

He gave a short laugh.

'So. A very long story, I am afraid – but we do arrive at the end, never fear.'

Within two or three years of the duke's death, Charles Edward Stuart had begun to make a nuisance of himself, and Jacobite hysteria had once more swept the country, rising to a peak upon the Bonnie Prince's arrival in the Highlands.

'Whereupon Hal promptly raised the standard of our father's old regiment, spent a fortune in reconstituting it, and marched off to the Highlands in the service of the king. The king was in no position to refuse such service, any more than his father had been when my father did the same thing thirty years before.'

He said nothing of the immensity of Hal's effort. At the time, he had been barely fifteen and ignorant, not only of the true dimensions of the scandal, but of his brother's response to it. Only now, looking back, could he appreciate the tremendous energy and almost maniacal single-mindedness that had enabled Hal to do what he'd done.

Melton, grimly intent upon restoring the family's lost honor, had met the Highlanders – and defeat – with Cope at Prestonpans. Went on to hold his own in the less decisive battle at Falkirk – and then at Culloden . . .

Grey's voice dried in his throat, and he paused, mouth working to find a little saliva.

'A famous victory!' Percy said, his voice respectful. 'I read of that, at least, in the newspapers.'

'I hope you never see one like it,' Grey said shortly. He curled his left hand into a fist, feeling

Hector's sapphire ring press against the leather of his glove. Hector had died at Culloden. But he did not mean to speak of Hector.

Percy glanced at him, surprised by his tone, but did not reply. Grey breathed deeply, the air cold and heavy in his chest. They had been walking slowly, but had come through the park and were now within sight of Lady Jonas's house; he could see guests coming in ones and twos, being welcomed at the door by the butler.

With unspoken consent, they stopped, a little way down the street. Wainwright turned to face him, his eyes still warm, but serious.

'Your mother does not style herself Duchess?' he asked, and Grey shook his head.

'My brother became head of the family at my father's death; she would do nothing that might seem to undermine his authority. She uses the title Dowager Countess of Melton.'

'I see.' Wainwright studied Grey with open curiosity. 'And yet you have continued to call yourself . . .'

'Lord John. Yes, I have.'

The corner of Wainwright's mouth tucked back.

'I see that your brother is not alone in being stubborn.'

'It runs in the family,' Grey replied. 'Shall we go in?'

Chapter 5

Genius and Sub-Genius

Grey noted at once that Percy was not entirely comfortable.

His color was high, and while he handed his cloak to the butler with aplomb, he looked quickly round the drawing room to which they were taken, as though searching for acquaintance, then glanced back at Grey uncertainly. His face brightened, though, as he spotted their hostess, and he hastened forward, Grey in his wake.

He bowed to Lady Jonas, and introduced Grey to her; she greeted them kindly, but with that air of distraction that attends a hostess in search of more-distinguished guests. They kissed her hand in turn and retired to the drinks table.

'You don't do this often, do you?' Grey murmured to Percy.

'Does it show?' Wainwright cast him a glance of half-comic alarm, and he laughed.

'Not at all,' he assured Percy. 'It is only that no one save Lady Jonas has spoken to you since we entered. How do you come to know her?'

Wainwright shrugged a little, looking embarrassed.

'She stepped on my foot at a ball. At Sir Richard Joffrey's house – the general had taken me there to meet Colonel Quarry. But Lady Jonas apologized most gracefully, asked my name – she knew the general, of course – and ended by inviting me to her salon, with any friend I might choose to bring. She said' – Percy blushed, avoiding Grey's eye – 'that beautiful boys were always welcome.'

'I have found that generally to be the case in society,' Grey said, tactfully ignoring both the blush and the implied compliment. 'Regardless of sex.' He nodded at the Honorable Helene Rowbotham, whose swanlike neck and doelike eyes were exciting their usual admiration near the window where she had placed herself so as to take best advantage of the pale winter sun.

'On the other hand,' he said lightly, 'a party at which the guests are all of the beautiful persuasion tends to be dull indeed, as they have no conversation that does not pertain to themselves. A successful gathering requires a number of the ill-favored but clever. The beautiful are but ornaments – desirable, but dispensable.'

'Indeed,' Percy said dryly. 'And in which camp do you place yourself here? Beautiful and dull, or homely and clever?'

'Oh,' Grey said lightly, and touched Percy's wrist, 'I'll be wherever you are . . . Brother.'

The blush, which had receded, surged back full force. Wainwright had no chance to reply, though, before Grey perceived Lady Beverley drifting toward them, an intentness in her eye at sight of Percy.

'Light-frigate off the starboard bow,' he said under his breath. Percy frowned in bewilderment, but then saw the direction of his glance.

'Really? She looks most respectable,' Percy murmured, he having evidently spent enough time with General Stanley in military circles as to have acquired familiarity with such terms as 'light-frigate' for a woman of easy virtue.

'Don't go into an alcove with her,' Grey murmured back, already nodding and smiling at the approaching lady. 'She'll have her hand in your breeches before you can say – Lady Beverley! Your servant, madam – may I present you my new step-brother, Percival Wainwright?'

Seeing the hint of hesitation in Percy's eye, he grasped Lady Beverley's trailing hand and kissed it, thus signaling to Percy that, yes, she *was* married, reputation notwithstanding, then gracefully relinquished the appendage to Wainwright for the bestowal of his own homage.

'Mr. Wainwright.' Lady Beverley gave him a look of approval, then turned the force of her not inconsiderable charm on Grey. 'We are obliged to you, Lord John! Monstrous kind of you, to bring such an ornament to decorate our dull society. Do come and have a glass of punch with me, Mr. Wainwright, and tell me what you think of Mr. Garrick's new role – you will have seen it, I'm sure. For myself . . .'

Before either man could draw breath to answer, she had got Percy's hand firmly trapped between her elbow and her yellow silk bodice, and was towing him purposefully toward the refreshment table, still talking.

Wainwright cast Grey a wide-eyed look, and Grey sketched a small salute in return, suppressing a smile. At least Wainwright had been warned. And if he took care to keep Lady Beverley out in the public view, she would be good company. Already she had drawn him into the circle around the guest of honor, which she cleft like the Red Sea, and was introducing him to the French philosopher.

He relaxed a bit, seeing that Percy seemed able to hold his own, and deliberately turned his back, not to embarrass his new relation with undue scrutiny.

'Lord John!' A clear voice hailed him, and he looked round to find his friend Lucinda, Lady Joffrey, smiling at him, a small leather-bound book in one hand. 'How do you do, my dear?'

'Excellently well, I thank you.' He made to kiss her hand, but she laughed and drew him in, standing on tiptoe to kiss his cheek instead.

'I crave a favor, if you please,' she whispered in his ear, and came down on her heels, looking up at him, expectant of his consent.

'You know I can deny you nothing,' he said, smiling. She reminded him always of a partridge, small, neat, and slightly plump, with a kind, soft eye. 'What is your desire, Lady Joffrey? A cup of punch? Sardines on toast? Or had you in mind something more in the way of apes, ivory, and peacocks?'

'It may well be pearls before swine,' she said, dimpling, and handed him the book. 'But the fact of the matter is that I have a . . . relation . . . who has written some verses – negligible, I am sure, but perhaps not without a certain charm. I thought to present them to Monsieur Diderot . . .' She cast a glance toward the window where the distinguished man of letters held court, then turned back, a faint blush mantling her cheeks.

'But I find my nerve fails me.'

Grey gave her a look of patent disbelief. Small and demure she might be in appearance; by temperament she had the guile of a serpent and the tenacity of a sticking plaster.

'Really,' she insisted, both dimple and blush growing deeper. She glanced round to be sure they were not overheard, and leaning close, whispered, 'Have you by chance heard of a novel entitled *Les Bijoux Indiscrets*?'

'I have, Lady Joffrey,' he said, with mock severity, 'and I am shocked to the core of my being to discover that a woman of your character should be acquainted with such a scandalous volume. Have you read it?' he inquired, dropping the pose.

'La, everyone's read it,' she said, relaxing into comfortable scorn. 'Your mother sent it to me last year.'

'Indeed.' He was not surprised; his mother would read anything, and maintained friendships with several similarly indiscriminate ladies, who kept up a constant exchange of books – most of which would have shocked their husbands, had those worthy gentlemen ever bothered to inquire about their wives' pastimes.

'Have you read it?' she asked.

He shook his head. *Les Bijoux Indiscrets* was an erotic novel, written some years before by M. Diderot for Madeleine le Puisieux, his mistress at the time. It had been published in Holland, and for a time, there had been a mania in England for smuggled copies. He'd seen the book, of course, but had done no more than flip through an illustrated copy, looking for the pictures – which were indifferently executed. Perhaps the text was better.

'Prude,' she said.

'Quite. Am I to infer that these . . . verses . . . share something of the sentiments of that particular volume?' He weighed the book in his hand. It was both small and slender, befitting poetry.

'I believe they were inspired by certain of the events depicted therein,' Lady Joffrey said, circumspect. 'The, um, author of the verses wished to present them to Monsieur Diderot as an acknowledgment of the inspiration, I believe – a tribute, if you will.'

He raised a brow at her, and opened the cover. *Certain Verses Upon the Subject of—*

'Jesus,' he said, involuntarily, and shut the book. He immediately opened it again, cautiously, as though afraid it might spit at him.

By an Admirer of the Works of that Urgent Genius,
Monsieur Denis Diderot, who in Humility stiles himself
'Sub-Genius.'

'You didn't write them yourself, did you?' he asked, glancing up. Lady Joffrey's mouth fell open, and he smiled. 'No, of course not. My apologies.'

He thumbed slowly through the book, pausing to read here and there. The verses were actually quite competent, he thought – even good, in spots. Though the material . . .

'Yes,' he said, closing the book and clearing his throat. 'I see why you might hesitate to present this personally – he *is* a Frenchman, though I believe he's said to be quite faithful to his present mistress. I suppose you hadn't looked at the contents before coming here?'

She shook her head, making the pheasant's feathers she wore in her powdered hair sweep across her shoulder.

'No. He – the relation I spoke of – had brought it to me early in the week, but I'd had no chance to look at it. I read it in the carriage on the way – and then, of course, was at a loss what to do, until most fortunately I saw you.' She looked over her shoulder at the group by the window, then back at Grey. 'I did promise to deliver it. Will you? Please?'

'I don't know why your husband does not beat you regularly,' he remarked, shaking his head. 'Or at least keep you locked up safely at home. Has he the slightest idea . . . ?'

'Sir Richard is a most accomplished diplomat,'

she replied with complacence. 'He has a great facility for not knowing things that it is expedient not to know.'

'I daresay,' Grey replied dryly. 'Speaking of knowing – do I know your relation?'

'Why, I am sure I could not say, I have so many,' she answered blandly. 'But speaking of relations – I hear that you are to acquire a new brother? I am told that he is amazing handsome to look at.'

Hearing Percival Wainwright referred to as his brother gave him a slightly odd feeling, as though he might in fact be contemplating incest. He ignored this, though, and nodded toward the table.

'You may judge of that for yourself; there he stands.'

Wainwright had moved away from the throng around the philosopher, and was now surrounded, Grey was pleased to see, by a small group of his own, both men and women, all seeming much amused by his conversation – particularly Lady Beverley, who hung upon both his words and his arm. Wainwright was telling some story, his face alight, and even across the room, Grey felt the warmth of his presence. As though he sensed their scrutiny, Percy glanced suddenly in their direction, and shot Grey a smile of such delight in his surroundings that Grey smiled back, delighted in turn to see him manage so well.

Lucinda Joffrey emitted a hum of approval.

'Oh, yes,' she said. 'And quite good style, too. Did you dress him?' she inquired.

No, but I should like very much to undress him. He cleared his throat.

'No, he has excellent taste of his own.'

'And the money to support it?'

He was not offended. A man's means were generally of more interest than his face, and everyone would be wondering the same thing of a newcomer – though not everyone would ask so bluntly. Lucinda, though, *did* have a great many relations, of whom at least half were female, and felt it her moral duty to help her sisters and cousins to good marriages.

'Unfortunately not. His father – you collect he is the general's stepson? – was a minister of some kind. Family poor as church mice, I gather. The general has settled a small sum upon him, but he has no property.'

Lucinda hummed again, but with less approval.

'Looking for a rich wife, then, is he?' she said, with a degree of resignation. She came from an old and estimable family, but one without wealth.

'Early days for that, surely.' Grey thought he had spoken lightly, but she gave him a sharp look.

'Ho,' she said. 'Does he fancy himself in love with someone unsuitable?'

Grey felt as though she had pushed him suddenly in the chest. He had forgotten just how acute she was. Sir Richard Joffrey was indeed a good diplomat – but no little degree of his success was the result of his wife's social connexions and her ability to ferret out things that it *was* expedient to know.

'If so, he has not told me,' Grey said, achieving, he thought, a good simulation of indifference. 'Have you met the great man yourself? Will I present you?'

'Oh, Monsieur Diderot?' Lucinda turned to eye the guest of honor speculatively. 'I did meet him, some years ago in Paris. A very witty man, though I think I should not care to be married to him.'

'Because he keeps a mistress?'

She looked surprised, then waved her fan in dismissal.

'Oh, no. The difficulty with witty people is that they feel compelled to exhibit their wit *all the time* – which is most tedious over the breakfast table. Sir Richard,' she said with satisfaction, 'is not witty at all.'

'I suppose it wouldn't do in a diplomat,' Grey agreed. 'Will I fetch you some refreshment?'

Lady Joffrey assenting, he made his way through the crowd, the book she had given him still in hand. The room buzzed with conversation and the excitement of a successful salon, but a freak of sound brought him Diderot's voice clearly – nasal, like all Frenchmen, but rich and pleasant. He seemed to be speaking of his wife.

'She has conceived the idea, you see, that all novels are vulgar trash, and desires me to read to her only material of a spiritually uplifting sort – commentaries upon the Bible, the works of – *haha!* – Burke and the like.'

A number of his listeners laughed with him, though Edmund Burke was popular.

'So,' the warm voice went on, audibly amused, 'I have taken to reading her the most ribald stories I can obtain. The value of the lesson is thereby doubled, as she not only hears the stories, but then reports every detail again in horror to her friends!'

A gust of laughter resulted from that, obliging Grey to signal his desire to the servant at the refreshment table, who nodded understanding and gave him a silver cup of punch and a small plate of savories. Balancing these with the book of poetry, he made his way back across the room, only to find Lucinda Joffrey already supplied with refreshment by a new escort, whom he recognized as an influential Member of Parliament.

Lucinda flicked a glance at him over the MP's shoulder, and made a slight gesture with her fan, which he interpreted as a signal that she was engaged in confidential transaction. He nodded understanding and retreated to a convenient window ledge, where he sat in the shelter of the damask draperies and consumed the savories himself with enjoyment, meanwhile observing the ebb and flow of society.

He had not been in the London tide for some time, and found it pleasant to sit and hear the grossest trivialities mingled with the loftiest of philosophical ideas, and to watch the social commerce being conducted under his nose – matches made and unmade, business connexions forged and uncoupled, favors given, acknowledged, and traded. And politics, of course – always politics – talked to death amidst expressions of outrage or approbation, depending upon the company.

And yet he knew there was real power here, could feel the pulse of it throbbing beneath the chatter and clothes. For most of those present, such salons were what they seemed: a source of entertainment at worst, at best a chance to be seen, perhaps to be taken up and made the vogue of the moment. But in the quiet corners, things were said that had the potential to alter lives – perhaps to affect the course of history.

Was it in such places that his own parents' fates had been sealed? It was at an evening musicale that his mother, a young widow, had been introduced to his father, he knew. Why had he been there? Gerard Grey had no ear for music. Had he come for the sake of politics and met love unaware? Or had his mother been part of it, even then?

He'd heard the story of his parents' meeting often as a child; it had been at her brother's house. His mother had three brothers, and a great quantity of ill-defined cousins, half cousins, and persons who were no blood relation but held the status of brothers, having been fostered by the family in that peculiar custom of the Scottish aristocracy.

One uncle was dead now, another living in exile in France. The third had retreated to his Border fortress, far from the public eye. Some cousins had survived the scandal, others had not. Politics was a risky game, and the stakes were high – sometimes mortal.

He felt the shiver of a goose crossing his grave, and shook it off, quaffing the punch in one swallow. He hadn't thought of these things in years, deliberately. But it was his family history; Percy should be told, as much for his own safety as anything else, if he was to move in society – and plainly he wished to. If there was a public connexion between himself and Grey . . . Some people had long memories.

He scanned the faces of the crowd, but luckily saw no one against whom Percy need be warned just yet.

Rising from his hiding place, he nearly collided with Diderot, heading purposefully for the *pissoirs* behind the screen at the end of the room.

'Your pardon, *Monsieur.*' They had clutched each other's arms to keep their feet, smiled and spoke together, then laughed.

The philosopher's face gleamed with sweat, and he mopped carelessly at his forehead with a sleeve. Grey pulled his handkerchief from his pocket to offer it, and felt something fall at his feet.

'Ah.' He stooped to pick it up. '*Permettez-moi, Monsieur. Un petit cadeau – pour Madame votre épouse.*'

Diderot's brows rose a little as he accepted both handkerchief and book; he dabbed absently at his cheeks as he flipped open the book with his thumb, read the title page, and broke into a most infectious grin, no less charming for a missing tooth.

'Your servant, sir,' he said. 'My wife will be *most*

obliged to you, *Monsieur*!' With a wave of the hand, he strode off, the open book still in his hand, and a moment later, wild peals of laughter came from behind the ornamental screen.

Heads were beginning to turn in Grey's direction, and he realized that Percy Wainwright had come up beside him, looking curious.

'Whatever did you give him?'

'Ah . . .' It dawned upon Grey that in his haste to accomplish his errand, he had neglected to inform M. Diderot that he was not himself the author of the verses, which were at the moment causing a murmur of baffled amusement to sweep through the room, people sniggering faintly from sympathy, though quite ignorant of the cause.

He could not in countenance join M. Diderot to explain, not with all eyes fixed upon that end of the room – Diderot was now loudly declaiming one of the verses, evidently for the edification of another gentleman whose head Grey briefly glimpsed above the edge of the screen. Ripples of outright laughter were running through the room, and Grey caught sight of Lucinda Joffrey, open fan pressed over her mouth, eyes wide in what might be hilarity or horror. He didn't wish to find out which.

'Let's go.' He seized Percy by the arm, and with the barest of bows to Lady Jonas, they made a hurried escape.

Outside, it had begun to snow in earnest. They stopped, breathless, to struggle into their greatcoats and cloaks in the shelter of the trees at the edge of Hyde Park.

'I had no idea, Lord John.' Percy Wainwright was red-cheeked with cold and laughter. 'I knew you for a man of wit, but not of letters. The subject matter, though . . .'

'You cannot possibly think I wrote that! And for God's sake, call me John,' he added.

Percy looked at him, snow spangling his dark hair – for he had lost most of his powder in the heat and crush of the salon – and gave him a smile of surpassing sweetness.

'John, then,' he said softly.

It was well on to evening. Candlelight glowed from the windows of the houses across the street, and the air was full of mystery and excitement, white flakes pelting down in utter silence, so quickly hiding the cobbled streets and leafless trees and the common-place filth of London. Despite the cold, he felt warmth pulsing through him; did it show? Grey wondered.

'It is early,' he said, looking down as he brushed a few flakes of snow from his hat. 'What would you say to a supper at the Beefsteak, perhaps a hand or two of cards? Or if you are so inclined, there is a new play . . .'

Glancing shyly up, he saw Percy's face fall.

'I should like it of all things. But the general has engaged us to dine with Colonel Benham; I cannot beg off, as it is on my account.'

'No, of course,' Grey said hurriedly, unreasonably disappointed. 'Another time –'

'Tomorrow?' Percy's eyes met his, direct. 'Perhaps . . . in my rooms? I live very plainly, I fear. Still, it is . . .' Grey saw Percy's throat move as he swallowed. 'It is . . . quiet. Our conversation would be undisturbed.'

The generalized warmth Grey had been feeling coalesced quite suddenly, low in his abdomen.

'That would be – oh, damn!'

'You have suddenly recalled another engagement?' Percy cocked a brow, with a crooked smile. 'I am not surprised; I should imagine you are in great demand, socially.'

'Hardly that,' Grey assured him. 'No, it's only that I must leave in the morning for the Lake District. The funeral of a – of a friend.' Even as he said it, he was thinking how he might delay his departure – surely a day would make no difference? He might make up the time on the road.

He wanted very urgently to stay; imagined that he could feel the heat of Percy's body, even across the space of snowy air between them. And yet . . . better, surely, if they had time. This was not some stranger – or rather, he was, but a stranger who was about to become part of Grey's family, and whom he hoped might be a friend; not some attractive, anonymous body whom he would never see again. He wished very much to do the thing – but even more, to do it properly.

'I must go,' he repeated, reluctantly. 'I regret it

exceedingly. But I will, of course, be back in good time for the wedding.'

Percy looked searchingly at him for a moment, then gave him the faintest smile and lifted his hand. His bare fingers touched Grey's cheek, cold and fleeting.

'Godspeed, then,' he said. 'John.'

Could be worse, he reflected. Percy Wainwright's unavailability meant that his own evening was free. Which in turn meant that he could go and beard Hal now, rather than in the morning, and thus not delay his departure for Helwater. If the snow kept pelting down like this, he might not make it out of London in any case.

He turned into the park, head bent against the blowing snow. Lady Jonas's house lay near the parade ground, just past the Grosvenor Gate, while the Greys' family manor, Argus House, was nearly diagonal from it, on the edge of the park near the barracks. It was nearly a mile across open ground, without the shelter of buildings to break the wind, but faster than going round by the road. And his blood was sufficiently warm with wine and excitement as to save him freezing to death.

The memory of the pleasure of Percy Wainwright's company – and speculations based on the furtherance of their acquaintance – were nearly enough to distract him from the prospect of the impending conversation with Hal – but not quite.

Reliving the old scandals leading to his father's death for Percy had been painful, but in the way that lancing an abscess is painful; he felt surprisingly the better for it. Only with the lancing did he realize how deeply and how long the thing had festered in him.

The feeling of relief now emboldened him. He was no longer a twelve-year-old boy, after all, to be protected or lied to for his own good. Whatever secret was sticking in Hal's craw now, he could bloody well cough it up.

The scent of smoke cut through the air, acrid and heartening with its promise of heat. Surprised, he looked for the source, and made out a faint glow in the gathering dark. There were few people in the park – most of the poor who scraped a living begging or stealing near the park had gone to shelter in alleyways and night cellars, crowding into filthy boozing kens or garrets if they had a penny to spare, huddling in church porches or under walls if they had not. But who in his right mind would camp in the open during a snowstorm?

He altered his path enough to investigate, and found the glow came from a clay firepot burning in the lee of a crude lean-to, propped against a tree. The lean-to was deserted – was, in fact, too small to shelter anything larger than a dog. He had no more than an instant to think this odd, when instinct made him turn and look behind.

There were two of them, one with a club, the other unarmed. Stocky shapes, black and ragged, hunched under split burlap sacks that covered heads and shoulders, hiding their faces.

'Stand and deliver!' said a hoarse Irish voice.

'Else we squash yer head in like a rotten turnip!' said another just like it.

He hadn't worn a sword to the salon. He did have his accustomed dagger, though, worn beneath his waistcoat.

'Bugger off,' he said briefly, unbuttoning his coat and producing this. He made small circles with the blade, the metal gleaming dull in what little light there was.

A dagger was not the weapon of choice when facing someone armed with a club, but it was what he had. He backed slowly, jabbing the blade at them, hoping to acquire enough distance to turn and run before they charged him.

To his surprise, they seemed turned to stone at his words.

'It's him, so 'tis!' one of them hissed to the other. 'The major!'

'O'Higgins?' he said, straightening in disbelief. 'O'Higgins!' he bellowed. But they had fled, uttering Irish blasphemies that floated back to him through the snow.

He replaced the dagger and rebuttoned his greatcoat, fumbling a bit, his fingers shaking a little from the shock of the encounter.

The bloody O'Higgins brothers. Grossly misnamed by their pious mother for a pair of archangels, their baptismal names of Raphael and

Michael shortened for common use to Rafe and Mick. Not twins, but so similar in appearance that they often masqueraded as each other in order to escape trouble. And worked in concert to get into it.

He was morally sure they were deserters from the Irish Brigade, but the recruiting sergeant had given them their shillings and their uniforms before Grey had set eyes on them. They weren't the worst of soldiers, though given to more alarming varieties of free enterprise than most.

He squinted through the gloom in the direction they had taken. Sure enough, Hyde Park barracks lay that way, though he couldn't see the buildings through the trees, dark as it was by now. At a guess, the O'Higginses had come to dice and drink with friends quartered there – or to attend some social event such as a cockfight – and realizing a sudden need for cash, had improvised in their usual slipshod but imaginative manner.

Shaking his head, he kicked the firepot over and scattered the glowing coals, which hissed red and died in the snow. He'd deal with the O'Higginses in the morning.

By the time he reached the Serpentine road, he was thickly plastered with snow, his blood had chilled appreciably, and he was beginning to regret not having picked the firepot up and taken it with him, the detriment to his appearance notwith-standing. Despite his gloves, his fingers had gone numb, as had his face, and the stiffness of his cheeks reminded him of the man lying on the pavement outside White's the night before.

The royal swan-keepers had removed the swans for the winter, and the lake was frozen, but not so hard that he would trust his weight to it. Covered with snow, soft patches would be invisible, and all he needed now was to crash through the ice and be submerged in freezing water and decaying duckweed. Sighing, he turned left to make his way round the lake.

Well, perhaps he would remember to ask Hal whether the man's identity and fate had been determined, once the other matter was settled. And while he was asking . . . the events of the afternoon had almost made him forget his mother's odd behavior at breakfast. In the shock of learning of Geneva's death, he had not at once thought of connecting her reaction to the mention of Jamie Fraser with the appearance of the journal page in Hal's office, but from his present perspective, it seemed not only likely, but probable.

Had Hal spoken to her already, then? If he had come to Jermyn Street, he had done so very surreptitiously, either late the night before or very early in the morning. No. Not late, or Grey, stewing by his window, would have seen him. And not early; his mother had been in her wrapper at breakfast, blinking and yawning as was her morning habit, clearly fresh from her bed.

Another thought struck him; perhaps his mother had also received a page from his father's missing journal? Perhaps in the morning post? He slowed a little, boots beginning to crunch in the inch of snow that now covered the ground. Had she opened another letter, after the one from Lady Dunsany? He could not remember; his attention had been focused on Olivia.

The thought of another page filled him with simultaneous alarm and excitement. It would account for his mother's sudden agitation, and her violent reaction to the mention of his Jacobite prisoner. And if such a thing *had* arrived this morning, Hal likely didn't know about it yet.

A surge of blood burnt his frozen cheeks. He brushed away the flakes that clung melting to his lashes, and strode through the deepening snow with renewed determination.

He was the more startled and discomfited to be greeted at the door by Hal's butler with the news that his brother had gone to Bath.

'He really has,' his sister-in-law assured him, appearing behind the butler. She dimpled at his upraised eyebrow, and flung out a hand to indicate the hall behind her. 'Search the house, if you like.'

'What the devil has he gone to Bath for?' Grey demanded irritably. 'In *this* weather?'

'He didn't tell me,' Minnie said equably. 'Do come in, John. You look like a snowman, and you must be wet to the skin.'

'No, I thank you. I must—'

'You must come in and take supper,' she said firmly. 'Your nephews miss their uncle John. And your stomach is grumbling; I can hear it from here.'

It was, and he surrendered his wet outer garments to the butler with more gratitude than he cared to show.

Supper was delayed for a bit, though, in favor of a visit to the nursery. Six-year-old Benjamin and five-year-old Adam were so raucously pleased to see their uncle that three-year-old Henry was roused from sleep and shrieked to join the fun. Half an hour of playing knights and dragon – Grey was allowed to be the dragon, which let him roar and breathe fire, but compelled him to die ignominiously on the hearthrug, stabbed through the heart with a ruler – left him in much better temper, but monstrously hungry.

'You are an angel, Minerva,' he said, closing his eyes in order better to appreciate the savory steam rising from the slice of fish pie set in front of him.

'You won't think so if you call me Minerva again,' she told him, taking her own slice. 'I've a nice Rhenish to go with that – or will you rather like a French wine?'

Grey's mouth was full of fish pie, but he did his best to indicate with his eyebrows that he would be pleased to drink whatever she chose. She laughed, and sent the butler to bring both.

Obviously accustomed to men's needs, she didn't trouble him with conversation until he had finished the fish pie, a plate of cold ham with pickled onions and gherkins, some excellent cheese, and a large helping of treacle pudding, followed by coffee.

'Minnie, you have saved my life,' he said, after his first sip of the fragrant hot black stuff. 'I am your most devoted servant.'

'Are you? Oh, good. Now,' she said, sitting back with an expression of pleased command, 'you may tell me everything.'

'Everything?'

'Everything,' she said firmly. 'I haven't been out of the house in a month, your mother and Olivia are too taken up with wedding preparations to visit, and your wretched brother tells me nothing whatever.'

'He doesn't?' Grey was surprised at that. Minnie was Hal's second wife – acquired after a decade of widowerhood – and he had always thought the marriage a close one.

'Your brother does, of course, speak to me on occasion,' she admitted, with a small gleam of amusement. 'But he subscribes to the peculiar notion that expectant women must be exposed to nothing in the least stimulating. I haven't heard any decent gossip in weeks, and he hides the newspapers – fearing, no doubt, that I will read some lurid confessional from Tyburn Hill, and the child be born with a noose round its neck.'

Grey laughed – though with the belated memory of the broadsheet in his coat pocket, felt that his brother might be well advised in the matter of newspapers, at least. He obligingly recounted his experiences at Lady Jonas's salon, though, including the incident of the Sub-Genius's book of verse, which made Minnie laugh so hard that she choked on her coffee and was obliged to be pounded on the back by the butler.

'Never fear,' she said, wiping her eyes on her napkin. 'I shall worm the author's identity out of Lucinda Joffrey, when next I see her, and let you know. So, you went with the new brother, did you? What is he like?'

'Oh . . . very pleasant. Well bred, well spoken. What does Hal think of him?' he asked curiously.

Minnie pursed her lips in thought. She was a pretty woman, rather than a beautiful one, but pregnancy agreed with her, lending a shine to mousy hair and a glow to her apple-dumpling cheeks.

'Hmm. He rather approves, though Melton being Melton, he is inclined to watch sharply, lest new brother pocket the teaspoons and put them up the spout to finance his habit of opium-eating and his three mistresses.'

'I see that Hal has waited much too long to forbid you newspapers,' Grey said, very pleased indeed to hear that Hal approved of Percy, in spite of the small awkwardness between them at first meeting. 'But you must have had some visitors yourself of late; who has come to call?'

'My grandmother, two aunts, six cousins, a rather nice little woman collecting money for the relief of widows of brickmakers – she actually *did* pinch one of the teaspoons, but Nortman caught her and shook it out of her, quite fun, such an amazing quantity of things she had stuffed into her bodice.' She dimpled at the butler, who inclined his head respectfully. 'Oh, and Captain Bates's lady came this afternoon. She came to see Hal, of course, but he wasn't in, and I was bored, so invited her to stay to tea.'

'Captain Bates's lady?' Grey repeated in surprise. 'I had not heard that he was married.'

'He isn't; she's his mistress,' she said frankly, then laughed at his expression. 'Don't tell me you are *shocked*, John?'

He was, but not entirely for the reasons she supposed.

'How do you know?' he asked.

'She told me – more or less.'

'Meaning what?'

Minnie rolled her eyes at him in exaggerated patience.

'Meaning that she was so agitated that she could not contain the purpose of her desire to speak with Melton, and so told me of her concern for the captain – I hear he has been arrested, did you know?'

'I had heard something of the matter.' Grey put aside his cup, waving away Nortman, hovering with the coffeepot. 'But—'

'And I knew she must be his mistress and not his wife, because I'd met her before – with her husband.' She took a demure sip of her freshly filled cup, eyes dancing at him.

'Who is . . . ?' he prompted.

'A Mr. Tomlinson. Very wealthy. Member of Parliament for some nasty little borough whose name I forget, in Kent. I met him just the once, at a subscription ball. He's fat, and hasn't two words to rub together; little wonder his wife's taken a lover.'

'Little wonder,' Grey murmured, thinking furiously. *Tomlinson, Tomlinson* . . . The name rang no bells for him at all. Could he possibly have anything to do with the conspiracy Hal had told him of?

'What was her concern?' he asked. 'And why did she come to Hal?'

'Well, the captain was arrested on Thursday,' Minnie said reasonably. 'She naturally wants him released. And evidently Hal is a good friend of the captain's – not that he'd ever mentioned it to *me*, of course.'

Not that he mentioned it to me, either, Grey thought cynically. *And what is our supposedly shirt-lifting captain doing with a mistress?* Hal had certainly not mentioned that aspect of the matter to Minnie, though, and a few more questions failed to elicit anything further in the way of information. Mrs. Tomlinson had been distraught, but hadn't known anything beyond the fact that Captain Bates had been arrested.

'She doesn't even know where he is, poor thing.' Minnie's wide, fair brow crinkled in pity. 'Do you think you could find out, John? I could send her a note, at least. Anonymously,' she added. 'I suppose Melton wouldn't like me to sign it.'

'A very reasonable supposition. I'll see what I can find out tomorrow – oh. I forgot; I am leaving in the morning for the Lake District. But I will see what I can discover before I leave.'

'The Lake District?' Minnie stared at him, then at the closed drapes, where the window glass rattled faintly in the wind behind its layers of lace and blue velvet. 'In *this* weather? What is it, a form of family dementia? Next thing you know, your mother will announce her departure for Tierra del Fuego in the midst of a hurricane.'

Grey smiled at her, realizing that it would be injudicious to mention Geneva Dunsany's death to an expectant mother.

'A prisoner of mine, from Ardsmuir, is paroled there. I must interview him, concerning a few administrative matters' – 'administrative' was a word sure to extinguish interest in even the most curious; sure enough, Minnie's eyes showed a faint glaze – 'and I must go now, to be sure of returning in time for the wedding, since the regiment will be departing for France soon thereafter.'

'Mr. Fraser? Melton told me about him. Yes, you will have to hurry.' She sighed, unconsciously pressing a hand over her abdomen. Hal had said the child was expected in the autumn; there was a good chance that it would be born before his return.

Grey did his best to distract Minnie from this distressing prospect with the story of his encounter with the O'Higginses in Hyde Park, and succeeded in getting her to laugh again.

When he left at last, she stood a-tiptoe at the
door to kiss his cheek, then looked up at him with
unaccustomed graveness.

'You will be careful, John? My daughter will need
her godfather, you know.'

'Daughter?' He glanced involuntarily at her still-
flat midsection.

'She has to be. I really can't bear another man to
worry about – going off to the ends of the earth to
be cut to pieces or die of flux and plague, wretched
creatures that you are.' She was still smiling, but he
heard the tremor in her voice, and touched her
shoulder gently.

'Godfather?' he said.

'Don't mention it to Melton; I haven't told him
yet.'

'Your secrets are safe with me,' he assured her,
and her smile grew more natural.

'Good. But you *will* be careful, John?'

'I will,' he said, and stepped into the swirling
whiteness, wondering as he did so whether it was
James Fraser or himself who carried the air of doom
that impelled both his mother and Minnie to urge
him to carefulness.

He had it in mind to ask his mother just that,
amongst other questions, but discovered upon his
return to Jermyn Street that Minnie had perhaps
been more astute than he thought in her discern-
ment of a family mania for travel; the countess had

indeed departed. Not for Tierra del Fuego, true; merely for a play in Drury Lane – the one which he had hoped to see with Percy Wainwright, ironically enough – after which she proposed to spend the night at General Stanley's house in town, because of the snow.

The effect upon his own intentions was the same, though, and he was obliged to content himself with writing a brief note to Hal, informing him of his own proposed absence, the date of his return, and a firm statement that he expected to be apprised of any further discoveries apropos the document of interest – meaning the journal page.

He considered mentioning the possibility that the countess had received a similar page, but dismissed it. Hal had said he would speak with their mother about the page; if she had received another, she would presumably tell him. And Grey had every intention of speaking with the countess himself upon his return from Helwater.

He was putting down his quill when he recollected the matter of the O'Higginses, and with a sigh, took it up again, this time to write a brief note to Captain Wilmot, under whose authority the O'Higginses theoretically fell – though in fact, he was privately inclined to consider them more a force of nature than properly disciplined parts of a military engine.

'It's stopped snowing, me lord!' Tom Byrd's voice came faintly to him, and he glanced aside, to see his valet's lower half protruding from the open window.

A cold draft wound its way about his ankles like a ghostly cat, but the wind had died. Evidently the storm had passed.

He came to stand behind Tom, who pulled his head in, red-cheeked from the cold. Everything outside was still, pure and peaceful in a blanket of white. He scooped a bit of fresh snow from the windowsill with his finger and ate it, enjoying the granular feel of it on his tongue as it melted, and the faint taste of soot and metal that it seemed to carry. There was no more than an inch or two upon the sill, and the sky was now clear, a cold deep violet, full of stars.

'Sun in the morning, I'll be bound,' Tom said with satisfaction. 'The roads will be clear in no time!'

'The roads will be mud in no time, you mean,' Grey said, but smiled nonetheless. Despite the grim nature of their errand, he shared Tom's lightening of the heart at thought of a journey. It had been a long winter indoors.

Finished with the packing, Tom had now picked up Grey's discarded greatcoat, coat, and waistcoat, and was turning out the pockets in his usual methodical fashion, putting loose coins into Grey's pocketbook, tossing crumpled handkerchiefs into a pile of dirty linen, setting aside loose buttons to be sewn on, and looking askance at various of the other items contained therein.

'It's a pritchel,' Grey said helpfully, seeing Tom's brows go up over a small pointed metal implement.

115

'Or part of one. Thing for punching nail holes in a horseshoe.'

''Course it is,' Tom said, laying the object aside with a glance at Grey. 'Does whoever you lifted it from want it back, you reckon?'

'I shouldn't think so; it's broken.' A pritchel was normally about a foot long; the bit on his desk was only two or three inches, broken from the pointed end.

Grey frowned, trying to think where on earth he had acquired the fragment. It was true; he had a habit of stuffing things unconsciously into his pockets, as well as a habit of picking up small objects and turning them over in his fingers while talking to people. The result being that he not infrequently came home with the proceeds of inadvertent petty theft in his pockets, and was obliged to return the items via Tom.

Tom examined a small pebblelike object critically, sniffed it, and determining it to be a lump of sugar from the Balboa, thriftily ate it before picking another object out of a handful of squashed papers.

'Well, now, this 'un's Lord Melton's,' he said, holding up a Masonic ring. 'Seen it on him. You been with him today?'

'No, yesterday.' Memory thus jogged, he came to look over Tom's shoulder. 'You're right, it is Melton's. I'll send it round to his house by one of the footmen. Oh – and I'll keep that. You can burn the rest.' He caught sight of the folded broadsheet he had taken from the coffeehouse, and retrieved it from the pile of paper scraps.

A faint smell of coffee wafted from the page as he unfolded it, and he experienced a vivid recollection of Percy Wainwright's face, flushed from the heat of the coffee he was drinking. Dismissing the faint sense of warmth this brought him, he turned his attention to the article concerning Ffoulkes.

The gist of it was much what Hal had told him. Prominent barrister Melchior Ffoulkes, discovered dead in his study by his wife, thought to have perished by his own hand . . . assorted remarks by persons who had known deceased, general shock and consternation . . . coroner's inquest to be held . . . but only vague allusions to what might have caused the man's suicide, and no hint whatever of treason or sodomitical conspiracies, and no mention of Captain Michael Bates, let alone the other fellow Hal had mentioned – Otway? *So far,* Grey thought cynically, crumpling the newspaper into a ball and tossing it into the fire.

The thought, though, recalled to him what Minnie had said about the visit of Captain Bates's mistress. It wasn't impossible, he supposed; there were men who enjoyed the favors of both men and women – but it wasn't common, and such persons as he knew of that bent generally displayed a sexual indiscriminacy that seemed at odds with the notion of such a settled relationship as the word 'mistress' implied.

Well . . . what of it, if Bates were in fact not

inclined to men? As he had said to Hal, sodomitical conspiracies were the common resort of any newspaper in need of news. People did love to read about depravity, and if the usual daily reports of arrests, trials, and pillorying for that vice began to pall . . .

'Will you need aught else, me lord?' Tom's voice broke his train of thought, and he looked up to see his valet hovering, arms filled with dirty linen and heavy-eyed, obviously longing for his bed.

'Oh. No, Tom, I thank you. Oh! Perhaps one thing . . .' He picked up the volume of his father's journal from his desk. 'Will you put this on its shelf in the library as you go?'

'Certainly, me lord. Good night, me lord.' Tom dexterously shifted his load in order to free a hand for the book and went out. Grey closed the door behind him and stretched, suddenly overcome by a desire for his own bed. He bent to extinguish the candle, then stopped short.

Damn, he'd forgotten that he'd promised Minnie to try to discover Captain Bates's whereabouts. Stifling a groan, he uncapped his inkwell and sat down again. Harry Quarry, he thought, would be best placed to discover Bates's circumstances; Harry knew everyone, and liked Minnie. And Harry was a sufficiently intimate friend that he could write bluntly of the matter, without niceties or circumspections.

Send me word of your discoveries as well, if you will, he wrote, and added the direction for Helwater.

As he pressed the half-moon signet he wore on his right hand into the sealing wax, he noticed that Hal's Masonic ring and the broken pritchel still lay on his desk. He picked up the ring and rolled it idly between his palms, trying to think if there were any further missives that might come between himself and bed.

A momentary urge to write to Percy Wainwright flickered in his brain – only a line, to express regret for his absence, a renewed desire to meet upon his return – but the church bells were tolling the hour of midnight, and his mind had grown so fatigued that he doubted his ability to put down even such a brief sentiment coherently.

His hands relaxed, and the Masonic ring rolled into his left palm, clinking against his own ring. Hector's sapphire.

Hal shared Grey's nervous habit of fiddling with things as he talked, but was most given to taking his rings on and off – this wasn't the first time he'd lost one. Grey, in contrast, never removed his rings, save to wash.

He turned his closed hand, so the sapphire glinted in the candlelight, a soft, true blue. The color of Hector's eyes.

Do you mind? he thought suddenly. *About Percy?* It was impulse; he expected no reply, and received none.

Now and then he wished ardently that he had faith in a merciful God and an afterlife in which the dead might live on – Jamie Fraser had such faith;

burned with it, in a way that excited both Grey's curiosity and his envy. But Grey was a rationalist. He accepted the existence of God, but had no conviction of the nature of such a being, and no sense that his creator took a personal interest in him. Just as well, considering.

He flicked Hal's ring idly onto his own middle finger – where it slid down, hanging loosely round his knuckle.

He frowned at it for a moment, feeling something obscurely wrong, but not realizing what. Then his hand curled tight in reflex.

His brother's hands were the same size as his own; they routinely took each other's gloves in mistake. Hal wore his ring on his own middle finger. Ergo, it wasn't Hal's ring.

He took it off and turned it over, squinting in the candlelight, but there was no inscription within, no mark of ownership. He was not a Freemason himself, but had many friends who were; this was a common style of ring.

'Well, where the devil did I pick *you* up, then?' he said to it, aloud.

SECTION II
Helwater

Chapter 6

✦

Breakage

Every time, he thought it would be different. Removed, caught up in the boredom and intermittent terror of a soldier's life, apart from simple daily things, the normal intercourse of humanity – it was understandable that in these circumstances, he would think of Jamie Fraser as something remarkable; use the image of the man as a talisman, a touchstone for his own emotions.

But surely the effect should lessen, should disappear entirely, when he actually saw the man? Fraser was a Scot, a Jacobite, a paroled prisoner, a groom – no one that he would normally take notice of, let alone regard especially.

And yet, every time, it was the same, the bloody same. How? Why?

He would ride up the winding drive at Helwater, and his pulse would already be beating in his ears. He would greet Dunsany and his family, talking cordially of this and that, accepting refreshment, admiring the women's gowns, Lady Dunsany's latest painting. All in an increasing agony of impatience, wanting – *needing* – to go out to the stables, to look, to see.

And then to spot him at a distance – exercising a horse, working at the pasture fences – or to come upon him unexpectedly face to face, emerging from the tack room or coming down the ladder from the loft where he slept. Each time, Grey's heart leapt in his chest.

The lines of neck and spine, the solid curve of buttock and columned thigh, the sun-darkened flesh of his throat, sun-bleached hair of his arms – even the small imperfections, the scars that marred one hand, the pockmark at the corner of his mouth – and the slanted eyes, dark with hostility and wariness. It was perhaps no surprise that he should feel physical arousal; the man was beautiful, and dangerous in his beauty.

And yet his excitement quieted at once when he was actually in Fraser's presence. A calm descended upon him, a strange content.

Once he had looked into those eyes, been acknowledged by them – then he could return to the house, go about his business, make conversation with other people. It was as though he was anxious, lest the world have changed in his absence, then reassured that it had not; Jamie Fraser still stood at its center.

Would it be that way again? It shouldn't be. After all, there was Percy Wainwright now, to divert his attention, engage his interest. And yet . . . he nodded to Tom, and turned his horse's head into the winding road that led upward to Helwater, feeling an aching in his chest, as though the cold air pressed upon it.

It shouldn't be, he repeated silently to himself.

And yet . . .

Lord Dunsany had been diminished by his daughter's death. The death of his son during the Rising had aged him suddenly, runnels appearing in the flesh of his face like dry valleys carved by unshed tears. Yet the old nobleman had stood like a rock then, strength for his wife and daughters.

Now . . . Dunsany stood to greet Grey, who was so much alarmed by his appearance that he dropped his hat on the floor of the library and hurried to embrace his friend, moved as much by fear that Dunsany would crumple and fall as by shared grief.

The old man's wig brushed his cheek, rough and unpowdered; surely Dunsany had been taller, before. The earl's arms were still firm; they clutched Grey with desperate strength, and he felt a deep subterranean quiver run through the desiccated body pressed to his.

'John,' Dunsany whispered, shocking him, for the viscount had never used his Christian name before. 'God forgive me, John. It is all my fault.'

'Nonsense, nonsense,' he murmured. He had no notion what Dunsany might mean, but gently patted the old man's back, breathing in the dusty scent of his coat, the slight sourness of unwashed skin. He glanced up discreetly; the butler who had opened the door to him stood a few feet away, Grey's hat crushed in his hands and distress at his employer's condition plain on his face.

'A little brandy, perhaps?'

The butler vanished with alacrity, in spite of Dunsany's feeble protest that it was barely noon.

'Noon of a bloody cold, wet, filthy day,' Grey said firmly, escorting Dunsany back to the chair from which he had risen. He cleared his throat, for the tears he had not shed for Geneva had risen at sight of her father's pitiable state. He blinked several times, and bent to pick up the poker.

'Do you call this a fire?'

'I do, yes.' Dunsany was making a gallant effort to recover himself, and managed a wavering smile. 'What do you call it?'

'Completely inadequate.' It *was* a small fire, almost niggardly, though there was a quantity of dry wood, and a basket of peat, as well. Moved by impulse, he stirred the fire recklessly, then tossed two of the peats onto the wakened blaze. The smell of it rose at once in the room, musky, dark, and ancient. It was the smell of Scotland, and a shiver that had nothing to do with the chill of the day ran through Grey's body.

'That's better.' He pulled another chair up to the hearth and sat down, rubbing his hands with affected briskness, meanwhile wondering what on earth to say.

Dunsany saved him the trouble.

'It is so good of you to come, John.' He made another attempt at a smile, this one better. Almost despite himself, he stretched out frail hands to the fire. 'Was it a very dreadful journey? This incessant rain . . .'

'Not at all,' Grey said, though in fact the roads had been liquid mud – where they still existed – and what would normally have been a four-day journey had taken nearly a week. He was in stocking feet at the moment, having left his encrusted jackboots in the hall with his drenched and filthy cloak, but Dunsany appeared not to notice. 'Your wife – she is . . . ?'

The faint traces of life that had warmed Dunsany's cheeks vanished at once, like a snuffed candle.

'Ah. Yes. She is . . . a rock,' Dunsany said softly, eyes on the fire, which had begun to smolder with the low blue flame characteristic of peat. 'A rock,' he repeated, more firmly. 'Her fortitude has sustained us all.'

Oh, has it? Grey thought. Something was wrong here. Lady Dunsany had never failed to greet him within moments of his arrival, but she was nowhere in sight. Neither had he ever known her to be far from her husband's side – yet as they spoke, he became aware that the desolate feel of the room was not due entirely to the meager fire. It was clean and orderly, but its usual warm appeal – due largely to the bits of clutter and careless ornament that Lady Dunsany strewed in her wake – had quite gone.

'I look forward to paying my respects to Lady Dunsany,' Grey said, cautious.

'Oh, she will be so pleased to – oh!' Realization struck the elderly nobleman, and he began to struggle out of his chair. 'I am so stupid today, Lord John, do forgive me. I have quite forgot to send Hanks to tell her you are here!'

Dunsany had barely regained his feet, though, when Grey heard voices in the corridor and stood, as well. Hanks had evidently taken matters into his own hands; the butler opened the door, bowing Lady Dunsany and her daughter Isobel into the room, following them with the tray of brandy.

'Lord John! Lord John!'

The advent of the women had much the same effect as his stirring up the fire; the room seemed at once warmer, the cold staleness of Dunsany's lonely lair dissipated in a wave of feeling and high-pitched voices.

They were in mourning, of course, and yet they brought with them a sense of movement and animation, like a very small flock of starlings.

Isobel was weeping, but as much in gratitude for his presence, he thought, as with grief. She flung herself upon his bosom, and he folded her gently in his arms, grateful himself for the opportunity to provide even this simple service. He feared he had much less to offer either of her parents.

Lady Dunsany was patting his arm, smiling in welcome, though her face was pale and set. Still, he caught sight of the grief lurking in her eyes, and moved by impulse, reached out an arm and drew her into his embrace, as well.

'My dears,' he murmured to the women. 'I am so sorry.'

He was terribly conscious, as they must be, of the sadly diminished state of the little family. Memories of other meetings swept him, when both Gordon and Geneva were with them, their friends filled the house, and his own coming was an occasion filled with delight and unceasing talk and laughter.

Hanks had taken it upon himself to pour the brandy, and had placed a glass in Lord Dunsany's hand with gentle insistence. The old man stood blinking at it, as though he had never seen such a thing before. He did not look at his wife or daughter.

Grey became aware, in the midst of this tumult, that Lord Dunsany's description of his wife had been neither admiring nor metaphorical; he had been stating a physical fact. Lady Dunsany *was* a rock. She accepted his embrace, but did not yield to it. 'But you have a grandson, I understand, Lady Dunsany?' he said, drawing back a bit in order to look down at her. 'I hope the child is well.'

'Oh, yes.' Her lips trembled a bit, but she smiled, nonetheless. 'Yes, he is a lusty dear boy. Such a – such a comfort.'

He noticed the brief hesitation. She was dry-eyed, and did not glance at her husband – though Lord John could not recall any occasion on which Lord Dunsany's welfare had not been her chief concern. Yes, something was quite wrong here, beyond the tragedy of Geneva's death.

It is all my fault, Lord Dunsany had blurted.

He began to understand his own role here. He was neutral ground, no-man's-land. Or everyone's.

Isobel did not appear at tea, later.

'She is shattered, poor thing,' Lady Dunsany said, her own lips trembling. 'She was so much attached to her sister, and the circumstances – there was hellish weather, and we arrived almost too late. She was terribly affected. But she will be heartened by your company; so good of you to come.' She did her best to smile at him, but it was a ghastly attempt.

'I'm sure that once the funeral is over . . .' She trailed off and her face seemed to collapse upon itself, as though the thought of the funeral oppressed her physically.

He began to have an odd feeling, as the evening drew in. The Dunsanys had always been a close and affectionate family, and he was not surprised that they should be deeply affected by Geneva's death. He had known them in such affliction before, when Gordon died. But on that occasion, their grief had been shared, the members of the family drawing together, supporting each other in their mourning.

Not now. He sat between his host and hostess at the tea table, and might as well have sat on the equator, between two frozen poles of ice and snow. Both spoke pleasantly and with great courtesy – to him. Watching carefully, he thought that the constraint between them was composed of a sense of blame on her part, clearly guilt on his – but why?

He had been cold, he thought, since the moment of his arrival. There was a good fire, of course, hot tea, coffee, toasted bread – but the chill of the day, the house, and the company mortified his bones.

'Oh!' Lady Dunsany started, rather as though she had sat upon a drawing pin. 'I had forgot, Lord John. There is a letter for you, come this morning.'

'A letter?' Grey was startled. No one save his family knew he had come to Helwater. What urgency might have compelled them to send a letter upon his heels? The messenger must have passed him on the road.

Thoughts of Hal, the journal page, the conspiracy, flitted through his mind. But what could have happened that would not abide his return? He took the folded paper from Lady Dunsany, expecting to see either Hal's jaggedly impatient lettering, or his mother's untidy scrawl – no one in the family wrote with any grace at all – but the direction was in an unfamiliar hand, round and clear.

The seal was plain; he broke it, frowning – and then felt an extraordinary warmth flow through him, reaching even his chilled toes.

There was no salutation. The note was brief:

*I had wished to send you a sonnet, but I am no
poet, and would not borrow someone else's words –
not even the verses of your friend the Sub-Genius,
filled with meaning as they are.*

*I wish you well in your errand of compassion. I
hope it may be quickly fulfilled, and your journey
home accomplished even more quickly.*

I cannot stop thinking of you.

He stared at this in astonishment, broken only
when Lord Dunsany bent, grunting slightly, to pick
up something from the carpet near his feet.

'What is this?' He held it up, a faint smile
momentarily easing the rigidity of his grief. That
was a rhetorical question, as it was perfectly obvious
that the object he held was a short, curling lock of
dark hair, bound with red thread.

'It fell when you opened your letter,' he
explained, handing it to Grey with the shadow of a
you-sly-dog look. 'I didn't know you had a sweetheart, Lord John.'

'A sweetheart?' Lady Dunsany's look of interest
deepened, and she leaned to peer closely at the lock
of hair in his hand. 'A dark lady, I see. It is not that
Miss Pendragon of whom your mother wrote, is it?'

'I think it very unlikely,' Grey assured her,
suppressing a brief shudder at thought of Elizabeth
Pendragon, a Welsh heiress with a very loud voice
and immense feet. 'However, I am afraid I am in
complete ignorance myself – the missive is
unsigned.'

He flashed the paper quickly before her eyes, not allowing time for her to read it, before tucking it safely into his waistcoat.

'You're blushing, Lord John!' Lady Dunsany sounded faintly amused.

He was, curse it.

He refused the footman's offer to see him to his room after tea; he knew the house well. His path took him past the nursery, though, and he was surprised to see the door standing open, a strong draft blowing out of it that stirred the drapes on the window on the other side of the hallway.

Peering in, he at first thought the room empty. The door to an inner room, doubtless where the child and his nurse slept, was shut; the outer room still showed its history as schoolroom to the Dunsany children. A long, scarred table stood against one wall, shelves full of ragged, much-loved books against another, and faded maps of the world, England, and her colonies fluttered dimly in the light of a guttering rush dip perched beside the door. The window on the far side of the room was open, pale curtains billowing, and he hurried to close it.

A gust of wind carried the curtains sideways for an instant, though, and he saw the slight figure standing in the window, her hair and skirts aswirl in the wind.

'Isobel!' He was seized by a momentary panic, suddenly gripped by the notion that she meant to throw herself out, and he lunged forward, grasping her arm so hard that she shrieked.

'Isobel,' he said, more gently. 'Come away. You'll catch your death.'

'I want to,' she said in a muffled voice, refusing to look at him, though she let him pull her into the room. Her clothes were damp with rain, her hair hanging wild about her face, and her flesh was very cold. Grey glanced at the hearth, but the fire had not been lit. Without comment, he took off his coat and wrapped it round her shoulders.

'I am so sorry, my dear,' he said quietly, and reached to close the window. The wind died and the curtains fell limp, half soaked. She stood unmoving, a small, draggled thing, like a mouse rescued from a cat – perhaps too late. He touched her shoulder.

'Let me take you downstairs,' he said. 'You should have something hot, some dry clothes . . .' She should have her mother, he thought. But of course – she had chosen to hide her grief here, in order not to distress her parents.

She raised her head suddenly, her face a grimace of bewildered grief.

'My sister is dead,' she said in a small, choked voice. 'How shall I live?'

He put his arms round her and held her close, making the sorts of soothing noises one made to injured dogs or frightened horses. She was making much the same sort of sound as an animal in distress, for that matter; small whimpers of pain, with now and then a great, tearing shudder of breath. Had she been a horse, he would have seen the pain ripple through her flanks. He felt it, coming in waves that beat against his body.

She did not resemble Geneva at all, being small and gently rounded, blond like their mother; Geneva had taken after Lord Dunsany, tall and lean, with thick chestnut hair. Isobel's head fit neatly just below his chin.

'It will be better,' he whispered to her. 'Bearable. The pain doesn't go away – but it grows more bearable. It does.'

She jerked back out of his grasp, face contorted.

'But what am I to do *now*? How shall I live until it does?' She choked, wiped her streaming nose on her sleeve, and turned a wild-eyed look on him. 'How can I? What can I *do*?'

He hesitated, wanting urgently to tell her something useful, knowing there was nothing.

'I . . . er . . . used to smash things,' he offered tentatively. 'When my father died. It helped. A bit.'

She blinked, shuddering and trembling, and let out a small, hysterical giggle, instantly quelled with a hand across her mouth. Slowly she drew it away.

'Oh, I do so want to smash something,' she whispered. 'Please, please.' Wide blue eyes spiked with tear-clotted lashes implored him to find something suitable.

Flustered, he looked round the schoolroom for something breakable and cheap. Not the ewer or basin, the candlestick was pewter . . . For lack of a better notion, he took down the rush dip from above the door, and lit the chamber stick from it. He would have blown out the wick, but she seized the little pottery vessel from him before he could, and, opening the window, hurled it with all her strength into the dark.

Leaning out beside her, he saw it smash on the wet slates below in a satisfying explosion of fragments. A slick of spilled oil burned briefly, a small tongue of blue flame that wavered for a moment in the windy rain, and went out.

The stronger light of the new candle in the chamber stick showed him her face. Her fair skin was blotched, her eyes were closed, her mouth a little open in slack relief. She tottered, knees giving way, and he hastily grabbed her arm, pulling her back from the window.

'Thank you,' she said, and took a long, shuddering breath. 'That . . . *is* better. A bit. I can't go on breaking things, though, can I?'

Groping for inspiration, he found one.

'Your father has a couple of good fowling pieces. Tom Byrd and I will go out with you tomorrow, and I'll teach you to shoot clay pigeons. They break very nicely.'

She wiped a hand beneath her nose, like a small child. He fished a handkerchief out of his sleeve and handed it to her.

'Not tomorrow,' she said, and blew her nose. 'There's the f-funeral tomorrow.' She closed her eyes for a moment, and seemed to sway. 'I think – I think that if only I can live through *that,* perhaps it will be . . .' She stopped speaking, as though she had simply found it too great an effort to continue.

'It will be better,' he said firmly. *It had to be,* he thought. *None of them will survive, otherwise.*

Isobel eventually suffered him to lead her to her chamber, where a frightened-looking maid drew her in, and he continued on to his own room, wishing that his sense of duty would allow him to send down word that he was indisposed, and take supper in his chamber.

His sense of foreboding was not eased by Tom Byrd, who was as usual a fount of disturbing information, gleaned from the servants over their own tea.

'Not surprised to hear *that,*' he said, of Grey's brief account of Isobel's response to her sister's death. 'Lady Ellesmere was almost dead when they got there, and Miss Elspeth said the bed was soaked right through with blood, and the carpet all round, too. Squished up into your shoes when you stepped on it, she said.'

Grey repressed a brief shudder at the thought.

'The hangings, too, all splashed about, like a butcher's shop,' Tom continued, evidently determined to give a full report. 'She said—'

'Who is Miss Elspeth?' Grey interrupted, not wanting to hear any more grisly details. 'Was she there?'

'Yes, me lord. She's Lady Ellesmere's and Miss

Isobel's old nurse. She went with Lady Ellesmere at her marriage, but when she died, she came back here to help care for the little 'un. Nice old stick.'

Tom hovered in front of the armoire, assessing the possibilities.

'You're to be pallbearer for the countess, me lord?'

'Yes. The dark gray do, do you think? Black velvet seems rather dramatic.'

'Oh, no, me lord.' Tom shook his head decidedly. 'You wouldn't, in London, but this is the country. They'll expect black, and the more dramatic, the better.'

Grey smiled briefly.

'I suppose you're right. You've become very skilled at valeting, Tom.'

Tom nodded matter-of-factly at the compliment.

'Yes, I have, me lord. Not but what you could wear red silk and a diamond in your nose like the Earl of Sandwich. They'll be talking of this funeral for months.'

Grey caught the slight emphasis on 'this,' and looked sharply at Tom.

'Because of the tragic nature of the countess's death, do you mean?'

'Aye, that – but more because of the earl. Did you know, me lord, the talk is that he ... er ... laid hands upon himself?' Tom spoke delicately, avoiding looking at Grey – which told Grey just how accurately the servants' gossip at Jermyn Street had

138

informed his valet regarding the Greys' own family scandal. How long had Tom known about it? he wondered.

'I hadn't, no.' So that was what was behind at least some of the Dunsanys' agitation. 'Does everyone know? The public at large, I mean, not just the servants here?'

'Oh, yes, sir! Jack the footman says the betting is five to three down the Bells, as how vicar will cut up rough tomorrow when they bring him in. Not let him be buried in hallowed ground, aye?'

'The vicar . . . what, is the earl being buried tomorrow, too?' He was momentarily staggered. He couldn't think how he had overlooked the earl's death – or rather, he could. No one had spoken of the late earl, or his untimely and coincidental demise. All the talk was of Geneva; none of the Dunsany household had mentioned the earl or his funeral at all, and he had unconsciously assumed that it had already taken place.

'Yes, me lord.' Tom looked pleased at being the bearer of interesting news. 'The old earl hadn't any kin, and Lord Dunsany was all for burying him on the quiet, like; tuck him safe away under the chapel floor up at Ellesmere. But Lady Dunsany wouldn't have it. *She* said,' he lowered his voice portentously, 'as how it would look fishy, see?'

'I am completely sure Lady Dunsany said nothing of the sort, but I take your meaning, Tom. And so?'

'And so she got her way. Ladies usually do, you

know,' Tom informed him. 'You want to be careful of that Lady Joffrey, me lord. She's got her eye –'

'Yes, I know. So it was Lady Dunsany's idea to bury the earl together with his wife?' Brazen it out with a lavish public funeral, and dare anyone to claim the earl's death was not an accident. It was not a bad idea, he'd grant her that. It would give rise to more talk in the short run, of course – but if the vicar could be coerced into burying the earl in consecrated ground, it would put paid to the rumors of suicide, and the talk would die a natural death, with no lingering whiff of scandal to follow her grandson.

The coroner's jury had brought back a verdict of accident, he knew. Such a jury was bound to be sympathetic to the Dunsanys, who were popular in the district. But if the vicar chose to make a scene . . . No wonder the Dunsanys were on edge.

'Yes, me lord. They was back and forth about it, and it wasn't decided for sure until this morning, Mr. Hanks says. But the vicar will have heard. They'd have to send him word, if they meant him to do the funeral.'

Yes, and doubtless the vicar would be grappling with his own conscience through the night, if he had doubts about the matter.

Tom was hesitating, evidently wanting to ask something, but unsure how it might be received. Grey raised a brow, inviting Tom to speak.

'They said – is it true, me lord, as how if a nobleman does himself in, the Crown can take the estate?'

Grey felt a tightening of the belly, but answered calmly. That, of course, was why the jury had brought it in as accident.

'Yes. On the grounds that self-murder is a crime against God, and against the state, as well. But it is not an invariable consequence. The king may choose not to exercise confiscation, or the . . . suicide may be ruled to have taken place while the person's mind was deranged, thus relieving him of the onus of crime.' He took a deep breath and turned round, looking directly at his valet. 'That's what was said of my father. That he was insane.'

Tom stared at him, expressionless, but with such a depth of sympathy in his eyes that Grey was obliged to turn away again, pretending to rummage for something in one of the saddlebags that had been brought up.

'I'm that sorry, me lord,' Tom said at last, so softly that Grey had the option of pretending not to have heard him. He thrust a hand into the saddlebag, feeling about at random, and closed his fist on something hard. It didn't matter what. He closed his eyes and squeezed it as hard as he could, until the bones of his knuckles popped.

'Thank you,' he said, just as softly.

When he opened his eyes again, he was alone.

Chapter 7

Penance

He could not sleep. It had been late when he left
Dunsany, the old gentleman having reached a
state of near insensibility over a decanter of claret
after supper. Grey had given Dunsany over to the
care of the viscount's own valet, who got the old
man to his feet and led him gently off to bed,
shuffling and murmuring. Grey then sought his own
bed, with the feeling that this day had lasted several
years and was long overdue to be expunged by sleep.

Sleep, however, perversely declined to come knit
up the raveled sleeve of care. Instead, the bad fairy
of insomnia chose to take up residence on the foot
of his bed, cozily recalling everything from Tom's
gory description of Geneva's death to her father's
drunken self-reproaches, in which he blamed himself repeatedly for everything from arranging the
marriage to allowing Geneva too much freedom.

His room was the same they always gave him.
The Blue Room, it was called, for the patterned silk
paper on the walls, repeated scenes of Dutch life,
Delft blue on a cream background. Masculine in
aspect, its furnishings luxurious, its hearth

generous, it was one of the most comfortable rooms in the house. And yet he felt chilled and restless, at odds with his surroundings.

He was tired to the point of exhaustion, but found himself unable to relax into the comforts of the feather bed, despite the wine and the lateness of the hour. Tom had left a jug of hot milk on the table, wrapped in a towel. He smiled a little at that, touched by Tom's thoughtfulness – though he hadn't drunk warm milk in twenty years and didn't feel sufficiently desperate as to start now.

He lay down on the bed again, hoping that recumbency might lead to a gradual relaxation, but didn't put out the candle. For some time, he watched the glow from the fire animate the scenes on the wallpaper, his hand flat on the empty space beside him. How many times had he seen those calm blue scenes? He had been a regular visitor at Helwater since the early days of his commission, when the Dunsanys' son, Gordon, had invited him to stay. Gordon had been killed in the Jacobite Rising, and the Dunsanys, in their grief, had adopted Grey as a sort of foster son. Now they had lost a daughter, as well.

How old had Geneva been, the first time he had come? Four? Five?

'Do you see that one?' he whispered, as though to an invisible companion. 'The one with the sailing boat? That's my favorite. I can imagine sailing down the Dutch canals, seeing all the windmills turn.'

What's a windmill, sir? The whispered words were

only in his mind, but his arm bent, curling in memory around a little girl who'd crept into his room in the middle of the night, frightened by a nightmare.

'A great tall mill, something like the mill by the river. Grindstones, you know. But it has no wheel for the water to turn. Instead, there are large sails, four of them, like arms, on the top of the mill. The wind makes them go round, and thus the corn is ground. There's one on the wall – do you see it?'

But he heard no answer; only the quiet pop and hiss of damp in the burning peat. His arm relaxed, and he smoothed the coverlet gently with his hand, as though it were a small girl's disheveled, silky hair, to be tucked back within her nightcap.

He stayed thus for some time, thoughts drifting, staring at the flickering blue shapes on the wall. Became aware that he was still stroking the coverlet, slowly, but that the image in his mind was no longer that of a child's hair. Soft, but coarser. Springy curls. Dark. And an imagined sense of warmth from the skin beneath.

'Jesus,' he said, and curled his hand into a fist. Rising, he crossed the room and jerked open the armoire. He groped, searching in the dimness for the pocket of his coat, felt no crackling of paper and gripped the cloth in sudden alarm, before catching sight of the letter, neatly set beside his hairbrushes on the shelf where Tom had placed it.

He took it up, heart beating faster, and tilted the

paper. The lock of hair fell out into his hand. Dark, a single curl, tied with red thread.

I cannot stop thinking of you.

He unfolded the letter and read the line again, for the pleasure of seeing the words upon the page. Gazed at them for several moments, then carefully folded the paper again, and set it back in place.

In all truth, the words caused him as much disturbance as pleasure. He had not expected thoughts of Percy to follow him to Helwater, and was not sure of his feelings. He hoped, to be sure, that they might discover something between them. But what that something might be, or come to be, he had no notion. If it happened at all, though, he envisioned it happening in London. London was a separate world, almost as though he were a different person there.

He did, on the other hand, know very well what his feelings were for Jamie Fraser. And being at Helwater, no more than a hundred yards from Fraser's physical presence, was sufficiently disturbing in itself. He had the irrational feeling that to take such pleasure in Percy's note was in some way a betrayal – but of what, for God's sake?

Moved by impulse, he drew back the heavy blue-velvet drapes at the window. It was a cloudy night, a thick rain still falling, but the sky held a faint sullen glow, the diffuse light of a hidden moon. He could see the dim outline of the stable roof through the streaks of rain on the windowpane.

'Hell,' he said softly, left the window abruptly,

and wandered round the room, picking up objects at random and putting them down again. He tried to return to his earlier thoughts – or to abandon all thought, purging the mind for sleep – but his efforts were bootless. James Fraser remained stubbornly in the center of his mind's eye. Grey had seen him once since his arrival – he had taken Grey's horse to the stables – but had had no opportunity to speak to him.

For God's sake, John, be careful.

His mother's words rang abruptly in his ear, and he shook his head, as though to dislodge an annoying mosquito.

And what, for God's sake, had his mother meant by *that*? Plainly, she meant Fraser; it was mention of the man and his Jacobite connexions that had frightened – yes, frightened – her. Why? What on earth did she think he might ask of Fraser? Or learn from him?

Something regarding his father's death. *Those* words came cold, from the dark recesses of his own mind. He shoved them reflexively away. His father had been dead for nearly seventeen years. He thought now and then of his father, but never of his death. And didn't mean to think of it now.

Such mortal thoughts, though, reminded him suddenly again of Geneva. Where was she tonight? Not in a spiritual sense – he trusted vaguely that she must be in heaven, though he had no concrete notion of the place – but in the physical?

The funeral would be tomorrow. Her body . . .

He glanced uneasily at the black night outside his window, as though she might be floating there, pale face staring in at him, her chestnut hair pasted to her skull by the pouring rain.

He pulled the curtains firmly shut. She would be in her coffin, ready for the procession to the church in the morning. Was she somewhere in the house? Surely she did not lie in some hogg house or desolate shed on the grounds?

The chapel. Of course. The thought came to him at once. He had never been in the chapel at Helwater; it dated from a much earlier century, when the Viscounts of the Wastwater had been Catholic, and it had been disused for years. He knew where it was, though; Geneva herself had shown him, waving a careless hand toward the small stone chamber that clung barnaclelike to the west side of the house.

'That's the old chapel,' she had said. 'We have a ghost there, did you know?'

'Well, I should hope so,' he had replied, jesting. 'All respectable families have at least one, do they not?'

She had looked at him queerly for a moment, but then laughed.

'Ours is a monk, a young man who kneels in prayer in the chapel at night. What kind of ghost has your family, then, Lord John?'

'Oh, we are not sufficiently respectable as to have an actual ghost of our own,' he assured her gravely. 'Nothing but the odd skeleton in the closet.'

That had made her laugh immoderately – little

did she know how true his remarks had been, he reflected, with a slight smile at the memory. The smile faded at the realization that he would not hear her laugh again.

He felt her absence suddenly and keenly. He had been so occupied with the grief of her family that he had felt her loss only as theirs, terrible, but experienced at a safe remove; now, in the deep solitude of the night, he understood it as his own. He stood for a moment, bereavement a sudden, small tear in his soul.

Unable to bear this for long, he reached with sudden decision for the armoire and found his cloak, threw it round his shoulders, pushed his feet into felt slippers, and went out into the corridor, easing the door softly to behind him. He would say farewell to her, at least, in private.

Discovering from within a room he had only seen from without was something of a challenge; Helwater, like most old houses, had been built in fits and starts as the finances and whimsy of successive viscounts allowed. Thus, it was a huge place – Lady Dunsany had told him that the entire east wing was closed in winter – and no passage went straightforwardly anywhere.

He had a good sense of direction, though, and knew that the chapel was at the northwest corner of the house. He worked his way through the twisting corridors as he would a maze, keeping a running count in his head of the turns, in order that he might find his way back again, and found that the exercise allowed him to keep his emotions at bay, if only for the moment.

The rain had kept up steadily all day, in that dismal winter downpour that darkens the spirit as it weights the land. The wind had come up now, and rain beat upon the shuttered windows in fitful bursts, marking his passage along the darkened corridors. He had brought a taper from his room, a faint glow to light his path. Something moved in the shadows and he stopped short.

Green eyes glowed for an instant and disappeared as the cat – it was only a cat – twined past his feet and vanished, silent as smoke. Was that Geneva's cat? She had had a kitten once, he knew. Would she not have taken it to Ellesmere? Perhaps her mother had brought it back. Perhaps . . . perhaps he was trying to occupy his mind with pointless trifles in order to avoid thinking of Geneva dead, even as he made his way toward her bier.

Heart still beating like a drum, he wondered what he thought he was doing, but he had come thus far; to turn back now would seem an abandonment of her. He closed his eyes for an instant, reestablishing the map of the house he was building in his head, then opened them and set off again with purpose.

Several more turnings brought him abruptly to what seemed an outer wall of the house, its lichened blocks pierced by an arched lintel of honey-colored stone.

This was clearly the chapel's entrance; the figures of saints and angels were carved into the arch. They had escaped the mutilations of Cromwell's vandals in the last century – he made out the figure of what must be Michael the archangel in the center of the arch, flaming sword held aloft. Below him, Adam and Eve cowered behind crude fig leaves, Eve's hands crossed modestly over her generous breasts. Not saints, after all. On the other side of the arch, a serpent hung in looping coils from the branches of an apple tree, looking smugly amused.

Blessed Michael defend us. The words came to him suddenly, though he was neither Catholic nor even religious. It was a common saying among the Scottish prisoners at Ardsmuir, though. He had heard it in the Gaelic, many times, and finally had asked Jamie Fraser for the English meaning, one night when they had dined together.

Plainly he had found the right place. A small oil lamp burned in the passage, throwing the archangel's visage into stern relief, and the flicker of candlelight was visible through the crack between the wooden doors under the archway. Wondering anew just what he was doing here, he hesitated for a moment, then shrugged and murmured 'Blessed Michael defend us.' He passed beneath the arch.

The chapel was tiny, and dark save the tall white candles that burned at head and foot of the closed coffin. It was draped in white silk, and glimmered like water.

He took a step toward it. Something large stirred in the darkness at his feet.

'Jesus!'

He dropped the taper, clapping a hand to his belt – where, alas, he had not placed his dagger.

A dark figure rose immense, very slowly, from the flags at his feet.

Every hair on his body stood erect and his heart thundered in his ears, as recognition tried vainly to overcome shock. The taper had gone out, and the man was visible only as a dark silhouette, haloed with the fire of the candles behind him.

He swallowed hard, trying to force his heart from his throat, and groped for words that were not altogether blasphemous.

'Bloody . . . Christ,' he managed, after several incoherent tries. 'What in the name of God Himself are *you* doing here?'

'Praying,' said a soft Scots voice, its softness no disguise for the shock in it – and an even more patent anger. 'What are *you* doing here?'

'Praying?' Grey echoed, disbelief in his voice. 'Lying on the floor?'

He couldn't see Fraser's face, but heard the hiss of air through his teeth. They stood close enough to each other that he felt the cold emanating from Fraser's body, as though the other had been carved from ice. Christ, how long had the man been pressed to the freezing flags? And why? His eyes adjusting, he saw that the Scot wore nothing but his shirt; his long body was a shadow, the candlelight glowing dim through threadbare fabric.

'It is a Catholic custom,' Fraser said, his voice as stiff as his posture. 'Of respect.'

'Indeed.' The shock of the encounter was fading, and Grey found his voice come easier. 'You will pardon me, Mr. Fraser, if I find that suggestion somewhat peculiar – as is your presence here.' He was growing angry now himself, feeling absurdly practiced upon – though logic told him that Fraser had risen as he did only because Grey would have stepped on him in another moment, and not with the intent of taking him at a disadvantage.

'It is immaterial to me, Major, what you find peculiar and what ye do not,' Fraser said, his voice still low. 'If ye wish to suppose that I have chosen to sleep in a freezing chapel in company with a corpse, rather than in my own bed, you may think as ye like.' He made a motion as though to pass, obviously intending to leave the chapel – but the aisle was narrow, and Grey was not moving.

'Did you know the – the countess well?' Curiosity was overcoming shock and anger.

'The countess . . . oh.' Fraser glanced involuntarily over his shoulder at the coffin. Grey saw him draw breath, the mist of it briefly white. 'I suppose she was. A countess. And, yes, I kent her well enough. I was her groom.'

There was something peculiar about *that* remark, Grey noted with interest. There was a wealth of feeling in that statement, 'I was her groom,' but damned if he could tell what sort of feeling it was.

He wondered for an instant whether Fraser had been in love with Geneva – and felt a surprising sear of jealousy at the thought. Knowing Fraser's feeling for his dead wife, he would suppose . . . but why in God's name would he come at night to pray by Geneva's coffin, if not – but no. That 'I was her groom' had been spoken with a tone of . . . hostility? Bitterness? It wasn't the respectful statement of a loyal and grieving servant, he'd swear *that* on a stack of Bibles.

Grey dismissed this confusion and took a breath of cold air and candle wax, imagining for an instant that he smelt the hint of corruption on the frigid air.

Fraser stood like a stone angel, no more than a foot from him; he could hear the Scot's breathing, faintly hoarse, congested. My God, had he been weeping? He dismissed the thought; the weather was enough to give anyone the catarrh, let alone anyone mad enough to lie half naked on freezing stones.

'I was her friend,' Grey said quietly.

Fraser said nothing in reply, but continued to stand between Grey and the coffin. Grey saw him turn his head, the candle glow sparking red from brows and sprouting beard, limning the lines of his face in gold. The long throat moved once, swallowing. Then Fraser turned toward him, his face disappearing once more into shadow.

'Then I leave her in your hands 'til dawn.'

It was said so quietly that Grey was not sure he'd heard it. But something touched his hand, light as a cold wind passing, and Fraser moved past him and was gone, the muffled thud of the chapel door the only sound to mark his leaving.

Grey turned in disbelief to look, but there was nothing to be seen. The chapel was dark, and silent save for the sound of rain thrumming on the slates of the roof.

Had that remarkable encounter really happened? He thought for an instant that he might be dreaming – must have fallen asleep in his chair by the fire, lulled by the rain. But he put a hand on the end of the pew beside him and felt hard wood, cold under his fingers.

And the coffin stood before him, stark and white in the candlelight. The flames quivered, the air in the chapel disturbed, then settled, pure and steady. Keeping watch.

Not quite knowing what to do, he sat down in the front pew. He should pray, perhaps, but not yet.

What was it Fraser had said? *I suppose she was. A countess.*

So she had been – for the brief months of her marriage. And now there was nothing left of her or her husband, save that small, enigmatic morsel of flesh, the ninth Earl of Ellesmere.

I leave her in your hands 'til dawn.

Had Fraser himself meant to keep watch all night, prostrate before her coffin? Plainly he meant Grey to stay through the remaining hours of cold dark. Grey shifted uneasily on the hard wood, aware that he could not now bring himself to leave.

He shivered, then wrapped his cloak more tightly, resigned. The chill of the slate floor was seeping through his slippers; his feet had gone numb already. He thought of Fraser in his shirt, and shivered again at the thought of pressing his own bare flesh against the icy slates.

Respect, Fraser had said. It scarcely seemed respectful, such an extraordinary act. What, he wondered, would have happened, had he actually stepped on the man? He still held that over-whelming impression of Fraser's presence, towering, cold as stone, and pushed aside a fleeting thought of what that frozen flesh might feel like, had he touched it. Restless, he stood and went forward, drawn like a moth to the glimmering white of the coffin.

More like something from the Middle Ages, he thought, and snorted, breath white in the dark air. Those Catholic buggers who walked barefoot through Paris or flagellated themselves to bloody shreds as an act of penance.

An act of penance.

He felt the words drop into place in his mind, like the tumblers of a lock. Recalled his sense of the Dunsanys, that some deep uneasiness tinged their grief.

'Oh, Geneva,' he said softly.

He saw again that vision of her at his window, pale-faced, wide-eyed, adrift in the night. So cold, and all alone. The outline of the stable behind her. From somewhere in the house, he thought he heard the creak of footsteps, and a far-off infant's cry.

'Oh, my dear. What have you done?'

Chapter 8

Violent Hands

I am the Resurrection and the life, saith the Lord. He that believeth in me, though he were dead, yet shall he live; and whosoever liveth and believeth in me, shall never die.

Well, he hoped so, to be sure. The words hadn't yet been spoken, but repeated themselves in his mind, a comforting refrain. Though another bit from the Book of Common Prayer whispered a counterpoint in the background.

. . . not to be used for any that die unbaptized, or excommunicate, or have laid violent hands upon themselves.

He hadn't gone to his father's funeral – didn't know if there had been one.

In spite of the weather, the church was full. The Dunsanys were liked by their tenants, friendly with most of the country gentry, and kind to their servants; everyone wished to comfort the family in its grief. Besides, it was the country, and entertainment was rare; no one would miss a good funeral, even if they were obliged to tramp through waist-deep snow to attend it.

Grey glanced over his shoulder, to see whether the tall figure of Jamie Fraser loomed among the crowd of grooms and chambermaids who stood at the back of the church, but there was no sign of the Scot. Fraser was, of course, forbidden to leave the boundaries of Helwater, but surely he would have been given leave to attend the funeral with the other servants – if he wished to.

Grey still felt the chill of his night watch in the chapel in his bones, but this deepened as he heard the rustle of anticipation at the door, and turned with everyone else to see the coffin of Ludovic, eighth Earl of Ellesmere, being brought in.

He made no attempt not to stare. Everyone was staring. The minister had come forth, and was waiting, stone-faced, at the altar, where Geneva's coffin already stood. Grey himself had helped to carry that, dreadfully conscious of the silent weight within.

What was causing his bones to freeze within him now, though, was the sight of Jamie Fraser, tall and grim, serving as pallbearer with five other sturdy manservants.

Someone had given him coat and breeches of a cheap black worsted, very ill-fitting. He should have looked ridiculous, bony wrists protruding from the too-short sleeves, and every seam strained to bursting. As it was, he reminded Grey of a description he had read in *Demonologie*, a nasty little treatise discovered in the course of researches undertaken after his experience with the Hellfire Club.

The men set down the earl's coffin and retreated to a bench set under the gallery. Grey was not surprised in the least to see Fraser sitting alone at one end, the other men bunched unconsciously together, as far away from him as they could get.

The vicar cleared his throat with an ominous rumble, the congregation rose, flustered and murmuring, and the service began. Grey heard not a word, his responses entirely mechanical.

Could he be right? He went back and forth on the matter, unsure. On the one hand, the thought that had come to him in the darkness of the chapel seemed incredible. A complete delusion, born of grief, fatigue, and shock. On the other . . . there was Lady Dunsany's behavior. Grief-stricken, certainly, but grief covering a rocklike determination. Determination to put the past behind her and raise her grandchild? Or determination to perpetrate a daring deception in order to protect him?

And Lord Dunsany, the target of his own blame – and his wife's. For arranging the marriage with Ellesmere, he'd said . . . but also for allowing Geneva too much freedom. What the devil had he said, mumbling in his cups? Something about her horse, spending hours roaming the countryside, alone on her horse. *Not alone, surely. In the company of her groom,* said a cynical voice in his mind.

And then there was said groom himself, and that remarkable encounter in the middle of the night. Even though Grey had not slept, it still seemed the product of a dream. He turned deliberately in his seat and looked at Fraser. Nothing whatever showed on the Scot's face. He might have been looking back at Grey – or at something a thousand miles beyond him.

Isobel was seated next to Grey, her small, cold, black-gloved hand held in his for support. She was no longer weeping; he thought she had simply passed the point of being able to.

Not a one of the Dunsany family had so much as glanced at Fraser, though most of the congregation had gawked openly, and many were still darting looks at him where he sat on the bench, upright and menacing as a corpse candle.

Yes, there was evidence. But his knowledge of James Fraser was evidence, as well – and he found it inconceivable that Fraser could or would have seduced a young girl, no matter what the circumstances. Let alone the daughter of his employer.

His eyes settled on the pair of coffins at the front of the church, identical beneath their white shrouds. So tragic, so . . . solidly marital.

Yes, and you bloody knew Geneva, too, he thought.

The rain had turned to snow. It wouldn't stick, sodden as the ground was, but the wind drove it against the windows, bursts of hard, dry pellets that struck the glass like bird shot.

Snowflake upon snowflake, silently accumulating

into a drift of what seemed like certainty – but, he reminded himself, could as easily be pure illusion.

He was light-headed from lack of sleep, and the snow-darkened windows lent the church a mournful dimness. He'd sat through the predawn hours in the freezing chapel, watching the flicker of the candle flames, and thinking.

Was his refusal to believe it purely the product of his own pride, his own guilt? Not only his belief in Jamie Fraser's honor, a refusal to believe he could be so mistaken in the man – but the knowledge that if it *were* true, he himself must bear a good part of the blame. He had introduced Fraser into the Dunsany household, his own honor surety for Fraser's.

He hadn't eaten this morning, too chilled and exhausted to think of food after his vigil in the chapel.

'Out of the deep have I called unto thee, O Lord. Lord, hear my voice.'

Fraser had closed his eyes, quite suddenly, as though unable to bear what he saw. What *did* he see? Grey wondered. The Scot's face remained blank as granite, but he saw the big hands curl slowly, gathering fabric and flesh together, fingers digging so hard into the muscle of his thigh that they must leave bruises.

Was it Geneva he mourned – or his dead wife? The trouble with funerals was that they reminded one of loss. He had not seen his father's funeral, and yet had never sat through one without thought of his father, the wound of his loss healing, growing smaller through the years, but always reopened.

And if ever I saw a man bleeding internally . . . he thought, watching Fraser.

> 'Give courage and faith to those who are bereaved, that they may have strength to meet the days ahead in the comfort of a reasonable and holy hope, in the joyful expectation of eternal life with those they love.'

Well, that expectation would be a comfort, to be sure. He had no such expectation himself – only something too vague to be called hope – but he did have one certainty to anchor himself in this fog of grief and indecision. The certainty that he would get at least one answer from Jamie Fraser. Maybe two.

It was only four o'clock, but the winter sun had set, leaving a thin slice of pale light above the fells. The temperature had dropped and the snow had thickened; already the highest rocks showed a rime of white, and large, wet flakes struck Grey's coat and stuck melting to his hair and lashes as he made his way to the stables.

He had seen the other two grooms helping to bring round horses and harness teams for those nearby funeral guests who were departing today, but there had been no sign of Fraser. Not surprising; Lord Dunsany preferred 'MacKenzie' to remain out of sight when there was company. His size, his aspect, and, above all, his Highland speech tended to unnerve some people. Grey had heard some comments regarding the tall, red-haired servant who bore Ellesmere's coffin, but most did not realize that he was Dunsany's servant, rather than that of the Earl of Ellesmere – and few, so far as he knew, had realized that the man was Scottish, let alone a paroled Jacobite.

Sure enough, he discovered Fraser in the stable block, pitching feed for the stalled horses, and came up beside him.

'May I speak with you, Mr. Fraser?'

The Scot didn't turn, but lifted one shoulder.

'I dinna see any way of preventing ye, Major,' he said. Despite the words, this did not sound unfriendly; only wary.

'I would ask you a question, sir.'

He was watching Fraser's face closely, in the glow of the single lantern, and saw the wide mouth tighten a little. Fraser only nodded, though, and dug his fork into the waiting mound of hay.

'Regarding some gentlemen intimately connected with the Stuart cause,' Grey said, and received a sudden startled look – mingled with an undeniable impression of relief.

'The Stuart cause?' Fraser repeated, and turned his back on Grey, shoulders bunching as he dug the fork into a pile of hay. 'To which . . . gentlemen . . . do ye refer, Major?'

Grey was conscious of his heart beating heavily in his chest, and took especial care that his voice might be under his control at this delicate juncture.

'I understand that you were an intimate friend to—' he nearly said, 'to the Young Pretender,' but bit that off and said instead, 'to Charles Stuart.'

'That—' Fraser began, but stopped as suddenly as he had begun. He deposited the forkload of hay neatly into one manger, and moved to pick up another. 'I knew him,' he said, voice colorless.

'Quite. Am I to understand also that you knew the names of some important supporters of the Pretender in England?'

Fraser glanced at him, face inscrutable in the lantern light.

'Many of them,' he said quietly. He looked back to the fork in his hands, drove it down into the hay. 'Does it matter now?'

Not to Fraser, surely. Nor to Hector, or the other dead of Culloden. But to the living . . .

'If any of them are still alive, I imagine it matters,' he said. 'Those who did not declare themselves at the time would scarcely wish their connexions exposed, even now.'

Fraser made a noise of soft derision through his nose.

'Oh, aye. I shall denounce them, I suppose, and thus gain pardon from your king?'

'Your king, as well,' Grey said pointedly. 'It is

possible that you could.' More than possible. The anti-Jacobite hysteria of the years before the Rising had eased somewhat – but treason was a crime whose stain did not fade; he had good reason to know it.

Fraser straightened. He let go of the fork and looked directly at him, his eyes so dark a blue that they reminded Grey of cathedral slates – darkened by age and the tread of feet, nearly black in the pooling shadows, but so enduring as to long outlast the feet that trampled them.

'If I would trade honor for my life – or for freedom – would I not have done it at my trial?'

'Perhaps you could not, then; you would have lain in danger from those Jacobites still at large.'

This attempt to goad Fraser was in vain; the Scot merely looked at him, with the expression of one regarding a turd in the street.

'Or perhaps you realized that such information as you possessed was not of sufficient value to interest anyone,' Grey suggested, unwilling – or unable – to give up. Fraser would have been compelled to swear an oath of loyalty to King George when he was given his life following Culloden, but Grey knew better than to try an appeal to *that*.

'I have said nothing regarding it, Major,' Fraser replied coolly. 'If what I ken has value to anyone, it is to yourself, I should say.'

'What makes you say that?' Grey's heart was hammering against his ribs, but he strove to match Fraser's even tone.

'It is a dozen years past the death of the Stuart cause,' Fraser pointed out. 'And I havena been besieged by persons desiring to discover my knowledge of those affairs connected with it. They asked at my trial, aye – but even then, without great interest in my answer.'

The dark blue gaze roved over him, detached and cynical.

'Do your own fortunes fare so badly, then, that ye seek to mend them wi' the bones of the dead?'

'With the—' Belatedly, he realized that Fraser spoke poetically, rather than literally.

'This has nothing to do with my own fortunes,' he said. 'But as to the dead – yes. I have no concern for those Jacobites still alive. If there are any left, they may go to the devil or the Pope as they please.'

He felt rather like a boy he had once seen at a zoological garden in Paris, who had poked a stick into a dozing tiger's cage. The beast had not snarled, nor thrown himself at the bars, but the slanted eyes had opened slowly, fixing upon the child in such a manner that the benighted urchin had dropped his stick and stood frozen, until his mother had dragged him away.

'The dead,' Fraser repeated, eyes fixed on Grey's face in that intent, unnerving fashion. 'What is it that ye seek from the dead, then?'

'A name. Just one.'

'Which one?'

Grey felt a sense of dread come over him that

paralyzed his limbs and dried his tongue. And yet it must be asked.

'Grey,' he said hoarsely. 'Gerard Grey. Duke. Duke of Pardloe. Was he—' Saliva failed him; he tried to swallow, but could not.

Fraser's gaze had sharpened; the dark blue eyes were brilliant, narrowed in the dimness.

'A duke,' he said. 'Your father?'

Grey could only nod, despising himself for his weakness.

Fraser grunted; impossible to tell if it was with surprise – or satisfaction. He thought for a moment, eyes hooded, then shook his head.

'No.'

'You will not tell me?'

It *was* surprise. Fraser frowned a little at him, puzzled.

'I mean the answer is no. I have never seen that name written among those of King James's supporters, nor have I ever heard it spoken.'

He was regarding Grey with considerable interest – as well he might, Grey thought. He could see unspoken questions moving in the Scot's eyes, but knew they would remain unspoken – as would his own, regarding Geneva Dunsany.

He himself felt something between vast relief and crushing disappointment. He had steeled himself to know the worst, and met only a blank wall. He longed to press Fraser further, but that would be pointless. Whatever else Fraser might be, Grey had no doubt of his honesty. He might have refused to answer, but answer he had, and Grey was compelled to accept it at face value.

That the answer still left room for doubt – perhaps Fraser had not been sufficiently intimate with the inner councils of the Jacobite cause as to be told such an important name, perhaps the duke had died too long before Fraser joined the cause – or perhaps the duke had been clever enough to remain successfully hidden from everyone save the Stuarts themselves . . .

'The Stuart court leaks like a sieve, Major.' The voice came quietly from the shadows. Fraser had turned his back again, resuming his work. 'If your father had any connexion whatever with the Stuarts and remained unknown – he was a verra clever man.'

'Yes,' Grey said bleakly. 'Yes, he was. I thank you, Mr. Fraser.'

He received no answer save the rustle of hay, and left the stable, followed by the whickering of horses and Fraser's tuneless whistle. Outside, the world had turned a soft, featureless white.

The fact that Fraser *had* answered him reinforced Grey's suspicions regarding Geneva. The encounter in the chapel was not mentioned, but the memory of it was clear between them. His honor would not permit him to mention it, lest it be taken as a threat – but the threat was implied. Had he made it explicit, Fraser's honor – and his temper – would likely have caused him to throw it back in Grey's face, stubbornly refusing to say a word and daring him to take action.

So he had something. It wasn't proof, either of Fraser's relationship with Geneva or of his own father's innocence – but food for thought, nonetheless.

He kept thinking, and while he did not see Fraser again before his departure, those thoughts moved him to one final trial of curiosity.

'Might I pay my respects to the new earl before I go?' he asked, hoping that he sounded as though he were jesting.

Lady Dunsany looked startled, but Isobel of course found nothing odd in his request, assuming that naturally the world shared in her admiration for her new nephew, and led him happily up to the nursery.

The sun was shining – a pale and watery winter sun, but still sun – and the nursery seemed peaceful and calm. The curtains hung motionless in the schoolroom, and Isobel did not glance at the window where he had shown her how to break things.

The ninth Earl of Ellesmere was lying in a basket, swaddled to the chin in blankets, a woolly cap pulled snugly down over his ears. The child was awake, though; it thoughtfully inserted a fist in its mouth, round eyes fixed on Grey – or possibly on the ceiling; it was difficult to tell.

'May I?' Without waiting for the nurse's permission, Grey scooped the child carefully up into his arms. He was noticeably heavy. He said as much, which caused both Isobel and the nurse to go off into raptures regarding the infant's voraciousness, capacity, and various other revolting details not suitable for discussion in mixed company, in Grey's opinion.

Still, he let them chatter, interjecting the occasional, 'Ah?' of interest, and looking covertly into the child's face. It looked like a pudding, slightly wet and glistening. It had eyes, to be sure – and he thought them blue, but his cousin Olivia had informed him that all children's eyes were blue at birth. Its other features appeared negligible at best.

The woolly cap had strings, tied beneath the infant's chin, and he nudged these with a thumb, thinking that he might be able to pry them up over the chin and thus dislodge the cap for a moment.

This seemed to annoy the infant, though; he contorted his face, went red, and emitted a high-pitched shriek, which caused Nanny Elspeth to snatch him protectively from Grey's arms. She patted the little back soothingly, giving Grey a look of marked disapproval.

'I only wondered – has he any hair?' Grey asked, in desperation. That produced a complete alteration in the women's attitude; from reproach, they turned all eagerness, vying with each other to remove the baby's cap and demonstrate the virtues of its scalp.

The child *did* have hair. A soft darkish slick that ran down the center of its head like the stripe on a Spanish donkey.

'May I?'

The nurse looked as though she would prefer to hand the child over to a convicted ax murderer, but as Isobel nodded encouragingly, she reluctantly surrendered the little creature to Grey's dubious care again.

He took a firm hold on the infant, making soft whistling noises through his teeth; that usually worked on strange dogs. He strolled to and fro across the room, joggling it gently, meanwhile maneuvering the little creature as unobtrusively as possible, so as to get the light behind it.

He *thought* there was a reddish tinge to the hair – but could not swear to it.

'Is he not lovely?' Isobel petted the tiny stripe of hair lovingly. 'I think he will look like my sister – see? He has her hair, I'm sure of it.'

With a sense of chagrin, Grey realized that, indeed, Geneva *had* had hair of a deep chestnut color. No answers here, then. He was trying to think how to return the child to the women without rudeness, but the boy settled the matter himself, by emitting a loud belch and decanting a remarkably large quantity of partially digested milk over Grey's shoulder.

'Does he not make you wish to marry at once and have children of your own?' Isobel asked, fondly patting the baby's back as the nursemaid – with bad grace – swabbed the offending mess from Grey's clothes.

'I do believe I can contain my impatience,' he

said, and both women laughed as though he had made some clever jest.

'Oh, look!' Isobel peered at the infant in delight. 'He's smiling, Lord John. He likes you!'

'Well, in fact . . .' the nursemaid began, eyeing the child's rapidly reddening face thoughtfully, 'I do believe . . .'

'Oh, dear!' said Isobel. A most unusual odor – sweet but foul – filled the air.

'I'm sure the sentiment is mutual,' Grey said politely, and bowed toward the infant. 'Your servant, sir.'

It was not until he and Tom were halfway back to London that it occurred to him that he had never thought to ask the infant's name.

SECTION III

Mixed Loyalties

Chapter 9

Unnatural Acts

Grey returned from the stark silence of the fells to a London in ferment.

As Hal had predicted, the printers had got hold of Ffoulkes's French family connexions and unearthed the hints of unsavory conspiracy; Ffoulkes's wife had fled the country and was presumably in France; another conspirator, a lawyer named Jeffords, had been arrested and was to be tried along with Captain Bates and Harrison Otway on a variety of charges ranging from lewd conduct to sodomy, conspiracy to commit unnatural acts, and, as a definite afterthought, conspiracy to assassinate various justices and ministers – presumably those who had been most outspoken about the need to crush this abominable vice.

'Not, I see, on charges of treason,' Grey remarked to his brother, crumpling a broadsheet with a cartoon illustrating two of the conspirators engaging in one of these unnatural acts and tossing it into the fire in Hal's office. 'As you suspected.'

Hal shrugged moodily.

'Doesn't take a fortune-teller to see that Bernard

Adams and that lot would strongly prefer a nice sodomitical conspiracy to outrage the public and keep them distracted than alarming news of a gang of traitors who came damned near to cutting Adams's throat and did manage to pass a great deal of damaging information to their master in France. To say nothing of fifteen thousand pounds – though I take leave to doubt that it all went to France.'

'They did?'

'They did. It's been kept very quiet, but Bates sent a note to Adams, cool as dammit, and inveigled him into meeting privately in the yard of a tavern in Lambeth, saying he – Bates, that is – had something of advantage to confide. Adams *went,* the idiot, and only escaped being killed because Bates missed his footing on a patch of mud, allowing the fool time to shout for help. Adams was wounded, and Bates escaped, of course, but they caught him – trying to make it to Ireland, evidently.'

'Yes, I gather he has an Irish mistress.'

Hal blinked at him.

'He does? Who told you that?'

Realizing that it might be impolitic to reveal his conversation with Minnie, Grey merely shrugged, as though it were common rumor.

'Who told you all this?' he asked.

'Harry. Likely got it from his half brother, Joffrey.'

'Much more likely from Lady Joffrey,' Grey observed, and Hal made a brief grimace of agreement.

A sudden grinding noise made Grey's head jerk round. In the corner stood a large wooden cabinet, which to this point he had assumed to be part of one of Mr. Beasley's futile efforts to bring some semblance of order to Hal's office. The doors to this swung slowly open, revealing a figure inside, and he clapped a hand to his dagger with an exclamation.

'It's all right.' Hal was still cross, but his voice showed a tinge of amusement. 'It's only an automaton.'

This was by now apparent; the cabinet contained a life-size figure, or rather half of one; the thing ended at the waist, the bottom half of the cabinet presumably being filled with the clockwork mechanism whose whirring had attracted Grey's attention. Going closer to examine this object, he discovered the figure to be made of wax, wood, and metal, gaily painted to resemble the popular conception of a native of India, complete to kohl-rimmed eyes, red lips, and gauzy turban.

He put out a hand to touch it, then jerked the hand back as a loud clank came from the machine. The figure leaned abruptly toward him in sinister fashion, but proved only to be inserting a stiff hand into a jar placed before it. More clanking and whirring, a long pause . . . and the figure snapped back into its original position, one arm swinging up so violently that it nearly struck Grey in the face.

'What the devil?'

'It's a fortune-teller,' Hal said, quite unnecessarily. He was openly amused by this time.

'So I see.' The figure's metal fingers held out a bit of folded paper, which Grey took gingerly and opened.

'The greatest danger could be your own stupidity,' he read aloud. He refolded the paper and dropped it back in the jar. 'Very nice. Where on earth did you get this?'

'Sergeant-Major Weems confiscated it from the O'Higginses,' Hal said. 'Put it in here for safekeeping until he can discover whom they stole it from.'

'You'd think it wouldn't be difficult to trace the owner.' Grey walked round the cabinet, examining it. It was battered and scarred, though originally of very good manufacture.

Hal shrugged.

'They claim they won it in a dice game.'

'Yes, well.' Grey dismissed the automaton and sat down again. 'You said the conspirators did succeed in getting material to France?'

'Adams says they did. Whilst he was frolicking on the river with Bates, Otway and Jeffords evidently burgled his house and took the contents of his safe, which included roughly fifteen thousand pounds: the property of His Majesty, intended to be handed over next day to the paymasters of two regiments bound for France. In the kerfuffle over all this, several offices in Whitehall discovered they were also missing assorted bits of important paper – though my personal suspicion is that they've leapt at the opportunity to blame any lapses in their bookkeeping on this so-called conspiracy.'

'Rather enterprising for a gang of sodomites,' Grey remarked, fascinated. 'What are they supposed to have intended doing with the money – holding orgies of disgusting vice?'

'God knows. The last newspaper I read speculated that they proposed emigrating to France – using the stolen money to insure their welcome – where presumably disgusting vice flourishes unchecked in the streets.'

'Were the documents and money recovered?'

Hal leaned back in his chair.

'No, they weren't. None of the conspirators had any suspicious material on them when they were arrested, and it wasn't found in Ffoulkes's house following his suicide – so the supposition is that Louis of France now has it.' Hal grimaced, as though his breakfast hadn't agreed with him. 'And speaking of France . . .'

Grey looked up sharply, hearing a new note in his brother's voice.

'Yes?'

'We aren't going there.'

'What?'

'The regiment's orders have been changed. Read that.' Hal extracted a letter from the mess on his desk and threw it in front of Grey. It was from the Ministry of War, and in a few curt lines, ordered the 1st/46th to join with the forces of Duke Ferdinand of Brunswick, in Prussia.

'No explanation?' Grey raised a brow at his brother, who glowered back.

'No. Not that I need one. It's frigging Twelvetrees's doing.'

Twelvetrees. That name rang bells of warning, and within a moment, Grey had recollected why. 'Nathaniel Twelvetrees?' Grey hazarded. 'The gentleman with whom you –'

'Nathaniel Twelvetrees is dead, and so is the matter to which you refer.' Hal's voice was flat, but his eyes dared Grey to say more on pain of death. 'This is his elder brother. Colonel in the Royal Artillery.'

'I see.'

Which he did. While Hal had succeeded in regaining something of the family honor by his military efforts, he had done it with the assistance of capable men, dedicated soldiers such as Harry Quarry, whom he had lured away from the Buffs with the promise of higher rank and freedom of authority. Other regiments – such as the Royal Artillery – boasted officers of privilege and noble family, if not any pronounced military skills. Such men would want nothing to do with Lord Melton's disgrace, or his regiment. Consequently, Hal could not rely on so many of the favors and connexions that gave some other regiments preferment.

Evidently, Colonel Twelvetrees thought the French campaign offered more scope and opportunity for distinction in battle, and wished to deprive the 46th of such opportunity. From what Grey knew of the war in Prussia, it was likely to be a long, drawn-out affair, with the Duke of

Brunswick's troops – which they would be joining as allies – at a numerical disadvantage.

Likewise, the English formed a smaller part of the army on the Prussian front, and would therefore have less influence in the management of the campaign.

'Well,' Grey said at last. 'The beer is better.'

Hal's bad temper at last gave way, and he laughed, if reluctantly.

'Yes, that's something. And at least you speak German. I'll need you by me, so they don't slip anything past us.'

'Percival Wainwright speaks German, as well,' Grey said, and his heart jumped. He touched his waistcoat pocket, where the lock of dark hair lay curled in secrecy.

'Does he?' Hal was interested. 'Good. Will you have time to show him his business? He signed his papers of commission this morning. I can turn him over to Wilmot or Brabham-Griggs, if you'd rather, but as you seemed to get on with him—'

'No, I can do that,' Grey assured him, rising. 'Do you know where I might find him today? Is he at the barracks?'

'No. Actually, he's at Mother's house, being fitted with a suit for the wedding. I narrowly escaped myself. Oh – which reminds me: Olivia said if you turned up here, I was to send you home at once to be measured.'

'All right.' This suited him excellently well, though he had his reservations regarding Olivia's taste. 'She isn't insisting upon yellow velvet, is she?'

'No, but she said something about persimmon waistcoats.'

Grey glanced suspiciously at his brother, who looked back with a perfect bland innocence.

'You wouldn't recognize a persimmon if you sat on it,' Grey said, 'and nor would Olivia.'

He was nearly out the door, when he remembered.

'That page of Father's journal,' he said abruptly, turning back. 'Did you speak to Mother? Have you learned any more about it?'

Something flickered in his brother's eyes, and then was gone.

'No,' Hal said casually, returning his attention to the stack of papers on his desk. 'Not a thing.'

Grey did not go home immediately, in spite of the presence there of Percy Wainwright. Instead, he crossed the courtyard and went upstairs to see if Harry Quarry was in his own office.

He was, leaning back in his chair, and apparently asleep, a half-dried quill stuck to a blotted page in a copybook on the desk before him.

'Practicing your penmanship, Harry?' Grey said, in a normal tone of voice. Quarry opened one bleary eye, reached out a hand, and flipped the book closed, the quill still inside it.

'Don't bellow, there's a good chap,' Quarry said,

pressing both hands against his temples, apparently in hope of keeping the contents of his head from escaping.

'Late night, was it?' Grey pulled up a stool and leaned on the desk, eyeing his friend.

'I believe I've eaten something that disagreed with me,' Quarry said with dignity, and stifled a belch by way of illustration.

'Really? What was her name?'

Quarry burst into a violent coughing fit that left his wig askew and his face empurpled.

'You *hound*,' he said hoarsely, tenderly patting his chest. 'What the devil d'you want, anyway?'

Grey rocked back a little on the stool.

'Since you ask – Harry, do you happen to know how one Nathaniel Twelvetrees died?'

Quarry's eyes flew open. He drew breath, and coughed some more. Grey waited patiently. Quarry frowned, pursed his lips, sighed – and gave up.

'Died following a duel with your brother. Not a secret; a good many people know.'

'You were there?' Grey asked, picking up something in Quarry's voice. Harry grimaced.

'I was Melton's second. Twelvetrees shot first, mind. Nicked Melton in the thigh, but he didn't fall. Staggered a bit, to be sure, but managed his aim and got Twelvetrees through the upper arm. Honor satisfied all round, should have been the end of it and no one the wiser. Only Twelvetrees's wound turned septic and he died.' Harry shrugged. 'Bad luck. Still, Twelvetrees insisted on his deathbed that it was a private affair, and it stayed that way. They're an honorable family. Cold as death,' he added fairly, 'but honorable.'

'I don't suppose I need ask what was the cause of the duel.' Grey rubbed a hand over his face, feeling suddenly tired. He needed a shave.

'No, I don't suppose you do. I heard you'd seen the betting book at White's.'

'Who told you that?'

'Oh, twenty or thirty people, so far.' Harry adjusted his wig, eyeing Grey. 'Melton wasn't one of them.'

'No, I don't suppose he would be.' Grey made no attempt to disguise the edge in his voice. 'Why did he challenge Twelvetrees? Obviously the duel happened after the wager was made. Dr. Longstreet told me Hal had wanted to fight Twelvetrees and the rest to begin with, but cooler heads prevailed – that would be you, perhaps, Harry?'

Quarry's heavy brows went up.

'How do you know he challenged Twelvetrees, and not t'other way around?' Harry asked.

Grey shrugged. The choice of weapon had to have been Twelvetrees's; Hal would always fight with a sword, if he could.

'Why did he do it after all? What did Twelvetrees do?'

'That,' Quarry said definitely, 'is not my secret to tell. Ask your brother, if you want to know.'

Grey made a rude noise.

'I couldn't get the name of his tailor out of him

with a corkscrew in his present mood. Tell me this, then – did he tell you about the page from my father's journal?'

Quarry's eyes opened wide, startled and blood-shot.

'About *what*?'

'Oh, he didn't.' Grey felt obscurely pleased at that. At least he wasn't the only one excluded from Hal's confidence. He stood up and shook his coat into order.

'All right, then. I'm going home. You know Percy Wainwright's bought in?'

'God have mercy on his soul,' Quarry said, but the jest was automatic. He reached across and gripped Grey's arm.

'John,' he said, his voice unexpectedly gentle, 'leave it. Your father's long dead.'

'Thank you, Harry,' Grey said, and meant it. He detached his arm from Quarry's grip, patting his friend's hand. 'But I'm not,' he whispered, and went out.

He left his horse in the barracks stable and walked to Jermyn Street, managing by the exercise both to work out the kinks of riding and to ease his mind a little. If Hal thought he could be brushed off like an annoying insect, Hal could think again. Still, Hal hadn't told Harry about the journal page, so it wasn't only himself his brother was keeping secrets from. Harry had not been with the regiment much above a year – he'd come over from the Buffs – but he was one of Hal's oldest friends.

At least he would have the upper hand in Germany, he thought. He was himself just as pleased by the change of orders; he liked many things about Germany – beer among them – and had numerous friends among the Prussians and their allies. And as Percy Wainwright *did* speak German, as well . . . The thought of Wainwright quite restored his good humor, and he swung whistling down the street and in at his mother's gate.

He found Percy Wainwright with Olivia, a sempstress, the sempstress's assistant, and Olivia's maid, all in a state of hilarity over the fitting of Percy's suit, which did not appear to be going well.

His first sight, in fact, was of Percy's bum, clad in linen drawers and exposed to view as Percy bent to touch his toes, indicating a tendency of the so-far sleeveless and skirtless coat to pull across the back.

'You see?' Percy was saying. The women, seeing Grey in the doorway, burst into laughter.

'Well, yes, I do,' Grey said, endeavoring not to laugh himself, but failing, as Percy shot upright and whirled round, wide-eyed. Grey bowed, hand on heart. 'Your servant, sir.'

'I fear you take me at a disadvantage, sir,' Percy said with mock dignity, whipping a pair of half-finished cream silk breeches off the settee and wrapping his loins in them.

If we were alone, I certainly would, Grey thought,

and allowed some hint of this to show in his smile. Percy caught the hint; a higher color rose in his cheeks, already flushed. He held Grey's eyes for a fraction of a second, his own alight with speculation – and acceptance – before joining in the general laughter.

'Johnny! How quick you've been! I didn't think you'd come 'til teatime.' Olivia waddled forward and went a-tiptoe, straining over her bulge to kiss his cheek. 'Here, *you* try this coat. Perhaps it will fit you better.'

He felt his own face grow warm at the notion of publicly disrobing – even partially – in the presence of Percy Wainwright, but the latter was grinning at his discomfiture, and he allowed himself to be stripped of his uniform coat and waistcoat, though he did retain his shirt and breeches. Catching, as he did so, a brief glimpse of Percy, bare-legged and clad only in drawers, as the latter wrapped himself in Grey's banyan, Olivia having evidently stolen this garment from his room.

Grey turned his back hastily, thrusting an arm randomly through what he hoped was the proper hole of the coat the sempstress held for him. The fabric was a heavy silk velvet of a midnight blue, and it was still warm from Percy's body. He bit the inside of his cheek, and tasted blood.

The sempstress, herself flushed and laughing, but still attentive to business, was circling him with a bit of chalk and a calculating eye, making him raise and lower his arms, move to and fro. Breaking out in a dew of sweat, he bent over at her order, remembering too late that he'd worn the stained doeskin breeches for riding.

Further outbreaks of hilarity, this time at his expense, but he didn't mind. He had a momentary qualm when the sempstress knelt at his feet to pin a waist seam, but she merely flushed a little more and cast her eyes modestly down, her shy smile making it evident that she considered it a personal compliment; she was a handsome young woman, and likely had had such before.

Percy Wainwright knew where the compliment lay. He laughed with the girls, teasing and making comments, but his gaze kept returning to Grey, alive with interest. He had left off his wig, and at one point, he casually ran a hand through his short-clipped hair, as though to order the dark curls, and glanced at Grey.

Did you get it, then? his upraised eyebrow said.

Grey raised his own.

Percy grinned at him, but glanced away a moment too soon, and when he looked back now and then, Percy was always engaged in conversation with Olivia, a maid, or Tom – who had arrived belatedly and was experiencing loudly audible mortification over Grey's breeches.

What was this? he wondered. He was not mistaken in the attraction; he knew that for certain. And he had not had any indication during their previous conversations that Percy was either light-minded or flirtatious in the least. Perhaps it was only caution, he told himself – a reluctance, lest anyone notice what was going on between them.

When they had at last resumed their usual garments and the sempstress and her assistant departed with armloads of blue velvet, he made occasion to brush shoulders with Percy at the door of the drawing room.

'Melton tells me I am to have the honor to familiarize you with the ways of the regiment, your duties and the like. If you have time this afternoon . . . ?' For the first time, he regretted staying in his mother's house. Though officers' quarters in the barracks would not have been much better. How far away were Percy's rooms?

'I should like that more than I can say,' Percy replied. 'But I am, alas, engaged.' The regret in his voice seemed real, but Grey experienced it as a small blow, nonetheless.

'Perhaps tomorrow—' he began, but saw Percy grimace in apology.

'My engagement is in – in Bath,' he said quickly. 'I shall not be back for two or three days. I should in fact have left this morning – I will be very late – save that I hoped to have a chance of seeing you before I left,' he added softly. He looked directly at Grey as he said this, and Grey felt some easing of his disappointment, if not his baser urges.

Bath, my eye, he thought. But after all, the man was surely entitled to his privacy, if he did not wish to say what his engagement was. Percy owed him nothing – yet.

'Find me upon your return, then,' he said. He clapped Percy briefly on the shoulder. 'Safe journey.' He turned, and without looking back, went out in search of some privacy of his own.

Chapter 10

Salle des Armes

He returned in the evening, to discover that the dowager countess had likewise come back from her excursion. He went to her boudoir to pay his respects, and found her cheerful, if a little pale from her journey, and with a few lines of worry round her eyes. These, he took to be the natural effects of her discovery of the extent of Olivia's ambitions as a wedding planner.

He did his best to distract her, therefore, with the story of the afternoon's fitting, nobly sacrificing his own dignity in order to include his stained breeches and Percy's drawers.

'Oh, dear, oh, dear – poor Tom!' The countess made small snorting noises. 'He does take his position very seriously, God help the poor lad. I think you must be a very great trial to him.'

'Yes, he was in hopes that Percy Wainwright might be a macaroni – you could quite see visions of embroidered waistcoats and clocked silk stockings dance in his head – but I was obliged to dash his hopes, alas.'

The countess smiled afresh at that, but her voice was serious.

'Do you like Percy Wainwright?'

'Yes,' he answered, rather surprised that she would ask. 'Yes, we get on quite well together. Common interests, and the like.' He trusted that no hint of just how common those interests were showed on his face. He cleared his throat and added, 'I like the general, too, Mother – very much.'

'Oh, do you?' Her face softened. 'I'm glad of that, John. He's a very fine man – and so kind.' She pursed her lips then, though still with a look of amusement. 'I am not sure your brother is quite as taken with him. But then, Hal is always so suspicious, poor boy. I really think sometimes that he trusts no one but you and his wife. Well, and Harry Quarry, to be sure.'

The mention of his brother reminded Grey. In the flurry of his return from Helwater, the preparations for the wedding, and the regiment's new orders, he had momentarily forgotten. But surely Hal had had sufficient time to speak with her by now.

'Mother – did Hal mention to you the page from Father's journal that we discovered in his office?'

If he'd thought her slightly pale before, he'd been mistaken. He'd seen her pale with fatigue and white with fury. Now, though, the blood washed from her face in an instant, and the look of fear in her eyes was unmistakable.

'Did he?' he repeated, trying to sound casual. 'I

rather wondered whether perhaps you had had one, too. Delivered by post, perhaps?'

She looked up at him, her eyes quick and fierce.

'What makes you think that?'

'The way you spoke of James Fraser when I departed for Helwater,' he told her frankly. 'Something must have disturbed you quite suddenly, for you to take such note of the man; you have known of him for years. But since the only thing you do know of him is that he was once a prominent Jacobite . . . ?' He paused delicately, but she said nothing. Her eyes were still blazing like a burning glass, but she wasn't looking at him any longer. Whatever she was looking at lay a good way beyond him.

'Yes,' she said at last, her voice remote. She blinked once and looked at him, her gaze still sharp, but no longer burning. 'Your father always said you were the cleverest of the boys.' This wasn't said in a complimentary tone. 'As for "was once a prominent Jacobite" – there is no "was" about it, John. Believe me, once a Papist, always a Papist.'

He forbore pointing out that 'Papist' and 'Jacobite' were not invariably the same thing. When politics entered the room, principle often flew out the window. While most Papists had indeed supported the Stuart cause, there were not a few Protestants who had as well, either from personal opportunism or from a sincere conviction that James Stuart was the divinely appointed sovereign of Great Britain, his religion notwithstanding.

'So you did receive a page from that journal,' he said, making it a statement, rather than a question. 'May I see it?'

'I burnt it.'

'What for?' He all but barked at her, and she blinked again, startled. She eyed him then, obviously choosing her words.

'Because,' she said evenly, 'I did not wish to keep it. Have you heard the expression, John, "Let the dead bury the dead"? What's past is past, and I shan't cling to its remnants.'

He struggled for a moment against the impulse to say something regrettable – but then his eye fell upon the miniature on her dressing table. It had stood there since the day Gerard Grey had given it to her, and it was years since John Grey had ceased to notice it. Noticing it now, he was taken aback to see just how much the portrait resembled the image he saw in his shaving mirror. His father had been darker in coloring, but otherwise . . . So much for his mother's chance of forgetting the past, then, even if she wanted to.

'Really, Mother,' he said mildly, 'you are the most atrocious liar. What are you afraid of?'

'What? What the devil do you mean by that?' she exclaimed indignantly. She didn't curse often, and he invariably found it amusing when she did, but he suppressed his smile.

'I mean,' he said patiently, gesturing at the miniature, 'that if you wish to convince the world that you have lost all thought for my father, you ought to remove that from sight. And when you tell people you have destroyed something,' he added, nodding at her secretary, 'you ought not to glance at the place where you've hidden it.'

She opened her mouth, but found nothing to say, and closed it again. She looked at him, eyes narrowed.

'If you don't want that journal page,' he said, 'I do.'

'No,' she said at once.

'Does it contain something so dangerous, then? Have you shown it to Hal?' Despite himself, a tinge of anger was creeping into his words. 'I'm no longer twelve, Mother.'

She looked at him for a long moment, the oddest expression of regret flitting across her face.

'More's the pity,' she said. Her shoulders sagged then, and she bowed her head and turned away, rubbing two fingers between her brows.

'I'll think about it, John,' she said. 'More, I can't promise you. Now leave me, do; I've a dreadful headache.'

'Liar,' he said again, but without heat. 'I'll send your maid, shall I?'

'Please.'

He went out, then, but at the door turned back and stuck his head through.

'Mother?'

'Yes?'

'If you wish to convince someone that you aren't afraid – look them in the eye. Good night.'

Percy Wainwright, it transpired, had never so much as touched a sword, let alone used one with violent intent. In order to remedy this shocking lack, he agreed amiably enough, upon his return from Bath, to go with Grey and Melton to their usual weekly practice, for the purpose of basic instruction.

The *salle des armes* favored by the Greys was in Monmouth Street, a small, dingy building wedged between a pawnbroker's and a mercer's shop near St. Giles, and run by a small Sicilian gentleman whose skill with the blade was surpassed only by the individuality of his idiom.

'Gets you fat-fat,' *Signor* Berculi said without preamble, rudely poking Hal in his very flat stomach. 'No practice, two weeks! Some *pidocchio* do the business on you, stick a rapier up you fat arse.'

Hal, quite accustomed to *Signor* Berculi, ignored this pleasantry and introduced Mr. Wainwright as a new addition to the family and to the regiment.

The *Signor* circled Percy, shaking his head and biting his finger in dismay. Percy looked mildly apprehensive, but the glance he shot Grey was filled with amusement.

'So old, so old!' *Signor* Berculi mourned, halting in front of Percy and prodding him critically in the upper arm. He waved a small, callused hand at Grey. 'That one, sword in cradle. You? Pah!' He spat, shook himself violently, then crossed himself.

'Come,' he said, resigned, and seized Percy by the sleeve. 'You lunge. No stick you foot, all right?'

While Percy was rapidly stripped to his shirt and breeches, given a battered rapier with no point, and set to lunging, the Greys stripped for action.

'*En garde.*' Hal fell naturally into his stance, knee bent, rapier forward, the side of his body turned toward Grey, left hand held gracefully up behind his head.

'*J'ai regardé.*' Grey tapped his blade lightly against Hal's, and held it crossed. *Signor* Berculi, circling them with beady eyes narrowed for flaws in form, shouted, '*Commencez!*' and they began.

It was an exhibition of form to begin with, neither man seeking actual advantage but only an opening in which to try a *coupé* or *passe avant*, circling slowly as their muscles loosened.

Grey saw Percy's eyes upon them, interested, until *Signor* Berculi spotted his distraction and drove him back to his lunging with a bark.

He breathed deep, intoxicated by the smell of sweat, old and fresh, the metal tang of the swords, and the rub of the hilt on the heel of his hand. He loved to fight with the rapier; it was so light, he was barely conscious of it as anything more than an extension of his body.

He and his brother were evenly matched physically, being of a height, with Hal having a few pounds the advantage in weight, and Grey perhaps an inch more in reach. Despite this evident equality

– and the fact that Hal *was* a fine swordsman – Grey knew himself to be better.

He seldom demonstrated that knowledge in their practice bouts, knowing equally well that Hal hated to lose and would be in bad temper if he did. Now, though, he found himself pressing, ever so slightly, and realized with a glance at Percy and a small tingling of his flesh that he meant to win today, no matter what the consequence.

'Have you any further news of the conspirators?' Grey asked, as much in order to distract his brother as from curiosity.

Hal met his thrust with a strong riposte, beat, and went for a thrust in *quarte*, which failed.

'They go to trial this week,' he said briefly.

'I have' – a beat, beat back, feint in *prime,* and he touched Hal's shoulder, barely, and smiled – 'have not seen mention of it in the papers.'

'You will.' Grunting, Hal lunged, and he barely turned aside in time.

'They' – Hal was beginning to breathe hard by now, and the words emerged in brief bursts – 'decided to – do as I said – they would.'

'To suppress the political aspects of the case?' Grey was still breathing easily. 'Say "Peter Piper picked a peck of pickled peppers."'

'She sells – sea shells – by the frigging seashore! Damn your eyes!' A fusillade of beats and a vicious thrust that missed his chest so narrowly that Grey felt the blade glide along his shirtfront.

'Peter Piper picked a peck of pickled peppers,

Peter Piper picked a peck of pippled pickers, Peter P—' Laughing – and beginning to gasp himself – he left off, and fought.

Beat, beat, feint, a half skip back as Hal's point lunged past his face, another, Hal was leaning too far forward – no, he'd caught himself, jumped back in the nick of time as Grey's blade came up. A lunge in *tierce*, in *tierce* again without let, and dust flew up from the stamp of his foot on the boards.

Hal had caught what he was about; he could feel Hal's thoughts as though they were inside his own head, feel the edge of astonished annoyance change, anger rising, then the jerk as Hal caught himself, forced himself to restraint, to something colder and more cautious.

Grey himself had no such restraint. He was happily off his head, drunk with the lust of fighting. His body felt like oiled rope, tensile and slippery, and he was taking dangerous chances, completely confident that he could elude Hal's point, regardless. He saw an opening, dropped into a flattened lunge with a yell, and his buttoned point struck Hal's thigh and skidded across the fabric of his breeches.

'Jesus!' said Hal, and swung at his head.

He ducked, laughing, and popped up like a jack-in-the-box, grabbing the point of his rapier so the blade bowed between his hands, then let go and snapped it off Hal's, making the metal ring and the sword jump in Hal's hand.

He heard Berculi swear in Italian, but had no

attention to spare. Hal was fighting back in earnest now, beating at his blade fit to break them both. He skipped in at once, his arm running up Hal's and taking him by surprise, so they ended in embrace, sword arms linked and blades entangled, bodies pressed together.

He grinned at Hal, baring his teeth, and saw the spark leap in his brother's eye. He was faster, though, and the first to jerk loose, leaving Hal for an instant off balance. He dropped by instinct into a perfect *Passata-sotto,* and his button pressed against Hal's throat.

'*Touché,*' he said softly.

Hal's hands fell away, his rapier dangling, and he stood for a moment, chest heaving for breath, before he nodded.

'*Je me rends,*' he said gruffly. *I yield.*

Grey took away his point and bowed to his brother, but his eyes were on Percy. Percy had left off his lunging altogether in order to watch, and stood against the wall, eyes wide in shock and what Grey hoped was admiration.

Signor Berculi had snatched off his wig and was kneading it with excitement.

'You!' he said, brandishing the object in Grey's face. '*Never* you do that! Is no proper that what you do! You *insano*! But good,' he added, standing back a little and surveying Grey from head to toe as though he had never seen him before. He nodded, pursing his lips judiciously. 'Very good.'

Hal was rubbing his head and neck with a towel.

He was flushed, but for a wonder, seemed amused rather than angry.

'What brought *that* on?' he asked.

'Showing off for the new brother,' Grey replied flippantly, with a casual wave at Percy. He wiped a sleeve across his jaw. He was soaked; his shirt and breeches stuck to him, and his muscles jumped and quivered. 'Want another go?'

Hal gave him a look.

'Oh, I think not,' he said. 'I've a meeting.' He looked at Percy, and tossed the rapier to him. 'Here, you have a go, Wainwright. I've taken the edge off him for you.'

Percy's mouth fell open, and *Signor* Berculi burst into sardonic laughter. Percy turned the sword slowly round in his hands, not taking his eyes off Grey.

'Shall I?'

Grey's pulse was still hammering in his ears, and something exhilarating ran up his spine like champagne bubbles rising in a glass.

'Of course, if you like. You needn't worry,' he said, and bowed deep to Percy, rapier politely extended. 'I'll be gentle.'

An hour later, Grey and Wainwright bade farewell to *Signor* Berculi and the *salle des armes,* and turned toward Neal's Yard, where one of Grey's favorite chophouses did a bloody steak with roast potatoes and the proprietor's special mushroom catsup – an appealing prospect to ravenous appetites.

Grey was entirely aware that more than one appetite had been stimulated by the recent exercise. The art of swordsmanship obliged one to pay the closest attention to the body of one's opponent, reading intent in the shift of weight, the narrowing of an eye, looking for a weakness that might be taken advantage of. He'd been attuned to every breath Percy Wainwright had taken for the last hour, and he knew damned well where Percy's weakness was – and his own.

Blood thrummed pleasantly through his veins, still hot from the exercise. The day was sunny, with a chilly breeze that dried the sweat and felt good on his heated skin, and the afternoon lay alluringly before them, empty of obligation. He was meant to be taking Percy on a tour of the barracks, the store-rooms, the parade ground, and introducing him to such officers and men as they ran across in the course of it. *The devil with that,* he thought. *Time enough.*

'Did you really have a sword in your cradle?' Percy asked, with a sidelong smile.

'Of course not. No good having a sword if you haven't got any sense of balance,' Grey said mildly. 'I believe I had reached the advanced age of three years before my father trusted me to stay solidly on my feet.'

He was gratified by the disbelieving look Percy gave him, but raised his hand in affirmation.

'Truly. If you ever become intimate with my – with *our* brother,' he corrected with a smile, 'ask him to show you the scar on his left leg. Hal was very kind in teaching little brother to use a sword, but carelessly gave me his own rapier to try. It wasn't buttoned, and I ran him through the calf with it. He bled buckets, and limped for a month.'

Percy hooted with laughter, but quickly sobered.

'Is it terribly important, do you think? That I know how to use a sword, I mean. *Signor* Berculi seemed to think I lack any natural ability whatever, and I must say I'm forced to agree with him.'

This was patently true, but Grey did not say so, merely moving a gloved hand in equivocation.

'It's always a good thing to be adept with weapons, especially if the fighting is close, but I know any number of officers who aren't. Much more important to act like an officer.'

'How do you do that?' Percy seemed sincerely interested, which was the first step, and Grey told him so.

'Have a care for your men – but also for their purpose. They will look to you in battle, and in some cases, your strength of will may be the only thing enabling them to go on fighting. At that point, their physical welfare ceases to be a concern, either to them or to you. All that matters is to hold them together and see them through. They must trust you to do that.'

Seeing the look of concern knitting Percy's dark brows, he altered his plan for the afternoon.

'After luncheon, we'll go to the parade ground, and I'll explain the general order of drills. That's why you have drills and discipline; the men must be in the habit of looking to you at all times, of following your orders without hesitation. And then,' he said, rather diffidently, 'perhaps we might take a little supper. Your rooms are convenient to the parade ground, I believe. If you did not mind . . . we might fetch a bit of bread and cheese and eat there.'

Percy's face lightened, the frown of concern replaced by a slow smile.

'I should like it of all things,' he said. He coughed then, and took up another subject.

'What was Melton saying to you during your bout? About a conspiracy of sodomites?' There was a hint of incredulity in his voice. 'A conspiracy to do *what*?'

'Oh . . . create scandal, subvert the public morality, seduce children, bugger horses' – he smiled blandly into the face of an elderly gentleman passing, who had caught this and was staring at him, pop-eyed – 'you know the sort of thing.'

Percy made snorting noises and pulled him along by the arm.

'I do,' he said, still snorting. 'I grew up Methodist, remember.'

'I didn't think Methodists even admitted the possibility of such things.'

'Not out loud, certainly,' Percy said dryly. 'But why is your brother concerned with this particular affair?'

'Because—' he said, and got no further. A man

204

jostled him rudely, shoving him into a wall so hard that he staggered.

'What the devil do you—' He put a hand to his bruised shoulder, indignant, then saw the look on the man's face and dodged. He hadn't seen the knife, but heard the scrape of it as it dragged across the brick wall where he had been standing an instant before.

The man was already recovering, turning. He kicked at the footpad, aiming for the knee, but got him square in the shin, hurting his own foot. The man yowled nonetheless, and drew back. Grey seized Percy by the sleeve.

'Run!'

Percy ran, Grey after him, and they pelted down the street, ducking hot-chestnut stands, orange sellers, and a throng of slow-moving women who shrieked and scattered as the men plowed through them. Footsteps rang on the pavement behind; he glanced back over his shoulder and saw *two* men, burly and determined, pursuing.

He'd left his rapier at the *salle des armes,* God damn it. He had his dagger, though, and ducking aside into an alley, ripped open his waistcoat and scrabbled frantically to get hold of it. He had no more than a second before the first of the men rushed in after him, reaching for him with a gap-toothed grin. Too late, the footpad saw the dagger and dodged aside; the point scored his abdomen, ripping his shirt and the flesh beneath. Grey glimpsed blood, and pressed the attack, shouting and jabbing.

The man danced backward, looking alarmed, and shouted, 'Jed!'

Jed arrived promptly, popping up behind his fellow with a blackthorn walking stick. He slammed this across Grey's forearm, numbing it, than bashed it at his hand. The dagger spun away into the piles of refuse. Grey didn't wait to look for it.

He dodged another blow, and ran down the alley, looking for egress or shelter and finding neither.

They were both after him. He'd no time to wonder where Percy was. The brick wall of a building loomed up in front of him. Dead end.

A door – there was a door, and he threw himself against it, but it didn't yield. He banged on it, kicked it, shouting for help. A hand grabbed his shoulder, and he swung round with it, striking out with a fist. The footpad grimaced, drew back, slapping at him like a baited bear.

Jed and his frigging stick were back, wheezing with the run.

'Do 'im,' said the first footpad, falling back to make room, and Jed promptly seized the blackthorn in both hands and drove the head of it into Grey's ribs.

The next blow got him in the balls and the world went white. He dropped like a bag of tossed rubbish and curled up on himself, barely conscious of the wet cobbles under his face. He realized dimly that he was about to die, but was unable to do anything about it. Kicks and blows from the stick thudded into his flesh; he barely felt them through the fog of agony.

Then it stopped, and for a moment of blessed relief, he thought he'd died. He breathed, though, and discovered he hadn't, as pain shot through him, sudden and searing as the spark from a Leyden jar.

'It *is* you,' said a gruff Scottish voice from somewhere above. 'Thought so. Are ye hurt bad, then?'

He couldn't answer. Enormous hands grabbed him beneath the armpits and sat him up against the wall. He made a thin breathy noise, which was all he could manage in the way of a scream, and felt bile flood his throat.

'Oh, like that, is it?' said the voice, sounding resigned, as Grey bent to the side and vomited. 'Aye, well, bide a wee, then. I'll fetch my jo wi' the chair.'

The very young apothecary squinted earnestly at Grey's forearm and prodded it gingerly.

'Oh, bad, is it?' he said sympathetically, at the resulting hiss of breath.

'Well, it's not *good*,' Grey said, ungritting his teeth with some effort. 'But I doubt it's broken.' He turned his wrist very slowly, tensed against the possible grating of bone ends, but everything moved as it should. It hurt, but it moved.

'Tellt ye it wasnae more than bruises.' Rab MacNab shifted his bulk, uncrossing his arms and leaning forward from his post against the wall. 'Agnes wouldnae have it but we get a doctor to ye, though. Tellt her 'twas a waste of money, aye?'

Despite his words, the big chairman cast a fond glance at his diminutive wife, who sniffed at him.

'I dinna mean to have his lordship die on my premises,' she said briskly. 'Bad for business, aye?' She nudged the apothecary aside, and bent to peer earnestly at Grey's face. Bright brown eyes scanned his battered features, then creased with her grin.

'Enjoy the ride, did ye?'

'I was much obliged to your husband, ma'am,' he said. While he was naturally relieved to have been discovered and rescued by an acquaintance, being thrown into MacNab's sedan chair and carried at the trot for a mile had been very nearly as excruciating as the original injury.

'My congratulations on your new premises,' he added, wishing to change the subject. He struggled upright and swung his legs off the divan, forcing the young apothecary – the boy couldn't be fifteen, surely – to let go of his arm.

'Thank ye kindly,' Nessie said, looking gratified. He couldn't help but think of her as 'Nessie,' as he had first met her under this name, before her apotheocis from whore to madam – and wife. She patted the respectable white kerch that bound her mass of curly dark hair, and looked contentedly round the tiny salon. It was furnished with a few bits of ramshackle furniture, all showing signs of heavy use – but it was scrupulously clean, and a good wax candle burned in a solid brass chamber stick.

'Small it is, but a good place. Three girls, all clean and willing. Ye'll recommend us to your friends, I hope. Not but what we'd be pleased to accommodate your friend here *gratis*,' she added, turning graciously to Percy. 'If ye'd care to pass the time, until his lordship's fettled? Janie will be free in no time.'

Percy, who had been listening to the noises behind the wall – presumably involving Janie, as the gentleman with her was panting that name repeatedly – with patent interest, bowed to Nessie with grave decorum.

'I do appreciate the offer, ma'am. I'd not wish to tire Mistress Jane unduly, though. Surely she must have some rest.'

'Och, no. Go all day and night, oor Janie will,' MacNab assured him proudly, though he seemed relieved at Percy's further polite refusal.

'I'll be off, then. But shall I come again?' the chairman inquired, straightening up. 'To carry his lordship home, once he's fit?'

'No, no,' Grey said hastily. 'I believe I am quite recovered. Mr. Wainwright and I will walk.'

Percy's brows rose, and everyone in the room looked askance at Grey, causing him to think that the damage to his face must be worse than he'd thought.

'You really should be bled, my lord,' the apothecary said earnestly. ' 'Twould be dangerous to go out into the cold without, and you injured. A terrible strain upon your liver. You might take a chill. And the bruises on your face – a good leeching would do the world of good, my lord.'

Grey hated being bled, and disliked leeches more.

'No, I am quite well, I assure you.' He shoved himself to his feet and stood swaying, brilliant dots of light blinking on and off at the corners of his vision. A chorus of dismayed exclamations informed him that he was falling, and he put out his hands just in time to catch himself as he plumped back down on the divan.

Anxious hands grasped his shoulders and eased him down into a supine position. Cold sweat had come out on his forehead, and a gentle hand wiped it away with a cloth as his vision cleared.

To his surprise, the hand was Percy's, rather than Nessie's.

'You stay and be bled like a good boy,' Percy said firmly. One corner of his mouth tucked back, repressing a smile. 'I'll go and find a coach to take us home.' He straightened up and bowed to Nessie and MacNab.

'I am so much obliged to you both for your kind assistance and hospitality. Do allow me to take care of this gentleman's fee.' He nodded at the apothecary, his hand going to his purse.

'That's all right.' Grey groped for his coat, which someone had folded tidily and put under his head. 'I've got it.'

'Ye do?' MacNab's heavy brows rose in surprise.

'I made sure yon thugs would ha' made awa' wi' your purse.'

'No, it's here.' It was; so far as he could tell, everything was still in his pockets that should be.

'Errr . . .' The apothecary had reddened, casting an agonized look at Nessie. 'That's all right, gentlemen. I mean – my fee – that's –'

An ecstatic shriek burst through the wall beside Grey's ear.

'I promised him an hour wi' Susan,' Nessie said, looking amused. 'But if ye'd care to cover *her* fee, your lordship . . .'

'With pleasure.' He fumbled his purse open and extracted a handful of coins.

'Ahhh . . .'

He looked at the apothecary, now a bright scarlet.

'Could I have Janie instead?' the boy blurted.

Grey sighed and added another florin to the coins in Nessie's hand.

It was only as he lay back and allowed the apothecary to fold back his sleeve that it occurred to him to wonder. He, too, had assumed the motive of the attack to be robbery. But it must have been plain to the footpads that he was incapable of resistance after that second blow. And yet they had not rifled his pockets and run – they'd beaten him until MacNab's timely appearance frightened them away.

Had they meant to murder him? That was a thought as cold as the fleam pressed into the bend of his elbow. He grimaced at the sting of the blade and shut his eyes.

No, he thought suddenly. *They had a knife.* The first attempt had been with a knife; there was no mistaking the grating of metal on brick. If they'd meant to murder him, they might have cut his throat without the slightest difficulty. And they hadn't.

There was a feeling of warmth as the blood welled and trickled over his arm; it felt almost soothing.

But if they had meant only to administer a beating . . . why? He did not know them. If it was meant as warning . . . of what?

Chapter 11

Warnings

What with one thing and another, it hadn't occurred to Grey to wonder what his mother's response to his misadventure might be. If it had, he might have expected her to peer at him in sympathy, pour him a stiff drink, and leave for a play. He would *not* have expected her to go white as a sheet. Not with fear for his well being – with anger.

'The *bastards*!' she said, in a tone barely above a whisper – a sign of great fury. 'How dare they?'

'Rather easily, I'm afraid.' Grey was sitting – gingerly – in her boudoir, examining himself in her enameled hand glass. The apothecary had been right about the leeching; while his jaw was sore, the swelling was much reduced, and only a faint blue tinge of new bruising showed, circling one eye and extending up into his temple. There was a cut on his cheekbone, though, and a trickle of blood had run down his neck onto his neckcloth and the neckband of his shirt. There was also a sizable rent in his coat, to say nothing of the filth from rolling in the alley; Tom would be annoyed, too.

'Did you recognize them?' The countess's hands

had been clenching a chair back. The first shock receding, she let go, though her fingers curled convulsively, wanting to strangle something. Hal got his temper from their mother.

'No,' he said, laying down the looking glass. 'Your ordinary ruffians. It's quite all right, Mother. They didn't even manage to rob me.' He pulled the cuff of his coat down a bit, hiding his right hand, which, not having been leeched, looked much worse than his face.

Her lips pressed together, nostrils flaring. Motherlike, unable to attack the miscreants who had harmed her offspring, her annoyance was shifting itself to said offspring.

'Whatever were you doing in Seven Dials, John?'

He started to raise an eyebrow at her, but it hurt and he desisted.

'Hal and I took Percy Wainwright to the *salle des armes*. He and I were on our way to luncheon.'

'Oh, Percy Wainwright was with you? Was he hurt?' Her fair brows drew together in concern.

'No.'

'I swear I shall be relieved when you all are off to Germany,' she said tartly. 'I shall worry about you much less, if you're merely standing in front of cannon batteries and charging redoubts full of grenadiers.'

He laughed at that, though carefully because of his ribs, and stood up, also carefully. Doing so, he felt a small hard object in his pocket, and was reminded.

'Father was a Freemason, was he not?'

'Yes,' she said, and a fresh uneasiness seemed to flare in her eyes. 'Why?'

'I only wondered – could this be his ring?' He fished it out and handed it to her. He might have picked it up carelessly in the library; there was a tray of the duke's small clutter, kept there by way of memoriam, though he did not recall ever seeing a ring among those objects.

He saw her eyes flick toward the little inlaid secretary that stood in the corner of the room, before she reached for the ring. Which told him that the duke had indeed had such a ring – and that she had kept it. So much for the dead past, he thought cynically.

She tried the ring gingerly on her left hand; it hung loose as a quoit on a stick, and she shook her head, dropping it back into his palm.

'No, it's much too big. Where did you get it? And why did you think it might be your father's?'

'No particular reason,' he said with a shrug. 'I can't remember where I picked it up.'

'Let me see it again.'

Puzzled, he handed it over, and watched as she turned it to and fro, bringing it to her candlestick in order to see the inside. At last, she shook her head and gave it back.

'No, I don't know. But . . . John, if you do recall where you found it, will you tell me?'

'Of course,' he said lightly. 'Good night, Mother.' He kissed her cheek and left her, wondering.

He declined Tom's suggestion of bread and milk in favor of a large whisky – or two – by the library fire, and had just reached a state of reconciliation with the universe when Brunton came to announce that he had a caller.

'I won't come in.' Percy Wainwright smiled at him from the shadows of the porch. 'I'm not fit to be indoors. I only came to bring you this.'

'This' was Grey's dagger, which Percy put gingerly into his hands. Percy hadn't been exaggerating about his fitness for civil surroundings; he was wearing rough clothes, much spotted and stained, and he bore about his person a distinct odor of alleyways and refuse.

'I went back to look for it,' he explained. 'Luckily, it was under a pile of dead cabbages – sorry about the smell. I thought ... you might need it,' he concluded, rather shyly.

Grey would have kissed him, damaged mouth notwithstanding, save for the lurking presence of Brunton in the hall. As it was, all he could do was to press Percy's hand, hard, in gratitude.

'Thank you. Will I see you tomorrow?'

Percy's smile glimmered in the dark.

'Oh, yes. Or shall I say, "Yes, *sir*?" For I believe you're now my superior officer, aren't you?'

Grey laughed at that, bruises, bleeding, and his mother's odd behavior all seeming inconsequent for the moment.

'I suppose so. I'll arrange a commendation for you in the morning, then.'

Chapter 12

Officers and Gentlemen

'We aren't like the Russians, you see,' Quarry explained to Percy, kindly. 'Bloody officers never go near their troops, let alone take them into battle.'

'They don't?' Percy looked wary, as though thinking this might be a good idea. He had spent the week prior being taught the duties of an ensign and a second lieutenant, which consisted of attending parades, drills, roll calls, and mountings of the guard, keeping exact lists of accoutrements and stores – Captain Wilmot had complimented his penmanship, before excoriating him in round terms for misplacing a gross of boots and misdirecting ten barrels of powder – supervising the care of the sick in hospital – luckily there were relatively few of these at this season – and touring the soldiers' accommodation.

'Look out for factions,' Quarry added. 'We've two battalions – one fights abroad whilst the other reequips and brings up its strength – but we aren't as large as some, and many of our common soldiers are longtimers, who've learnt to rub along together.

There'll be an influx of new men over the next month, though, and they tend to be sucked into one group or another. You can't afford that – you'll be watched, because of the family attachment, and there cannot be any sense of favoritism toward any group, save, of course, that you must always champion those companies directly under your command – you have four of them. Clear on that?'

'Oh, yes. Sir,' Percy added hurriedly, making Quarry grin.

'Good lad. Now bugger off to Sergeant Keeble and learn which end of a musket the bullet goes in.'

'Keeble's on the square with a company,' Grey interrupted, having paused to deliver a sheaf of papers to Quarry's office. 'I have a moment; I'll run him through the musket drill.'

'Good. What's this lot?' Quarry picked up his spectacles and squinted through them at the papers. His eyes widened and he snatched off the spectacles, as though unable to believe his eyes. *'What?'* he bellowed.

Grey plucked at Percy's sleeve.

'You're dismissed,' he whispered. 'Come on.'

Percy cast a last, apprehensive glance at Quarry, who had gone puce with rage and was addressing the sheaf of papers in loudly blasphemous terms. Quarry wasn't looking at him, but Percy saluted briskly and turned on his heel to follow Grey.

'What was *that* about, or am I allowed to know?' he asked, once outside.

'Nothing.' Grey shrugged. 'Instructions from the

War Office, contradicting the last set. It happens once a week or so. How are you getting on with things?' More than busy with his own duties, he'd barely seen Percy during the week.

'Well enough. Or at least I hope so,' Percy said dubiously. 'People do shout at me a lot.'

Grey laughed.

'Being shouted at is actually quite high on your list of duties,' he assured Percy.

'No one shouts at *you*.'

'I am,' Grey said complacently, 'a major. No one is allowed to shout at me – within the regiment, of course – save Harry, Colonel Symington, and my brother. I don't mind Harry, I keep the hell out of Symington's sight, and I tread with extreme care around Melton; I advise you to do the same. Have you toured the barracks this morning?'

'Yesterday. Ah . . . is there anything I should look for especially, in terms of brewing trouble?'

Grey had gone with him for the first round of such tours, but now explained the finer points.

'For those in barracks, look for signs of drunkenness – which is not difficult to spot, I assure you – excessive gambling, or a disposition to excessive whoring. For those in billets in the town—'

'How do you know what's excessive?'

'If a man is missing important bits of his uniform or equipment, he's gambling excessively. If he's missing important bits of his anatomy from the syphilis, or if you find a whore actually in his bed, that's considered above the odds. Pox and the clap are more or less all right, provided he can stand up straight.'

'Easier said than done. Ever had it?'

'No,' Grey said, edging aside and giving Percy a stare. 'Have you?'

'Once, in my younger years.' Percy shuddered. 'Only time I ever bedded a woman. If I hadn't already known what I was, that would likely have been enough to seal the matter.'

'Was she a whore?' Grey inquired, not without sympathy. He had himself bedded several whores over the years, partly from necessity, and partly – at first – from a curiosity as to whether the experience might suddenly trigger some dormant desire for the female.

'No,' Percy said. 'In fact, she was a rather well-known lady with a marked reputation for piety. A good deal older than myself,' he added delicately.

'Is she dead?' Grey asked, with interest. 'Do I know her?'

'Yes, you do, and no, she isn't, worse luck, the old baggage. Anyway, what am I looking for when Colonel Quarry says, "the looks of the men"?'

'Oh—' Grey waved a vague hand toward the distant parade ground, where a mass of new recruits were being chivvied into awkward lines by barking corporals. 'If they seem thinner or paler than usual, not themselves.'

'And how would I know that?' Percy protested. 'I've only seen most of them once!'

'Well, you visit them every week – oftener, if

you have reason to think there's trouble brewing,' Grey said patiently. 'You ought to know all their names by the end of the second week, and the names of their mothers, sisters, and sweethearts by the third.'

'After which I will perhaps have mastered the duties of ensign, and be allowed to forget them all, as a second lieutenant?'

'You won't forget them,' Grey said with confidence. 'An officer never forgets his men. Never worry – I have the greatest faith in you.'

'Well, I'm glad you think so,' Percy said, in tones of extreme doubt, following Grey into the armory. 'And these are muskets, are they?'

Despite Percy's protestations of ignorance and ineptitude, he proved to be a more than adequate shot. Grey had taken him out to the edge of London, to an open field, to try his hand without witnesses, and was agreeably surprised.

'And these are muskets, are they?' he mimicked, poking a finger through the center of a target, the cloth shredded by multiple shots.

Percy grinned, unabashed.

'I didn't say I'd never held a gun before.'

'No, you didn't.' Grey rolled up the target. 'What kind of gun?'

'Target pistols, for the most part. Fowling pieces, now and again.' Percy didn't go into detail, shrugging off Grey's praise with modesty. 'What Colonel

Quarry said – about the family connexion . . .' He hesitated, not sure how to express his question.

'Well, there will be a bit of jealousy amongst the other officers,' Grey said, matter-of-factly. 'They all view each other as rivals, and of course will suspect you of preferment. Not a great deal you can do about it, though, save do your job well.'

Percy rubbed a handkerchief over his face to remove the powder stains.

'I mean to,' he said with determination. 'What other skills ought I to possess, do you think?'

'Well,' said Grey, with a glance at Wainwright's graceful form, 'you must be able to dance. Can you dance?'

Percy looked at him in disbelief.

'Dance?'

Grey looked back in similar disbelief, but this wasn't mockery. He tended to forget, given Percy's ease in society, that he had not been born to that world but rather into a family of strict Methodists. He knew nothing of Methodists, but supposed they considered dancing sinful.

'Dance,' Grey said firmly. 'Dancing is most necessary for any man of good education, and the more so for an officer. And I quote from a well-known authority: "Fencing endows a man with speed and strength, while dancing brings elegance and dignity to carriage and movement."'

'In that case, I am doomed.'

'Well, dancing is somewhat less lethal in intent,' Grey said, rubbing a finger beneath his nose in an effort not to laugh. 'Come with me.'

'Where are we going?' Percy gathered up the musket, cartridge box, shot pouch, powder horn, and other impedimenta of shooting.

'To my brother's house. My sister-in-law employs a very good dancing master for her sons, and I'm sure will make arrangements for you to be tutored discreetly.'

Minnie was charmed by Percy, whom she had not yet met; still more charmed that he should seek her help. Grey had noticed this female paradox before: women who swooned at the notion of powerful men who would protect them at the same time liked nothing better than an open admission of helplessness on the part of any male within their sphere of influence.

He left Percy to Minnie, who was – in spite of her pregnancy – demonstrating steps and figures with considerable deftness, and went to the library.

Hal's collection of military historians, tacticians, and theorists was considerable, and Grey helped himself without compunction to those volumes he thought might be of most service in Percy's military instruction.

Flavius Vegetius Renatus – known chummily as 'Vegetius' to his intimates – who wrote *Epitomae Rei Militaris* sometime between A.D. 385 and 450. One of Hal's favorites, a good place to start.

'Few men are brave; many become so through care and force of discipline,' Grey murmured, tucking the book into the crook of his arm.

There was Mauvillon's *Histoire de la Dernière Guerre de Bohème*, in three volumes. Very popular, and quite recent, having been published only two years before, in Amsterdam. Only volumes I and II were present – Hal must be reading volume III – but he took the first one.

He hesitated among Marcus Aurelius, Tacitus, and Vauban, but on impulse added Virgil's *Aeneid*, for some relief. That would do for now; after all, Percy had very little time to read these days – no more than Grey himself did.

He turned from the bookshelf at the sound of a step, and found his brother had returned.

'Stealing my books again?' Hal asked, with a smile.

'Retrieving my own.' Grey tapped the *Aeneid*, which was in fact his. 'And borrowing Vegetius for Percy Wainwright, if you don't mind.'

'Not in the least. Quarry says he's shaping well,' Hal remarked. 'I see – or rather, I hear – that Minnie's teaching him to dance.' He inclined his head toward the drawing room, where the sound of laughter and the counting of steps indicated the satisfactory progress of the first lesson.

'Yes. I think he'll do very well,' Grey said, pleased at hearing Harry's good opinion.

'Good. I'm sending him in command of a company down to Sussex tomorrow, to fetch back a shipment of powder.'

Grey felt an immediate urge to protest, but stifled it. His opposition to the suggestion was based more on the fact that he and Percy had agreed to a private rendezvous next day than to any doubt of Percy's ability to manage such an expedition – or to his knowledge of the inherent dangers of any expedition involving kegs of black powder and inexperienced soldiers.

'Oh, good,' he said casually.

He was beginning to feel, like Percy, that perhaps he was doomed. To involuntary celibacy, if nothing else.

'Where have you been?' he asked curiously, noticing as Hal put off his cloak that his brother was in traveling clothes, rather than uniform.

Hal looked mildly disconcerted, and Grey, with interest, saw him rapidly consider whether to tell the truth or not.

'Bath,' he said, with only an instant's delay.

'Again? What the devil is in Bath?'

'None of your business.'

Suddenly, and without warning, Grey lost his temper. He dropped the books on the desk with a bang.

'Don't tell me what is my business and what is not!'

If Hal was taken aback, it was for no more than an instant.

'Need I remind you that I am the head of this family?' he said, lowering his voice, with a glance at the door.

'And I am bloody *part* of this family. You can't fob me off by telling me things are none of my business. You cannot ship me off to Aberdeen to prevent my asking questions!'

Hal looked as though he would have liked to do precisely that, but he controlled himself, with a visible effort.

'That was not why you were sent to Aberdeen.'

Grey pounced on that.

'Why, then?'

Hal glared at him.

'I decline to tell you.'

Grey hadn't hit Hal for a number of years, and had lost the fight on the last occasion when he'd tried it. He gave Hal a look suggesting that he wouldn't lose this one. Hal returned the look and shifted his weight, indicating that he would welcome the chance of relieving his feelings by violence. That was interesting; Hal was more upset than he appeared.

Grey held his brother's gaze and ostentatiously unclenched his fist, laying his hand flat on the desk.

'I hesitate to insult your intelligence by pointing out the fact that I am a grown man,' he said, politely.

'Good,' Hal said, very dryly indeed. 'Then I won't insult yours by explaining that it is the fact that you are indeed a man that prevents my telling you anything further. Be on the square at ten o'clock tomorrow.'

He left the room without looking round, though there was a certain tenseness about his shoulders that suggested he thought Grey might conceivably throw something at him.

Had there been anything suitable within reach, he likely would have. As it was, Grey was left with the blood thundering in his ears and both fists clenched.

A flurry of mutually contradictory instructions from three Whitehall offices, an outbreak of fever in the barracks, and the sudden sinking – in harbor – of one of the transport ships meant to carry them to Germany kept Grey too busy for the next week to worry about what might be happening in Sussex, or to pay more than cursory attention to the news that the sodomite conspirators had been condemned to death.

He was sitting in his own small office at the end of the day, staring at the wall, and trying to decide whether it was worth the trouble to put on his coat and walk to the Beefsteak for supper or whether he might simply send the door guard to bring him a Cornish pasty from the street, when the door guard himself appeared, come to ask if he would receive a visitor – a Mrs. Tomlinson.

Well, that resolved his immediate dilemma. He would have to put on his coat to receive this woman, whoever she was.

A soldier's wife, perhaps, come to beg him to get her husband out of some difficulty or to advance her his pay. Tomlinson, Tomlinson . . . he was running mentally through his roster, but failing to recall any Tomlinsons. Still, there were always new recruits –

oh, no. Now he remembered; this Tomlinson woman was Minnie's acquaintance, the mistress of the Captain Bates who had just been condemned to death. He said something which caused the door guard to blink.

'Bring her up,' he said, settling his lapels and brushing crumbs from his luncheon pasty off his shirt ruffle.

Mrs. Tomlinson reminded Grey – not unpleasantly – of his favorite horse. Like Karolus, she had a strong jaw, a kind eye, and a pale mane, which she wore in a bundle of tight plaits, as though on parade. She dropped into a low curtsy before him, spreading her skirts as if he were the king. He took her hand to raise her, and kissed it, taking advantage of the gesture to think uncharitable thoughts about his sister-in-law.

No hint of these thoughts showed in his voice, though, as he begged her to be seated and sent Tom for wine and biscuits.

'Ah, no, sir,' she said hurriedly. 'I'll not stay. I've come only to thank your lordship for discovering Captain Bates's whereabouts for me – and to beg a further favor of your lordship.' A becoming color rose in her cheeks, but she held his gaze, her own pale hazel eyes clear and direct. 'I hesitate to impose upon you, my lord. Will you believe me that only the most urgent necessity impels me?'

'Of course,' he said, as cordially as possible under the circumstances. 'What may I have the pleasure of doing for you, madam?'

'Will you go and see him?'

He stared at her, uncomprehending.

'Captain Bates,' she said. 'Will you go and see him?'

'What,' he said stupidly, 'in Newgate?'

The faintest of smiles lifted her long, solid jaw.

'I'm sure he would wait upon your honor here, and he was able,' she said, very respectful. 'I'm sure he would prefer it.' She had the faintest trace of an Irish accent; rather charming.

'I'm sure he would,' Grey said dryly, recovered from the surprise. 'Why ought I to go and see him? Beyond, of course, the simple fact of your request.'

'I think he must tell you that himself, sir.'

He rubbed his own jaw, considering.

'Do you . . . wish me to carry a message for you?' he hazarded. The kind eyes widened.

'Ah, no, my lord. No need; I see him every day.'

'You do?' It wasn't impossible; even the most depraved felons received visitors. But . . . 'Does your husband not object?' Grey said, as delicately as possible.

She neither blushed nor looked away.

'I haven't asked him, my lord.'

He thought of inquiring exactly where her husband *was,* but decided that it was no business of his.

Hal would doubtless advise against it, but Grey's own curiosity was strong. It was likely the only opportunity he might get to hear any unfiltered details regarding the affair. Between the highly colored public version of events in the newspapers and Hal's coldly cynical view was a substantial gap; he would like very much to know where the truth lay – or, if not the truth, another view of matters.

What the devil could Bates want with him, though? He hesitated for a moment longer, fixed by those large hazel eyes, but at last capitulated. No harm to hear what Bates had to say.

'Yes, all right. When?'

'Tomorrow, my lord, if you can. The time is short, you see. The ha— the execution is set for Wednesday noon.' Only with the word 'hanging' did her composure desert her momentarily. She paled a little and her hand went unthinking to her throat, though she snatched it away again at once.

'Very well,' he said slowly. 'May I—' But she had seized his hand and, falling to one knee, kissed it passionately.

'Thank you,' she said, and with a hard squeeze of the hand, was gone in a flurry of petticoats.

Chapter 13

A Visit to Newgate

Entering a prison is never a pleasant experience, even if such entrance be accomplished voluntarily, rather than under duress. Grey had been governor of Ardsmuir Prison for more than a year, and he had never entered the place – even his own quarters – without a deep breath and a stiffening of the spine. Neither had he enjoyed visiting the Fleet in search of recruits who would accept army service to escape debt, nor any of the smaller prisons and gaols from which it had been his occasional duty to abstract errant soldiers. Still, Newgate was notable, even for a connoisseur like himself, and he passed under the portcullis at the main gate with a sense of foreboding.

Henry Fielding had described it in one of his recent novels as 'a prototype of hell,' and Grey was inclined to think this description admirably succinct.

The room to which he was shown was bleak, nothing but a deal table, two chairs, and an empty hearth, surrounded by walls of discolored stone that bore many laboriously chiseled names, and a number of disquieting scratches, suggesting that more than one desperate wretch had attempted to claw his – or her – way out. Outside the room, though, the prison teemed like a butcher's offal pile, rich with maggots.

He'd brought a vial of spirits of turpentine, and applied this periodically to his handkerchief. It numbed his sense of smell, which was a blessing, and might perhaps keep pestilence away. It did nothing for the noises – a cacophony of wailing, cursing, manic laughter and singing second only to Bedlam – nor for the sights.

Through the barred window, he could see across a narrow courtyard to a large opening that apparently provided light and air to an underground cell, and was likewise barred. A woman stood upon the inside sill of this opening, clinging precariously to the bars with one hand, the other being used to lift her ragged petticoats above her waist.

Her privates were pressed through the opening between the bars, for the convenience of a guard who clung, beetlelike, to the outside of the bars. His jacket hung down far enough as to obscure his straining buttocks, but the droop of his breeches and the rhythmic movements of his hips were plain enough.

Prisoners passing through the courtyard ignored this, walking by with downcast eyes. Several guards also ignored it, though one man stopped and said something, evidently an inquiry, for the woman turned her head and made lewd kissing motions toward him, then let go her skirts in order to extend a hand through the bars, fingers curling in enticement – or perhaps demand.

The sound of the door opening behind him tore Grey's fascinated gaze from this tableau.

Bates was decently dressed in a clean uniform, but heavily shackled. He shuffled across the room and collapsed into one of the chairs, not waiting for introduction or invitation.

'Thank God,' he said, sighing deeply. 'Haven't sat in a proper chair in weeks. My back's been giving me the very devil.' He stretched, groaning luxuriously, then settled back and looked at Grey.

His eyes were a quick, light blue, and he was shaved to perfection. Grey looked him over slowly, noting the pristine linen, neatly tied wig, and manicured nails.

'I didn't know one could procure the services of a valet in here,' Grey said, for lack of a better introduction.

Bates shrugged.

'It's like anywhere else, I imagine; you can get almost anything – provided you can pay for it.'

'And you can.' It wasn't quite a question, and Bates's mouth turned up a little. He had a heavy, handsome face, and a body to match; evidently he wasn't starved in prison.

'Haven't a great deal else to spend my money on, have I? And you can't take it with you – or so that very tedious minister tells me. Did you know they force you not merely to go to church on a Sunday here but to sit beside your coffin at the front?'

'I'd heard that, yes. Meant to encourage repentance, is it?' He could not imagine anyone less repentant in outward appearance than the captain.

'Can't say what it's *meant* to do,' the captain said judiciously. 'Bloody bore, I call it, and a pain in the arse – literally, as well as metaphorically. No proper pews; just filthy benches with no backs.' He pressed his shoulders against his chair, as though determined to extract as much enjoyment from his present circumstances as possible.

Grey took the other chair.

'You are otherwise well treated?' Not waiting for an answer, Grey withdrew the flask of brandy he had brought, unstoppered it, and passed it across.

Bates snorted, accepting it.

'The buggers here who think I'm a sodomite are bad enough; the buggers who *are* sodomites are a damn sight worse.' He gave a short laugh, took a healthy swallow of brandy, and breathed slow and deep for a moment. 'Oh, God. Will you send me more of this for the hanging? They'll give you brandy here, if you pay for it, but it's swill. Rather die sober.'

'I'll see what can be done,' Grey said. 'What do you mean, the sodomites are worse?'

Bates's eyes roamed over him, sardonic.

'The sodomites . . . They had me chummed for a bit with a decorator from Brighton, name of Keyes. Woke me in the middle of the night, jabbing his yard at my fundament like a goddamned woodpecker. Offered to smash his teeth in, he didn't leave off *that* business, whereupon he has a go at *my* privates, slobbering like a dog!' Bates looked both affronted and mildly amused, and Grey began to be convinced that Minnie's opinion was correct.

'I take your point,' Grey said dryly. 'You are not yourself a sodomite.'

'That's right,' said Bates, leaning back in his chair. 'Just your basic traitor. But that's not what I'll be hanged for.' For the first time, a tinge of bitterness entered his tone.

Grey inclined his head. Evidently Bates took it for granted that Grey knew the truth of the matter. How? he wondered, but his mind automatically supplied the answer – Minnie, of course, and her sympathetic acquaintance with Mrs. Tomlinson. So Hal *did* talk to her.

'Yet you've chosen not to make that public,' Grey observed. 'There are any number of journalists who would listen.' He'd been obliged to fight his way through a crowd of them outside the main gate, all hoping for the opportunity to get a private interview with one or more of the infamous conspirators.

'They'd listen if I told them what they want to hear,' the captain observed caustically. 'The public has made up its mind, d'ye see. And there are too many voices from Whitehall whispering in Fleet Street's ear these days; mine wouldn't be heard past the door of this place. I'm a convicted sodomite conspirator, after all – obviously, I'd say anything.'

Grey let this pass; he was likely right.

'You sent for me,' he said.

'I did, and I thank you for coming.' Bates raised the flask ceremoniously to him, and drank, then leaned his head back, studying Grey with interest.

'Why?' Grey said after a moment.

'You're an officer and a gentleman, aren't you? Whatever else you may be.'

'What do you mean by that?' Grey kept his voice calm, though his heart leapt convulsively.

Bates looked at him for a long moment, a half smile on his face.

'One would never guess, to look at you,' he said conversationally.

'I'm afraid I don't take your meaning, sir,' Grey said politely.

'Yes, you do.' Bates waved a hand, dismissing it, and took another drink from the flask. 'Not to worry. I wouldn't say a word – and if I did, no one would believe me.' He spoke without rancor. 'You know a man named Richard Caswell, I imagine. So do I.'

'In what capacity, may I ask?' Grey inquired, out of personal curiosity as much as duty. Caswell was the proprietor of Lavender House, an exclusive club for gentlemen who preferred gentlemen – but he undoubtedly had other irons in the fire. And if the suborning of treason was one of those . . .

'Moneylender,' Bates said frankly. 'I gamble, d'ye see. That's what's brought me to this pass; need of money. My old granny said as the cards were the devil's pasteboards, and they'd lead me straight to hell. I wonder if I shall get to see her and tell her she was right? Though if so, I suppose she'll be in hell, too, won't she? Serve her right, the prating old bizzom.'

Grey declined the offered distraction.

'And Richard Caswell mentioned my name to you? In what connexion, may I ask?' He was more than surprised to hear that Caswell had spoken of him, and in fact, doubted it. Dickie Caswell would have died a long time ago were he that careless with the secrets he held.

Bates gave him a long, shrewd look, then shook his head and laughed.

'Play cards, do you, Major?'

'Not often.'

'You should. I see you aren't easily bluffed.' He shifted his feet, the irons clanking.

'No, Caswell didn't mention your name. He had one of those beastly coughing fits of his and was obliged to rush into his chamber for his medicine. I took the opportunity to rummage his desk. His diary was all in code, the wily beast, but he'd written *Lord John Grey* on the margin of his blotter. Didn't know who you were, but happened by chance to be at cards with Melton that night, and he spoke of his brother John. Susannah knew your brother's wife, had heard the story of your title, and . . . *voilà.*' He smiled at Grey, all good-fellowship.

Grey felt the fist in his midsection relax by degrees. It clenched again at the captain's next words.

'And then of course, Mr. Bowles's assistant mentioned you in my hearing, sometime later.'

The word 'Bowles' went through him like an electric shock. Followed by a slightly lesser one at the word 'assistant.'

'Neil Stapleton?' he asked, surprised at the calmness of his own voice.

'Don't know his name. Fairish chap, pretty face like a girl's, sulky-looking?'

Grey managed to nod.

'You were with Mr. Bowles at the time?' he asked. Dickie Caswell dealt in secrets. Hubert Bowles dealt in lives. Presumably on behalf of the government.

'That would be telling, wouldn't it?' Bates put back his head and drained the last of the brandy. 'God, that's good!'

'I know nothing of the particulars against you,' Grey said carefully. 'The material you passed to Melchior Ffoulkes – this came from Mr. Bowles?' And if so, what sort of game was Bowles playing?

Bates stifled a belch with his fist, and gave him an eye.

'I may be a cardsharp, a traitor, and a scoundrel in general, Grey. Doesn't mean I've no sense of honor, you know. I won't betray any of my associates. Believe me, it's been tried. No one swings on my word.'

He turned the empty flask over. A single drop fell onto the table, its warm pungency a welcome relief from the cold scent of turpentine. Bates put his finger in it, and licked it thoughtfully.

'What is it they say – "Live by the sword, die by the sword"? I imagine you know that one, don't you?'

'I know that one, yes.' Grey's mind was working like a Welsh miner at the coal face, great black chunks of supposition mounting in a dirty pile round his feet. He essayed one or two further questions regarding Bowles and Stapleton, but was met with shrugs. Bates had given him Bowles's name, but would go no further. Had that been his only purpose? Grey wondered.

'You did send for me,' he pointed out. 'Presumably there is *something* you wish to tell me.'

'No. To ask you. A favor. Or rather, two.' The captain looked him over, seriously, as though evaluating a questionable hand that might still be played to advantage.

'Ask me what?'

'Susannah,' the captain said abruptly.

'Mrs. Tomlinson?'

'The same, and bad cess to the mister, as Susie's fond of saying.' A brief smile flickered, then disappeared. 'She was wed to him young, and he's a right bastard.'

'My sister-in-law says he's a bore.'

'He is, but the two aren't exclusive. He beats her – or he did, before she took up with me. I put the fear of God into him – wish I'd killed the sniveling little shit when I'd the chance. . . .' Bates brooded for a moment on lost opportunities, but then shook off his regrets.

'Well, plainly once I'm gone, she'll be at his mercy again – if he's not already at it.'

'And you wish me to step into your place and threaten Mr. Tomlinson with bodily harm if he mistreats his wife? I should be pleased to do that, but I fear—'

'No, I want you to get her away from him,' Bates interrupted. 'She's a brother in Ireland, in Kilkenny. If she can reach him, he can protect her. But she's no money of her own, and I'm in no position to give her any.'

Grey looked at him sharply.

'A nice choice of words,' he observed. 'Rather than saying that you haven't any, either.'

Bates returned his stare.

'Let us merely say that if I had funds available, I should turn them over to you on the spot, to use in her behalf, and leave it at that, shall we?'

Grey gave a brief nod of assent, chucking that into the pile at his feet for later analysis.

'And the second favor that you mentioned?'

'Ah. Well, I suppose that's Susannah, as well – in a way of speaking. She insists she'll come to the hanging.'

For the first time, the captain appeared to experience some perturbation at the thought of his demise.

'I don't want her there, Grey,' he said. 'You know what it'll be like.'

'Yes, I do,' Grey said quietly. 'No, you don't want

her there. Do you wish me to see her? Explain, as gently as I can—'

'I've explained, and not gently,' Bates interrupted. He grimaced. 'That only made her more insistent. She says that she can't stand the thought of me dying alone in a crowd of people convinced that I'm a disgusting pervert. She says—' His voice thickened momentarily, and he paused to cough heavily into his handkerchief, in order to cover the lapse. 'She says,' he continued more firmly, 'that she wants someone to be there who knows why I'm really dying, and what I really am. Someone for me to look at from the gallows, and know.' He looked at Grey, a faint smile on his lips.

'I don't know what you are, Grey, and I don't care. But you do know what I am, and the truth of why I'm dying here. You'll do.'

Grey felt as though someone had suddenly snatched the chair out from under him.

'You want me to attend your hanging?'

His tone must have contained some of the incredulity he felt, for the captain gave him an impatient look.

'I'd have sent an engraved invitation, had I time,' he said.

Grey wished he'd brought an extra flask for himself. He rubbed a knuckle slowly down the bridge of his nose.

'And you expect that I will accede to these – you will pardon my characterizing them as peculiar, I trust – requests . . . why?'

Bates smiled crookedly.

'Let's put it this way. You swear to see Susie safe to her brother in Ireland, and to see me safe to wherever I'm going – and I undertake to see to it that Hubert Bowles never sees your name in my handwriting.'

Grey blinked.

'Saying what?'

Bates raised one fair brow.

'Does it matter?'

It took the space of one breath for Grey to come to a conclusion regarding the possibilities.

'No, it doesn't. Done.' He paused for an instant. 'You trust my word?'

'Officer and gentleman,' Bates repeated, with a tinge of ruefulness. 'Besides, I haven't a great deal of choice in the matter, do I?'

There seemed no more to say after that. He nodded, considered offering his hand to Bates in farewell, and thought better of it. Then something else occurred to him.

'One last question, Captain – if you will allow me?'

Bates made an expansive gesture.

'I've all the time in the world, Major. Until Wednesday, that is.'

'I respect your determination to safeguard the names of any associates still at large. But perhaps you will tell me this: are any of them Jacobites?'

The blank surprise on Bates's face was so patent that it would have been laughable under other circumstances.

'Jacobites?' he said. 'God, no. Why would you think that?'

'The French *are* involved,' Grey pointed out. Bates shrugged.

'Well, yes. But it isn't always religion with the frogs, no matter what old Louis tells the Pope, and the Stuart cause is deader than I'll be on Wednesday. Louis's a merchant at heart, and not about to throw good money after bad. Besides, he never wanted James Stuart on the English throne, and never expected him to take it – just wanted the distraction, while he got on with quietly pocketing Brussels.'

'You know a great deal about what King Louis wants.'

Bates nodded, slowly.

'And you know what I want, Major. We have our bargain. But if Mr. Bowles should be moved to seek one of his own . . .' He quirked a brow, and Grey saw a nerve twitch in his jaw. 'He's got four days left.' But it was said without hope.

Grey bowed and put on his hat.

'I'll see you on Wednesday.'

He had nearly reached the door, when he stopped and turned for a moment.

'I'll send the brandy Tuesday night.'

Percy Wainwright was expected to return from his journey on Wednesday. Grey thought of sending him a note, of asking for his company, but didn't. He did know what it would be like.

Chapter 14

Place of Execution

Grey had always thought the roar of a mob to be one of the worst sounds possible. Worse than the howl of a hurricane or the clap of thunder that follows in the wake of nearby lightning. And the mob itself every bit as random and as lethal as other forces of nature. The only difference, Grey thought, was that you would not call a mob an act of God.

He spread his feet a little, to keep his footing against the waves of people who were lapping up the slopes of Tyburn Hill, and kept one hand on his sword hilt, the other on his dagger. He'd considered for some time whether to wear his uniform or not, but at last had decided that he must. Soldiers were not universally popular, by any means, and it was not unknown for a maddened crowd to turn on them. But if the point of his presence was to give some reassurance to Michael Bates, then he must be recognizable. To which end, he'd worn uniform, chosen a spot as near to the gallows as he could get, and held it grimly against all comers.

He hoped the brandy had arrived in time, but there was no way to tell. He'd gone direct to

Tyburn, rather than follow the cart from Newgate as many spectators did. By the time it rumbled into view, the three prisoners in it were so plastered with mud and filth that they might have been bears, bound for a baiting.

And a baiting it was.

The noise rose, hungry, at sight of the prisoners, and a hail of rocks and debris arched out of the crowd – most of it falling back onto said crowd, distance preventing the missiles from reaching their targets. Cries of pain or protest were swallowed by the immense thrum, menacing as the sound of a hornet's nest.

He felt it in his bones, and along with it, an echo of the terror that must afflict those who were its focus.

The minister who walked behind the condemned cart was heavily splashed with mud himself, though his grim face was still visible through the smears. A final bombardment of rocks drove him back, clutching his Bible to his chest as though it might be a literal as well as spiritual shield.

'Crush the mon-sters! Crush the mon-sters!' The chant was coming from a group of gaily clad prostitutes, who had linked arms against the surge of the crowd and were throwing their bodies to and fro in unison, in rhythm to their chant. A rival group was brandishing ill-spelt placards denouncing *Efemnit CUNTS!* He recognized Madame Mags, resplendent in black taffeta and gold brocade, and a number of her girls. Luckily, they were all much too busy enjoying themselves to notice him.

Other chants, of much more offensive content, poked rudely through the noise of the mob. Most of the rocks, he saw, were being flung by women – not prostitutes: housewives, barmaids, servant girls, with faces made ugly by hate under their respectable caps.

The prisoners were being helped down from the cart, a few of the sheriff's men pushing back the crowd with sticks and halberds. The men scuttled for the steps, as though the gallows was a place of sanctuary. Doubtless it was.

Now he could make out Bates, a stocky figure in the center, shoulders back, head up. The colors of the Horse Guards uniform were just visible beneath the coating of filth.

The slender youth on the right also wore uniform; that must be Otway, and the small, hunched man in ordinary clothes no doubt Jeffords. A rock struck Bates in the chest and he staggered back a step, but then caught himself and stepped firmly forward, teeth bared at the crowd in what might have been a grin or a snarl. The response was a fresh shower of dung and shouted vitriol. Some criminals came to their end at Tyburn in glory, accompanied by fiddlers and flowers; not sodomites.

Grey shoved between two 'prentices who tried to squeeze in front of him, and elbowed one of them in the side hard enough that the youth squealed and pulled away, cursing. He could see Bates's gaze roaming over the crowd, and against his better judgment, waved his arms, shouting, 'Bates!'

By a miracle, the man heard him. He saw the sharp eyes fix on him, and something like a smile beneath the mud and scratches.

He felt a stealthy hand at his pocket and grabbed at it, but it was a small hand, and the would-be pickpocket – a child of seven or eight – wriggled free of his grasp and dived into the crowd. He was barely in time to keep the child's accomplice from making away with his dagger while he was thus distracted, and by the time he was able to place his attention on the gallows once again, the executioner was moving the men into place beneath the dangling nooses.

Otway screamed, a high, thin sound barely audible over the crowd. Nonetheless, the crowd caught it and took it up, wailing melodramatically and catcalling, as Otway struggled and kicked in terror, wild-eyed as a spooked pony.

Grey found his fists clenched hard on the hilts of sword and dagger. For God's sake! he thought, in agonized impatience, can you not die like a man, at least?

Thin white bags were placed over the prisoners' heads, the nooses adjusted; the minister walked slowly behind the men, reading aloud from his Bible, his words inaudible. Everything seemed to move with the horrid slowness of nightmare, and Grey suffered from the sudden illusion of having forgotten how to breathe.

Then the traps were sprung and the bodies fell, ending with a hideous jerk. Cheers and screams rose from the crowd. Otway hung limp, his neck broken clean. The other two were dancing, knees churning the air for purchase.

Grey looked wildly for the neck-breakers, the men who would – for a price – seize the legs of a half-hanged man and pull to hasten his death. He had paid for someone to perform this office for Bates, should it be necessary. But no one ran forward, and he saw the Newgate guards watching contemptuously, spitting, as Bates twirled and jerked upon his rope.

He didn't think. He battered his way through the people before him. The guards, surprised, saw his uniform and let him pass.

One of Bates's flailing feet struck him in the ear, the other in the chest. He jumped, clasped the frenzied, muscular thighs with his arms, and clung like death, his weight pulling him down toward the earth. The parting of Bates's neckbones vibrated through him like the twang of a stretched rope, and he tumbled into the mud below the gallows.

Chapter 15

A Delicate Errand

At his mother's door, he bade farewell and thanks to Captains MacNeill and MacLachlan, two officers of the Scotch Greys who had rescued him from the mob at Tyburn.

'No but what I'm sure 'twas kindly meant,' MacNeill said to him, for perhaps the fourth time. 'But to risk your life to send a pederast to hell a moment faster, man? Havers!'

MacLachlan, a dour man of few words, shook his head in agreement.

'Still, I should like to get a good grup o' yin or twa o' the rascals,' MacNeill went on with gloomy relish. 'I'd teach them to ken what they're aboot!'

Grey was not sure which rascals MacNeill meant – whether pederasts, or the yahoos in the crowd who had tried to drown him in a puddle. It didn't seem worth inquiring. He tried to press a bit of money upon them to drink his health, but was starchily informed that both were Presbyterians and abstainers, whereupon he thanked them once again and limped inside.

His cousin Olivia, massively pregnant, was

edging down the stairs. She stopped when she saw him, and put a hand to her mouth, eyes wide with horror.

'John! What's happened to you?'

He opened his mouth to explain, and thought better of it.

'I, er . . . I was run down by a coach in the street.' He pressed against the wall to let her past, realizing too late that he was leaving filthy smudges on the wallpaper. Olivia peered at him with concern, then called to the butler.

'Brunton, go and fetch a doctor!'

'No, no! I'm fine, quite all right. I'll . . . I'll just . . . have a bath and go to bed.' He was about to escape past her and up the stairs, when the door to the drawing room opened and Percy Wainwright came out.

His brows shot up at sight of Grey, but he said nothing, merely turned on his heel, went back into the drawing room, and reappeared almost at once with a glass of wine, which he thrust into Grey's hand.

'I'd come to talk with you and Melton about the regiment,' Percy said, eyeing him with a concern equal to Olivia's. 'But I shall come again another day.'

Grey shook his head, mouth full of wine, and swallowed.

'No, stay,' he said hoarsely. 'Hal's coming?'

The front door opened and his brother came in, stopping dead at sight of Grey.

'Yes, I know,' Grey said wearily. 'Go talk to Wainwright, will you? I'll be down in a moment.'

Hal ignored this, and came close, frowning at him.

'What the devil happened to you?'

'He was run down in the street by a coach!' Olivia leapt in, indignant on her cousin's behalf. 'Did they not even stop to see if you were all right, Johnny?'

'You were run down by a coach?' The countess, drawn by the hubbub, appeared at the top of the stairs, looking alarmed. 'John! Are you all right?'

Grey rubbed his brow. A fine reward for his good intentions, he thought bitterly.

'I'm quite all right,' he said, speaking carefully, because his lower lip was split and his jaw swollen. The teeth on the left felt loose, but would probably be all right. 'No, they didn't stop. I doubt the driver saw me. It was a mail coach,' he added, in a moment of inspiration, and saw the lines between his mother's brows relax a bit, though she went on looking worried.

She was by this time at the foot of the stair, examining him in detail, and while he was touched by her solicitude, he really wanted nothing more than a stiff drink and a bath, and said so.

'Yes, a bath,' the countess agreed, wrinkling her nose. 'And burn those clothes!'

This sentiment was put to a popular vote and unanimously passed. Meanwhile, Brunton, who had actually been paying attention, quietly manifested himself beside Grey, removed the glass of wine from his hand and replaced it with a glass containing Scotch whisky, a liquid whose restorative qualities Grey had learnt to appreciate while at Ardsmuir. He leaned against the wall – what were a few more smudges, after all? – and inhaled a mouthful, closing his eyes in thanks.

Meanwhile, attention had shifted to Hal, who was explaining that he was not stopping, as he was summoned to a meeting at Whitehall, but had merely paused on his way there in order to deliver Percy Wainwright's commission papers, now officially countersigned and sealed with the Royal seal. These he produced with a flourish and handed over to general applause.

Percy flushed up like a peony, to Grey's amusement, and bowed to the company, papers held to his chest.

'I thank you, my lord,' he said to Hal. 'And I'm sure I will hope to be a credit to you and to the regiment.'

'Oh, you will be,' Hal said, smiling. 'If it kills you.'

There was laughter at Percy's faint look of alarm, and his concern faded into an answering smile.

'You think I'm joking, don't you?' Hal said, still smiling. 'Ask my brother. In the meantime – congratulations, sir, and welcome to our company!' He bowed briskly, and with a wave of farewell, strode out to his waiting coach.

'You'll track mud everywhere, John,' the countess said, returning her disapproving attention to Grey's state. 'Do step into the drawing room and take your clothes off; I'll send Tom down to take care of you.'

'I'll keep you company.' Percy, tucking his commission papers away in his coat, opened the door for Grey, who limped through, clutching his whisky. What with one thing and another, lust was the last thing on his mind at the moment, but he was nonetheless glad to be alone with Percy, if only for a short time.

'You know,' Percy said, closing the door and eyeing him. 'I begin to be convinced that you do this on purpose, to avoid my company.'

Grey leaned against the mantelpiece with a faint groan, unable to sit down on any of the furniture.

'Believe me,' he said, 'I should prefer the company of an organ-grinder's monkey, let alone yours, to that of the persons I was obliged to consort with this afternoon.'

'Were you really run down by a coach?' Wainwright asked, peering curiously at him.

'Why do you ask?' Grey parried.

'Because I've seen people run down by coaches,' Percy replied bluntly. 'If you'd been only knocked aside and rolled in the gutter, you'd be bruised and filthy – but you look as though you've been beaten within an inch of your life. If you'll pardon my frankness.' He smiled, to indicate that no offense was meant by this, before going on.

'And if you'd actually been run over by a mail coach, you'd be dead, or close to it. You'd certainly have broken bones. To say nothing of wheel marks on your clothes.'

Grey laughed, despite himself. There was no need to shelter Percy from the truth, after all – and it was dawning on him that, in fact, there were aspects of the situation that he could share with Percy Wainwright that he couldn't tell even his brother.

'You're right,' he said, and proceeded to give Percy an abbreviated, but truthful, version of his afternoon's activities. Percy listened with the greatest attention and sympathy, refilling Grey's glass when it got low.

'So you were beaten by a mob who objected to your going to the help of a gentleman whom they thought a sodomite – who in fact wasn't,' Wainwright observed, at the end of it. 'Rather ironic, isn't it?'

'Bates was a brave man, and he died very horribly,' Grey said shortly. 'I am not inclined to find humor in the situation.'

Wainwright's expression sobered at once.

'You are right; I do apologize. I meant no offense, either to you or to Captain Bates.'

'No, of course not.' Grey softened his tone. 'And in all justice, the captain himself would doubtless have appreciated the irony. He was that sort of man.'

'You liked him,' Wainwright observed, with no hint of surprise.

'I did.' Grey hesitated. He did not yet know Wainwright very well, for all he was about to become a member of the family. And yet . . . 'Have you ever been to Ireland?' he asked abruptly.

Wainwright blinked, surprised.

'Once. Several years ago.'

Grey considered for an instant longer – but the man could always say no, after all.

'The captain entrusted me with a particular errand, of importance and delicacy. I have promised to see it done, but – well, let me tell you.'

By the time he had finished his explanation, Wainwright's mobile face was a study: shock, sympathy, curiosity, and – no doubt about it – a desire to laugh.

'You have the greatest talent for awkward situations,' he said, the corner of his mouth twitching. 'Have you any idea why the captain should have selected *you* for this particular enterprise?'

Grey hesitated again, but answered honestly.

'Yes, I do. He thought I could be blackmailed.'

All humor vanished from Wainwright's face. He lowered his voice, though they were quite alone.

'*Has* he blackmailed you? You are in danger of exposure if you do not perform his errand?'

'No, no, nothing like that,' Grey said hurriedly. 'He did not know – that is – no.' Nothing would induce him to utter the name of Hubert Bowles, even if it were possible to explain how he had come to know the man, which it wasn't.

'It was nothing to do with . . . that,' he said. 'Another matter, which I am not at liberty to explain. But the end of it is that I did agree to perform the captain's request. I did like him,' he added, half-apologizing. 'And yet I cannot leave London at present; I have duties to the regiment, and for me to ask leave would cause a great deal of attention and comment. I must find someone suitably discreet to accompany Mrs. Tomlinson to Ireland – and do so quickly, before her husband discovers the plan or has a chance to injure her further.'

Wainwright rubbed a thoughtful finger below his lip, and glanced at Grey.

'Would you trust me to do it? I am commissioned, but my service does not become effective with the regiment for ten days yet; I presume you could give me leave?' He smiled, eyes dancing. 'And I can assure you of my discretion.'

Grey's heart lightened at once, though he protested.

'I cannot ask such a thing of you. The danger—'

'Oh, I don't see how you can expect me to resist such an opportunity.' Percy's smile grew wider. 'After all, if there is one thing I never expected to do in life, it's to abscond with a man's wife!'

His laughter was infectious, and Grey couldn't help smiling, though it reopened the cut in his lip. Before he could take up his handkerchief to blot it, Percy had whipped out his own, and pressed it to Grey's mouth. He had stopped laughing, but still smiled, his fingers warm even through the linen cloth.

'I shall undertake your errand with pleasure,

John,' he said. 'Though I would appreciate it very much if you can contrive not to be beaten to a pudding again before I come back.'

Grey would have replied, but at this point, there was a discreet knock at the door, which opened to reveal Tom Byrd, a banyan and towel over his arm, who nodded to Wainwright before turning a minatory eye on Grey.

'You'd best undress, me lord. Your bath is getting cold.'

Chapter 16

In Which an Engagement is Broken

Despite his injuries, Grey slept like the dead, and rose late. He was enjoying a leisurely and solitary breakfast in banyan and slippers when Tom Byrd appeared in the dining-room doorway, his face registering an excited alarm that made Grey drop a slice of buttered toast and rise to his feet.

'What?' he said sharply.

'It's the general, me lord.'

'Which general? Sir George, do you mean?'

'Yes, me lord.' With a hasty glance behind him, Tom stepped in and shut the door.

'What on earth—'

'Brunton doesn't know what to do, me lord,' Tom interrupted, in a hoarse whisper. 'He daren't let the general in, but he daren't turn him away, neither. He asked him to wait a moment, and sent me to run fetch you, fast.'

'Why the devil would Brunton not let him in?' Grey was already heading for the door, brushing crumbs from his sleeves.

'Because the countess told him not to, I reckon,' Tom said helpfully.

Grey stopped in his tracks, unable to believe his ears.

'What? Why should she do such a thing?'

Tom bit his lip.

'She, um, broke the engagement, me lord. And Sir George, he says he wants to know why.'

What can she mean by this, Lord John?' Sir George, rescued from the stoop, was a study in agitation, wig awry and his waistcoat misbuttoned. 'She gives no reason, no reason whatever!'

'She wrote to break off your understanding?'

'Yes, yes, she sent a note this morning. . . .' Sir George fumbled at his pockets, searching, and eventually produced a crumpled bit of paper, which indeed said nothing beyond a simple statement that the countess regretted that she found their marriage impossible.

'I am not a handsome man,' Sir George said, peering rather pathetically into the looking glass above the sideboard, and making a vain attempt to straighten his wig. 'I know I am nothing to look at. I have money, but of course she does not need that. I had quite expected that she would refuse my proposal, but having accepted me . . . I swear to you, Lord John, I have done nothing – *nothing* – that might be considered reprehensible. And if I have somehow offended her, of course I should apologize directly, but how can I do that, if I have no notion of my offense, and she will not see me?'

Grey found himself in sympathy with Sir George, and baffled by his mother's behavior.

'If you will allow me, sir?' He gently turned the general toward him, unbuttoned his waistcoat, and rebuttoned it neatly. 'They, um, do say that women are changeable. Given to fits of irrational behavior.'

'Well, yes, they do,' the general agreed, appearing a little calmer. 'And I have known a good many women who *are*, to be sure. Had one of them sent me such a note, I should merely have waited for a day or two, in order to allow her to regain her composure, then come round to call with an armful of flowers, and all would be well.' He smiled bleakly.

'But your mother is not like that. Not like that at all,' he repeated, shaking his head in helpless confusion. 'She is the most logical woman I have ever met. To a point that some would consider unwomanly, in fact. Not myself,' he added hastily, lest Grey suppose this to be an insult. 'Not at all!'

This was true – his mother was both logical and plainspoken about it – and gave Grey fresh grounds for bemusement.

'Has something . . . happened, quite recently?' he asked. 'For that is the only circumstance I can conceive of which might explain her taking such an action.'

Sir George thought fiercely, his upper lip caught behind his lower teeth, but was obliged to shake his head.

'There is nothing,' he said helplessly. 'I have been involved in no scandal. No *affaire*, no duello. I have not appeared the worse for drink in public – why, I have not even published a controversial letter in a newspaper!'

'Well, then there is nothing for it but to demand an explanation,' Grey said. 'You have a right to that, I think.'

'Well, I thought so, too,' Sir George said, exhibiting a sudden diffidence. 'That is why I came. But I am afraid . . . the butler said she had given orders . . . I do not wish to make myself offensive. . . .'

'What do you have to lose?' Grey asked bluntly. He turned to Tom, who had been making himself inconspicuous by the door, intending to tell him to have the countess's lady's-maid come down. He was forestalled, though, by the opening of the door.

'Why, Sir George!' Olivia's face lighted at sight of the general. 'How lovely to see you! Does Aunt Bennie know you're here?'

She almost certainly did, Grey reflected. Whatever her present mental aberration, he was sure that his mother was still sufficiently logical as to have deduced the likely effect of her note, and would almost certainly have noticed Sir George's carriage drawing up in the street outside; it was elderly but solid, and of a sufficient size as to accommodate several passengers, and a small orchestra to entertain them *en route*.

That being so, she had probably also decided what to do when he *did* appear. And since she had given orders not to admit Sir George, the chances of Grey inducing her to come down from her boudoir and speak to the general without the use of a battering ram and manacles were probably slim.

Whilst he was drawing these unfortunate conclusions, Olivia had been eliciting the purpose of Sir George's visit from him, with consequent exclamations of dismay.

'But what can have made her do such an unaccountable thing?' Olivia turned to Grey, her agitation surpassing Sir George's. 'We have sent the invitations! The wedding is next week! All of the clothes, the favors, the decorations! The arrangements for the wedding breakfast – everything is ready!'

'Everything except the bride, apparently,' Grey observed. 'She has not had a sudden attack of nerves, I suppose?'

Olivia frowned, running her hands absently over her protruding belly in a manner that made the general turn tactfully away, affecting to reexamine the sit of his wig in the looking glass.

'She *was* a bit odd at supper last night,' she said slowly. 'Very quiet. I supposed she was tired – we'd spent all day finishing the fitting of her gown. I didn't think anything of it. But . . .' She shook her head, mouth firming up.

'She can't *do* this to me!' she exclaimed, and turning, headed for the stairs in the determined manner of a climber about to attempt the Hindoo Kush. Sir George, openmouthed, looked at Grey, who shrugged. Of them all, Olivia was likely the only one who could gain entrance to his mother's boudoir. And as he had said to Sir George, there was nothing to lose.

The general, relieved of Olivia's blatantly fecund presence, had left the looking glass and was pottering round the room, heedlessly picking things up and putting them down at random.

'You do not suppose this is meant as some sort of test of my devotion?' he asked, rather hopefully. 'Like Leander swimming the Hellespont, that sort of thing?'

'I think if she had meant you to bring her a roc's egg or anything of the kind, she would have said so,' Grey said, as kindly as possible.

Olivia had left the door ajar; he could hear raised voices upstairs, but could not make out what was being said. The general had halted in his erratic progress round the room, and was now staring at a potted plant in a morbid sort of way. He put out a hand to the mantelpiece, touching one of Benedicta's favorite ornaments, a *commedia dell'arte* figurine in the shape of a young woman in a striped apron. Grey was moved to see that the general's hand was shaking slightly.

'You are quite positive that nothing has happened?' he asked, more by way of distracting the general's mind than in actual hopes of discovering an answer. 'If there was an event, it must have been quite recent, for she was fitting her wedding gown yesterday, and she would not have done that, if . . .'

The general turned to him, grateful for the distraction, but still unable to conceive of an answer.

'No,' he repeated, shaking his head in bafflement. 'So far as I am aware, the only thing of note that has happened to *anyone* I know in the last twenty-four hours was your own adventure at Tyburn.' His eyes focused suddenly on Grey. 'Are you quite recovered, by the way? I beg your pardon, I should have inquired at once, but . . .'

'Quite,' Grey assured him, embarrassed. He could see himself in the glass over the general's shoulder, and while the night's sleep had improved his appearance considerably, he still sported a number of visible marks, to say nothing of a rough stubble of beard. 'How did you . . .'

'Captain MacLachlan mentioned it, when I saw him at my club last night. He . . . ah . . . was most impressed by your courage.' There was a delicate tone of question in this last remark, inviting Grey to explain his behavior if he would, but not requiring it.

'The captain and his friend were of the greatest assistance to me,' Grey said, and coughed.

The general was now regarding him closely, curiosity momentarily overcoming his worry.

'It was a most unfortunate affair,' he said. 'I knew Captain Bates quite well; he was my chief aide-de-camp, some years ago. Did you – that is, I presume that you were acquainted with him, also? Perhaps a club acquaintance?' This was put with the greatest delicacy, the general plainly not wishing to appear to link Grey in friendship with a convicted sodomite.

'I met him briefly, once,' Grey said, wondering whether the general was aware of the political machinations behind Bates's trial and conviction. 'A . . . most interesting gentleman.'

'Wasn't he,' the general said dryly. 'He was at one point a fine soldier. A great pity that he should end in such a manner. A very sordid affair, I am afraid. I am glad, though,' he added, 'that you were not badly injured. A Tyburn mob is a dangerous thing; I have seen men killed there – and with less provocation than you offered them.'

'Tyburn?' a shocked voice said behind Grey. He whirled, to find Olivia staring at him, mouth open in astonishment. 'You were at Tyburn yesterday?' Her voice rose. 'It was *you* who seized the legs of that dreadful beast, and was set upon by the crowd?'

'*What?*' Tom, who had tactfully retired to the hallway, appeared behind Olivia, eyes popping. 'That was *you*, me lord?'

'How did you hear of it?' Grey demanded, attempting to hide his discomfiture by dividing an accusatory glare between his cousin and his valet.

'My maid told me,' Olivia replied promptly. 'There's a broadsheet circulating, with a cartoon of you – though they didn't have your name, thank God – being drowned in the mud of perversion. What on *earth* possessed you, to do such a—'

'So *that's* what happened to your uniform!' Tom exclaimed, much affronted.

'And why were you at Tyburn in the first place?' Olivia demanded.

'I have not got to account to *you,* madam,'
Grey was beginning, with considerable severity,
when yet another form joined the crowd in the
doorway.

'What the devil have you been doing, John?' his
mother said crisply.

There was no help for it. So much, Grey thought
grimly, for trying to spare the feelings of his female
relations, both of whom were staring at him as
though he was a raving lunatic.

The countess listened to his brief account – from
which he carefully omitted Mrs. Tomlinson and his
own visit to Newgate – then sank slowly into a chair,
put her elbows on the table among the breakfast
things, and sank her head into her hands.

'I do *not* believe this,' she said, her voice only
slightly muffled. Her shoulders began to shake. Sir
George exchanged appalled glances with Grey,
then made a tentative move toward her, but
stopped, clearly not sure whether any attempt at
comfort might be well received. Olivia had no such
compunctions.

'Aunt Bennie! Dearest, you mustn't be upset;
Johnny's all right. Now, now . . .' Olivia hovered
over the countess for a moment, patting her
shoulder. Then she bent closer, and her look of
tender anxiety vanished suddenly.

'Aunt Bennie!' she said reproachfully.

Benedicta, Dowager Countess of Melton, sat up,

reached for a napkin, and mopped at what were clearly now revealed to be tears of laughter.

'John, you will be the death of me yet,' she said, sniffing and dabbing at her eyes. 'What on *earth* were you doing at Tyburn?'

'I was passing by,' he said stiffly, 'and stopped to see what was happening.'

She cast him a look of profound disbelief, but didn't take issue with this remark. Instead, she turned to Sir George, who had not ceased to gaze at her since her appearance.

'I owe you an apology, Sir George,' she said. She took a deep breath. 'And, I suppose, an explanation.'

'Oh, no, my dear,' the general said softly. 'You owe me nothing. Not ever.' But his heart was in his eyes, and she rose and came to him swiftly, taking his hand.

'I am sorry,' she said, low-voiced but clear. 'Do you still wish to marry me, George?'

'Oh, yes,' he said, and without taking his rapt gaze from her face, lifted her hand and kissed it.

'Well, I'm glad of that,' she said. 'But I shan't hold you to it, if you should change your mind as a result of what I tell you.'

'Benedicta, I would take you bankrupt, in your shift,' he said, smiling. His mother smiled back, and Grey cleared his throat.

'Tell us *what*, exactly?' he said.

'Don't presume upon my good nature,' his mother said, turning and narrowing her eyes at him.

'Part of this is your fault, telling feeble-minded lies about being run down by mail coaches. I thought you were trying to hide the fact that you had been attacked again. Without cause, I mean.'

'Indeed,' Grey said, provoked. 'Being attacked by a murderous crowd is quite all right, while being attacked by a random footpad is not?'

'That depends upon whether the attack on you and Percival Wainwright *was* random,' the countess said. 'Must we stand here in the midst of stale toast and kipper bones, or may we repair to a more civilized spot?'

Relocated to the drawing room and provided with coffee, the countess sat beside Sir George on the settee, her hand on his arm, and looked at Grey.

'After your father's death,' she said, 'I went to France for some time. Within a month of my return to England, I received three proposals of marriage. From three men whom I had reason to suspect of having been involved in the scandal that took your father's life. I refused them all, of course.'

The general had stiffened at this, the happiness of his renewed engagement fading.

'From whom did you receive these proposals of marriage?' Grey asked, before the general could. His mother's eye rested on him.

'I decline to tell you,' she said briefly.

'Do you decline to tell *me*, Benedicta?' The

general's tone was somewhere between outrage and pleading.

'Yes, I do,' the countess said crossly. 'It is my private business, and I don't want the two of you – or the three, I suppose, since one of you would certainly tell Melton and put the cat among the pigeons for good and all – to be poking into things that should be left alone. There may be nothing at all – I hope that is the case. If there *should* be any mischief afoot, though, I most assuredly don't want it to be made worse.'

Sir George was disposed to argue, but Grey succeeded in catching his eye, whereupon he subsided, though with an expression indicating that his acquiescence was momentary.

'Did the journal pages have anything to do with these men?' Grey asked. 'A page from my father's journal was left in my brother's office,' he explained to the general and Olivia. 'And, I rather think, another was sent to you, Mother?'

'As you so cleverly deduced, yes,' his mother said, still cross. 'Neither page referred to any of these three men, no. But your father did discuss things with me on occasion; I knew that he had suspicions regarding at least two of them. That being so, there was a possibility that he had written down his suspicions – perhaps with evidence confirming them – in his journal.'

'Because, of course, the journal disappeared after his death,' Grey said, nodding. 'Do you know when it was taken?'

The countess shook her head. She wore a simple calico gown, but her hair had not yet been dressed for the day and was simply covered by a linen cap. Her color was high, and Grey thought it no wonder that the general was smitten; she was tired and strained, but undeniably *was* handsome for her age.

'I never thought to look. It was ... some time before I felt able to read any of his – of Pardloe's journals. Even then, I thought it likely that you or Melton had borrowed it. Who else would want it, after all?'

'A man who thought he might be mentioned in it, to his disadvantage,' Grey said. 'Why the devil is he scattering pages of it round at this point?'

'To indicate that he has it,' his mother said promptly. 'As for why ... I assumed that it was the announcement of my marriage to Sir George that precipitated the action.'

Sir George jerked as though she had run a drawing pin into his leg.

'What?' he said incredulously. 'Why?'

The countess's fine-boned face showed the effects of what had likely been a sleepless night, but a glimmer of ironic humor showed in the curve of her mouth.

'*You* may be willing to take me in my shift, my dear. I did not think that the proposals I had received were based upon simple desire of my person. That being so, they were based upon one of two things: my money and position – or the possibility that I posed a threat to the gentlemen in question, by virtue of what they supposed I might know.'

Grey rubbed his knuckles over the stubble on his chin. The countess's money and position were considerable; her Scottish connexions were not so powerful as they had once been, in the wake of the South Sea scandal and the failed Risings, but the Armstrongs were still a force to be reckoned with.

'Were any of these gentlemen in a position to be tempted by your assets?' Grey asked.

'There are relatively few men who wouldn't be,' Olivia put in, with surprising cynicism. 'I have seldom met a man so rich that he didn't think he needed more.'

Olivia was young, but not stupid, Grey reflected. And while she seemed not to have been damaged by her earlier engagement to a Cornish merchant prince named Trevelyan, the affair had evidently taught her a few things about the workings of the world.

Benedicta nodded approvingly at Olivia.

'Very true, my dear. But while one of the gentlemen in question could undeniably have used both money and influence, the other two were sufficiently endowed with worldly goods that they could certainly have done better for themselves than a widow past childbearing.'

'So you assumed that their motive was to discover whether you were indeed a threat to their safety – and if so, to prevent it,' Sir George said slowly.

The countess nodded, reached for her coffee, and, discovering it to be cold, put it back with wrinkled nose.

'I did. But I refused them, as I say, and continued to live quietly. One of them returned to press his suit, but eventually he gave up, as well.'

The countess had not, so far as Grey knew, ever even considered remarriage, until she met Sir George.

'I can see why the journal pages should be distressing to you, Aunt Bennie,' Olivia said, frowning. 'But what purpose could they be intended to serve?'

Benedicta glanced at the general.

'At first, I wasn't sure. But then John was attacked and beaten in the street, to no apparent purpose, which alarmed me very much.' His mother's eye lingered on Grey's face, troubled. 'And when I thought it had happened again yesterday . . . I became sure that this was a warning, a threat to prevent my marriage.'

Grey was thunderstruck.

'What? You thought—'

'I did, no thanks to you.' His mother's look of concern had altered to annoyance. 'I didn't want you killed next time, so I thought I would break the engagement and let it be publicly known. If there were no more such warnings, I would know that my deductions were correct, and I could proceed on that assumption.'

'Whereas if you broke your engagement and I

was consequently murdered in the street, you could reform your hypothesis. Quite.' Heat rose in Grey's face. 'For God's sake, Mother! When – if ever – did you propose to tell *me* any of this?'

'I *am* telling you,' his mother said, with exaggerated patience. 'One such instance might well have been coincidence, and the risks of my telling you wouldn't justify my doing so. Two is another matter.

'As for not telling you of my suspicions after the first incident . . . if there was in fact no threat, I didn't want you or your brother going off and doing something foolish. I still don't. If you were in danger, though, then of course I had to speak. But as the second attack was in fact brought about by your own actions, it has no connexion, and we are back with an assumption of coincidence.

'If I'd known about your adventure at Tyburn' – and here her eye rested on him with the deepest suspicion; she knew damned well he wasn't telling her everything, no more than she was telling him everything – 'I shouldn't have felt obliged to break the engagement. You really ought to apologize to Sir George for the inconvenience to his feelings, John.'

The general had been increasingly restive through these explanations, and now burst forth.

'Benedicta! Should anyone – anyone! – be so rash as to offer violence to you or your sons, they will answer to me. Surely you know that!'

The countess regarded him with a sort of exasperated fondness.

'Well, that's a very gallant speech, Sir George, but the point is that I would prefer my sons to remain alive rather than to be avenged – though I am sure you would make an excellent job of vengeance, should that be necessary,' she added, evidently intending this as a palliative.

Grey was growing increasingly annoyed with the tone of these speeches, and put a stop to them by setting down his own coffee cup with a clatter.

'Why should anyone wish to prevent your marriage?'

It was Sir George who answered that, without hesitation.

'I said I would protect your mother and all that belongs to her – and am capable of doing so, I assure you. If Benedicta did know anything that might threaten one of these men, she might denounce them openly, once married to me.'

Grey was more than affronted at the blatant assumption that he and Hal would be incapable of protecting the countess, but retained sufficient self-control as not to say so. He would admit that, viewed objectively, the general commanded more resources toward this end – and he might possibly be in a better position at least to exert some form of persuasion, if not actual control, upon the countess's behavior, which he and Hal assuredly could not. The limits of the general's own influence were just beginning to dawn on Sir George, he saw.

'I . . . assume that you do *not* in fact know

anything that might be dangerous to one of these men?' the general asked the countess, hesitantly.

'If she does, she isn't going to tell you,' Grey informed him, forestalling his mother's answer. 'One question, Mother, if you please. Is any one of the men in question a member of the regiment?'

She looked startled at the idea, and blurted, 'God, no!' with such feeling as made it evident she spoke the truth.

'Well, then. As both Melton and myself will be embarking *with* the regiment in less than a month, I would suppose we can contrive to avoid being killed before that time, if in fact there *is* any threat. And once in Germany, we shall presumably be safe from attack.' He glanced at his cousin, who had been listening to all of this with her mouth half open, eyes moving back and forth between the speakers like the pendulum of a clock.

'Do you suppose that Olivia is under any threat?'

'I don't think so,' his mother said slowly. 'I doubt that any of them even know that she has come to reside here while Malcolm Stubbs is in America.'

'Then that leaves only your own safety to be secured,' Grey pointed out. 'You are bound for the West Indies, are you not, Sir George? If my mother were to accompany you, I daresay that you might be able to protect her from any malicious attempts?'

A look of genial ferocity was spreading across Sir George's face.

'I should like to see 'em try,' he said. He turned to the countess, his face flushed with animation. 'Will you, Bennie? Will you come with me?'

'What, and leave Olivia by herself?'

Olivia sat up straight, enthused.

'Oh, no! I could go to Minnie – she's often asked me. We should have such fun together – oh, do, Aunt Bennie, do go!'

The countess eyed her niece for a moment, assessing her sincerity, then sighed and turned to Sir George.

'I daresay I will be in much more danger from pestilence, seasickness, and vipers than from anything London can offer. But all right. Yes, I'll go.'

It was not yet noon, but the bell was rung and sherry sent for, and a general toast drunk to the renewed engagement. It was only as Grey finally went upstairs to get dressed that he recalled his mother's words regarding probability.

It hadn't occurred to him to connect his encounter with the O'Higginses in Hyde Park with the later attack by Jed and his companion in Seven Dials. The O'Higginses had, of course, indignantly denied being anywhere in the vicinity, and had produced at least sixteen witnesses to testify that they were virtuously engaged in a drinking bout in a shed behind the barracks at the time of the incident. And even if he was morally sure of their identity, there was nothing to say that they had lain in wait for *him;* in fact, their recognition of him had been what made them flee. But still . . .

276

One attack might be coincidence, the countess had said. *Two is another matter.*

Grey told Hal the next day about the breaking and reestablishment of the countess's engagement, with its consequent revelations.

'I heard about the business at Tyburn,' his brother remarked, eyeing him. 'Do you want to tell me what *that* was about? Because I don't for an instant think you just happened to be there.'

Grey was tempted to tell him about the conversation he had had with Captain Bates in Newgate, but there was no way to explain his acquiescence without mention of Hubert Bowles, which in turn might lead to questions neither of them would wish to have either asked or answered.

'No,' he said simply. 'Not now.'

Hal accepted this without further comment; he could be ruthless in pursuit of any matter he believed to be his business – but by the same token, was willing to let other people mind their own.

'Mother gave no hint of the identity of any of these men?' The automaton's cabinet was still in the corner, but Hal had the jar of mottoes and fortunes on his desk, and was dipping into it at random, drawing out a folded slip, reading it, and tossing it back.

'No. Do you think they exist?' That was a thought that had come to Grey in the night, that the countess might have invented these nebulous figures. Though in that case, he was at a loss to explain why she had broken the engagement.

'Oh, yes. I could put a name to two of them, I think.' Hal unfolded a new slip. *'He who throws dirt is losing ground,'* he read. 'Do you suppose the O'Higginses wrote these themselves?'

'Oh? Who?' Grey kept his voice casual, though his pulse leapt. 'As for the O'Higginses, I doubt they can write.'

'Good point.' Hal dropped the slip back into the jar, and shook it. 'Captain Rigby – Gilbert Rigby – and Lord Creemore. I happened to be in England when Mother came back from France, and called upon her almost every day. She had a good many visitors – but I tended to meet those two most frequently, and to find them alone with her.'

Grey reached into the jar, to hide the small flare of resentment he felt at this reference to a time in which he had been excluded from his family's affairs.

'He who laughs at himself never runs out of things to laugh at,' he read, and smiled reluctantly. 'I recall Captain Rigby, from before Father died, very vaguely – he brought his dog, as I recall – but I don't believe I know Lord Creemore.'

'Perhaps not by his title. His name is George Longstreet,' Hal said dryly. He plucked another fortune, read it, and, shaking his head, tossed it back.

'Why are you telling me about them now?' Grey asked, curious. 'The last time I inquired about the circumstances following Father's death, you declined to insult my intelligence by answering my questions.'

'*Do not mistake temptation for opportunity.*' Hal read a new one, dropped it, and leaned back in his chair, surveying his brother.

'I didn't want to tell you, because I knew if I did, you'd be off poking sticks into hornets' nests, and there was no point in stirring up things that have lain quiet for years. But now . . .' Hal looked him over slowly, taking in the remnant bruises, and shook his head. '*If* there's anything to Mother's theory that you were attacked as a warning to her to keep silence, there's a possibility of it happening again. If that's the case, you need to know as much as possible, for your own safety.'

'I'm touched at your concern,' Grey said dryly – but was, nonetheless. 'Since the regiment sails in a few weeks' time, I doubt I'll be able to molest many hornets.'

'Well, yes, there's that,' Hal agreed cordially. 'I don't propose to give you time to sleep, let alone roam about London overturning stones in search of long-hidden Jacobites.'

'You do, however, propose to tell me what you know about Mother's erstwhile suitors.' Grey fished out another motto, and unfolded it.

Hal chewed the inside of his cheek for a moment, thinking, then heaved a sigh.

'Right. I'm guessing about Rigby, but I know for a fact that Longstreet – as he was then – proposed to

Mother, because I caught him in the act of doing so.'

'Indeed,' Grey said, fascinated. 'You put a stop to it?'

Hal shot him a narrow look, then coughed.

'Indirectly,' he said, and hurried on. 'Rigby was one of Walpole's crowd at the time; Walpole came himself to call on Mother – kind of him; it would have been much worse without his making a show of his interest – and he sent his secretary and his aides frequently to the house, as his health kept him from going out. That's how Rigby came to know Mother, I think.'

'And Longstreet?'

'Never mind Longstreet,' Hal said shortly. 'I'll deal with him myself.'

'That remark about hornets' nests . . .'

'Exactly. Keep away from him.'

That was evidently all he was going to hear about Longstreet, at least for the moment. Grey allowed the subject to drop, returning to the larger issue.

'Does it seem at all plausible to you?' Grey asked. 'This theory of Mother's?'

Hal hesitated, then nodded.

'It does,' he said, 'but only if Mother actually *does* know something that could be injurious to someone.'

'Or if that someone thinks she does. But what can she know,' Grey added, 'that would be so dangerous as to justify this kind of hocus-pocus?'

Hal shook his head.

'I don't see how she can have evidence of anything concrete; if she had, surely she would have produced it at the time of the . . . the scandal. All she might know would be the identity of someone who was not only a Jacobite at the time, but a man who had substantial position – and likely still does.'

That made sense. Anti-Jacobite feeling had died down of latter years, with the defeat of Charles Stuart's army, but an accusation of Jacobitism was still an effective tarbrush, wielded by politicians or the press.

'Longstreet would have been vulnerable to a threat of exposure then, and would be now,' Grey said. 'What about Captain Rigby?'

Hal actually smiled at that.

'I suppose so,' he said. 'He's presently Director of the Foundling Hospital.' He unfolded another motto, laughed, and read it aloud: *'A conclusion is simply the place where one grows tired of thinking.'*

Grey smiled at that, and stood up.

'Then I suppose we've reached a conclusion for now. Will you tell me what you discover regarding Longstreet?'

A flicker of something passed through his brother's eyes, but was gone too quickly for Grey to interpret it.

'I'll tell you anything you need to know,' Hal said. 'In the meantime, haven't you business to do?'

'I have,' Grey said, and left. Hidden in his hand, he carried the last slip of paper he had taken from the automaton's jar. *The one you love is closer than you think*, it said.

Six days until the wedding. Four days – perhaps five – until Percy Wainwright returned from Ireland.

Hal had not been joking about allowing him no time to sleep. Grey could feel the regiment beginning to rise from winter quarters and prepare for war, like a bear shaking off the sleep of hibernation, feeling the first rumblings of appetite. And men, like bears, must be fed.

Unlike bears, they must also be clothed, housed, armed, trained, disciplined, and moved from place to place. And then, of course, there was the military hierarchy, a many-headed beast with voracious appetites of its own.

Grey's days were a blur of activity, rushing from Whitehall offices to shipping offices, holding daily councils of war with the other officers, receiving and reviewing daily reports from the captains, writing daily summary reports for the colonels, reading orders, writing orders, hastily donning dress uniform and dashing out to leap on a horse in time to take his place at the head of a column to march through the London streets in a guildhall procession to the cheers of a crowd, then throwing the reins to a groom and brushing the horsehair from his uniform in a carriage on his way to a ball at Richard Joffrey's house, where he must dance with the ladies and confer in corners with the gentlemen, the ministers who ran the machine of war, and the merchants who greased its gears.

The one redeeming aspect of such affairs was that food was served, often his only opportunity to eat since breakfast.

It was at one such gathering that Hal came up beside him and said quietly, 'Lord Creemore is ill.'

Such was Grey's state of starvation and mental preoccupation that he didn't recall at once who Lord Creemore was, and said merely, 'Oh? Pity,' without taking his attention from the sardines on toast he had accepted from a passing footman.

Hal gave him a narrow look, and repeated with some emphasis, 'Lord Creemore is ill. Very ill, I'm told. He hasn't been out of his house in two months.'

'Ah!' said Grey, realization dawning. 'George Longstreet.' He ate the sardines in two bites and washed them down with a gulp of champagne. 'Probably not in any condition to hire thugs and plant documents, you think?'

'I think not. Here comes that tedious ass Adams; you talk to him – if I do, I'll throttle him.' With a perfunctory nod, Hal strode past the Ordnance minister and shouldered his way into the crowd. Sighing, Grey drained his champagne glass, put it on a passing tray, and took a fresh one.

'Mr. Adams,' he said. 'Your servant, sir.'

'Wasn't that Lord Melton?' Bernard Adams, who was short of sight, squinted dubiously toward the end of the room where Hal had made his escape. 'I wanted to speak with him, regarding the extravagance of his request for . . .'

Grey drained another glass, listening to the tall clock in the corner chiming midnight, and thought how pleasant it would be to turn into a pumpkin and sit inert at Adams's feet, impervious to the man's blather.

Instead, he fixed his eyes on the mole to the right of Adams's mouth, nodding and grimacing periodically as he worked his way methodically through three more glasses of champagne and a plate of bacon savories.

Dropping into bed three hours later, in a haze of fatigue and alcohol, he managed to remain awake for a few seconds, in which he wondered whether he would recognize Percy Wainwright upon his return from Ireland, let alone remember what to do with him.

Chapter 17

In Which a Marriage Takes Place, among Other Things

On the 27th of February, the marriage of General Sir of George Stanley and Benedicta, Dowager Countess Melton, was celebrated at the church of St. Margaret's, the parish church of Westminster Abbey.

It was not a large wedding, but one done in the best of taste, as Horace Walpole, one of the guests, remarked approvingly. Olivia had had the church decorated simply with evergreen boughs, done up in ribbons of gold tissue, and the scent of pine and cedar lent a welcome freshness to the atmosphere of ancient wax and bodies kept too long enclosed. Composed in equal parts of military dignitaries, politicals, and social ornaments, the congregation shone nearly as brightly as the four hundred candles, a-glimmer with gold lace and diamonds.

'With my goods I thee endow, with my body I thee worship . . .'

Grey, in the front pew with Percy Wainwright, was close enough to see the expression on the general's face, which surprised him with its soft intensity. He was the more surprised – and not a little taken aback – to catch an answering flash of response from the countess's eyes.

He experienced that peculiar crawling of the flesh that attends any child's sudden realization that a parent must not only have engaged at some comfortably primeval date in the theoretical carnal act that resulted in his own existence – but was capable of doing it again in the all-too-physical present.

He glanced quickly at Percy, to see whether this *frisson* of horror was shared, but saw only an expression of subdued wistfulness on Percy's mobile face. Of course it would not be the same, he reminded himself; the general was in fact not Percy's father. There would be no bar to his imagining – he choked *that* line of thought off at the root, staring hard at Percy in order to avoid looking at the wedding couple.

The light from one of the stained-glass windows caught a few tiny dark bristles, missed in shaving, just beneath Percy's lower lip. It shone through the amber irises of his eyes and touched his flesh with rose and gold.

Grey sincerely hoped that his new brother was not thinking – Percy looked suddenly sideways and met his eyes. Grey took a deep breath and looked away, fixing his gaze on a stained-glass window illustrating the martyrdom of Saint Lawrence, roasted on a gridiron.

They stood close together, the full skirts of their

coats brushing. He felt a stirring among the folds of blue velvet, and Percy's hand brushed his.

No more than a touch, but he breathed deep, and embarrassment faded into awareness.

Tonight.

They had made a solemn pact, the two of them. After the wedding breakfast, they would go away and spend the rest of the day – and the night – together, though hell should bar the way.

Grey crooked one finger round one of Percy's, very briefly, then let go. He realized that his thoughts had gone well beyond the limits of what was suitable in church, and tried to force his attention back to the solemn spiritual event being enacted in front of him. Though why the church had thought to put things like 'with my body I thee worship' into the service . . .

He caught sight of Olivia, discreetly lurking behind one of the slender stone pillars – far too slender to hide her current grand proportions. He smiled, then noticed that her face was pale, set in a pained grimace. No doubt recalling her own nuptials and missing Malcolm, he thought sympathetically.

It might be two years before the gallant Captain Stubbs returned, by which time his first offspring would be—

Olivia's grimace deepened, and her face went purple. Grey gripped the back of the pew in sudden consternation, and Percy glanced curiously at him. Grey lifted his chin, trying to indicate Olivia's alarming behavior, but Percy's view of her was blocked by the pillar and a carved wooden screen. He frowned at Grey in puzzlement, and Grey leaned forward a bit, trying to see whether— but Olivia had disappeared.

The bishop was discoursing comfortably upon the honorable estate of marriage and looked well set to continue upon this course for some time. Grey tried by means of various small jerks of the head and grimacing of his own to alert one of the women on the other side of the aisle, but – beyond frowns of puzzlement from the elderly Havisham sisters and a flirtatious glance behind her fan from Lady Sheridan – was unable to elicit any response.

'What is it?' Percy whispered.

'Don't know.' She couldn't possibly have fainted without someone noticing. Perhaps gone outside for air?

'Maybe nothing. Stay here,' he whispered back, and slipping past Percy, left the pew as quietly as he might and walked rapidly down the side aisle, head lowered and the back of his hand pressed to his mouth, as though he might be indisposed.

He reached the vestibule and flung open the heavy outer door, causing a premature flurry of 'hurrahs!' and a smart clash of swords from the waiting honor guard, who snapped into formation, making an archway for the happy couple.

Contorting his face into what he hoped was apology, Grey made abortive waving motions at the indignant swordsmen and shut the door hastily upon a chorus of disgruntled oaths.

Muttering a few of his own, he made his way back into the church and along the right-hand aisle, glancing furtively into the alcove that held the baptismal font, up into the crowded galleries – for God's sake, an enormously pregnant woman could not simply vanish in the midst of a crowded church!

He ducked into the secluded side chapel, but no one was there. A single candle burned before the statue on the altar, a rather blank-faced thing with outspread hands – Christ Intercessor, he thought Olivia had said it was. At this point, though, he'd take help where he could get it.

'Ah . . . perhaps you wouldn't mind lending a hand?' he whispered, not knowing any official prayers for the purpose. 'If you please.' With a polite nod, he withdrew and resumed his hunt, this time going back down the nave toward the door. What if she had meant to go out, but been overcome before reaching the egress?

He scanned the pews covertly as he passed, in case she might merely have gone to sit down with friends, but received nothing save curious looks from the inhabitants. He reached the door to the vestibule again, and hesitated, unsure where to search next. Whether by heavenly intercession or luck, at this point he spotted a small wooden door set inconspicuously in the shadows beneath the organ gallery.

He tried the door, and finding it unlocked, pushed it cautiously inward – only to have it stick halfway. He was about to give it a healthy shove, when he perceived the foot just beyond it, clad in a lemon-yellow silk slipper.

'Olivia!' He thrust his head through the opening, and found his cousin seated on the bottom step of a small stairway, looking like an untidy heap of lemon-yellow laundry. Seeing him, she withdrew her foot, allowing him to open the door enough to sidle through.

'Olivia! Are you unwell?'

'No!' she hissed. 'For heaven's sake, keep your voice down, John!'

'Shall I fetch someone to you?' he whispered, bending down to look at her. There was not much light here, only what filtered down the stairwell from the loft above. As the light was coming through a window over the loft, it fell down the stairs in a wash of the most delicate hues, with watery lozenges of pink and blue and gold that made Olivia appear to be sitting at the foot of a rainbow.

'No, no,' she assured him. 'I only felt tired and wanted to sit down for a bit.'

He glanced skeptically at their surroundings.

'And you decided to sit down here, rather than in a pew. Quite. Will I go and fetch you some water?' The nearest water to hand was likely the baptismal font, and the only vessel in which he could carry it was his hat, which he had inadvertently brought away with him. Still . . .

'I don't need—' Her voice broke off and she arched her back a little, eyes and lips squeezing shut. She put one hand behind her, pressing a fist into her lower back. Her face had gone purple again; he could see that, despite the light.

He wished to rush back into the church and fetch a woman to her at once, but was afraid to leave her thus in mid-spasm. He'd been in the general vicinity of women birthing – soldiers' wives and camp followers – but had never witnessed the process at close quarters. His impression was that it involved a good deal of screaming, though; Olivia wasn't doing that. Yet.

She blew out air through pursed lips, relaxed, and opened her eyes.

'How long have you been doing . . . that?' He gestured delicately at her bulging midsection. Not that the answer would be of help; he hadn't any notion how long this process was meant to take.

'Only since this morning,' she assured him, and put a hand to the small of her back, grimacing again. He wished she wouldn't; she looked like nothing so much as one of the gargoyles on the pediment outside. 'Don't worry, everybody says first babies take ages. Days, sometimes,' she added, letting out held breath in a gasp.

'In your position, I think I would not find that an encouraging thought at the moment.' He turned, hand to the door. 'I'm going to fetch someone.'

'No!' She sprang to her feet, surprising him extremely, as he hadn't thought she could move at all, let alone so fast. She clung ferociously to his arm. '*Nothing* is going to interfere with this wedding, do you hear me? *Nothing!*'

'But you—'

'No!' Her face was an inch from his, eyes bulging in a commanding stare that would not have disgraced a sergeant conducting drills on the square. 'I've worked over these arrangements for six months, and I won't have them undone now! Don't you take one step out there!'

He paused, but she clearly meant it. And she wasn't letting go of his sleeve, either. He sighed and gave in – for the moment.

'All right. For heaven's sake, though, sit down.'

Instead, she clenched her teeth and pressed suddenly hard against the door, grinding her back against the wood. Her belly had firmed up in some indefinable fashion, so that it seemed even larger, if such a thing was possible. There was so little room at the foot of the stairs that the enormous swell of it brushed against him, and the air was filled with the smell of sweat and something sweetly animal, completely overpowering the feeble scents of powder and eau de toilette.

She was clenching her hands, as well as her teeth, and he found that he was doing precisely the same thing. Also holding his breath.

She relaxed and exhaled, and so did he.

'For God's *sake,* Olivia!'

She was leaning against the door, feet braced, hands cupping her enormous belly, her eyes still closed, breathing. She opened one eye and looked at him.

'You,' she said. 'Be quiet.' And closed it again.

He eyed her bulk. He couldn't escape to fetch help, with her leaning against the door. In normal circumstances, he could have removed her, but the circumstances were anything but normal. She had wedged herself solidly into the doorframe, and he could see no convenient way of getting to grips with her.

Besides, she was panting like a bellows. What if she had another of those alarming spasms, just as he was in the act of dragging her from the – a draft of cool air struck the back of his neck, and he glanced up, startled.

Up. He glanced back at Olivia, whose eyes were still closed in a frown of the most ferocious determination, then wheeled and sprinted up the stair before she could stop him.

He popped up next to the child working the bellows, who gaped at sight of him and left off pumping. A hiss from the organist started him again, though he continued to stare at Grey. The organist, hands and feet poised over manuals, pedals, and stops, ignored him completely, peering instead into a small mirror mounted on the organ, which allowed him to see the proceedings at the altar below.

Grey went hastily to the railing, just in time to see General Stanley sweep his mother into an embrace of such exuberant and obvious affection that the congregation broke into applause. Frantic, Grey jabbed his hands into his pockets, looking for some small missile, and came up with a paper of the boiled sweets he had bought for Percy, who had a sweet tooth.

Who? Anyone, he thought. Any woman, at least. All heads were turned toward the altar, where the bishop was raising his hands for the final blessing. Taking a deep breath and commending his soul to God, Grey pegged one of the sweets into the congregation. He'd aimed to strike the pew near Lady Anthony, one of his mother's close friends seated near the back. Instead, he struck her husband, Sir Paul, squarely in the back of the neck. The baronet jerked and clapped a hand to the spot, as though stung by a bee.

Sir Paul glared wildly round, looking in every direction but up. Grey picked another sweet and was searching for a better target, when a small stir toward the front made him look there. Percy Wainwright had made his way out of the pew, and was heading for the back of the church, nearby heads turning curiously to follow him.

Abandoning his strategy, Grey raced past the organist and down the stairs. Almost too late, he saw Olivia, collapsed again at the foot of the stairs. Panicked at the thought of help escaping, he put both hands against the narrow walls and vaulted over her, coming down with a thump at the foot of the stair. He snatched open the door, just in time to find Percy outside it, looking startled.

He leaned out, seized Percy by the sleeve, and yanked him into the tiny space.

'Help me get her out!'

'What? My God! All right. Where shall we take her?' Percy was sidling round Olivia's feet, evidently trying to decide what to take hold of. A peculiar whooshing noise made him shy back.

'Oh, Jesus!' Grey said, looking in horror at the spreading pool of liquid at his feet. 'Olivia, are you all right?'

'It isn't blood,' Percy said dubiously, trying without success to keep clear of the puddle.

'My new dress!' Olivia wailed.

'I'll buy you a new one,' Grey promised. 'Two. Olivia, you have to stand up. Can you stand up?'

'Shall I fetch someone? A doctor?' Percy made a tentative motion toward the door, but was fore-stalled by Olivia's seizing the skirt of his coat.

'Just . . . wait,' she said, sitting up and panting. 'It's all right. It's—' Her face went quite blank, and then suddenly assumed a look of the utmost concentration. Her hand fell from Percy's coat and went to her belly. Her eyes went round, and so did her mouth.

If she screamed, it was drowned by a blast of organ music.

'Oh, God.' Grey was on his knees, pawing through an unending mass of yellow silk. Now there *was* blood, though not a great deal. 'Oh, God, are you all right, Olivia?'

'I don't really think so, John.' Percy was shouting to be heard over the music, squashed in beside her on the step, frantically trying to stroke her hair and mop her face with his handkerchief simultaneously.

'Is she meant to—' His words were lost as the organist hit the pedals, the great diapasons opened above, and the staircase shook with the sound.

Grey had located a leg under the silk, straining with effort. Its fellow had to be there somewh— there. He gripped Olivia's knees in what he hoped was a reassuring fashion, trying not to look at what might be happening between them.

Suddenly Olivia slid down, pressing back against Percy so hard that Grey heard his grunt above the music. Percy gripped her by the shoulders, bracing her disheveled head against his chest. Grey felt a sort of subterranean shudder go through her body, rather like the waves of sound that beat on them, and looked down involuntarily.

There was a crash nearby as the outer doors were flung open, and to the clash of swords and the cheers of soldiers, a long purple object slithered out into Grey's hands, accompanied by a gush of fluids that did his cream silk breeches no good at all.

You must both be godfathers,' Olivia informed them, from the bower of her bed at Jermyn Street. She looked fondly down at the infant glued to her breast.

Grey glanced at Percy, who was beaming at mother and child, as though he were a Renaissance artist specializing in studies of *Madonna e bambino*.

'We should be honored,' he told his cousin, smiling. 'And now I think you must rest. And we must go to the Turkish baths. You realize this will be the second suit of clothes I've burned this month?'

Olivia disregarded this, lost in admiration of the little boy in her arms.

'What do you think? John Percival Malcolm Stubbs? Or Malcolm John Percival?'

'Call him Oliver,' Percy suggested, cleaning his hands with the remnants of a very stained handkerchief.

'Oliver?' Olivia looked puzzled. 'Why Oliver?'

'Cromwell,' Grey explained, understanding instantly what Percy meant. 'He's got the roundest head I've ever seen.'

Olivia gave him a cross-eyed look, then revelation dawned.

'Oh, *Cromwell*!' she said, but instead of laughing, squinted thoughtfully at the child. 'Cromwell Stubbs? I quite like it!'

Chapter 18

Finally

The room was small and clean, but had very little in the way of amenities beyond a bed, a basin, and a pot. It did, however, *have* a bed, and that, at the moment, was the only real consideration.

He saw it over Percy's shoulder, as his new stepbrother pushed open the door – which had a lock, still better – and crossed the narrow room to push back the curtain. Cool gray snow light flooded in, making the room – and Percy's flesh – seem to glow, dark as it was.

'Damned cold,' Percy said, turning toward him with a grimace of apology. 'I'll light the fire . . . shall I?' He moved toward the tiny hearth as though to do so, but stopped, hand hovering over the tinderbox, dark eyes fixed on John's.

Grey felt his pulse throb painfully through his chilled hands, and fumbled a little as he drew off his gloves and dropped them. He threw off greatcoat and coat together in a thump of snowy weight, crossed the narrow room in two paces and seized Percy in his arms, sliding his hands under Percy's cloak, his coat, jerking the shirt from the waistband of his breeches, and sinking his freezing fingers into the warmth of Percy's skin.

Percy yelped at the cold abruptness of his touch, laughed and kneed him in the thigh, then pushed him back, and with one hand began to unbutton Grey's shirt, the other, his own. Grey interrupted him, hastily jerking at his own buttons, popping one off in reckless haste, so eager to resume his acquaintance with that lovely, warm smooth flesh.

Their breath rose white, mingled. He felt the gooseflesh rough on Percy's shoulders, the shiver of frozen air on his own bare ribs, and half clad, dragged Percy whooping into the icy bed, breeches still about his knees.

'What?' Percy protested, laughing and squirming. He kicked madly at the bedclothes, trying to free himself from the breeches. 'Are you nothing but a beast? May I not have even the smallest kiss before—'

Grey stopped his words with his own mouth, feeling the rasp of Percy's beard, its tiny bristles, and nipped at the soft, full lip, still stained with wine.

'All you like,' he gasped, breaking the kiss for a gulp of air. 'And, yes, I am a beast. Make the best of it.' Then returned to the fray, struggling to get closer, desperate for the heat of Percy's body.

Percy's own cold hand slid down between them, grasped him. Cold as the touch was, it seemed to burn. He felt the seam of his breeches give as Percy shoved them roughly down and wondered dimly what he would tell Tom. Then Percy's prick rubbed hard against his own, stiff, hot, and he stopped thinking.

Neither of them had thought to lock the door. That was the first conscious thought to drift through his mind, and alarm brought him upright. The house was still, the room quiet save the whisper of the snow against the window and the comforting sound of Percy's breathing. Still, he slid out of the cozy warmth of the bedclothes, and picking up Percy's cloak from the floor, wrapped it about his naked body and went shivering to lock the door.

The rattle of the key disturbed Percy, who rolled over in the bed with a groan of sleepy yearning.

'Come back,' he whispered.

'I'll light the fire,' Grey whispered back.

The heat of their efforts had taken the frozen edge from the air, but the room was still achingly cold. The luminous glow from the window gave enough light for him to make out the dark shape of the basket that held Percy's meager supply of wood and kindling. He felt beside it and groping, knocked away the small, cold square of the tinderbox; it slid across the slate of the hearth, and was furred with ash and dust when he picked it up. No one had swept the room in some time; he supposed that Percy's means did not allow him to employ a woman to clean, though his sheets and linen were laundered.

He was acutely conscious of Percy as he worked. Small memories of the body lingered on his mouth, in his hands, making them uncertain with steel and flint. He felt Percy's eyes on his back, heard the small rustlings of quilts as that lithe bare body shifted in the bed.

His mouth tasted of Percy. Each man has his own taste; Percy tasted, very faintly, of mushrooms – wood morels, he thought; truffles, perhaps. Something rare, from deep in the earth.

The steel chimed and sparks flew, glowed brief against the char but didn't catch. He had tasted himself once, out of curiosity; faintly salt, bland as egg white. Perhaps Percy would think differently?

A spark caught, its red heart swelling, and he thrust a straw hastily upon it. There. Fire caught at the tip, burst suddenly gold along its length, and he dropped it onto the careful pile of straw and paper he had built, reaching for the sticks that would usher the infant flame into full birth.

He stood then, stretching cramped legs, waiting to be sure the fire was well and truly caught. He heard Percy draw breath behind him, as though to speak, but he didn't.

He wanted to speak himself, say something in acknowledgment of what they had shared – but found himself unaccountably shy, and turned instead to the window, looking out at the white-covered roofs of London, humped like slumbering beasts, silent under the falling snow.

The exudations of their mingled breath, their sweat, ran in rivulets down the window.

The sky was an unearthly grayish-pink, suffused with light from the hidden moon; light shone like crystal in the droplets of moisture. He touched one with his finger and it disappeared, a small clear circle of wetness on the glass. Slowly, he drew a heart, standing a little aside so Percy could see – and then put his own initials, Percy's below. He heard a soft laugh from the bed, and seemed to feel warmth flow between them.

He'd had Percy's arse twice, and loved every second of it, from the first tentative slick probings to the piercing sense of conquest and possession – so thrilling that he would have prolonged it indefinitely, save for the irresistible onrush that emptied him so completely he forgot himself and Percy both.

The fire had caught well. He stooped and thrust a good-size stick of wood into it, then another.

He was chary of lending his own arse, and seldom did, not liking the sense of being so dominated by another.

He'd been raped once, years ago, and managed to dismiss the memory as a minor misfortune. But there was always since a moment, an instant of something not quite panic, when he felt his flesh obliged to yield so suddenly to that demand. Hector, of course – but Hector had come before.

He could feel Percy waiting for him, but delayed,

torn between desire itself and the urge to wait, so that desire gratified should be that much more delight.

The warmth of Percy's body called him, and the thought of that long – longer than his own, but not much – silken prick. Large-knobbed, he thought. He'd not seen it yet. What would it look like, come daylight?

Daylight was a good way off. The muffled reverberation of a church bell reached him and he waited, counting. They were deep in the night; hours yet of darkness. Privacy.

The bedclothes rustled, restive.

Should he? He thought Percy would not insist. But simple decency... He grimaced, not quite smiling at the irony of such consideration, in a situation where no normal person would even think the word 'decency.'

A louder rustle of bedclothes, and Percy's breath. Was Percy coming to him? No, he'd stopped. Afraid to presume, he thought, shy of pressing a desire that might not be welcomed. He turned, then, and looked at Percy.

The lively face was still, eyes no longer warm but hot as the embers of the growing fire at his back. Heat embraced his legs, touched his buttocks. He let the cloak fall and stood naked, the hairs of his body stirring in the rising air.

His own long hair was disheveled, but still bound. Percy's curls were clipped short, to allow of a wig, but now standing on end, damp, and spiked as the devil's horns. Slowly, he reached back and pulled the ribbon from his hair.

'Do you want me?' Grey asked, voice low, as though he might be heard beneath the sleeping roofs outside.

'You know that I do.' Percy's answer was softer still, and his gaze burned where it touched him.

He breathed deeply, turned, crossed his arms upon the chimneypiece, and bent his head upon them, braced. He spread his bare feet apart, feeling grit beneath his soles.

'Come, then,' he said. And waited, eyes closed, the breath of the fire fierce on his balls.

Shall I tell you a great secret?' Percy's voice was soft, breath warm in his ear. Grey reached a hand through the sheets, slid it over the high round of a still warmer buttock.

'Please,' he whispered.

'My name is not Percival.'

His hand stayed where it was, but he turned his head. Percy's face was turned away from him, half buried in the whiteness of the pillow.

'Really,' Grey said slowly, not sure if this were meant as a jest or . . . if not a jest, what? 'What *is* your name, then? Are you confessing that you are in actuality Desperate Dick, the highwayman? Or younger brother to the Pretender? Because if so—'

Percy rose suddenly in a flurry of sheets and hit him hard on the arm.

'Oh,' he said, in a different tone of voice. He fumbled through the sheets again and laid his hand on Percy's thigh. He squeezed in apology, and waited.

He could hear Percy's breath, deep and uneven, and feel the tension in the leg under his hand.

'I . . . told you that my father was minister to a particular sect of Methodists,' Percy said at last.

'You did,' Grey replied cautiously.

'I rather think you have not many Methodists among your acquaintance, John?'

'None, that I know of.' Where on earth was this leading? The one thing he was sure of was that it was no joke. The spot on his upper arm where Percy had hit him throbbed; he'd have a bruise come morning.

Percy made a sound, not quite a laugh.

'I am not surprised. Methodists are rather severe in outlook; my father's sect particularly so. They would consider you and your family most frivolous and ungodly.'

'Would they, indeed?' Grey spoke a little coldly. He would admit to a general laxness in churchgoing – his mother and cousin attended to that end of things – but frivolous? *Him?*

'My father would have considered the Archbishop of Canterbury frivolous, John,' Percy said, plainly perceiving the affront. He laughed a little unsteadily, took a deep breath, and lay down on his back, drawing the sheet up over his chest.

'My name is Perseverance,' he said in a rush.

'Per—' Grey lay completely still, holding his breath and concentrating fiercely on his belly muscles.

'Go ahead and laugh,' Percy said from the dark, with exceeding dryness. 'I won't mind.'

'Yes, you would,' Grey said, but was still unable to quell the bubble of mirth that rose up the back of his throat, and being there firmly suppressed, emerged through his nose in a strangled snort. To keep from committing further offense, he said the first thing that came into his mind.

'What's your middle name?'

Percy laughed, sounding a little easier, now that the dreadful confession was made.

'Middle names are a useless ostentation, an ornament of arrogance, and a mark of the damnation to be visited upon those who fester in the surfeit of their pride. One Christian name is enough for any God-fearing soul,' Percy replied with mock severity. 'I imagine you've got two or three of them, haven't you?'

'No, just the one,' Grey assured him, rolling over to face him. 'And not even anything sinfully exotic like Achilles or Oswald, I'm afraid – it's a very pedestrian William. Jesus,' he said, struck by a sudden realization. 'What am I to call you now? I *can't* call you Percy anymore, not with a straight face.' Something else occurred to him.

'Does the general know?'

'He does not,' Percy said, with certainty. 'Since my mother died, no one at all has known it, save myself.'

'She wouldn't have told him?'

'No,' Percy said softly. 'She knew how I . . . She knew. She never called me anything but Percy.'

Grey wondered for a moment whether Percy meant that his mother had known . . . but surely not. Even if so, that was a discussion for another time. Just now, he was realizing exactly the magnitude of the gift Percy had given him.

He was the only one who knew. Percy had been right; it was a great secret, and John felt the weight of his lover's trust, warm on his heart.

He groped for Percy's hand and found it, slightly cold. They lay silent for a bit, side by side, holding hands, bodies warming to each other.

A church bell chimed the hour, then struck. He counted out the long, slow strokes, and felt Percy doing the same thing beside him. Midnight. A long time yet 'til dawn.

The bell fell silent, and the air shivered and rippled, falling still around them like the water of a pool.

'Shall I tell you a great secret?' Grey whispered, at long last. The room was dark, but his eyes were well accustomed to it by now; black beams criss-crossed the whitewashed ceiling above, so close that he might touch one if he sat up.

'Please.' Percy's hand tightened on his.

'My father was murdered.'

'I found him, you see.' The words came with surprising ease, as though he had told the story many times – and he supposed he had, though only to himself.

'He was in the conservatory. The conservatory had doors that led out into the garden; it was the easiest way to come and go from the house without being seen – I used it all the time.'

He'd used it the night before, in fact, to steal out for an illicit excursion to the river with the son of a local poacher. He'd left the conservatory door carefully jammed, to ensure an inconspicuous return at dawn, and when he came back in the soft gray light, wet to the knees, his pockets full of interesting stones and dead crayfish, a live baby rabbit tucked in his shirt, the door had seemed just as he'd left it. A careful look round in case the gardeners should be stirring early, and he had slipped inside, heart thumping with excitement.

'It was so quiet,' he said, and saw it in memory, the glass panes of the ceiling beginning to glow but the huge room below still slumbering. Everything was gray and shadowed, dreamlike.

'It wasn't yet full day. No noise from the house proper, all the ferns and vines and trees still – and yet, you know the way plants seem to *breathe*? They were doing that. I didn't see him – see the body – just at first. My foot struck the gun; it was lying just inside the door, and went spinning off with a terrible clatter.'

He'd stood transfixed, then ducked hastily behind a row of potted acacias, in case someone should have heard the racket. Apparently no one had, though, and he peeped cautiously out from his refuge.

'He was – he was lying under the peach tree. A ripe peach had fallen and smashed on the stone floor beside him; I could smell it.'

Smelt it, rich and sweet, above the jungle damp of the plants, mingled with the richer stink of blood and bowels. That was his first exposure to the smell of death; it had never troubled him on battlefields, but he could not eat peaches.

'How far . . . ? The, um, the . . . gun?' Percy spoke with the greatest delicacy. Grey squeezed his fingers to show that he appreciated it.

'No, he couldn't have dropped it. He lay twenty feet away, at least, with a bench and several big pot-plants between.'

He'd known at once that it was his father. The duke was wearing his favorite old jacket, a shabby thing of checkered wool, not fit for anything beyond puttering.

'I knew from the first glimpse that he was dead,' he said, staring up into the white void above. 'But I ran to him.'

There was no way in which to describe his feelings, because he hadn't had any. The world had simply ceased in that moment, and with it, all his knowledge of how things were done. He simply could not see how life might continue. The first lesson of adult life was that it, horribly, did.

'He'd been shot in the heart, though I couldn't see that, only a pool of blood on the floor under him. His face was all right, though.' His own voice seemed remote. 'I hadn't time to look further. The door into the house opened just then.'

Sheer instinct, rather than thought, had propelled him back behind the acacias, and he had crouched there, frozen like the rabbits he had hunted in the night.

'It was my mother,' he said.

She'd been in her wrapper, not yet dressed for the day, and her hair hanging over her shoulder in a thick plait. He'd seen the first light from the glass panes overhead strike her, glowing from the dark-blond plait, showing up her wary face.

'Gerry?' she'd said, voice low.

The baby rabbit in John's shirt had stirred then, roused by his own immobility. He was too shocked to do anything about it, too frightened to call out to the duchess.

She looked about her, and called once more, 'Gerry?' Then she saw him, and what dim color the growing light had lent her vanished in an instant.

'She went to him, of course – fell on her knees beside him, touched him, called his name, but in a sort of desperate whisper.'

'She expected to find him there,' Percy said, intent. 'And she was shocked to find him dead – but . . . not surprised, perhaps?'

'Very astute of you.' Grey rubbed at his ribs, feeling in memory the scratch of the rabbit's sharp claws, a pain ignored. 'No. She wasn't surprised. I was.'

The duchess had remained for a few moments crouched over her husband's body, rocking to and fro in an agony of silent grief. Then she had sat back on her heels, arms wrapped about herself, her white face set like stone, and tearless.

The rabbit's scrabbling at his belly drew blood, and he clenched his teeth against a hiss of pain. Fumbling madly and silently, he pulled the tail of his shirt free and the little thing tumbled to the stone floor of the conservatory, where it stood frozen for an instant, then shot out of the acacias, toward the outer door.

The duchess recoiled from the sudden movement, hand clamped across her mouth. Then she saw the rabbit, quivering in a small puddle of early light, and her shoulders shook.

'Oh, God,' she said, still quietly. 'Oh, dear God.'

She'd stood up then, the skirt of her wrapper stained with blood, and walked across the conservatory. Keeping her distance from the rabbit, she pushed the door ajar with one outstretched arm, then stepped back and stood watching, apparently deeply absorbed, as the rabbit stayed for a long, nose-twitching second before bolting for freedom.

'I might have come out then,' Grey said, and drew a deep breath. 'But just then, she saw the gun. I hadn't known it was a gun myself – only that my foot had struck something – but when she picked it up, I saw it was a pistol. A dueling gun, one of my father's. He'd a pair of them, chased silver – very beautiful.'

His father had let him shoot with one, once. Seeing the silver of the barrel glint as his mother lifted it, he'd felt the shock of recoil in his arm, heard the sharp bang, and his empty stomach had risen up, choking him with bile.

'She stood there for a moment, just staring at it. Then her face . . . changed. She looked at my father's body, at the gun, and – I knew she'd made a decision of some kind.'

She had crossed the floor like a sleepwalker, stooped, and put the pistol in her husband's hand. She'd laid a hand, very lightly, on his head and stroked his hair. Then rose swiftly and walked quickly away into the house, closing the door gently behind her.

John had stood up, light-headed from the sudden movement, and staggered to the outer door. He'd shoved it open and, leaving it hanging ajar, ran through the garden and out the gate, across the back fields – running without thought or destination, only running, until he tripped and fell.

'There was a hayrick near. I crawled to it, and burrowed in. After a bit, I went to sleep.'

'Hoping that it wouldn't be real when you woke,' Percy said softly. Somewhere in the telling, Percy had gathered him into his arms, and held him now, close against his body. His head lay in the hollow of Percy's shoulder, and the curly hairs of Percy's chest brushed soft against his lips when he spoke.

'It was, though. The farmer found me near sunset; I'd slept nearly the day through, and everyone was in a panic, looking for me.'

Percy's hand smoothed the hair away from John's face, gentle.

'Your mother likely thought whoever'd killed your father had got you, too.'

'Yes, she did.' For the first time in the telling, a lump came into his throat, recalling his mother's face when she'd seen him, filthy, trailing hay and mud across the Turkey carpet in her boudoir. 'That's – the only time she cried.'

Percy's arm tightened round his shoulders. He could hear Percy's heart, a muffled, steady thump beneath his ear.

'And you?' Percy said at last, very quietly. 'Did you weep for your father?'

'I never did,' he said, and closed his eyes.

Chapter 19

Pictures at an Exhibition

Grey had one precious day of leave, following the wedding. He was greatly tempted to spend it in bed with Percy. But it was his only chance to go and have a look at Gilbert Rigby, erstwhile soldier and suitor of widows, presently guardian to London's foundlings. And there was the minor consideration that flesh had its limits.

He and Percy had reached them twice more, waking in the night in a musky tangle of limbs. The memory of warm, wet mouths in the darkness and the taste of wine and wood morels had been enough to make him slide out of bed at dawn when he saw Percy, naked, dousing his face with water at the basin, and seize him from behind.

He would have felt guilt at his own rough manners, had Percy not made it clear as day that such usage suited him.

'Don't worry,' Percy had whispered, when he had tried to say something afterward – apologize, perhaps. Percy's face was buried in his shoulder, but he felt the smile against his skin. 'You'll have your full share.'

He hadn't realized what *that* meant, but it became clear soon enough; such slow and tender use as Percy put him to was nonetheless thorough – and lasted a very long time. It brought him to the edge again, held him trembling there, gasping and whimpering, and finally dropped him over the side of a sheer precipice he had never suspected was there. He came to himself bathed in sweat and so shattered that his eyes barely focused, only to find that Percy still held him, was still inside him. He had made some small sound, and Percy laughed.

Percy was laughing now, and the sound of it, deep and infectious, made him hard on the instant, blood rushing through him like a spring tide, rich with salt, surging through and stinging his abraded flesh.

'Look at that!'

He turned to see where Percy was pointing, and saw a small pug dog trotting through the crowd, its tail curled up tight as a spring and a grin on its face. Everyone who saw it was grinning, too; the animal was wearing a black velvet jacket with silver buttons and yellow silk butterflies embroidered round the edge, a small brimmed hat tied to its head with a string beneath its chin.

The dog was attracting a great deal more attention than the portraits on display. They were in the inner court of the Foundling Hospital, where an artists' exhibition to raise funds for support of that institution was in progress. No better opportunity, Grey had thought, for laying eyes on Doctor Rigby, while still enjoying Percy's company.

The women, in particular, were in ecstasies over the pug, and from their remarks, Grey gathered that the pug's owner, a tall, lean man with a dignified air, was indeed the director himself. Rigby was evidently conducting a sort of royal progress, moving slowly through the crowd, greeting people and pausing to chat for a moment.

Rigby would reach them within a few minutes, Grey saw, and so turned to examine the pictures at hand. The Dilettante Society had organized an ongoing exhibition, making this the first public art gallery in London. The painters of the society had lent a number of their own canvases, as did some of the richer governors and noble patrons of the Foundling Hospital. Among the modern paintings by Reynolds, Hogarth, Casali, and Rybrack was a rarity – a portrait from an earlier century.

'Look at that,' he said, nudging Percy.

It was the famous Larkin portrait of George Villiers, first Duke of Buckingham. The duke, slender as a sylph in white silk hose, and bejeweled like a dagger hilt, gave them back a grin of slightly frenetic gaiety, below a pair of knowing eyes.

After a long moment, Percy turned to him, with a nod at the portrait.

'What do you think?'

'No doubt about it, I should say.'

They looked at the portrait together, standing

quite close; he could feel the warmth of Percy's arm brushing his.

'Odd, how it shows on some men, but others—' Percy shook his head, then glanced at Grey with a smile. 'Not you, John.'

'Nor you.'

In fact, most of the men he had encountered who shared their 'abominable perversion' gave not the slightest indication of their appetites in the outward person. Those few who did tended to be of the very effeminate, doe-eyed sort; pretty in youth, but they aged badly.

He cast a look back, as they moved on. George Villiers had not had the opportunity to age, badly or no. Villiers had been not only a nobleman but the favorite of a king, and as such, immune to prosecution. He had been killed by a naval officer at the age of thirty-six – not because of his private behavior, which was notorious, but because of his military incompetence. Grey wondered what Michael Bates would have thought of that, and for a fraction of an instant, wished the captain there.

But Dr. Rigby was approaching them now, cordiality stamped upon his saturnine features.

'Good day, gentlemen!' the doctor said, coming up to them. 'You are enjoying the exhibition, I trust? It is so kind of you; we appreciate your support more than I can say.'

'Your servant, sir.' Grey bowed, unable to keep from returning Rigby's smile, which seemed to hold a genuine warmth and sincerity, for all he had doubtless been employing it without respite for the last hour.

'We are honored to be able to be of any help,' Percy said, with a depth of feeling that surprised Grey a little. He bowed, too, and held out his knuckles to the pug, to be sniffed. 'Your servant, sir,' he said gravely to the dog.

Rigby laughed.

'Thank the gentleman, Hercules,' he said, whereupon the pug put forth one foot and executed a gracious bow, then licked Percy's hand, wagging enthusiastically.

Rigby had given no indication whatever that he recognized Grey. For his own part, Grey might or might not have recognized the former Captain Rigby in the hospital's director; he had met Rigby a few times at his parents' house, but then Rigby had always been in uniform, and with no attention to spare for a ten-year-old boy.

'I am directed to give you my mother's compliments, sir,' he said to Rigby. 'The Dowager Countess of Melton?'

Rigby frowned as though unable to place the name, and Grey swiftly added, 'Though I believe you knew her as the Duchess of Pardloe.'

Rigby's face went comically blank for a moment, then he recovered himself, and seized Grey by the hand.

'My dear sir!' he exclaimed, pumping the hand. 'My apologies! I should have known you at once – you resemble your father very strikingly, now that I realize. . . . But of course it is many years since I knew him. Such a sad loss . . .' The doctor was stumbling, flushing with embarrassment. 'I mean . . . I do not wish to recall you to such a . . . How *is* your dear mother?'

'Very well,' Grey said, smiling. 'Though in fact, she is no longer Countess of Melton, either. She was married yesterday, to Sir George Stanley.'

Rigby appeared genuinely astonished by the news; either he had had no idea, or he was a splendid actor.

'You must offer her my heartiest congratulations,' he said, pressing Grey's hand warmly. 'Do you know, I once asked her to marry *me*?'

'Really?'

'Oh, yes.' Rigby laughed, the wrinkles of his face drawing up in such a way as to destroy the illusion of dignity. 'She very wisely refused me, saying that she thought I was quite unfit for marriage to anyone.'

Grey coughed.

'Ah . . . I am afraid my mother is sometimes—'

'Oh, she was entirely right,' the doctor assured him. 'She correctly perceived – some time before I did – that I am a natural bachelor, and much too fond of my own company and habits to make the adjustments required by marriage. But perhaps you are married yourself, sir?'

Grey was taken entirely unaware by the wash of heat that flooded his face at the question.

'Ah . . . no, sir. I am afraid not.' He glanced

unobtrusively aside for Percy, but his stepbrother had gone to one of the windows that overlooked the grounds and was watching something outside. 'Nor is my stepbrother,' he added, nodding at Percy. 'General Stanley's son, Perc – Percival Wainwright.'

'Time enough, sir, time enough.' Rigby smiled indulgently, then became aware of the hovering presence of several ladies, awaiting their turn to be introduced to Hercules, who was wagging the entire rear half of his body and panting at them in friendly fashion.

'I must go,' the doctor said, clasping his hand once more. 'How pleased I am to have met you, Lord John – it is Lord John, is it not, and your brother's name is Harold? Yes, just so, I thought I remembered. Allow me to say that while your mother was entirely correct in her refusal of me, I should have taken the greatest pride in being your stepfather, and I offer my most sincere congratulations to Sir George in his entering that office.'

His departure left Grey with the feeling of one who has had a warm blanket removed and finds the cool air surprising. He felt somewhat disconcerted, but oddly touched by the meeting, and strolled over to join Percy by the window.

There were a number of children on the open ground, bundled in coats and shawls against the chill, running about in some sort of game under the eyes of a pair of nurses.

'Do you like children, particularly?' he inquired, surprised at seeing Percy's attention fixed on them.

'No, not particularly.' Stirred from his reverie, Percy turned and smiled at him, his face touched with ruefulness. 'I was only wondering what their life is like here.' He glanced around them, at the high walls of brick and gray stone. The place was clean, and certainly not without elegance, but 'homely' was not the adjective one would choose to describe it.

'Better than it would have been otherwise, I suppose.' Some of the foundlings were orphans, others given up by mothers who could not feed them.

'Is it?' Percy gave him a crooked smile. 'My mother tried to have me admitted here, when it opened. But I was much too old – they didn't take children older than two.'

Grey stared at him, aghast.

'Oh, God,' he said softly. 'Perseverance, my dear.'

'It's all right,' Percy said, his smile becoming better. 'I didn't hold it against her. My father had died the year before, and she was desperate. But tell me, what did you make of the good doctor?' He nodded at Rigby, now some distance down the gallery, his cordiality as indefatigable as Hercules's wagging tail.

Grey would have said more, but Percy was plainly disinclined to pursue the subject of his early life, so Grey obliged with his impressions of Doctor Rigby.

'I cannot think he has anything to do with the matter,' he concluded. 'He was plainly taken completely unaware by my appearance, and unless he is most remarkably devious, he had no inkling of my mother's marriage.'

A fresh inrush of people caught them up at this point, preventing private conversation, and they made their way slowly along the gallery, carried along with the crowd into a special room where the permanent exhibition of William Hogarth's paintings were kept – Hogarth being one of the principal benefactors of the hospital – and out again, each alone with his thoughts.

They came back again along the main gallery, but Doctor Rigby and Hercules had disappeared.

'Do you ever wish—' Percy began, and then stopped, a small frown visible between his brows. Thick, silky brows, the sable of a painter's brush; Grey's thumb itched with the urge to smooth them.

'Do I ever wish?' he prompted, and smiled. 'Many things.' He let a hint of such things as he wished show in his voice, and Percy smiled back, though the frown did not disappear altogether.

'Do you ever wish that you were . . . not as you are?'

The question took him by surprise – and yet he was somewhat more surprised to realize that he did not need to think about the answer.

'No,' he said. He hesitated for a moment, but Percy's asking of the question was enough. 'You do?'

Percy glanced back at the portrait of Villiers, then looked down, dark lashes hiding his eyes.

'Sometimes. You must admit – it would make some things less difficult.'

Grey glanced thoughtfully at a nearby couple, evidently courting; the young woman was flirting expertly over her fan, giggling as her swain made faces, imitating the stuffed-frog expression of one portrait's subject.

'Perhaps. And yet it depends, I think, much more upon one's position in life. Were I my father's heir, for instance, I should feel the pressure of an obligation to marry and reproduce, and should likely consent. As it is, my brother has met his obligations in that regard nobly, and thus it is a matter of indifference whether I should ever wed.'

He shrugged, dismissing the matter, but Percy was not willing yet to let it go.

'*You* may be indifferent,' he said, with a sideways smile. 'The women are not.'

Grey lifted one shoulder briefly.

'There is the issue of consent. They will scarce abduct me and wed me by force.'

'Oh, Lady Joffrey would see it done, I assure you.' Percy rolled his eyes expressively. He had met Lucinda Joffrey at Lady Jonas's salon and been impressed by her force of character, which was considerable. 'Never turn your back upon her; she will have you knocked on the head and carried out in a roll of carpet, only to wake in Gretna Green as a new husband!'

Grey laughed at that, but conceded the point.

'She would. You are in as much danger as I,

though, surely – Lady Joffrey has eight cousins and nieces to marry off!' Then he caught a glimpse of the wry twist to Percy's mouth, and realized what he had meant by making some things less difficult.

'Oh, she has had a stab at you already, has she?' he asked, suppressing a smile. 'Which one did she throw at you?'

'Melisande Roberts,' said Percy, his mouth drawing down in an expression of mild distaste.

'Oh, Melly?' Grey glanced down, hiding a smile. He had known Melisande all his life; they had played together as children. 'Well, she is good-tempered. And kindness itself. And she has a modest income.'

'She is the size of a hogshead of ale, and approximately the same shape!'

'True,' Grey allowed. 'And yet – it would make no difference to *you*, surely, if she were a great beauty?'

Percy, who had been looking sulky, gave a lopsided smile at this.

'Well . . . no. Not in terms of . . . no. But I shouldn't want to go about with a plain woman on my arm, as though I could get no better!'

'Shall I consider myself flattered,' Grey inquired, 'that you consent to be seen in public with me, then?'

Percy glanced at him and uttered a short laugh.

'Oh, you would be a catch, my dear, were you bankrupt and common as dirt – or as I am.'

'I am exceeding flattered,' Grey said politely, and

took Percy's arm, squeezing until his fingers sank past cloth and flesh and touched bone. 'Shall we go?'

Percy caught breath, but nodded, and they went out, walking in a silence of unshared thoughts down High Holborn Street. They had planned to see Mecklin's performance as Shylock in *The Merchant of Venice* and have supper at the Beefsteak; Grey was anticipating the evening – and the night to come thereafter – but Percy's thoughts were evidently still focused on their conversation.

'Do you think it true,' he said suddenly, in a low voice, 'that we are damned?'

Grey was not of a theosophical turn of mind, nor yet much concerned about the stated tenets of religion. He had many times heard his father's uncensored opinions of an earlier sovereign, Henry, and the effects of that worthy's sexual itch and dynastic ambitions upon the Church of Rome.

Yet Percy's eyes were deep and troubled; Grey would ease that trouble, if he could.

'I do not,' he said, as lightly as possible. 'Men are made in God's image, or so I am told. Likewise that we differ from the animals in having reason. Reason, therefore, must plainly be a characteristic of the Almighty, *quod erat demonstrandum*. Is it reasonable, then, to create men whose very nature – clearly constructed and defined by yourself – is inimical to your own laws and must lead inevitably to destruction? Whatever would be the point of that? Does it not strike you as a most capricious notion – to say nothing of being wasteful?'

Plainly, the notion of a reasonable God – let alone a thrifty one – had not struck Percy before. He laughed, his face lightening, and they spoke no more of the matter then.

Percy did return to the matter a few days later, though. No doubt it was a matter of Percy's own upbringing in a religious milieu, Grey reflected. Or perhaps it was only that Percy had never been with a man willing to discuss philosophy in bed. Grey hadn't, himself, but found the novelty mildly diverting.

They had left the barracks separately and met in Percy's rooms for a few stolen hours. Where, after the initial delights of the flesh had been tasted, Grey found himself with his head pillowed on Percy's stomach, being read to from a collection of legal opinions, published a year or two previous.

> 'If any crime deserve to be punished in a more
> exemplary manner, this does. Other crimes are
> prejudicial to society; but this strikes at the being
> thereof: it being seldom known that a person who
> has been guilty of abusing his generative faculty so
> unnaturally has afterwards a proper regard for
> women. For that indifference to women, so
> remarkable in men of this depraved appetite, it may
> fairly be concluded that they are cursed with
> insensibility to the most ecstatic pleasure which

human nature is in the present state capable of
enjoying. It seems a very just punishment that such
wretches should be deprived of all tastes for an
enjoyment upon which they did not set a proper
value; and the continuation of an impious
disposition, which then might have been
transmitted to their children, if they had any, may
be thereby prevented.'

'So,' Grey remarked, 'we must be exterminated, because our pleasures are insufficiently ecstatic?'

Percy's brow relaxed a bit, and he closed the book.

'And lest we pass on this deplorable lack to our children – which we are hardly likely to have, under the circumstances.'

'Well, as to that – I know more than one gentleman who seeks no pleasure in his wife's bed, but goes there in the course of duty nonetheless.'

'Yes, that's true.' Percy still frowned, though with thoughtfulness, rather than unease. 'Do you think it's actually different? Between a man and a woman? Not merely in mechanical terms, I mean, but in terms of feeling?'

Grey had seen enough of marriages arranged among the nobility and the wealthy as to know that the emotions and mutual attraction of the persons involved were usually considered irrelevant, if indeed they were considered at all. Whereas such ongoing relations as he had from time to time contracted himself involved nothing else, being quite free of the requirements of society. Still, he considered the matter, enjoying the peaceful rise and fall of Percy's breathing beneath his cheek.

'I think a gentleman conducts his affairs with kindness and with honor,' he said, at last. 'That being so, if the recipient is a woman or a man – does it matter so much?'

Percy gave a short laugh.

'Kindness and honor? That's all well – but what of love?'

Grey valued love – and feared it – too greatly to make idle protestations.

'You cannot compel love,' he said finally, 'nor summon it at will. Still less,' he added ruefully, 'can you dismiss it.' He sat up then, and looked at Percy, who was looking down, tracing patterns on the counterpane with a fingertip. 'I think you are not in love with me, though, are you?'

Percy smiled a little, not looking up. Not disagreeing, either. 'Cannot dismiss it,' he echoed. 'Who was he? Or is he?'

'Is.' Grey felt a sudden jolt of the heart at the speaking of that single word. Something at once joyful and terrible; the admission was irrevocable.

Percy was looking up at him now, brown eyes bright with interest.

'It is – I mean, he – you need not worry. There is no possibility of anything between us,' Grey blurted, and bit his tongue to keep back the sudden impulse to tell everything, only for the momentary ecstasy of speaking of Jamie Fraser. He was wiser than that, though, and kept the words bottled tight in his throat.

'Oh. He's not . . . ?' Percy's gaze flicked momentarily over Grey's nakedness, then returned to his face.

'No.'

It was late in the day; light skimmed across the room from the high attic windows, striking the dark burnished mass of Percy's curling hair, painting the lines of his face in chiaroscuro, but leaving his body in the dimness of shadow.

'Is friendship and sincere liking not enough for you?' Grey was careful to avoid any tone of pettishness or accusation, making the question merely one of honest inquiry. Percy heard this, and smiled, lopsidedly, but with answering honesty.

'No.' He stretched out a hand and ran it up Grey's bare arm, over the curve of his shoulder, and down the slope of his breast, where he spread his palm flat over the nipple – and took a sudden grip of the flesh there, fingers digging into the muscle.

'Add *that*, though . . .' he said softly, 'and I think it will suffice.'

They saw little of each other during the days, Grey being busy with the increasingly frantic preparations for departure, and Percy consumed by the rigors of his own training and the needs of the four companies under his command. Still, in the evenings, they could go about quite openly together in public, as any two men who happened to be particular friends might do – to supper, to a play, or a gaming club. And if they left such venues together, as well, it caused no comment.

No one at Jermyn Street would question Grey's occasional absence at night, for he often slept in the barracks or at the Beefsteak, if he had been kept late on regimental business or out with friends. Still, to be gone every night would cause notice, and so the nights they spent together in Percy's rooms were doubly precious – for their scarcity, and for the realization that they were coming to an end.

'We must be circumspect in the extreme,' Grey said. 'On campaign. There is very little privacy.'

'Of course,' Percy said, though given what he was doing at the time, Grey thought he was not paying particular attention. His fingers tightened in Percy's hair, but he did not make him stop. Time enough to repeat the warning – and he was no more eager than Percy to contemplate the inevitable interruption of their intimacy.

An intimacy of more than body – though God knew, that was sufficiently intimate.

Percy had taken him at his offer on their first night, again the next morning, and had used him with the greatest gentleness – a gentleness that unnerved him, even as it brought him nearly to tears.

He had not made that particular offer again, disturbed as much by the experience as he had been by the long-ago rape, though in a very different –

and admittedly more pleasant – way. Percy never pressed him, never asked; only made it clear that should Grey wish it . . . And perhaps he would, again. But not yet.

The unexpected intimacy of mind between them was as intoxicating – and occasionally as unsettling – as that of the flesh.

Percy had not referred directly to the story Grey had told him regarding the duke's murder since the night they had first lain together. He knew his friend must be thinking of it, though, and was therefore not surprised when Percy mentioned the matter a few days later. Not pleased – he did not precisely regret telling Percy the truth, but was surprised at himself for having done so after keeping the secret for so long, and felt a sort of lurking unease at the secret he had guarded for so long being now shared by another – but not surprised.

'But what happened afterward?' Percy demanded. 'What did you do? Did you not tell anyone? Your mother?'

Grey felt a flash of annoyance, but recognized in time that the cause of it was not Percy's question but the memory of his own helplessness.

'I was twelve years old,' he said, and Percy glanced at him sharply and drew back a little, sensing the edge in his voice, despite its calm. 'I said nothing.'

The gardener had found the duke's body, later in the morning. A hastily convened coroner's jury had found a verdict of death while the balance of mind was disturbed, and two days afterward Grey had been sent north, to stay with distant cousins of his mother's, in Aberdeen. The duchess, with a prudence he did not appreciate until years later, had left, too, to live in France for several years.

'Could she not have taken you with her?' Percy asked, echoing Grey's own anguished – but unspoken – question at the time.

'I believe,' he said carefully, 'she considered that there might be some risk to her own life.'

He believed – though very much *ex post facto* – that she had in fact courted such risk.

'Courted it?' Percy echoed in surprise. 'Whatever do you mean by that?'

Grey sighed, rubbing two fingers between his brows. There was an unexpected relief, and even pleasure, in the intimacy of talking, finally, about all this – but this was balanced by the equally unexpected distress of reliving those events.

'It's a gray place, Aberdeen.' Grey was sitting up in bed, arms round his knees, watching the last of the night evaporate from the roofs of the city. 'Stone. Rain. And Scots. The bloody Scots.' He shook his head in recollection, the sound of their talk like the rumble of carriage wheels on gravel.

'I didn't hear much. Scandals in London . . .' He shrugged. 'Not of interest in Aberdeen. And I imagine that was the point; to shield me from the talk. My mother's cousins were kind enough, but very . . . remote. Still, I overheard a few things.'

The duchess – or the countess, as she had taken

to styling herself – had apparently been very visible in France, to the murmurous disapproval of her Scottish Lowland relations. Not young, she was still a very handsome woman, and rich.

'There were rumors that she had to do with some of the French Jacobites. And if there is one thing of which I am certain, it is that my mother harbored – and harbors – no sympathy whatever for that cause.'

'You think she was looking for the man who killed your father.'

Grey nodded, still looking out the window, seeing not the lightening sky above London but the gray rain clouds of Aberdeen.

'I don't know if she found him,' he said softly. 'I convinced myself after a time that she had. Had killed him in turn – or in some other way contrived his destruction.'

Percy raised an incredulous eyebrow.

'You think – or thought – that your mother had *killed* him?'

'You think women are not capable of such things?' Grey didn't quite laugh, but turned his head so that Percy could see the half smile on his face.

'Not generally, no. *My* mother could certainly not . . .' Percy trailed off, frowning, evidently trying to visualize Benedicta Grey in the act of murder. 'How? Poison?'

'I don't know. She's rather direct, my mother. Much more likely a stab to the heart. But in fact, I don't suppose she ever found the man – if indeed she was searching for him. It was just . . . something I told myself she was doing.' He shrugged, dismissing the memory. 'What happened to *your* father?' he asked curiously.

Percy shook his head, but accepted the change of subject, an expression of wry humor on his face.

'Believe it or not, he was run over by a mail coach.'

'Ass!'

'No, I mean it, he was.' Percy shrugged, helpless. 'He was standing in front of a public house in Cheltenham, preaching at the top of his lungs and quite oblivious to his surroundings. We heard the coach coming—'

'You were *there*?'

'Yes, of course. He'd take me along, to give out tracts or pass the hat when he preached in public. Anyway, I pulled at his coat – I could see the coach then, and how fast it was coming – and he cuffed me away, absently, you know, like one would brush away a fly, too absorbed in his vision of heaven to notice anything on earth. He stepped forward, to get away from me. Then it was on us and I jumped back, out of the way. And . . . he didn't.'

'I'm sorry,' Grey said.

Percy glanced at him, mouth half turned up.

'I wasn't. Self-righteous, heavy-handed bastard. My mother wasn't sorry, either, though his death made it very hard for her.' He flipped a hand, indicating that he wished to waste no more conversation on the subject. 'Going back to your much more sincerely lamented father – I have been thinking about what you told me. Do you – do you mind?'

'No,' Grey said cautiously. '*What* have you been thinking?'

Percy cleared his throat. 'I'll tell you, but since you mentioned the, um, inquest. You are quite, quite positive that your father did not . . . uhh . . .'

'No, he didn't, and yes, I am sure.' Grey heard the edge in his own voice and made a small gesture of apology. 'Sorry. I . . . haven't spoken of it before. It's—'

'Raw,' Percy said softly. Grey glanced up and saw such a warmth of understanding in Percy's eyes that he was obliged to look away, his own eyes stinging.

'Yes,' he said. Like a fresh-cut onion.

Percy squeezed his leg comfortingly, but said no more of Grey's feelings, returning to his line of thought.

'Well, then. If – I mean, *since* that is the case, we know something important, do we not?'

'What?'

'The murderer himself didn't seek to disguise the death as suicide. Your mother did that. Do you know why, by the way? I suppose you never asked her.'

Grey managed a wry smile at that.

'Could you have asked *your* mother such a thing?'

Percy frowned, seeming to consider the question, but Grey didn't wait for an answer.

'No. I've never spoken to my mother regarding the matter. Nor Hal.'

One of Percy's smooth dark brows rose high.

'Really. You mean – neither of them knows that *you* know that your father's death was not a suicide?'

'I suppose they don't.' It occurred to him for the first time, with a small sense of shock, to wonder whether Hal knew the truth of their father's death. He had always supposed that he must, that their mother had told Hal the truth – and resented the thought that she had but had not told him, owing to his youth. But what if she hadn't told Hal, either?

That thought was too much to deal with at the moment. He pushed it away, returning to Percy's question.

'I'm reasonably sure why she did it. She feared some danger – whether to herself, Hal, or even me – and that fear must have been exigent, since she preferred to allow my father's name to be disgraced rather than risk it.'

Percy caught the underlying note of bitterness in this.

'Well, she *is* your mother,' he said mildly. 'A woman might be excused for valuing her sons' lives above their father's honor, I suppose. The point I was getting at, though, is this: the murderer didn't kill your father in order to deflect suspicion from himself by making your father appear to be a traitor. So why *did* he do it?'

He looked at Grey, expectant.

'To keep my father from revealing the murderer's own identity as a Jacobite traitor,' Grey said, and shrugged. 'Or so I have always supposed. Why else?'

'So would I.' Percy leaned forward a little, intent. 'And whoever did it is also presumably the same person who took your father's journal, do you not think?'

'Yes,' Grey said slowly. 'I imagine so. I didn't know at the time that the journal had been taken, of course . . .' And not knowing, had never taken that into account, during all those long gray hours of brooding, alone in Aberdeen. 'You think – oh, Jesus.' His mind skipped the next obvious question – might the duke have written of his suspicions in his journal – and darted to the point Percy had been coming to.

'He *wasn't* in the habit of writing in his journal in the conservatory, then?' Percy was reading the progress of Grey's thoughts across his face, his own face alight with cautious excitement.

'No, never.' Grey took a moment to breathe. 'The conservatory wasn't lighted, save for parties. He always wrote in his journal in the library, before retiring for the evening – and put the journal back into the bookcase there. He wrote on campaign, of course – but otherwise, no. I never saw him write in his journal anywhere else.'

Which meant two things: whoever had shot his father had known him well enough to be aware that he kept a journal and where it was – and whoever had done it was sufficiently well-known to the household that he had been able to enter the library and abstract the journal.

'Do you think he took it . . . before?' Percy asked. 'Might that be *why*, do you think? That the murderer read the journal, saw that he was exposed – or about to be – and thus . . .'

Grey rubbed a hand over his face, the bristles of his sprouting beard rasping his palm, but shook his head.

'Even assuming that my father was foolish enough to write down such suspicions in plain language – and I assure you he was not – how could someone have read it? No one looked at his journals – not even my mother; she teased him about them – and he didn't leave them lying about.'

Restless, he got out of bed and stood by the window, trying to remember. He was trying to reconstruct in his mind the library at their country house. They called it 'the library' more by way of jest than anything else; it was a tiny, book-lined closet, lacking even a hearth, with barely room for a chair and a small writing desk. Not the sort of room in which his father would have entertained visitors.

'I do agree that it's more likely that the man took the journal after the murder.' Percy rubbed absently at his shoulders, cold in spite of his woolen banyan. 'A visitor – coming to leave his condolences? Might he not have found opportunity to abstract it then?'

Grey grappled with the notion. He was unwilling to relive the horrible days following his father's death, but obliged perforce to recall them. The quiet, hurried arrangements, the low-voiced conversations, always suspended when he came in sight.

There *had* been a few visitors, friends who came to support the duchess in her grief, and a few of Hal's particular friends – Harry, Harry Quarry had come, he recalled that. Who else? Robert Walpole, of course. He remembered the First Lord, gray-faced and ponderous, coming slowly up the walk, leaning on his secretary for support, the shadow of his own approaching death clear upon his face.

He closed his eyes, fingers pressed against the lids, trying to think. Faces flitted past, some with names, some strangers, all fractured by remembered shock. Bar Harry and Walpole, the only people he could recall with any clarity from that dreadful week were—

He dropped his hand, opening his eyes.

'It might not have been a visitor,' he said slowly.

Percy blinked, and pursed his lips.

'A servant?' he said, shocked at the idea. 'Oh, no.'

Grey felt a coldness at the heart at the thought himself. The servants had all been with his parents for years, were trusted implicitly. To consider that one of them, someone who had shared the family's house, the intimacies of its daily life, might all the while . . .

He shook himself, dismissing the idea.

'I can't think anymore,' he said. 'I can't.' Tiredness pressed on his shoulders, and his neck ached with the weight of recalled sorrow and anger. His eyes were burning, and he leaned his forehead against the frozen windowpane, welcoming the cold pressure of it on his face. Dawn was coming up in the east; the ice-blurred glass glowed with a faint yellow light.

There was a rustle of bedclothes, and he felt Percy's hands, warm on his shoulders. He resisted for a moment, but then let Percy pull him away from the window, hold him close, body to body.

'Don't be sorry that you told me.' Percy spoke quietly in his ear. 'Please.'

'No,' he murmured, not sure whether he was sorry or not. At the moment, he wished he had kept silent, only because to speak of it was to be forced to think of it again. He'd kept the secret buried for so long – he hadn't realized that he had kept it buried in his own flesh, as well as his mind. His joints ached as though he was being slowly pulled apart.

'You're cold; you'll make yourself ill. Come to bed.'

He suffered Percy to put him to bed and draw the blankets up under his chin. He closed his eyes obediently when told to, and listened to the sounds of Percy stirring up the fire, adding wood, using the pot. Then opened them again when he heard Percy break the ice in the ewer and splash water into the tin he used to heat his shaving water.

'Where are you going?' he demanded. Percy turned from the hearth and smiled at him, hair standing on end, his face darkly rakish with its bristling beard.

'Some of us must work for a living, my dear,' he said. 'And I have it on good authority that I shall be cashiered and broken – if not actually strung up by the thumbs and flogged – should I not appear promptly on the square with my companies in good order by nine of the clock.'

'That's right – am I not inspecting your companies at nine o'clock?' Grey sat up, but Percy waved him back into the pillows.

'Given that the bells have just rung half six, and that *you* have nothing to do save shave, dress, and stroll in a leisurely fashion to the parade ground, I think you may take your ease for a bit.' Percy picked up his shaving mug and bent to peer into the tiny square of his looking glass, mouth half open in concentration as he applied the lather.

Grey lay slowly back, and watched him go about the business of shaving and dressing, neat and quick. A little of Percy's warmth remained in the bedclothes; it thawed him, slowly, and he felt a great lassitude steal over him. His mind felt soggy, and tender, like a bruised fruit.

The room was still dark, dawn some way off. He could see Percy's breath as he bent to pull on his boots, fastened the hooks of his coat.

Wig in place, Percy paused by the bedside, looking down at him.

'Do you think she knew? Who it was?'

'I'm sure she did not,' Grey said, with what firmness he could muster.

Percy nodded and bending, kissed him on the forehead.

'Try to sleep,' he said. 'The bells will wake you.'

He left, closing the door gently behind him.

The warmth now enclosed Grey in a snug pocket, though the end of his nose was as cold as if he still pressed it against the windowpane. He was heavy-limbed, blanketed with the fatigue of a long day and a sleepless night – but he knew he would not sleep, bells or no.

He was going to have to talk to Jamie Fraser again.

SECTION IV

The Regiment Rises

Chapter 20

Ye Jacobites by Name

Helwater
The Lake District

He spent as little time as politeness required with the Dunsanys, before discovering that he had left something he required in his saddlebag.

'No, no – I'll fetch it. Won't take a moment.' He stopped Lady Dunsany, her hand on the bell rope, and was out of the library before she could protest.

His heart beat faster as he approached the stable, but for once, it had little to do with the physical presence of Jamie Fraser.

Dinner had been served; the stable was filled with the peaceful sounds of chewing and the smell of fresh-broken hay. One or two of the horses lifted a head to look at him, wisps of hay straggling from the champing jaws, but for the most part, they ignored him, noses firmly planted in the mangers.

Fraser was at the far end of the stable, mucking out. The huge door there had been slid aside, and he was silhouetted against the pale light of the fading spring sky. He must have heard Grey's footsteps on the brick floor, but didn't break the rhythm of his work.

He stopped, though, and straightened when Grey came up to him. It was cold in the stable, but there was a sheen of moisture across his jaw, and the linen shirt clung to his shoulders. He smelled of clean sweat.

'Leaks,' Grey said abruptly. 'You said "leaks."'

Fraser rested the manure fork on its tines, wiped his face with a sleeve, and regarded him quizzically.

'I dinna recall having done so, Major, but I suppose it's possible – I do ken the word.'

'When you spoke of the Stuart court at our last meeting,' Grey amplified. 'You said, and I quote, "The Stuart court leaks like a sieve." I am convinced that you understand the niceties of English grammar sufficiently as to use the present tense correctly, Mr. Fraser.'

Fraser raised one thick red brow, though no expression of concern showed on his face. Grey sighed.

'It leaks like a sieve,' he repeated. 'How do you know that it does, unless you are presently in contact with someone there?'

Fraser rubbed a finger under his nose, regarding him, then turned back to his work, shaking his head.

'Your brain's like to burst, Major, and ye dinna give over thinking so much,' he said, not unkindly. He shoved the pitchfork under a mound of manure-matted straw and heaved the muck out through the open door. 'Ye ken well enough that the terms of my parole dinna permit any such thing.'

That was quite true; Grey had written those

terms, and Fraser had signed them. He recalled the occasion vividly; it was the first – but not the last – occasion on which he had been sure that only the presence of armed guards kept Fraser from breaking his neck.

It was apparent from the Scot's ironic expression that he recalled the occasion, too.

'And if I wasna sufficiently honorable as to abide by those terms, Major,' he added evenly, 'I should have been in France a week after setting foot in this place.'

Grey forbore to take issue with the notion of someone of Fraser's striking appearance being able to travel the roads without being noticed, or to cross fifty miles of open fell on foot, without cloak, food, or shelter – not least because he was convinced that the man quite possibly could have done so.

'I would never suggest a breach of honor on your part, Mr. Fraser,' Grey said, and was mildly surprised to find that true. 'I apologize if my question might have implied any such suggestion.'

Fraser blinked.

'Accepted, Major,' he said, a little gruffly. He paused, gripping the fork as though about to return to his work, but then the muscles of his shoulders relaxed.

'I said that the Stuart court leaks like a sieve, Major, because both King James and his son are still alive, and the same men still surround them. So far as I am in a position to know,' he added, with a glint of dry humor.

'You don't think they've given up?' Grey asked curiously, choosing not to notice that 'King James.' 'Surely they have no hope—'

'No, they have nay hope, and no, they've not given up,' Fraser interrupted him, the dry note more pronounced. 'They're Scots, for all they live their lives in the shadow of St. Peter's. They'll cease plotting when they're dead.'

'I see.' He did. Eighteen months as governor of Ardsmuir was enough to have given him a useful estimation of the Scottish character. The Emperor Hadrian had known what he was about, he thought; pity later rulers of England had been less prudent.

With that thought in mind, he chose his words carefully.

'May I ask you a question, Mr. Fraser?'

'I see no way to stop ye, Major.' But there was no rancor in Fraser's voice, and the light in his eye was the same that appeared when they played chess. Wariness, interest – and readiness.

'If I were to release you explicitly from that provision of your parole – and were to forward any letter you cared to send, wherever you chose to send it, without question – would you be able to contact someone who would know the names of prominent Jacobites in England? It would have been someone active in 1741.'

He'd never seen Fraser drop-jawed, and didn't now, but the Scot plainly couldn't have been more taken aback had Grey suddenly kissed him on the mouth.

'That—' he began, then broke off and shook his head. 'Do you—' He paused again, so patently appalled at the suggestion that words failed him.

'Do I know what I ask? Yes, I do, and I am sorry for it.' Silence hung between them for a moment, broken by the champing of horses and the call of an early lark in the meadow beyond the stable.

'Please believe that I would not seek to make use of you in this fashion, were there any other choice,' Grey said quietly.

Fraser stared at him for a moment, then pushed the fork into the heap of soggy straw, turned, and went out. He walked off into the growing dusk, to the paddock, and there stood, his back turned to Grey, gripping the upper rail of the fence as though trying to reestablish his grip on reality.

Grey didn't blame him. He felt completely unreal himself.

'Why?' Fraser asked bluntly, turning round at last.

'For my father's honor.'

Fraser was silent for a moment.

'Do ye describe my own present situation as honorable, sir?'

'What?'

Fraser cast him an angry glance.

'Defeat – aye, that's honorable enough, if nothing to be sought. But I am not merely defeated, not only imprisoned by right of conquest. I am exiled, and made slave to an English lord, forced to do the will of my captors.

'And each day, I rise with the thought of my perished brothers, my men taken from my care and thrown to the mercies of sea and savages – and I lay myself down at night knowing that I am preserved from death only by the accident that my body rouses your unholy lust.'

Grey's face was numb; he could not feel his lips move, and was surprised to hear the words come clearly nonetheless.

'It was never my intent to bring you dishonor.'

He could see the Scot check his rising anger, with an effort of will.

'No, I dinna suppose that it was,' he replied evenly.

'I don't suppose you wish to kill me?' Grey asked, as lightly as possible. 'That would solve my immediate dilemma – and if you dislike your life as much as you appear to, the process would relieve you of that burden, as well. Two birds with one stone.'

With startling swiftness, Fraser plucked a stone from the ground, and in the same motion, hurled it. There was a sickening thump, and jerking round, Grey saw a fallen rabbit, legs kicking in frantic spasm beneath a bush.

Without haste, Fraser walked over, picked it up, and broke its neck with a neat snap. Returning, he dropped the limp body at Grey's feet.

'Dead is dead, Major,' he said quietly. 'It is not a romantic notion. And whatever my own feelings in the matter, my family would not prefer my death to my dishonor. While there is anyone alive with a claim upon my protection, my life is not my own.'

He walked off then, into the chilly twilight, and did not look back.

Grey left Helwater the next day. He did not see Fraser again – did not plan to – but carried a note to the stable at mid-morning. It was deserted, most of the horses gone, and the three grooms with them, as he'd expected.

He had taken some pains with the composition of the note, keeping it as formal and dispassionate as possible. He had, he wrote, informed Lord Dunsany that if Fraser chose to write any letters, to anyone whomsoever (that phrase underlined; he knew that Fraser wrote secretly to his family in the Highlands when he could), he was to be provided with paper and ink, and the letters dispatched under Dunsany's seal, without question. The letters would not, he added delicately, be read by any save their intended recipients.

He had thought to leave the note, addressed to Fraser, pinned to a railing or stall where it would be easily found. But now he reconsidered; he didn't know whether the other grooms could read, nor whether their respect for Fraser might restrain their curiosity – but neither he nor Fraser would want the matter to be generally known and talked about.

Ought he to leave the note with Dunsany, to be delivered personally? He felt some delicacy about that; he did not wish Fraser to feel any pressure of Dunsany's expectations – *only yours*, he thought grimly. He hesitated for an instant, but then climbed the ladder to the loft where he knew Fraser slept, heart beating like a drum.

The loft was dim, but even in the poor light, it was apparent at once which spot was Fraser's. There were three striped mattress tickings on the floor, each with a lidded wooden crate beside it for clothes and personal belongings. Two of these were scattered with pipes, tobacco pouches, stray buttons, dirty handkerchiefs, empty beer jugs, and the like. The one on the left, a little distance from the others, was starkly bare, save for a tiny wooden statue of the Virgin and a rush dip, presently extinguished.

He found himself holding his breath, and forced himself to walk normally, footsteps echoing on the boards.

There was a single blanket on the ticking, neatly spread, but speckled with straw. Heaps of matted straw lay around each mattress like a nest; the grooms must pull hay over themselves for extra warmth. No wonder; his breath was white, and the chill of the place numbed his fingers.

The impulse to lift the lid of the box and see what lay within was nearly irresistible. But he had done enough to Jamie Fraser; to intrude into this last small bastion of his privacy would be unforgivable.

With this realization came another; it wouldn't do. Even to leave the note atop the crate, or discreetly placed beneath the blanket, which had been his first thought, would let Fraser know that Grey had been here – an intimacy in itself that the man would find an unwelcome violation.

'Well, damn it all anyway,' he muttered to himself, and going down the ladder, found a bucket to stand on and pinned the note above the lintel of the tack room, in plain sight, but high enough that only Fraser would be able to reach it easily.

He looked up toward the fells as he left the stable, searching for horsemen, but nothing showed save rags of drifting fog.

Chapter 21

Cowardice

The sailing had been put back two weeks because all of the necessary food and equipment had not yet arrived. Grey arrived at Percy's rooms at nightfall, soaking wet and chilled to the bone from a day spent shivering in the rain on the docks, negotiating the terms under which the goddamned chandler from Liverpool would actually deliver the barrels of salt pork for which he had been contracted, and the terms under which the ship's crew – contracted to carry said barrels – would actually load the goddamned barrels into the goddamned hold of the goddamned ship and batten down the goddamned hatches on top of them.

Percy rubbed him dry, gave him fresh clothes, made him lie on the bed, listened to his grievances, and poured him a brandy, which made him think that perhaps he wouldn't die just yet.

'Do you suppose fighting will be easier than the struggle to get to the battlefield?' Percy asked.

'Yes,' Grey said, with conviction, and sneezed. 'Much easier.'

Percy laughed, and went down to fetch supper

from the tavern on the corner, returning with bread, cheese, ale, and a pot of something purporting to be oyster stew, which was at least hot.

Grey began to emerge from his condition of sodden misery, enough to talk a little and take note of his surroundings. To his surprise, he saw that Percy had been drawing; a cheap artist's block and charcoal had been pushed to one side, the top sheet showing the view from the window, roughed in, but rendered with considerable skill and delicacy.

'This is very good,' he said, picking it up. 'I didn't know you could draw.'

Percy shrugged, nonchalant, but clearly pleased by his praise.

'One of my mother's friends was an artist. He showed me a few things – though warning me that to become an artist was the only certain way to starve.'

Grey laughed, and mellowed by fire, hot food, and ale, made no demur when Percy turned to a clean sheet of paper and began to sketch Grey's features.

'Go ahead and talk,' Percy murmured. 'I'll tell you if I need you to be still.'

'Whatever do you want a drawing of me for?'

Percy looked up from his work, brown eyes warm but serious in the candlelight.

'I want something of you to keep,' he said. 'Just in case.'

Grey stopped, then set down his cup.

'I don't mean to leave you,' he said quietly. 'Did you think I would?'

Percy held his eyes, a faint smile on his lips.

'No,' he said softly. 'But you are a soldier, John, and we are going to war. Does it never occur to you that you might be killed?'

Grey rubbed a knuckle over his mouth, disconcerted.

'Well . . . I suppose so. But I – to tell you the truth, I seldom think about it. After all, I might be run down in the street, or take a chill and die of pleurisy.' He put out a finger and lifted his soggy shirt, hung over a stool to dry before the fire.

'Yes, you might,' Percy said dryly, resuming his work. 'The regimental surgeon told me that ten times more men die of the flux or plague or infection than ever are killed by an enemy. No reason you shouldn't be one of them, now, is there?'

Grey opened his mouth to reply to this, but in fact, there was no good answer.

'I know,' Percy said, head bent over the paper. 'You don't think about that, either.'

Grey sighed, shifting a little.

'No,' he admitted. 'Are you worrying?'

Percy's teeth were set in his lip, his fingers making short, quick lines. After a moment, without looking up, he said suddenly, 'I don't want you to think me a coward.'

Oh, that was it. He ought to have known.

He was inclined to offer a simple reassurance, but hesitated. He had asked the same question, or something very like it, once. And Hector, his first lover, four years older and a seasoned soldier, had not given him the reassurance he'd asked for, but rather the honesty he'd needed. He couldn't offer Percy less.

'It's sometimes not so bad,' he said, slowly, 'and sometimes it's very terrible. And the truth is that you'll never know what it's going to be like – and you never know what you'll do.'

Percy glanced up at him, eyes bright with interest.

'Have you ever run away?'

'Yes, of course. Doing your duty doesn't mean standing in front of a battery and being killed. Usually,' he added as an afterthought. 'And you must try to save your men, above all. If that means retreat, then you do – unless ordered to stand. If you do run, though, don't drop your weapon. Firstly, you'll likely bloody need it – and secondly, the quartermaster will stop the cost of it from your pay.'

Percy flipped open his sketchbook and set his pencil to the page, frowning intently.

'Wait, let me get that down. *Primum:* save . . . men. *Secundo:* do not . . . drop . . . weapon. *Tertio –* what's the third thing on this list?'

'Suck my prick,' Grey said rudely. 'Ass.'

Percy promptly flipped the sketchbook shut and came toward him, eyes brighter still.

'Wait! I didn't mean it!'

'Just following orders,' Percy murmured, pinning him to the bed with a deft knee on his thigh, and getting a hand on his flies. 'Sir.'

The brief and undignified struggle that followed – filled with muffled accusations of insubordination, high-handedness, disobedience, arrogance, contumacy, despotism, mutiny, and tyranny – ended in a truce that left the respective parties on the floor, breathless, flushed, disheveled, panting, and entirely satisfied with the negotiated terms of surrender.

Feeling boneless but peaceful, Grey struggled up from the floor and crawled onto the bed, where he lay half dozing as Percy tidied up the scattered remnants of their supper.

'Are you brave, John?' Percy drew a blanket over him, and kissed his forehead.

'No,' he said, without hesitation. 'The only time I ever *did* act from what I thought was courage ended in disaster.'

He was astonished to hear his own voice saying this.

He'd told the whole story – perforce – to Hal at the time, though he would infinitely have preferred to be shot for desertion or flogged at the triangle than do so. He could still remember Hal's face during that telling: relief, dismay, fury, laughter, renewed fury, and – damn him – sympathy, all shifting through his fine-boned face like water over rocks. And the rocks beneath – the deep-cut lines and smudges of exhaustion, signs of the sleepless night Hal had spent searching for him.

He'd never told anyone else, and felt for an instant as though he were on a sled, about to plunge down a steep, snowy slope with an icy abyss at its foot. But Percy's weight sank the mattress beside him, and his hand was warm on Grey's back.

'It was my first campaign,' he said, with a deep breath. 'The Stuart Rising. I hadn't got my commission yet; Hal took me with the regiment into Scotland, to have a taste of soldiering.'

Which he'd taken to like a duck to water. He'd loved the rough camp life, the routines and drills, the intoxicating scents of steel and black powder. The exciting sense of danger as they marched upward, pressed on into the bleak crags and dark pines of the Highlands, the men drawing closer, becoming more watchful, as civilization faded behind them. Most of all, the simple pleasure of the company of men, and the sense of himself as one of them.

He was quick, eager, and comfortable with weapons; had been taught to use a sword nearly as soon as he could stand, and to hunt with both gun and bow. He'd quickly made a place for himself as a forager and scout, and the men's wary regard of him as the colonel's younger brother ripened into a casual respect for him as a man. For a sixteen-year-old on his first campaign, it was more intoxicating than Holland gin.

He went out regularly with the other scouts, casting about in the evening to be sure there was no lurking threat as camp was made.

'Usually, we went out in pairs; I'd been out with a soldier named Jenks that evening. Decent fellow, but built like an ox. He'd get out of breath easily, and didn't care much for climbing in the steep mountains.' And so when Grey had thought he'd seen smoke, a half mile high above them in the Carryarick Pass, Jenks had assured him he hadn't.

'He might have been right; the light was going, and I couldn't be sure. We turned back to camp. But it niggled at me – what if I *had* seen it?'

And so he'd slipped out of camp after supper. Should have told someone, but didn't. He wasn't afraid of getting lost. And if it *was* nothing, he didn't want to be mocked for making a fuss or seeing shadows. He might have told Hector – but Hector had gone to the rear with a message for the captain of the Royal Artillery company that was traveling with them, bringing cannon for General Cope.

He did see shadows. Nearly three-quarters of a mile up the side of one of Scotland's crags, the wind brought him the scent of smoke. And creeping through brush and bracken, stealthy as a fox in the gathering gloom, he'd seen at last the flicker of a small fire and the movement of shadows against the trees of a clearing.

'And then I heard her voice. A woman's voice. An *Englishwoman's* voice.'

'What, on a mountainside in the Highlands?' Percy's voice reflected his own incredulity at the time. Even now, a decade and more past the Rising, the barbarian clansmen crushed or removed, the Highlands of Scotland remained a desolate wilderness. No one in his right mind would go there now

– save soldiers, whose duty it was. But a woman? Then?

He'd crept closer, sure his ears were deceiving him.

'It couldn't be Jacobite troops, in any case, I thought. It was only a single tiny fire. And when I got close enough to see . . .'

His heart had given such a lurch of excitement that he nearly choked on it. There was a man in the clearing, sitting on a log, relaxed.

He could so vividly recall his first sight of Jamie Fraser, and the fierce rush of emotions involved – alarm, panic, dizzying excitement. The hair, of course, first of all, the hair. Bound back loosely, not ginger but a deep red, a red like a stag's coat, but a red that glinted in the firelight as the man bent to push another stick into the fire.

The size of the man, and the sense of power in him. Plainly a Scot, by his dress, by his speech. He'd heard stories of Red Jamie Fraser – surely there couldn't be two like him. But was it, could it be, really?

He'd realized that he was holding his breath only when spots began to swim before his eyes. And, trying to breathe silently, had seen the woman come into view on the far side of the fire.

She *was* an Englishwoman, he could see it at once. More than that, a lady. A tall woman, crudely dressed, but with the skin, the carriage, the refined features of a noblewoman. And certainly the voice. She was addressing the man crossly; he laughed.

She called him by name – by God, it *was* Jamie Fraser! And through his haze of panic and excitement, Grey made out the man's reply and realized with horror that he was making indecent insinuations to the woman, stating a plain intent to take her to his bed. He had kidnapped her, then – and dragged her to this distant spot in order to dishonor her without the possibility of rescue or interference.

Grey's first impulse had been to retire quietly through the brush, then tear down the mountain as fast as possible and run back to camp to fetch some men to apprehend Fraser. But the presence of the Englishwoman altered everything. He dare not leave her in the Scot's grasp. He had so far had one experience in a brothel, and knew just how quickly immoral transactions could be accomplished. By the time he got back with help, it would be far too late.

He was sure his heartbeat must be audible at a distance, hard as it was hammering in his own ears.

'I'd come armed, of course.' He kept his eyes fixed on the ceiling, as though the egg-and-dart molding told some gripping tale. 'A pistol and a dagger in my belt.'

But he hadn't loaded the pistol. Cursing himself silently, he'd grappled for a moment with the problem: risk the delay of loading, the sound of the shot, plus the possibility of missing, or use the dagger?

'You didn't think of taking him prisoner?' Percy asked curiously. 'Rather than trying to kill him?'

'I did, yes,' Grey said, a slight edge to his voice.

'But I was reasonably sure that his own men were somewhere nearby. He was well known, one of the Scottish chiefs; the clans were gathering – he wouldn't be alone at all, if it weren't for the woman.

'And it was dark, *and* the clearing was completely surrounded by forest. You've never seen a Scottish pine forest – two steps into the trees, and a man has vanished from sight. If I tried to take him prisoner, he might either shout for help – and I certainly couldn't take on a horde of clansmen – or simply dive into the brush and be gone. Which would leave me and the woman as sitting ducks; his men would be on us long before I could get her down off the bloody mountain. But if I could kill him quietly, I thought, then I could get her away to safety before anyone knew. So I drew my dagger.'

'That's what you meant about courage.' Percy's hand tightened on his shoulder. 'My God, I wouldn't have had the nerve even to think of doing something like that!'

'Well, you would have been a good deal more intelligent than I was, then,' Grey said dryly.

His face felt hot, flushed both with embarrassment at the memory and with the memory itself, of blood pounding through his body at the prospect of his first kill.

He'd marked out the distance carefully – three paces, to be covered at a bound. Then fling his arm round the man's head and pull it back, rip the dagger hard across the stretched throat. That's what Sergeant O'Connell had instructed them to do, taking an enemy unawares in close quarters. They'd practiced, he and several of the younger soldiers, taking it in turn to play victim or killer. He knew just what to do.

'So I did it,' he said, with a sigh. 'I flung my arm round his head – and it wasn't there anymore. Next thing I knew, I was somersaulting through the air.'

The dagger went flying from his sweating fingers. He slammed hard into the earth and something fell on him. He'd fought back by instinct, dazed and breathless, but knowing that he fought for his life. Kicked, punched, clawed, bit – and for the most part, encountered only empty air.

Meanwhile, some elemental force had set about him, and a bone-cracking blow to the ribs drove the rest of the breath out of him. He reached out blindly, something grabbed his arm with a grip of steel and twisted it up his back. He lunged upward in panic, and his arm had snapped like a stick.

'Well . . . the long and the short of it is that the Englishwoman turned out to be Fraser's *wife,* curse her. And I, for my pains, ended up tied to a tree and left for my brother's men to find in the morning.'

'Jesus! All night, you were there? With your arm broken? You must have been in torment!'

'Well, yes,' Grey admitted reluctantly. 'It was more the biting midges, though. And needing desperately to have a pee. I didn't really notice the arm much.' He didn't mention the searing pain of the burn along the edge of his jaw, where Fraser had laid the hot blade of his dirk – or his raw back, where he'd rubbed most of the skin off, trying to free himself. None of this bodily discomfort had seemed important, by contrast with the agony of mind occasioned by the realization of the depth of the betrayal he had been led into.

'Meanwhile—' He cleared his throat, determined to finish. 'Meanwhile, Fraser and his men had crept round behind the camp, to the artillery park, taken all the wheels off the cannon, and burnt them. Using information I'd given them.'

Percy had been looking at him with sympathy. At this last confession, his mouth fell open. For an instant, shock showed in his eyes. Then he reached over and took Grey's left arm in both hands, feeling gently through the shirt. The bone was lumpy, where it had healed.

'What did he do to you?' Percy asked quietly. 'This Fraser?'

'It doesn't matter,' Grey said, a little gruffly. 'I should have let him kill me.' He had in fact been convinced that Fraser *did* mean to kill him – and hadn't spoken. The truth . . . well, he'd told Hal. He shut his eyes, but didn't pull his arm away. Percy's hands were warm, his thumbs gently stroking along the bone.

'It was the woman,' he said, resigned to complete humiliation. 'He threatened her. And I – idiot that I was – spoke, in order to save her.'

'Well, what else could you do?' Percy said, his tone so reasonable that Grey opened his eyes and stared at him. Percy smiled a little.

'Of course you would protect the woman,' he said. 'You protect everyone, John – I don't suppose you can help it.'

Astonished, Grey opened his mouth to contest this absurd statement, but was forestalled when Percy leaned forward and kissed him softly.

'You are the bravest man I know,' Percy said, his breath warm on Grey's cheek. 'And you will not convince me otherwise. Still . . .' He sat back, surveying Grey with interest. 'I admit to surprise that you did become a soldier, after *that* experience.'

'My father was a soldier, so was Hal. I never thought of being anything else,' Grey said, truthfully. He managed a crooked smile. 'And you do see the world.'

Percy's face lighted at that.

'I've never been outside the British Isles. I've always wanted to see Italy – pity there's no fighting there. Shall I like Germany, do you think?'

Grey recognized Percy's attempt to leave the subject of his humiliation, and gave him a look saying as much – but accepted it, nonetheless.

'Probably, if you don't catch the flux. The beer is very good. But as to Italy – perhaps we will go there. In the winter, when the campaigning is done. I should like very much to show you Rome.'

'Oh, I should like that of all things! You have been there – what do you recall most vividly?'

Grey blinked. In truth, his impressions of Rome were largely jumbles of ancient stone: the flat black paviors of the Appian Way, the marble baths of

Caracalla, the dark, grease-smelling pits of the cata-
combs, their heaps of dusty brown skulls seeming as
much a part of the cave as the rock itself.

'The seagulls on the Tiber,' he said suddenly.
'They call all night long, in Rome. You hear their
cries ringing from the stones of the streets. It's
strangely moving.'

'Seagulls?' Percy looked incredulous. 'There are
seagulls on the Thames, for God's sake.' Grey
glanced at the window, dark now, and streaked with
rain.

'Yes. It's ... different in Rome. You'll see,' he
said, and rising on his elbow, kissed Percy back.

Chapter 22

Shame

Life, as was its wont, became still busier. After their impromptu supper, Grey did not see Percy again for nearly a week, save for brief glimpses across the parade ground or a quick exchange of smiles as they passed in a corridor. He had no time to wish for more. The pressure of events was increasing, day by day, and he could feel responsibility wrapped like a strangling vine about his spinal cord, reaching eager fingers into the base of his skull.

He hadn't been home in three days, and was living exclusively on stale coffee, Cornish pasties, and the odd gulp of brandy. Something, he thought, was going to snap. He hoped it would be only his temper, when the time came, and not someone else's neck.

The tension was not limited to Grey, nor even to the officers. In the men, it was manifested as anticipation and exuberance, but with a nervous edge that gave rise to quarrels and petty conflicts, fights over misplaced equipment and borrowed whores. These were for the most part ignored, dealt with summarily by the sergeants, or settled privately between the aggrieved parties. But some things necessarily became public matters.

Two days before they began the march to Gravesend for embarkation, four companies were summoned to the square to witness a punishment. Crime, theft. Sentence, a hundred lashes – sentence reduced to fifty by the commanding officer, to insure that the man would be fit to march out with his companions.

Percy Wainwright was the lieutenant in charge, the commanding officer, though punishment was attended, as usual, by several senior officers – Grey among them.

He disliked the process, but understood its necessity. Usually, he simply stood, face impassive and eyes focused somewhere beyond what was happening. This time, though, he watched Percy.

Everything went smoothly. Percy seemed well in control of his men, the situation, and himself. And if he was white to the lips and openly sweating, that was nothing remarkable in a young commander performing this office for the first time.

Percy's eyes were fixed on the process, and despite himself, Grey could not help following them. It was not severe, as such things went, though the man's back was welted and bloody after a dozen strokes. Grey watched the rhythmic swing of the cat, heard the sergeant's chanted count, and began, with a sudden sense of disorientation, to feel the impact of each blow in the pit of his stomach.

He fought the impulse to close his eyes.

He began to feel ill, the residue of his black-coffee breakfast churning inside him, rising up at the back of his throat. He was sweating, and fighting the sudden illusion that it was rain that ran down his face and neck.

His eyes were still open, but it was no longer the spring sunshine of the parade ground he saw, nor the stocky young soldier, groaning and flinching at each blow. He stood in the gray stone yard of Ardsmuir Prison, and saw rain run gleaming over straining shoulders, run mixed with blood down the deep groove of Jamie Fraser's back.

He swallowed back bile and looked at his boots. Stood quietly, breathing, until it was finished.

The man was taken down from the triangle, helped away by his friends to the surgeon for a lathering of goose-grease and charcoal. Companies dismissed, leaving in an orderly fashion, quiet, as men tended to be after witnessing punishment. But when Grey turned to look for Percy, he had vanished.

Supposing that he required a moment's privacy – he'd looked as though he were about to vomit, too – Grey returned to his own work, but made a point of coming back later, to inquire casually how Percy did, perhaps offer a drink or advice, as needed.

He did not find Percy in any of the places a second lieutenant would normally be. Surely he had not simply left and gone home to his rooms in Audley Street? Not without telling anyone, Grey thought, and no one recalled seeing him after the flogging.

It took quite a bit of casual wandering about, poking into this and that, before he finally found Percy, in one of the storage sheds behind the parade ground, where spare equipment was kept.

'All right?' he inquired, seeing Percy sitting on a mounting-block. It was a bright day, and sunlight fell through the boards of the shed, striping him with red where the light caught his uniform coat.

'Yes. Just thinking.' Percy's face was in shadow, but his voice was calm.

'Ah. Don't let me interrupt, then.' Grey reached for the door, but wasn't surprised when Percy stood up.

'No, don't go. It was good of you to come look for me.' He put his arms round Grey for a moment, bending his head so that their cheeks brushed.

Grey stiffened for an instant, surprised and half-alarmed – but it was quiet outside; the parade ground was empty, everyone bustling to finalize their preparations for departure. He returned the embrace, comforted by the touch, arousal stimulated by the sense of danger – but then stepped back.

'Quite sure you're all right?' Percy had stopped sweating, and was no longer white, but was plainly still disturbed in mind. He nodded, though.

'That – reducing the sentence – was that all right?' he asked.

'Under the circumstances.' Grey paused, hand on the jamb. 'Do you need a moment?'

Percy shrugged, and moved restlessly round the confines of the shed, kicking at things.

'This – what's it called?'

'A whirligig.' A cylindrical cage made of slats, with a door in one side. It was used for minor punishments, lateness or missing equipment. 'You put a man inside, and two men spin it round.'

'Do you – do we – use these often?' Percy nudged the toe of his boot at the horse, a wooden thing like a child's rocking-horse – save that the back was not flat, but rose to a ridge.

'It depends.' Grey watched him, saw the disturbance in him, his usual grace lost as he moved about, restless, unable to settle. He felt the echo of it in his own flesh, and coughed, trying to dispel it. 'Some officers use punishment a great deal; others not so much. And sometimes there's no help for it.'

Percy nodded, but without looking at him. He stood for a few moments, looking at the shelves that ran along one wall, where various bits of equipment were stored. There were two baize bags there, where the cats were kept.

'Did you ever wonder what it's like?' he asked suddenly. 'To be flogged?'

Grey felt a clenching in his innards, but answered honestly.

'Yes. Now and then.' Once, at least.

Percy had been kneading one of the red baize bags, like a cat sharpening its claws. Now he let it fall to the floor, and took up the cat-o'nine-tails itself, a short handle with a cluster of leather cords.

'Do you want to find out?' he said, very softly.

'What?' An extraordinary feeling ran through Grey, half-fear, half-excitement.

'Take off your coat,' Percy said, still softly.

In a state of something like shock, Grey found his hand go to the buttons of his waistcoat. He felt as though sleepwalking, not believing any of it – that Percy had suggested it, that he was doing it. Then his shirt was off, and gooseflesh rose on his back and shoulders.

'Turn around,' Percy said, and he did, facing the horse.

The cords struck across his shoulders like the sting of a jellyfish, sharp and sudden. His hands closed tight on the horse's back.

'Again,' he said, half breathless.

He heard Percy shift his weight, felt his interest shift as well, from the sense of nervous excitement to something more.

'Sure?' said Percy softly.

He bent a little forward and spread his arms, taking a fresh grip, exposing the full reach of his bare back. The stroke caught him just below the shoulderblades, with a force that drove the breath out of him and stung to the tips of his fingers.

'More?' The word was whispered. He could feel Percy's breath, warm on the back of his neck, feel him close, the touch of a hand light on the naked skin of his waist.

God, don't touch me! he thought, and felt his

stomach clench as his gorge rose. But what he said, hoarse and low was, 'Again. Don't stop.'

Three more blows, and Percy stopped. Grey turned round to see him gripping the cat in both hands, face white.

'I've cut you. I'm sorry.'

He could feel the weal, a vivid line that ran from his right shoulderblade, angled down across the center of his back. It felt as though someone had pressed a hot wire into his skin.

'Don't be,' he said. 'I asked.'

'Yes, but—' Percy had seized his shirt, draped it across his bare shoulders. 'I shouldn't have started it. It – I didn't mean – I'm sorry.'

'Don't be,' Grey said again. 'You wanted to know. So did I.'

He dreamed of it, the night before they left.

Felt himself bound, and the dread of shame. Pain, disfigurement – but most of all, shame. That a gentleman should find himself in such case, exposed.

The men were drawn up in their square, eyes front. But he realized slowly that they were not looking at him. Somehow he became separate, and felt profound relief that after all it was not him.

And yet he felt the blows, grunting with each one, like a beast.

Saw the man taken down at the end, dragged away by two men who held his arms across their shoulders, his own feet stumbling as though he were drunk. Saw a stark-boned face gone slack with exhaustion, eyes closed and the water running, dripping, face shimmering with it, his hair nearly black, so saturated as it was with sweat and rain.

Spreading ointment across the torn and furrowed skin, his fingers thick with it so as to touch as lightly as possible. Fierce heat radiated from the man's back, though the skin of his arms was cool, damp with drying sweat. Picked up a linen towel to blot the sweat from the man's neck, untied the thong that bound his soaked hair and began to rub it dry.

He felt the hum of some tune in throat and chest, and felt great happiness as he worked. The man said nothing; he did not expect it. He smoothed the long thick strands of half-dry hair between his fingers, and wiped the curve of ears that reminded him of a small boy's, heartbreaking in their tenderness.

Then he realized that he was straddling the man, and that they were both naked. The man's buttocks rose beneath him, smooth and round and powerful, perfect by contrast with the bloody back. And warm. Very warm.

Woke with a dreadful feeling of shame, heavy in his belly. The sound of dripping water in his ears.

The dripping of rain. The drip of sweat, of blood and seed. Not tears. The man had never wept, even in extremity.

Yet his pillow was wet. The tears were his.

Through the rest of the day, as he rode at the head of the marching column, as they passed

through the streets of London, and down to the
Pool where they would embark, he would now and
then brush his fingers lightly beneath his nose,
expecting each time to catch a whiff of the
medicated salve.

Chapter 23

The Rhineland

Tom Byrd was in his element. He circled Grey like a vulture round a prime bit of carrion, visibly gloating.

'Very nice, me lord,' he said with approval, reaching out to tweak a small fold out of the buff lapel of Grey's best dress uniform, straighten the edge of a six-inch cuff, or rearrange the fall of an epaulet cord. 'Don't you think he looks well, sir?' He appealed to Percy, who was lounging against the wall, watching Grey's apotheosis.

'I am blinded by his glory,' Percy assured Tom gravely. 'He'll be a credit to you, I'm sure.'

'No, he won't,' Tom said, standing back with a sigh. 'He'll have gravy spilt down his ruffles before the evening's out. That, or he'll take a bet from someone and jump that big white bastard of a horse over a wall with his arms crossed, and fall off into a bog. Again. Or—'

'I did not fall off,' Grey said, affronted. 'The horse slipped when we landed, and rolled on me.'

'Well, it did your clothes no good at all, me lord,' Tom said severely. He leaned closer, breathed heavily on a silver button, and polished it obsessively with his sleeve.

Grey was indeed splendid, got up regardless, with his hair tightly plaited, folded round a lamb's-wool pad, bound in a club, and powdered. Boots, buttons, and sword hilt gleaming, and his officer's gorget polished to a brilliant shine, he was the very model of a British soldier. It was largely wasted effort; no one would look twice at an English officer in a room full of Prussians and Hanoverians, whose officers, even when not royalty or nobility, tended to a great deal of gold lace, embroidery, and plumes. He stood stiffly, hardly daring to breathe, as Tom prowled round him, looking for something else to poke at.

'Oh, I want to go to the ball, too!' Percy said, mocking.

'No, you don't,' Grey assured him. 'It will be speeches half the night, of the most pompous sort, and an endless procession of roast peacocks with their feathers on, gilded trout, and similar glorious inedibles.'

He would, in fact, much prefer a supper of eggs and beans in his tent with Tom and Percy. Normally, a mere major would not be invited to the dinner which celebrated the joining together of the new allied Hanoverian army under His Grace, Duke Ferdinand of Brunswick.

Hal must go, of course, not only as an earl in his own right – though English earls were small beer by comparison to the margraves, landgraves, electors, and princes who would be in attendance – but as colonel of his own regiment. Grey was invited because he was Melton's brother, but also because he was acting as lieutenant-colonel of the regiment, in the absence of the officer who normally fulfilled that office, who had succumbed to food poisoning halfway across the Channel. It would not do for Hal to appear in such august company completely unattended. Ewart Symington had pleaded indisposition – Symington did not speak German and hated social occasions – and so Grey and his best uniform were being pressed into service.

'Are you ready?' Hal poked his own powdered head in, inquiring.

'As I'll ever be,' Grey said, straightening himself. 'Tom, you won't forget about the bottles?'

'Oh, no, me lord,' Tom assured him. 'You can count on me.'

'Well, then.' He crooked an arm toward his brother, and bowed. 'Shall we dance?'

'Ass,' said Hal, but tolerantly.

The feast, held in the ancient guildhall, was exactly as Grey had predicted: long, eye-glazingly boring, and featuring course after course of roast pork, boiled beef, gravied mutton, roasted pheasants, sliced ham, braised quail, grilled fish, eggs in aspic and in pies, shellfish in soup, in pastry, and on the half shell, plus sundry savories, syllabubs, and sweets, all served on a weight of silver plate sufficient to purchase a small country and washed down with gallons of wine, drunk in a succession of endless toasts in honor of everyone from Frederick, King of Prussia, King George of England, and Duke Ferdinand down to – Grey was sure – the kitchen cat, though by the time this point in the proceedings was reached, no one was paying sufficient attention as to be sure.

The German officers were indeed splendid. Grey particularly noticed a tall, blond young Hanoverian, whose uniform was that of his friend von Namtzen's regiment – though von Namtzen himself was nowhere in sight. Contriving to have speech of the young lieutenant before dinner – and wondering to himself how the man came to be at such an affair – he learned that the young man's name was Weber, and that he was there as attendant to a senior officer of von Namtzen's Imperial Hanoverian Foot, owing to an outbreak of some plague amongst the regiment that had temporarily rendered most of the other senior officers *hors de combat*.

'Is Captain von Namtzen also afflicted?' Grey asked, covertly admiring the man's face, which, with its deep-set blue eyes and sensual mouth, looked like that of an angel thinking lewd thoughts.

Weber shook his head, a small frown marring the perfection of his features.

'Alas, no.'

'Alas?' Grey echoed, surprised.

'The captain suffered an accident, late in the autumn,' Weber explained. 'No more than a scratch, while hunting – but it festered, you know, and his *Blut* was poisoned, so the doctors had to take it off.'

'Take *what* off?'

'Oh, *Entschuldigung,* I am not clear.' Weber bowed in apology, and Grey caught a whiff of his cologne, something spiced and warm. 'It was his arm he has lost. His left arm,' he added, in the interests of strict accuracy.

Grey swallowed, shocked.

'I am so sorry to hear this,' he said. 'The captain – he is recovering?'

'Oh, *ja,*' Weber assured him, turning his head a little as the gong began to sound as signal for the men to take their seats. 'He is at his lodge. He will perhaps be well enough to join the campaign in another month. We hope so.' His eyes lingered on Grey's in friendly fashion. 'We meet again soon, perhaps?'

Grey nodded, and went to find Hal, unsettled by the news about von Namtzen, but glad to hear that at least Stephan was recovering. Just inside the door of the guildhall, a phalanx of trumpeters raised their horns and blew a salute that ruffled the banners that hung from the ceiling, announcing the ceremonious arrival of Duke Ferdinand.

'Well, now we're for it,' Hal muttered, watching a servant fill his glass in preparation for the first toast.

'Here is to our glorious victory!' said the man beside him in German, beaming.

'Here's to us being able to walk out of here without help,' Hal replied in English, smiling cordially.

The overall result of this affair was firstly that desired by the occasion – the introduction of the commanders to one another, and the creation of a sense of joint grandeur and invincibility. The secondary result was what might be expected after three hours of continuous drinking of toasts, during which it would be considered unthinkably discourteous for anyone to leave the table.

Grey was beginning to suffer serious discomfort, and to be sure that Tom had forgotten after all, when he felt the servant who stood behind his chair turn aside for a moment, then lean over. He moved his foot gently and found the empty magnum that had been placed beneath his chair.

'Thank you,' Grey said, in heartfelt relief. He grinned across the table at Hal, who was also looking somewhat tense, though keeping up appearances nobly. 'Do the same for my brother, would you?'

It was well past midnight by the time the dinner was concluded, and the commanders and senior officers of the allied Hanoverian army staggered out into the cool spring night, most of them dashing for the nearest sheltering wall or tree.

The Greys, in no such need, strolled with smug insouciance through the dark streets toward the inn where they were quartered, talking randomly of the evening, the personalities encountered, and their private opinions regarding the history, ability, and expected effectiveness of the aforementioned.

Grey was filled with a pleasant sense of well

being, brought on by two or three quarts of wine and spirits, and a sense of anticipation regarding the coming campaign. It was true that he and Percy would not have the sort of intimacy they had been allowed in London – but they would be in each other's company, sharing adventure and a camaraderie of the spirit. As for that of the body . . . well, opportunity did occur now and then – and at the worst, they had winter to look forward to, and the privacy and freedom of Rome.

Buoyed by these pleasant thoughts and the brilliant light of a full moon, it was some time before he realized that Hal was not sharing his elation, but was pacing along with his head down, evidently weighed down by some preoccupation.

'What's the matter?' Grey asked. 'Were we slighted in some manner that I didn't notice?'

'What?' Hal glanced at him, surprised. 'Oh. No, of course not. I was only thinking that I wished it had been France.'

'Well, France has its advantages,' Grey said judiciously, 'quite aside from the fact that it's full of Frenchmen. But I think we'll do well enough here.'

'Ass,' Hal said again, though without heat. 'It's nothing to do with the campaign; that's all right – we may be in the minority here, but I think we shall have a good deal more autonomy under Ferdinand than we might under Frederick. No,' he continued, frowning at the uneven cobbles in the street, 'I wanted France because of the Jacobite exiles there.'

'Oh?' The word 'Jacobite' pricked a hole in the

soap bubble of Grey's intoxication, and he put out a hand to ward off a passing tree. 'Why?'

He hadn't told Hal anything regarding his inquiries of Jamie Fraser; no need, unless they came to something. They had seen Sir George and Lady Stanley safely embarked for Havana, the week before their own sailing, and in the frantic rush of embarkation, Grey had not spared a single thought for the puzzle surrounding his father's death. No more journal pages had surfaced; no further attacks had been made. The whole business seemed to have vanished, as suddenly as it had begun.

'Nothing, probably. Only I had a name or two, from Bath—'

'Bath?' Grey said, stumbling slightly. 'What the bloody hell is in Bath?'

Hal glanced at him, then made a small gesture of resignation.

'Victor Arbuthnot,' he said.

For a few moments, Grey could not place the name, but then it came to him.

'Father's old friend? The one he did astronomy with?'

Hal snorted.

'He may have done astronomy, but his friendship is questionable. He was the man who presumably denounced Father as a Jacobite conspirator.'

'He – what?' Grey came to an abrupt halt, staring. The moon was bright enough that his brother's face was fully visible. He could see that Hal was at least as drunk as he was, though still able to walk and speak. 'You found him – and you let him live?'

Hal waved a hand impatiently, nearly over-balanced, and gripped a tree.

'Arbuthnot swears he did not. He gave a statement, yes, and bitterly regrets it. I might have done it, too, if they'd done to me what they did to him.' Hal's jaw tightened a little as he swallowed. 'He admitted to being a Jacobite himself, to conspiring with Catholics from Italy and from Ireland, thinking it was safe enough to give their names – but he swears he gave no names of men within England; no one who could be taken up and questioned. And definitely not Father.'

Grey didn't bother asking why Hal believed Arbuthnot. Plainly he did, and Hal was not a fool.

'Then how does he explain—'

'He doesn't know. He didn't write the statement himself – he couldn't.' Hal's mouth twisted. 'He only signed it – with a man named Bowles tenderly guiding his hand, he said.'

'Bowles,' Grey said slowly. His own insides had surged at the name, and he swallowed several times, to make sure they stayed put. 'You . . . know this Bowles?'

Hal shook his head. 'Harry does. Small sadist with a face like a pudding, he says. Intelligencer. You've met him?'

'Once,' Grey said, and pulled at his stock, wanting air. 'Just the once.'

'Yes, well, I don't know what he is now, and

Arbuthnot didn't know what he was then – an assistant of some kind, Arbuthnot said. I sent Mr. Beasley to look for the original statement,' Hal added abruptly. 'Not to be found.'

'Secret? Or destroyed?'

'Don't know. He couldn't find anybody who would admit even to having seen the thing.'

And yet that statement was the basis for the warrant of arrest issued for Gerard Grey, first Duke of Pardloe. The warrant that had never been served.

'Jesus.' They had stopped walking, and without the flow of air across his face, Grey felt his gorge rising. 'I think I'm going to puke.'

He did, and stayed bent over for a minute, hands on his thighs, breathing heavily. The purging seemed to have helped, though; he was somewhat light-headed when he stood up, but his mind seemed clearer.

'You said, "definitely not Father." Do you – or does he, rather – mean that Father *was* a Jacobite, but Arbuthnot didn't denounce him? Or that he wasn't a Jacobite at all?'

'Naturally he wasn't a Jacobite,' Hal said, angry. 'What are you saying?'

'Well, if he wasn't – and you know that for a fact – why do you want to talk to Jacobites in France?' He stared at Hal, whose face was pallid in the moonlight, his eyes dark holes.

'He wasn't,' Hal repeated stubbornly. 'I just – I just – wait.' He swallowed visibly, and Grey could see the sheen of sweat on his brow.

Grey nodded, and sat down on a low wall, trying not to hear the retching noises; his own stomach hadn't quite settled yet, and he felt pale and clammy.

A few minutes later, Hal came back out of the shadows and sat down heavily beside him.

'Damned oysters,' he said. 'You oughtn't to eat oysters in a month without an "R" in it, everyone knows that.' Grey nodded, forbearing to point out that it was March, and they sat still for a time, a cold breeze drying the sweat on their faces.

'You could have told me, Hal,' Grey said quietly. They were sitting on the wall of a churchyard, and the shadow of the church itself covered them in darkness. He could no longer see Hal as anything save an indistinct blur, but could sense him and hear him breathing.

Hal didn't answer for some time, but finally said, 'Told you what?'

'Told me that Father was murdered.' He swallowed, tasting wine and bile. 'I – should have liked to be able to speak of it with you.'

He felt the shift of Hal's weight as his brother turned toward him.

'*What* did you say?' Hal whispered.

'I said why could you not have *told* me – oh. Oh, Jesus.' His bones turned to water, as he belatedly grasped the horror in his brother's question. 'Jesus, Hal. You didn't *know*?'

His brother was absolutely silent.

'You didn't know,' Grey said, voice shaking as he

answered his own question. He turned toward Hal, wondering where the words had come from; he hadn't any breath at all. 'You thought he killed himself. I thought you knew. I thought you always knew.'

He heard Hal draw breath, slowly.

'How do you know this?' Hal said, very calmly.

'I was there.'

Hardly knowing what he said for the roaring in his ears, he told the story of that summer dawn in the conservatory, and the smell of the smashed peach. Heard the echo of that first telling, felt the ghost of Percy warm beside him.

At some point, he realized dimly that Hal's face was wet with tears. He didn't realize that he was weeping, as well, until Hal fumbled in his sleeve by reflex, pulled out a handkerchief, and handed it to him.

He mopped his face, scarcely noticing what he did.

'I thought – I was sure that Mother had told you. And that the two of you then had decided that I wasn't to know. You sent me to Aberdeen.'

Hal was shaking his head, back and forth, like an automaton; Grey could feel, rather than see it, though he made out the movement when Hal wiped his nose heedlessly on his sleeve. It occurred briefly to Grey that he didn't think he'd seen his brother cry since the death of his first wife.

'That . . . that cunning old . . . oh, God. That bloody woman. How could she? And alone – all these years, alone!' Hal covered his face with both hands.

'Why?' Grey felt breath beginning to move in his chest again. 'Why in God's name would she not tell you? I understand her wishing to keep the truth from me, given my age, but – you?'

Hal was beginning to get himself under control, though his voice still cracked, going raggedly from one emotion to another, relief succeeded by dismay, only to be replaced by horror, sorrow giving way to anger.

'Because she knew I'd go after the bastard. And, damn her, she thought he'd kill me, too.' Hal brought a fist down on the wall, making no sound. 'God *damn* it!'

'You think she knew who it was.' Spoken aloud, the words hung in the air between them.

'She knows at least who it might be,' Hal said at last. He stood up and picked up his hat. 'Let's go.'

The brothers walked the rest of the way in silence.

Chapter 24

Skirmish

As one of the battalion's two majors, Grey held responsibility for roughly four hundred troops. When the army was on the move, it was his duty to ensure that everyone turned up in the right place, more or less at the right time, suitably trained and equipped to do whatever they had been sent to do. As Hal's acting lieutenant-colonel, it was also his work to be actively in the field when the regiment was engaged, managing the logistics of battle, directing the movements of some twenty-six companies, and carrying out – to the best of his ability – such strategy and tactics as his orders gave him.

Through the entire month of April, the forces of Duke Ferdinand and his English allies had been on the move – but not engaged, owing to the cowardly disinclination of the Duc de Richelieu's French and Austrian troops to stand still and fight.

Consequently, the army had moved up, down, and sideways to the Rhine Valley for weeks, forcing the French gradually back toward their own border, but never managing to force an engagement.

Consequently, Grey's daily occupation consisted generally of sixteen hours of argument with Prussian sutlers, Hanoverian mule drivers, and English quartermasters, endless meetings, inspecting and approving – or not – each new campsite, housing, and culinary arrangement, dealing with outbreaks of flux and pox, and dictating orders to – and listening to the excuses for not following said orders – of twenty-six company commanders regarding the behavior, equipment, and disposition of their men.

Grey sought occasional relief from this tedium by going out on patrols with one or another company. The ostensible – and in fact the actual – purpose of this exercise was for him to judge the companies' readiness and the competence of their officers. So far as he was concerned, the principal benefit of such excursions was to keep him from losing either his temper or his mind.

He must rigorously avoid any appearance of favoritism, of course, and was in the habit of choosing which company to attend by dint of throwing a dart at the list hung on the wall of his tent. By the vagaries of chance, therefore, the lot did not fall on one of Lieutenant Wainwright's companies until late April.

He saw Percy himself often – they shared supper most evenings, whether in the officer's mess or privately, in Grey's tent – and of course inquired after his companies in the usual way – but most of their conversation was of a personal nature. He had not yet seen Percy work his men, save for drills, and thus went out on April 24 in a state of mingled anticipation and apprehension.

He rode a gelding called Grendel, whose mild temper belied his name, and the weather had obligingly adopted a similar disposition. The day was sunny and warm, and the men more than happy to be out and active. Percy was nervous, but hid it reasonably well, and everything went smoothly for most of the day. In early afternoon, though, the column found themselves perhaps six miles from camp, progressing along the edge of a bluff over the river.

The terrain was thickly wooded, but with a broad, grassy lip along the edge of the bluff, and a good breeze came up from the silver sheet of the Rhine below – a grateful relief to men who had made the steep climb up the bluff in full uniform and equipment. Then the wind changed, and Grendel's head came up, nostrils flaring. His ears went forward.

Grey reined up at once. Ensign Tarleton saw his movement and properly signaled the company to halt, which they did in a rather blundering, complaining fashion, muttering and stepping on each other's heels. Percy turned round to frown at them in rebuke.

'Tell your men to fall into firing order; I don't like something over there,' Grey said under his breath. He nodded at a copse, a hundred yards away. The wind was coming from that direction; it touched his face.

The other officers' horses were lifting their heads now, nickering uncertainly. Percy didn't ask questions but rose in his stirrups, calling orders. The sense of alarm spread like fire in straw; all complaint and disorder vanished in a moment, and the men snapped into a double line, their corporal shouting the orders to load.

A blast of musket fire burst from the copse, a stitchery of bright flashes through the trees and a sharp smell of powder smoke, borne on the breeze.

The men stood firm; Percy gave a quick glance down the line.

'No one hit,' he said, sounding breathless. 'Too far!'

Grey took one more fast look – good ground, open to the copse. It was a small copse; no chance of a regiment hiding in it. No artillery; if they'd had cannon, they'd have used it. Retreat or advance? The trail they'd come up was steep and rocky, a sheer drop to the river on one side, thicket on the other; infantry would cut them down, firing from the trailhead.

'They'll move closer. Charge them before they reload.' Grey had gathered his reins hastily into one hand as he spoke, preparing to draw his sword.

Instead, he was just in time to grab the reins of Percy's horse, as the latter threw them to him, slid to the ground, and bellowing, 'CHARGE!' at the top of his voice, rushed toward the copse on foot, grappling for the sword at his side.

The company, caught midway in reloading, flung

order and caution to the wind, abandoned the openmouthed corporal, and galloped after their lieutenant, roaring enthusiastically.

'Jesus Christ!' Grey said. 'Mr. Tarleton – stand fast!' Leaning across, he thrust both sets of reins into the ensign's startled hands, flung himself off, and ran – not after the charging company, but to the side, circling the copse.

He plunged into the trees, pistol in hand, trying to look everywhere at once. His worst fear – that there *was* a large company inside the copse – was dispelled at once; he caught sight of white uniforms, but no great mass of them. In fact, they seemed to have come upon a foraging party; Grey dodged round a bush and nearly collided with the group of donkeys whose scent had disturbed the horses, the small beasts heavily laden with nets of grass.

One donkey, equally startled, put back its ears, brayed shrilly, and snapped big yellow teeth an inch from his arm. He slapped it smartly across the nose and shoved through the brush, cursing his own idiocy, and that of the French commander, whoever the bloody-minded frog was.

What had possessed the Frenchman to fire on them at such distance? Sense would have been to keep quiet, or retreat unobtrusively through the trees. And why had *he* told Percy the French were coming toward them? More than likely, they had realized their folly and *were* about to retreat, being outnumbered and lightly armed.

As for Percy's idiocy . . . he could hear Percy

shouting somewhere ahead, hoarse and wildly elated. He had an overpowering desire to punch Lieutenant Wainwright, and hoped no Frenchman would deprive him of the chance to do so by killing Percy first.

A shriek came from his right and he jerked aside as someone charged him. Something tugged at his coat, pulling him off balance. He stumbled, grabbed at a tree branch to keep from falling, and fired by reflex at the man who had just tried to bayonet him.

The French soldier jerked, struck in the side, and turned the incredulous face of a young boy on him before falling. Grey swore silently to himself, teeth clenched as he reloaded. The boy wore a corporal's insignia; chances were that this fourteen-year-old nitwit was the commander of the foraging party.

He thrust the reloaded pistol into his belt, and picked up the musket the young corporal had dropped. The boy was still breathing; Grey could see his chest rise and fall. His eyes were closed, but his face was twitching with pain. Grey stood for an instant, hand on his pistol, then shook his head and turned again toward where he had last heard Percy's voice.

Percy's tactic had been unorthodox in the extreme – to say nothing of contravening every known principle of order and command – but it was amazingly successful. The dumbfounded French soldiers had been taken completely by surprise, and had scattered like geese. Most of them had fled – he could hear crashing at a distance – and the remainder were being efficiently felled by Percy's troops, quite off their heads at the ease of their first victory.

This was madness. The French should surrender at once, while there was something left to save – but of course, he'd just shot their commander; there was probably no one to surrender, or to call for it.

Just as he thought this, someone did. Percy, voice cracked from shouting, was yelling, 'Surrender, God damn you! You're beaten, for God's sake, give *up*!' He was shouting in English, of course.

Grey dashed aside a hanging branch, and was just in time to see Percy kill his first man.

A large French soldier feinted deftly to one side with his bayonet, then lunged upward with murderous intent. Percy lunged at the same moment, dropping into a perfect *Passata-sotto* – doubtless by accident, as he'd never been able to do it in practice. He looked completely astonished as the bayonet slid past his ear, and the point of his sword passed cleanly beneath the Frenchman's arm and into his body. The Frenchman looked still more astonished.

Percy let go of the sword, and the Frenchman took three small steps backward, almost daintily, sat down with a thump, and died, still looking surprised.

Percy walked away a short distance and vomited into a bush. Grey was watching him, and nearly missed the flicker of movement. He whirled by instinct, already swinging the musket by the barrel. The stock slammed the Frenchman – yes, white, he was French – in the back and knocked him sideways as the Frenchman's own gun went off with a bang and a bloom of black smoke.

Grey threw himself into the smoke and hit the man, shoulder first, fell with him, and rolled in the leaves. Came up gasping, punching, and yelling. Hit the man's face accidentally and felt something crunch in his hand; a shock ran up the bones of his arm and paralyzed it for an instant. The Frenchman's hand struck clawing at his face, caught him in the eye, and as he flinched back, the man twisted under him, seized his arm, and flung him off.

He hit the ground on hip and elbow. Eyes watering, he scrabbled one-handed for his dagger and thrust blindly up with all his strength. Cloth scraped his hand, body warmth and the reek of sweat, and he shoved as hard as he could through tearing cloth, hoping for flesh, fearing the jar of bone.

The man gave a gurgling scream, and staggered back. Grey covered his injured eye with one hand and through a haze of tears made out the Frenchman, doubled over, a dark stain in his crotch spreading beneath his clutching hands. Beyond him stood Percy, mouth open, pistol in hand.

'Will you fucking shoot the bastard?' Grey bellowed.

Like an automaton, Percy raised his pistol and did. He blinked at the sound of the shot, then stood, eyes wide, watching as the Frenchman fell slowly forward, still grasping his crotch, curling in on himself like a dried leaf.

'Thank you,' Grey said, and shut his eyes, pressing the heel of his hand hard into the injured socket. Colored pinwheels spun behind his eyelid, but the pain lessened.

After a moment, he took away his hand and rolled onto his hands and knees, where he paused for an instant, steadying himself, before being able to stand.

'Good,' he said to Percy, having got up at last. He sneezed and cleared his throat. 'That was good.'

'Was it?' Percy said faintly.

Both Grey's eyes were streaming and the injured one wouldn't stay open, but he could see well enough to summon the men back and begin to take stock. The French had fled, leaving six dead. The wounded, including the corporal, had either crawled into the brush or been dragged off by their companions; he was not disposed to spend time searching for them. He had Brett make a quick tally; no one injured, bar a slight wound in the thigh to Private Johnston, who was limping cheerfully round going through the pockets of the dead French.

Grey gave brisk orders for retirement – there was no telling how far the foraging party had been from their main company, nor how quickly they might return with reinforcements – and they collected the weapons and left, heading back to camp.

It was nearly dark when Grey returned at last to his tent, having sent out a scouting party, received reports from the regimental captains, waited for the scouting party's report, conferred with Ewart Symington, sent Ensign Brett with stiff remarks to the quartermaster regarding a cask of what purported to be salt beef, but which in fact appeared to be the remains of an extremely elderly horse, made his own report to Hal, and written orders for the next day, all with a wad of damp guncotton pressed over his wounded eye. His head throbbed, his hand hurt, and he was famished, but he felt happy nonetheless.

The same sense of anticipation and excitement that rose within his breast flowed through the camp around him; you could hear it in the scraping of whetstones, the clank of kettles and the singing. Soldiers nearly always sang in camp, save when completely exhausted or dispirited, but what they sang varied, and was a good indication of their feelings. Sentimental ballads and mangled bits of music hall were standard camp fare. Marching songs, not surprisingly, when marching.

But when anticipating battle, the songs tended to the comic and the bawdy, and the snatches he heard as he walked through the camp would have made a sailor blush. The news had spread. The French were close, and the troops smelt blood. He whistled under his breath as he walked.

He found Tom Byrd and Percy in his tent, conversing amiably. Both of them sprang up at once when they saw him and there was a certain amount of fuss made over the state of his eye, by Percy, and the state of his uniform, by Tom – who, once having satisfied himself that the eye had not actually been gouged out, seemed more concerned with a large tear in the skirt of the coat he had just shed.

'Look!' Tom thrust three fingers through the rent, and waggled them, looking accusingly at Grey. 'Gone right through the lining. What's done that, me lord – a sword?'

'I don't recall – oh, yes, I do. It was a bayonet.'

Tom inhaled, as though about to say something, but subsided, muttering, and set the coat aside.

'Sit yourself down, me lord,' he said, resigned. 'I'll fetch a bowl of barley water for your eye.'

Grey sank onto a camp stool, surprisingly glad to sit down. Appetizing smells of stew and hot bread drifted through the tent, and his stomach growled; he hadn't eaten since dawn. He hoped Tom would bring supper; the eye could wait a little longer.

'Your men—' he began, only to be stopped by Percy's snort.

'Fed, watered, brushed, curried, and stabled with ribbons braided into their little tails, or rather, getting drunk round the fires – I ordered them an extra ration of beer, was that right? – or slinking off into the bushes with the local whores, but they *have* been fed. Did you think I'd forget them?'

There might have been an edge to this, but it was said lightly, and Grey smiled, tilting his head to look at Percy with his good eye.

'I am quite sure you would overlook no detail of their welfare. I was going to say that they did very well today. They're a credit to you.'

Percy flushed up at this, but only said, 'Oh. Well, they're a good lot,' in an offhanded way. He cleared his throat; he was still hoarse. 'None of them much hurt, at least.'

'No. And you?'

Percy glanced quickly at him, then away.

'I can't stop shaking,' he said, low-voiced. 'Does it show?'

'No,' Grey said, choosing not to add that given his own present state of vision, he likely wouldn't have noticed had Percy been quaking like egg-pudding in a high wind. He reached out a hand, though, and put it on Percy's arm, which seemed solid enough. 'No,' he repeated, more strongly. 'You aren't. Not to look at.'

'Oh,' Percy said, and took a deep breath. 'It's just inside, then. Good. What did Melton say?'

Most of Hal's remarks wouldn't bear repeating, but Hal could convey his own opinions to Percy in the morning, by which time Hal would be considerably calmer, and Percy might have stopped shaking.

'Not a lot,' Grey said. 'Just flesh wounds. Don't worry about it.'

They talked of nothing in particular then, taking no great interest in the conversation, only glad to be in each other's company. This went on until Tom came back, carrying a flask of brandywine and a bowl of some cloudy liquid, which he claimed was warm barley water with salt, sovereign for sore eyes.

He handed this to Percy, and disappeared again in search of supper.

Grey leaned over the bowl and sniffed it.

'Am I to drink it, do you think? Or pour it over my head?'

'I don't mind what you do with it, but I strongly suggest you don't pour the brandy into your eye. It would sting, I expect. Besides, I need it.' Percy poured a generous portion of the latter liquid into a cup and pushed it across the table. He didn't bother finding another cup for himself, but drank directly from the flask, thus giving Grey an idea of just how much he likely *was* shaking internally.

Grey sipped his own. It wasn't good, but it burned pleasantly, and numbed the annoying pain in his eye a little. Still, he should do something with the barley water; Tom would be offended if he didn't. He groped for the handkerchief in his sleeve, inspected it critically, and decided it would do.

'You meant it, didn't you?' Percy said quietly, putting down the flask.

'Meant what?'

'When you said you were a beast.' Percy was looking at him with an expression that seemed somewhere between awe and mild revulsion. Grey didn't care for either.

'So are all soldiers,' he said shortly. 'All men, for that matter. Get used to it.'

Percy made a small huffing sound, which might have been amusement.

'You needn't tell *me* that, my dear,' he said dryly. He stood, took the cloth from Grey's hand, and dipped it in the bowl. 'Put your head back.'

His hand on Grey's neck was warm, his touch delicate.

'Can you open your eye?'

Grey tried, and managed a slit. Percy's face swam in a haze of tears, dark and intent.

'Not so bad,' he murmured. 'Here, relax.' Percy's fingers spread the lids of his injured eye, and squeezed the liquid from the cloth into it. Grey stiffened a little in reflex, but found that it didn't hurt much, and did relax a little.

'All I meant is that you are a great deal more honest about it than most.'

'I doubt it is any virtue.' A thought came to him, belatedly. 'Are you wondering whether you are sufficiently a beast, yourself? That you acquitted yourself well, I mean? You did. I should have said so.'

'You did.'

'I did?'

'Yes. You don't remember?'

'No,' Grey said, honestly. 'I was rather busy.'

Percy chuckled, low in his throat, and dipped the cloth again.

'I am sufficiently honest as to acknowledge my own inexperience, at least. You were right, about having no idea what you'll do in battle. Had you not shouted at me to shoot that fellow, I should simply have stood there gaping, until you got up and did it yourself.'

Grey opened his mouth to remonstrate, but Percy bent and kissed him quickly on the lips, his breath warm on Grey's water-chilled cheek.

'I don't seek reassurance, my dear, no need.' He stood upright and the cloth came over Grey's eyes again, with its soothing flood. 'I did not disgrace myself utterly, and perhaps will do better later. I meant only to say that I understand now what you told me. And that at the end of it' – the cloth drew away, and Grey blinked – 'the only thing important is that we are still both alive.

'That,' he added, his tone offhand as he turned to dip the cloth again, 'and that I am proud of you.'

Alarmed and stirred by the kiss, deeply embarrassed at the praise – and not a little shocked that Percy did not instinctively perceive the essential truth of the matter – Grey began to say the obvious: it was his duty. But Tom Byrd came in with the supper then, and in the end, he contented himself with no more than a feeble 'Thank you.'

Chapter 25

Betrayal

In early May, the Duc de Richelieu returned to France, replaced by the Comte de Clermont. The Comte de Clermont, reluctant to engage his troops in spite of their numerical superiority, continued to play at tag through the Rhine Valley. Brunswick, who understood these tactics well enough, continued patiently to answer them, flanking Clermont's sides, blocking an advance here, prodding there – little by little driving Clermont's army back toward the French border.

By late May, it was clear that the French had nowhere left to skip away to; within weeks, perhaps days, they must either turn and fight, or retreat into France with Brunswick baying at their heels. Clearly Clermont would fight.

That being so, Duke Ferdinand wisely chose to take time now to ready his troops and burnish his cannon, wishing to meet the attack, when it came, in a state of maximum readiness.

To this end, Grey spent much of his time in riding to and fro, inspecting companies, taking the reports of company commanders, arguing with quartermasters, giving orders for resupply, refitment where needed, the obtaining of more wagon mules (these in great demand, and thus both scarce and expensive), and the ten thousand other details that fell to a major's daily lot.

The only good thing about this process, Grey reflected, heading back toward the small village where he was presently quartered, was that he had no more than the ninety seconds between the time his head hit the pillow and his falling asleep, in which to experience sexual frustration. The ninety seconds were required in which to administer such palliative action as was possible; otherwise, he would be asleep in three.

He uncorked his canteen and drank deeply; it was a warm day in late spring, and the water seemed to taste not only of the tin and beechwood canteen, but of rising sap, half sweet and pungent. The Drachenfels loomed before him – the 'Dragon's Rock,' that stony peak on the shore of the Rhine, where Siegfried was said to have slain his dragon – romantically wreathed in river haze, its foot a-welter in greening vineyards.

The spring weather was affecting everyone; men walked dreamily into walls on sentry duty, put down their muskets and forgot them in the fields, took French leave and were found lazing under hedgerows or haystacks, often curled about a woman.

Grey might have thought it unfair that he was unable to do likewise – but he remembered his first campaign, when he and Hector had stolen away to find solitude and sweetness in nests of spring grass under skies that spun with stars, the heat of their young bodies more than compensating for the chill of the evenings. Rank had its privileges, but it undeniably had its drawbacks, as well. At least he did have the pleasure of Percy's company most evenings, if not the freedom to employ it fully.

Sighing, he corked the canteen and looked about for Richard Brett, the ensign accompanying him. Brett was the youngest of the ensigns, only fifteen, and normally bright and industrious, but suffering particularly from the effects of springtime – on account of his youth, Grey supposed.

At the moment, Brett was nowhere in sight, though his horse grazed contentedly along the lush green verge of the road, reins hanging. Nudging his own mount in that direction, Grey discovered an open gate in the wall of a farmhouse, and inside it, Mr. Brett, elbows leaned upon the coping of a well and his gaze fixed worshipfully upon the young woman who was hauling a bucket out of it, smiling at him.

The fact that Brett spoke no German and the young woman plainly had no English obviously posed no bar to an exchange of sentiments; the body had its own language.

Resigned but generous, Grey dismounted, letting his own horse graze as well. 'Ten minutes, Mr. Brett,' he called, and walking a little way off the road, found a grassy spot and lay down with his hat over his eyes.

The ground was warm beneath him, the sun warm above, and he felt bone and muscle melt, the tight-coiled springs of his mind relax like an unwound watch. He made a vain attempt to keep hold of the dozen things he should be paying attention to, but then gave up. It was spring.

It was still spring come evening, and Grey came back to the village thinking of doorknobs. One, in particular. Tom had secured him a small room at the top of the local *Gasthof*; small, but with a door that locked, a most unusual facility in such parts.

Or rather, the door *had* a lock. The key for it had not yet been found, but Grey was assured it existed, and would doubtless resurface momentarily.

Meanwhile, the doorknob – made of white china and slick as an egg – as though to compensate for the loss of the key, was inclined either to spin loosely round on its stem, or to jam fast, both conditions preventing the door from being opened from the outside. More than once, Tom had been obliged to go through the window of the adjoining garret, and worm across the front of the house in order to slide into the window of Grey's room and open the door from the inside.

There was an entertainment scheduled for tonight, a concert of sorts, with local dances performed, in the next village over. Most of the men and all of the officers in the area would be there, making the most of the mild weather and their temporary freedom. Given the obliging nature of his doorknob, Grey thought that perhaps he and Percy might make the most of the occasion, as well. A brief appearance at the festivities, and in the darkness, everyone well-laced with flowing wine, no one would notice if they left – separately for the sake of discretion – and slipped back to the inn.

The sun had begun to sink, washing the old walled *Gasthof* and its orchard in a haze of peach and apricot as he rode into the paved courtyard at the trot, his horse eager for home and hay.

Grey was feeling no less eager, and was not particularly pleased to be stopped in the courtyard by a Captain Custis, from the 9th, who hailed him as he dismounted.

'Hoy, Grey!'

'Custis.' He nodded to the ostler and gave over his horse, turning to see what the captain wanted. 'Were you wanting me?'

'Not so you'd notice,' Custis said cheerfully. 'Colonel Jeffreys says you promised to lend him your copy of Virgil, so I said I'd fetch it for him, as I was bound this way on an errand. As I was waiting for you, though, I found myself in conversation with *Herr* Hauptmann here' – he nodded at a small, dapper Prussian captain of infantry, who bowed and clicked his heels – 'and fancy my surprise to hear that there's a Maifest on in the next village tonight!'

'Fancy that,' Grey said, unable to repress a smile. He glanced at the brilliant horizon, where peach was deepening into coral and lavender. 'And of course it will be too late for you to ride back to camp tonight after you get the book, so you'll have to stay on. Pity, that.'

'Yes, isn't it. You're going?'

'Oh, yes. Bit later, though; I've orders to write first.'

'Hauptmann and I will save you a wineskin. But I mustn't forget the colonel's book.'

'Right, I'll get it.'

Custis and Hauptmann followed him up the narrow stair, discussing with some animation the virtues of a local vineyard, located at the foot of the Drachenfels.

'*Federweisser,* they call the new, uncasked wine. "Feather-white," and it is, too – white, very light – but by God! Three glasses, and you're under the table.'

'*You're* under the table, perhaps,' Grey said, laughing. 'Speak for yourself.'

'It *is* somewhat strong,' Hauptmann said. 'But you must drink the *Federweisser* with the *Zwiebelkuchen* that they make there also. That way, you do not suffer—'

Grey grasped the china knob, which turned properly for once, and pushed the door open. And stood paralyzed for an instant, before jerking it shut.

Not quite fast enough, though. Not fast enough to have prevented Custis and Hauptmann from seeing, over his shoulder. Not nearly fast enough to obliterate the image that reached his own eyes and burned directly through them into his brain: the sight of Percy, naked and facedown on the bed, being split like a buttered bun by a blond German officer, also naked, his pale buttocks clenched with effort.

Someone had given a cry of shock; he couldn't tell whether it was Custis, Hauptmann, or himself. Perhaps it was Percy. Not the other man; he had been too intent on his business, eyes shut and face contorted in the ecstasy of approaching climax.

Weber. The name floated through Grey's mind like an echo and vanished, leaving it completely blank.

Everything thereafter seemed to happen with remarkable slowness. His thoughts were like clockwork, clicking from one to the next with dispassionate quick logic, while everyone – himself included – seemed to move with a cumbersome sluggishness, turning slowly toward each other and away, the changing expressions of shock, bewilderment, horror flowing like cold treacle over faces that all looked suddenly alike.

You are the senior officer present, said the small, cold voice in his head, taking note of the confusion. *You must act.*

Things abruptly resumed their normal speed; voices and footsteps were coming from everywhere, attracted by the cry, the slam of the door. Puzzled faces, murmured questions, excited whispers,

English and German. He stepped forward and rapped on the door, once, sharply, and the voices behind him hushed abruptly. On the other side of the door there was a deafening silence.

'Get dressed, please,' he said very calmly through the wooden panel. 'Present yourselves in the courtyard in five minutes.' He stepped back, looked at the gathering crowd, and picked one of his ensigns' faces out of the swimming throng.

'Fetch two guards, Mr. Brett. To the courtyard, at the double.'

He became dimly aware of a hand on his arm, and blinking once, turned to Custis.

'I'll do it,' Custis said, low-voiced. 'You needn't. You mustn't, Grey. Not your own brother.'

The horrified sympathy in Custis's eyes was like the prick of a needle, rousing him from numbness.

'No,' he said, his own voice sounding strange. 'No, I have to—'

'You mustn't,' Custis repeated, urgent. He pushed Grey, half-turning him. 'Go. For God's sake, go. It will make things worse if you stay.'

He swallowed, and became aware of all the faces lining the stairway, staring. Of just how much worse the gossip would be, that extra touch of scandal, the *frisson* of horror, the *schadenfreude*, as word spread that he had been obliged to arrest his own brother for the crime of sodomy.

'Yes,' he said. He swallowed again, whispered, 'Thank you,' and walked away, going down the stairs, counting the wooden treads as they flickered past beneath the toes of his boots, one, two, three, four . . .

Went on counting his steps, ringing sudden on the bricks of the courtyard, one, two, three, four . . . muffled as he passed the gate, walking on strewn hay and wet earth, saw Brett and the guards coming toward him, raised a hand in acknowledgment but did not stop, one, two, three, four . . .

Walked straight down the main street of the village, heedless of mud, of horse dung, of screaming children and barking dogs, eyes fixed on the crag of the Drachenfels, rising in the distance. One, two, three, four, five, six, seven . . .

Chapter 26

Drinking with Dachshunds

Both men were turned over to the commanding officers of their respective regiments. Hal was at headquarters with Duke Ferdinand; in his absence, Percy was given over to the custody of Ewart Symington; Lieutenant Weber, the Hanoverian, was sent to the Graf von Namtzen's representative.

Symington, with more tact than Grey would have given him credit for, didn't mention Percy to him, and had evidently given orders that no one else should, either. The fact that no one spoke to *him* of Percy didn't mean that no one spoke of Percy, of course. The army was idle, awaiting a new round of orders from Brunswick. Idleness bred gossip, and Grey found the sudden cessation of conversations, the looks – ranging from sympathy to disgust – and the averted eyes of both men and officers so disquieting that he took to spending the days alone in his tent – he would not return to the inn – though it was by turns stifling or drafty.

Had he been in command, he would have had the men on the move – marching from point A to point B on daily drill, if necessary, but moving. Soldiers took to sloth like pigs to mud, and while such idleness was good for trade, from the points of view of local tavern keepers and prostitutes, it bred vice, disease, disorderliness, and violence among the troops.

But Grey was not in command, and the English troops sat, sunning themselves as the days slowly lengthened toward Midsummer Day. Dicing, drinking, whoring – and gossiping.

With no company save Tom and his own thoughts, which trudged in a weary circle from rage through fear to guilt and back again, Grey was left no social outlet save the occasional game of chess with Symington, who was an indifferent player at best.

Finally, unable to stand the growing sense of being mired hip-deep in something noxious, Grey in desperation asked Symington for leave. Stephan von Namtzen, the Graf von Erdberg, was a personal friend; Grey had been seconded to the Graf's regiment the year before, as English liaison officer. Von Namtzen's regiment was with Brunswick's troops, but the Graf himself had not yet come to the field; presumably he was still recovering at his hunting lodge, a place called Waldesruh. Only a day's ride from the present English position.

Grey wasn't sure whether his request for leave had more to do with his need to escape from the morass of silent accusation and speculation that surrounded him, the need of distraction from his own thoughts, or from a basely jealous urge to discover more about Percy's partner in crime and his fate. But Stephan von Namtzen was a good friend, and above all at the moment, Grey felt the need of a friend.

Symington granted his request without hesitation, and with Tom loyally in tow, he set off for Waldesruh.

Waldesruh was a hunting lodge – which by Hanoverian standards, probably meant that it employed fewer than a hundred servants. The place was surrounded by mile upon mile of brooding forest, and despite the continued weight on his mind and heart, Grey felt a sense of relief as he and Tom emerged at last from the woodland shadows into the sunlight of Waldesruh's exquisitely manicured grounds.

'Oi,' said Tom approvingly. The lodge, three-storied and built of the pale brown native stone with brick touches in red and green, spread itself before them, elegant and colorful as a pheasant. 'Does himself well, the captain, for a Hun. Do you suppose the princess is here, too?' he asked hopefully.

'Possibly,' Grey said. 'You must refer to him as the Graf von Erdberg, here at his home, Tom. "Captain" is his military title, for the field. Should you speak to him directly, say, "*Herr* Graf." And for God's sake—'

'Aye, aye, don't call them Huns where they can hear.' Tom did not quite roll his eyes, but assumed a martyred air. 'What's a Graf, then, did you say?'

'A landgrave. "Count" would be the English equivalent of the title.'

He nudged his horse and they started slowly up the winding drive toward the house.

Grey hoped the Princess Louisa – now the Gräfin von Erdberg – wasn't to home, despite Tom's obvious eagerness to renew his acquaintance with the princess's body servant, Ilse. He didn't know what the nature of von Namtzen's marriage might be, but it would be much easier to talk with Stephan von Namtzen without the prolonged social *pour-parlers* that the princess's presence would necessarily entail.

Still, if she were a devoted wife, she might well feel it incumbent upon her to hover over her wounded husband, tenderly nursing him back to health. Grey tried to envision the Princess Louisa von Lowenstein engaging in this sort of behavior, failed, and dismissed it from mind. God, if she were here, he hoped that at least she hadn't brought her unspeakable mother-in-law.

A small, grubby face popped out of the foliage just ahead of them, blinked in surprise, then popped back in. Shouts and excited rustlings announced their arrival, and a groom was already hurrying round the house to take charge of Tom and the horses by the time they reached the flagged steps.

Wilhelm, Stephan's butler, greeted Grey at the door, his long face lighting with pleasure. A number of dogs surged out with him, barking and wagging with delight as they smelt this new and interesting object.

'Lord John! *Willkommen, willkommen!* You will eat?'

'I will,' Grey assured him, smiling and patting the nearest furry head. 'I am famished. Perhaps I should make my presence known to your master first, though? Or your mistress, should she be at home,' he added, for the sake of politeness, for the presence of the dogs assured him that the princess was not here.

A pained look crossed Wilhelm's features at mention of his employers.

'The Princess Louisa is at Schloss Lowenstein. The Graf . . . yes, I will send word to the Graf at once. Of course,' he said, but with a sort of hesitancy that caused Grey to glance sharply at him.

'What is wrong?' he asked directly. 'Is it that the Graf is still unwell? Is he unfit to receive company?'

'Oh, he is . . . well enough,' the butler replied, though in such uncertain tones that Grey felt some alarm. He noticed also that Wilhelm didn't answer his second question, instead merely gesturing to Grey to follow him.

Had he harbored any doubts regarding the princess's residency, they would have disappeared the moment he stepped across the threshold. The lodge was immaculately clean, but still held the pleasantly frowsty air of a bachelor establishment, smelling of dogs, tobacco, and brandywine.

A pair of mud-caked boots was visible through a

parlor door, flung askew on the hearth – a good sign, he thought; Stephan must be somewhat recovered, if he were riding – and a small heap of stones, scraps of paper, pencil stubs, detached buttons, grubby bread crusts, coins, and other detritus recognizable as the contents of a man's pockets was turned out on a silver salver which elsewhere might be intended for visiting cards.

Speaking of which . . .

'Has the Graf entertained many visitors since his unfortunate accident?' he inquired.

Wilhelm cast a rather hunted glance back over one shoulder and shook his head, but didn't elaborate.

Not such a good sign; Stephan was normally a most sociable gentleman.

The butler paused at the foot of the staircase, as though trying to make up his mind about something.

'You are tired from your journey, *mein Herr*? I could show you to your room,' Wilhelm offered, making no move to do so.

'Not at all,' Grey replied promptly, taking up the obvious cue. 'Perhaps you would have the kindness to take me to the Graf? I would like to give him my respects at once.'

'Oh, yes, sir!' Palpable relief spread over Wilhelm's countenance, causing Grey to wonder afresh what the devil von Namtzen had been doing.

He had not long to wonder. Wilhelm shut the dogs in the kitchen, then escorted him, almost at the trot, through the lodge and out a door at the rear, whereupon they plunged into the forest and made their way along a pleasant, shady trail. In the distance ahead, Grey could hear shouts – he recognized Stephan von Namtzen's voice, raised in displeasure – and a remarkable thunder of hooves and . . . wheels?

'*Was ist*—' he began, but Wilhelm shook his head decidedly, and beckoned him on.

Grey rounded the next curve of the path on Wilhelm's heels and found himself on the edge of an enormous clearing, floored with sand. And rushing directly toward him, screaming like an eagle and wild-eyed as his horses, was what appeared to be one of the ancient German gods of war, driving a chariot drawn by four galloping dark horses, scarlet-mouthed and foaming.

Grey flung himself to the side, taking the butler to the ground with him, and the chariot slewed past with barely an inch to spare, a flurry of monstrous hooves spraying them with sand and droplets of saliva.

'Jesus!'

The quadriga – yes, by God, it was; the four horses ran abreast, threatening at every moment to overturn the chariot that bounced like a pebble in their wake – galloped on, held in perilous check by the one-armed maniac who stood upright behind them, a terrified groom with a whip beside him, clinging with one hand to the chariot and with the other to the Graf von Namtzen.

Grey rose slowly to his feet, staring and wiping sand from his face. They weren't going to make the turn.

'Slow *down!*' he bellowed, but it was much too late, even had they heard him over the thunder of the equipage. The chariot's left wheel rose, touched sand, skipped free again, and to a chorus of shouts and screams, left the ground altogether as the horses scrambled, getting in each other's way as they slewed uncontrolled and leaning into the turn.

The chariot fell sideways, spilling out its contents in a jumble of flailing limbs, and the horses, reins trailing, galloped on a few more steps before stumbling to a shuddering halt, fragments of the shattered chariot strewn behind them.

'Jesus,' Grey said again, finding no better remark. The two figures were struggling in the sand. The one-armed man lost his balance and fell; the groom tried to grasp his other arm, to help, and was cursed at for his trouble.

At Grey's side, Wilhelm crossed himself.

'We are so glad you have come, *mein Herr,*' he said, voice trembling. 'We didn't know what to do.'

And you think I do? Grey thought later, in silent reply. The groom had been bundled off with a broken arm, a doctor sent for, and the horses – fortunately uninjured – seen to and stabled. The erstwhile charioteer had cavalierly dismissed a large swelling over one eye and a wrenched knee and greeted Grey with the utmost warmth, embracing him and kissing him upon both cheeks before limping off toward the house, calling for food and drink, his one arm draped about Grey's shoulders.

They sat now sprawled in chairs before the fire, awaiting dinner, surrounded by a prostrate pack of heavily breathing dogs, their patience sustained by a plate of savories and a decanter of excellent brandy. A spurious sense of peace prevailed, but Grey was not fooled.

'Have you quite lost your mind, Stephan?' he inquired politely.

Von Namtzen appeared to consider the question, inhaling the aroma of his brandy.

'No,' he said mildly, exhaling. 'Why do you ask?'

'For one thing, your servants are terrified. You might have killed that groom, you know. To say nothing of breaking your own neck.'

Von Namtzen regarded Grey over his glass, mouth lifting a little.

'You, of course, have never fallen from a horse. And how is my dear friend Karolus?'

Grey made a sound of reluctant amusement.

'Bursting with health. And how is the Princess Louisa? Oh – I am sorry,' he said, seeing von Namtzen's face change. 'Be so kind as to forget I asked.'

Stephan made a dismissive gesture, and reached for the decanter.

'She is also bursting,' he said wryly. 'With child.'

'My dear fellow!' Grey was sincerely pleased, and

would have wrung Stephan's hand in congratulation, had there been one to spare. As it was, he contented himself with raising his glass in salute. 'To your good fortune, and the continued health of your family!'

Von Namtzen raised his own glass, looking mildly embarrassed, but pleased.

'She is the size of a tun of rum,' he said modestly.

'Excellent,' Grey said, hoping this was a suitable response, and refilled both their glasses.

That explained the absence of the princess and the children, then; Louisa would presumably want to remain with the ancient Dowager Princess von Lowenstein, her first husband's mother – though God knew why.

There was a bowl of flowers on the table. Chinese chrysanthemums, the color of rust, glowing in the setting sun. An odd thing to find in a hunting lodge, but von Namtzen loved flowers – or had used to. He pushed the bowl carelessly aside now, and a little water slopped on the table. Von Namtzen ignored it, reaching for a decanter on the tray. His left shoulder jerked, the missing hand reaching instinctively for his glass, and a spasm of irritation touched his face.

Grey leaned forward hastily and seized the glass, holding it for von Namtzen to pour. The smell of brandy rose sweet and stinging in his nose, a counterpoint to the clean, bitter scent of the flowers. He handed the glass to von Namtzen, and with a murmured *'Salut,'* took a generous swallow of his own.

He eyed the level of brandy in the decanter, thinking that as things looked, they were likely to need it before the evening was out. Von Namtzen outwardly was still a large, bluntly handsome man; the injury had not diminished him, though his face was thinner and more lined. But Grey was aware that something had changed; von Namtzen's usual sense of imperturbable calm, his fastidiousness and formality had gone, leaving a rumpled stranger whose inner agitation showed clearly, a man cordial and snappish by turns.

'Don't fuss,' von Namtzen said curtly to his butler, who had come in and was endeavoring to brush dirt from his clothes. 'Go away, and take the dogs.'

Wilhelm gave Grey a long-suffering look that said, *You see?*, then clicked his tongue, urging the dogs away to the kitchen again. One remained behind, though, sprawled indolently on the hearthrug. Wilhelm tried to make it follow him, as well, but von Namtzen waved him away.

'Gustav can stay.'

Wilhelm rolled his eyes, and muttering something uncomplimentary in which the name 'Gustav' featured, went out with the other dogs wagging at his heels.

Hearing his name, the dog lifted his head and yawned, exhibiting a delicately muscular, long pink tongue. The hound – Grey thought it was a hound, from the ears and muzzle – rolled to its feet and trotted over to von Namtzen, tail gently wagging.

'What on earth is *that*?' Grey laughed, charmed, and the strained atmosphere eased a little.

It was not, Grey supposed, more ridiculous than Doctor Rigby's pug – and at least this dog was not wearing a suit. It was impossible to regard the creature without smiling, though.

It was a hound of some sort, black and disproportionately long-bodied, with legs so stumpy that they appeared to have been amputated. With large, liquid eyes and a sturdy long tail in constant motion, it resembled nothing so much as an exceedingly amiable sausage.

'Where did you get him?' Grey asked, leaning down and offering his knuckles to the dog, who sniffed him with interest, the tail wagging faster.

'He is of my own breeding – the best I have obtained so far.' Von Namtzen spoke with obvious pride, and Grey forbore to pass any remark regarding what the rest of the Graf's attempts must look like.

'He is . . . amazing robust, is he not?'

Von Namtzen beamed at his appreciation, irritability forgotten, and scooped the dog up awkwardly in his one arm, displaying the dog's expanse of hairless belly and a tremendous chest, deep-keeled and muscular.

'He is bred to dig, you see.' Von Namtzen took one of the stubby front paws, broad and thick-nailed, and waggled it in illustration.

'I do see. To dig what? Worms?'

Von Namtzen and Gustav regarded each other

fondly, ignoring this. Then the dog began to squirm, and von Namtzen set him gently on the floor.

'He is marvelous,' the Graf said. 'Completely fearless and extremely fierce in battle. But very gentle, as you see.'

'Battle?' Grey bent to peer more closely at the dog, which promptly turned to him and, still wagging, gave a sudden massive heave which ended with the stumpy paws perched on his knees, the long muzzle sniffing interestedly at his face. He laughed and stroked the dog, only now noticing the healed scars that ran over the massive shoulders.

'What on earth has he been fighting? Cocks?'

'Dachse,' von Namtzen said, with immense satisfaction. 'Badgers. He is bred most particularly to hunt badgers.'

Gustav had tired of perching on his hind legs; he collapsed onto the floor and rolled onto his back, presenting a vast pink belly to be scratched, still wagging his tail. Grey obliged, raising a brow; the hound seemed so amiable as to appear almost feeble-minded.

'Badgers, you say. Has he ever killed one?'

'More than a dozen. I will show you the skins tomorrow.'

'Really?' Grey was impressed. He had met a few badgers, and knew of nothing – including human beings – willing to engage with one; the badger's reputation for ferocity was extremely well founded.

'Really.' Von Namtzen poured a fresh glass, paused for no more than an instant to sniff the vapor of the brandy, then tossed it back in a manner unfitting the quality of the drink. He swallowed, coughed, and was obliged to set down the glass in order to thump himself on the chest. 'He is bred to go to ground,' he wheezed, eyes watering as he nodded at the dog. 'He will go straight into a badger sett, and do battle with them there, in their own house.'

'Must be the devil of a shock to the badgers.'

That made Stephan laugh. For an instant, the tension left his face, and for the first time since his arrival, Grey caught a real glimpse of the friend he had known.

Heartened by this, he topped up Stephan's glass. He thought of suggesting a hand of cards after supper – he had found that cards usually soothed a troubled mind, provided one did not play for money – but on second thought, forbore. Stephan could doubtless manage to play well enough, but the actions involved were bound to emphasize his disability. As it was, Grey tried to avoid staring at the empty sleeve that fluttered limply whenever von Namtzen moved. The shoulder and the curve of the upper arm were still intact, he noted; the amputation seemed to have been done somewhere above the elbow.

Watching Stephan relax by degrees over their casual supper of eggs, *Wurst,* and toasted *Brötchen,* Grey found himself reluctant to bring up the true subject of his visit. Whether it were the loss of the arm, something to do with the Princess Louisa – for he noticed that von Namtzen barely mentioned her, though he spoke of his children with evident fondness – or something else, it was plain that Wilhelm had reason to be worried for his master.

Still, whatever was troubling Stephan, his own matter would have to be dealt with – and time was short. Was it better, Grey wondered, lighting a pipe for Stephan and handing it across, to wait 'til the morrow? Or would it be easier for both of them if he were to speak now, when the warmth of friendship renewed and the intimacy of oncoming night might cushion the harsh edges of the matter? That, and a fair amount of alcohol; they had shared a bottle of hock with supper, and the decanter now held a bare half inch.

He decided to wait just a bit longer, unsure whether this decision was the counsel of prudence or of cowardice. He poured the last of the excellent brandy, taking care to fill his own glass no more than halfway. Kept the conversation light, going from dogs and hunting to minor news from his cousin Olivia's last letter, and amusing stories from the field. He felt the rawness of his own emotions begin to numb, his thoughts of Percy recede to a tolerable distance, and decided that it had been prudence after all.

It was getting on for midsummer, and the sky stayed light far into the night. Through an increasing sense of muzziness, Grey heard the carriage clock strike ten. Wilhelm had come in a little while before to light the candles and refill the decanter, but he could still see von Namtzen's face by the fading light from the window.

The broad planes of it were calm now, though harsh lines that hadn't been there the year before cut deep from nose to mouth. The mouth itself had gone from its normal sweet firmness to a line whose grimness relaxed only when Grey succeeded in making him laugh. Grey had a sudden impulse to reach across, cup Stephan's beard-bristled cheek in his hand, and try to smooth those lines away with a thumb. He resisted the impulse, and let Stephan fill his glass again. Soon. He would have to speak soon – while he could still talk.

'The moon is nearly dark,' Stephan remarked, nodding toward the window, where the faint sickle of the waning moon shone in a lavender sky above the wood. 'The badgers come more often from their setts at the dark of the moon. We will take Gustav out tomorrow night, perhaps. You will stay some days, *ja*?'

Grey shook his head, preparing himself.

'Only a day or two, alas. I have actually come on an unpleasant errand, I fear.'

Stephan's gray eyes were slightly unfocused by this time, but he lifted his head from a contemplation of his own newly filled glass and turned a face of curiosity and owlish sympathy on Grey.

'Oh, *ja*? *Was denn*?'

'Ober-Lieutenant Weber,' Grey said, hoping that he sounded casual. 'Michael Weber.' The name felt strange, repellent on his tongue, and he fought back the unwelcome recollections that struck him when he heard or spoke Weber's name: the vision of Weber's muscular, pumping, pale backside, the rumpled fawn breeches on the floor – and the usual hot surge of anger that accompanied that vision. 'I wished to speak with him – if you have no objection.'

Von Namtzen frowned. Shook his head, swallowing, and grimaced as though the liquor hurt his throat.

'You do object?' Grey raised a brow.

Stephan shook his head again and set down his glass, wiping the back of his hand across his lips.

'He's dead.' The words came out hoarsely, and he shook his head again and cleared his throat explosively, repeating more clearly, *'er ist tot.'*

Grey had heard him the first time.

'What happened?' he asked. His heart had seized up at von Namtzen's words, and started again with a painful lurch.

Von Namtzen reached for the decanter, though his glass was still nearly full.

'I shot him,' he said, very quietly.

'You—' Grey choked off his exclamation, and took a deep breath. 'How?' he asked, as evenly as he could. 'I mean – *you* executed him? Personally?'

'No.' It was not overwarm in the room, but a dew of sweat had formed along Stephan's jaw; Grey saw the sheen of it as he turned his head away, groping for the decanter.

'You must understand. He would have been

executed – hanged, had he been court-martialed. The family would have been disgraced, utterly, and there are other sons in the army – they would be ruined. I . . . have known the family for a long time. His father is my friend. Michael . . .' He rubbed his hand fiercely over his lips. 'I knew this boy, knew him from the day of his birth.'

Gustav, sensing distress in his master, got up and padded over to sit by von Namtzen's foot, leaning heavily against his leg in an attempt to give comfort. Grey wished momentarily that he could act in such a straightforwardly sympathetic manner, but the best he could do at the moment was to keep silence.

Von Namtzen met his eyes directly for the first time, the depths of his wretchedness apparent in the bloodshot whites and swollen rims.

'I could not let such a thing happen to him – to his family.' He took a deep breath, his hand clutching his glass as though for support. 'And so I took him from the gaol where he was, saying that I would bring him to his village. On the way, we met with a company of French foragers – I knew where they were; my scouts had told me. There was a skirmish; I had given Michael back his pistol and sword – I ordered him to take his men and fall upon the enemy.'

Stephan fell silent, all too clearly reliving the event.

'He knew, do you think?' Grey asked, quietly. 'What you intended?'

Stephan nodded, slowly.

'He knew he was to die. I saw the thought kindle in his mind as we rode. He seized it then, let it burn in him. I saw, when it took him. You know it – that moment when a man throws everything away and there is nothing left but *der Kriegswahn*?' It was not a term with an exact English equivalent; 'the madness of battle,' perhaps. Not waiting for Grey's nod, he went on.

'The men knew, too. They had treated him with contempt, but at this order, they came together at once behind him, the picture of loyalty. Michael was a good soldier always – very brave. But this . . . He lifted his sword and charged toward the French, standing in his stirrups, screaming, all his men pouring after him. I have not before seen such ferocity, such courage, and I have seen much of such things. *Er war . . . ein Prachtkerl,*' he ended, so softly that Grey barely made out the final word.

Glorious, it meant; radiantly beautiful. And in the sense of intimacy that comes with mutual drunkenness, Grey felt he saw the man for an instant as Stephan had, glorious in his rush toward destruction, his warrior's end – and beneath this, Stephan's more personal sense of his beauty as a man; mortal, fleeting.

That gave him a deep pang, the sharp point of his own jealousy blunted by this final picture of the lovely boy, this Weber whose fallen-angel's face he had seen so briefly, embracing Stephan's gift of a noble death.

Von Namtzen let go of his brandy glass and

leaned down clumsily to pat the dog, who moaned in his throat and licked his master's hand.

'But he was not killed,' he said bleakly, his great blond head still bent over the dog. 'Not even wounded.'

He raised his head then, but would not look at Grey; his eyes fixed on the bowl of chrysanthemums, gone the color of dried blood in the shadows of the night-darkening room.

'He led his men well, killed three French with his own hand, and routed them completely. He stood quite alone for an instant then at the edge of a wood, all his men gone on in pursuit. And then . . . he turned to look at me.'

With a look of such terror, such despair, that von Namtzen had found himself fumbling for his own pistol, spurring his horse toward Michael, almost by reflex, so strong was the need to answer that wordless cry.

'I passed a few feet before him, and shot him in the heart. No one saw. I got down and picked him up in my arms; his clothes were damp, his flesh was still hot from the battle.'

Stephan closed his eyes. He released a sigh that came from his bones, and seemed to deflate, his broad frame collapsing.

'And so I put him across his saddle and took him home to his mother,' he said flatly. 'A dead hero, to be mourned and celebrated. Not a disgraced sodomite, whose name could never be spoken by his family.'

There was silence then, broken only by the sounds of a startled woodcock calling in the forest. Then an owl hooted, somewhere near, and its silent shadow passed the window, part of the gathering night.

Grey wished to speak, but anger and brandy and grief – for Weber, for Percy, for von Namtzen, and not least for himself – seized in his throat, bitter as the smell of the Chinese flowers.

'*Er war ein Prachtkerl,*' Stephan muttered suddenly again, low-voiced and choked. Pushing back his chair, he lurched to his feet and blundered from the room, his loose sleeve a-flutter, almost stumbling over the dog in his haste.

Gustav snorted in surprise and hopped to his feet, tail waving slowly as he hesitated, not sure whether to follow.

'Here,' said Grey, seeing the dog's puzzlement. His voice came thick, and he cleared his throat, repeating, '*Hier, Gustav,*' and held out a bit of cold *wurst.* 'You should like it. You look very much like a sausage yourself, you know,' he said, and immediately felt sorry for the insult.

'*Entschuldigung,*' he murmured in apology, but Gustav had taken no offense, and accepted the tidbit with grace, tail gently wagging to and fro, to and fro.

Grey watched this oscillation for a moment, then closed his eyes, feeling dizzy. He should call Wilhelm. He should go to bed. He should . . . The thought drifted away unformed. He crossed his arms on the table before him and laid his head upon them.

He was very drunk, and only half conscious of his body. All the same, his eyes burned and his joints ached, as though some ague was come upon him. He wished dimly that he could find relief in weeping, but with all he had drunk, his body was parched, his throat dry and sticky, and he felt obscurely that he did not deserve such relief.

A soft weight leaned against his leg, and the dog's breath warmed the flesh of his calf. He reached down blindly with one hand, and stroked the silky head, over and over, breathing the strong musky smell of the animal, the motion keeping thought at bay until brandy and fatigue assumed that duty and his body relaxed. He dimly felt the wood of the table beneath his cheek, and heard the owl again, hooting in the dark.

When Tom Byrd came to find him, he was sound asleep, Gustav the dachshund on the floor beside him, a long watchful muzzle resting on his boot.

The badger's sett was within a mile of the lodge, the gamekeeper assured them, and so they walked through the woods, enjoying the mildness of the evening. So near to summer, the sun remained in the sky well past nine, and so their badger hunt was conducted in a dim, glowing light that made Grey feel as though they were on an expedition to capture elves or faeries, rather than a ferocious small animal.

Nothing had been said between himself and von Namtzen during the day, but the awareness that there were things to be said hung between them. Still, the gamekeeper and his son walked nearby, keeping an eye on Gustav, who trotted stolidly along, long nose lifted to the scents of the evening air, and so such talk as there was dealt with small, impersonal matters.

He had not known quite what to expect of a badger hunt. The gamekeeper had partially excavated the sett, which lay in the side of a hill, so that the mouth of a dark tunnel was visible. Gustav began to quiver with excitement as the wind changed, bearing a scent so pungently pronounced that even Grey's feeble nose perceived it.

The dog's hackles rose all down his back, and he began to growl enthusiastically, then to bark, as though in challenge to the badger. If a badger was in residence, it failed to emerge, though, and at von Namtzen's sign, the gamekeeper loosed the dog, who shot for the tunnel's entrance, paused for a moment to dig madly, dirt flying from the stubby paws, and then wriggled his broad shoulders into the earth and disappeared from view, tail stiff with excitement.

Sounds of snuffling and scratching came from the hole, and Grey suffered a moment's nightmare, imagining what it must be like to go forward into darkness, enclosed, engulfed, swallowed by the earth, with the knowledge of teeth and fury lurking somewhere ahead, invisible.

He said something of this to von Namtzen, who laughed.

'Dogs, fortunately, are not hampered by imagination,' he assured Grey. 'They live in the moment. No fear of the future.'

This attitude held an obvious appeal – but as Grey noted, some of its benefit depended upon what was happening at the particular moment. Just now, Gustav appeared to be experiencing a moment with an angry badger in it, and von Namtzen, burdened with imagination, seemed to fear the worst, clutching Grey's arm with his one good hand and muttering German curses and exhortations, mixed with prayers.

Some one of these incantations must have proved effective, for after a heart-stopping period of silence, something moved at the entrance to the tunnel, and Gustav made his way slowly out of the bowels of the earth, dragging the body of his enemy.

The dog was allowed to disembowel his prey and roll on the gory remains in celebration, before being carried off in triumph by the gamekeeper to have a torn ear mended, leaving Grey and von Namtzen to follow as they would.

The sun had finally sunk below the trees, but the last of the fading light still washed the sky with a brilliant gold. It would be gray within moments, but for the space of a heartbeat, the branches of the forest were etched black against it, each twig, each leaf distinct and beautiful.

Grey and von Namtzen stood watching it, both

struck for an instant. Grey heard Stephan's breath leave him in a sigh, as the light began to fail.

'This is my favorite time of the day,' Stephan said.

'Really? You do not find it melancholy?'

'No, not at all. Everything is quiet. I feel . . . alone.'

'*Allein?*' Grey asked, as von Namtzen had spoken in English. '*Allein oder einsam?*' Alone, meaning 'lonely,' or 'in peace' – solitary?

'*Allein. In Ruhe,*' von Namtzen answered, smiling a little. 'I am busy always in the daylight, and in the evening, there are the people – official banquets, entertainments. But no one wishes me to do anything while the light falls. You like this?' He nodded at the prospect before them. They had emerged from the forest at the crest of a small hill, not far from the lodge. Waldesruh and its stable lay a little below them, their solid lines gone soft with twilight, so that the lodge seemed about to vanish into the earth and be covered over by the trees, flowing dark and silent down from the slope behind it.

Grey might have found the thought that everything might vanish and they be left alone to face night in the forest somewhat daunting. At the moment, though, he recognized Stephan's wistfulness, and shared it. To be quite alone, to lay one's burdens at the feet of the trees, and lose them – if only for a moment – in the deepening shadows there.

'*Ja,*' he said. '*Wunderschön.*' Yes, he had a liking.

They stood for several minutes then, not speaking. Watching the last trace of color fade from the sky, the lacework of the branches begin to blur and merge with the dark as night crept ineluctably upward from the earth.

'So,' von Namtzen said after a time, quite casually. 'What is it?'

Grey took a deep breath of the forest's cool green air and explained the matter as concisely as he could.

'Oh, how most distressing to your family! My dear fellow, I am so sorry.' Von Namtzen's voice was full of sympathy. 'What will happen to him, do you suppose?'

'I don't know. He will be tried, at a court-martial. And almost certainly will be found guilty. But the sentence . . .' His voice died away. The memory of Otway being dragged, screaming, to the gallows was one that haunted Grey daily, but he felt superstitiously that to speak of the possibility was to invoke it. 'I don't know,' he said again.

'He will be found guilty,' von Namtzen repeated, frowning. 'There were witnesses, I understand, besides Captain Hauptmann?'

'There were. An officer named Custis – and myself.'

Von Namtzen stopped dead, and dropped the sack containing the badger, in order to grip Grey by the arm.

'Grosser Gott!'

'Yes, I believe that sums up the matter very well.'

'They will make you speak – testify – to it?'

'Unless I manage to be killed before he is court-martialed, yes.'

Von Namtzen made a sound of deep consternation, shaking his head.

'What will you do?' he asked, after a bit.

'Live in the moment,' Grey said, nodding at the bloodstained bag. 'And hope that when my own moment comes, I, too, will walk out of the earth and see the sky again.'

Von Namtzen didn't quite laugh, but snorted through his nose, and led the way through a stand of flowering trees that scattered tiny white petals down on them like snow.

'I was most pleased, of course, to hear that your brother's regiment would be attached to Duke Ferdinand's troops,' he said, in an apparent attempt at casual conversation. 'Not only for their valuable assistance, but because I hoped to have the chance of resuming our friendship.'

'I, too,' Grey said honestly. 'I am only sorry that we cannot meet solely as friends, free of such unpleasant considerations as those I have brought you.'

Von Namtzen gave a lopsided shrug.

'We are soldiers,' he said simply. 'We will never be free of such things. And it is part of our friendship, is it not?'

Grey was not sure whether he meant their shared profession, or their shared involvement in recurrent unpleasantness, but it was true, in either case, and he laughed ruefully.

'Still,' von Namtzen went on, knitting his heavy brows, 'it is most unfortunate.'

'Yes, it is.'

'Not only the . . . the occurrence.' Von Namtzen made a brief gesture with his missing arm, which unbalanced him, so that he stumbled, but recovered with a muttered *'Scheisse!'*

'No,' he resumed. 'It is unfortunate that it involved both English and Prussian troops. Had it been our men, and only our own officers who witnessed the crime, it could have been dealt with . . . more quietly.'

Grey glanced at him. This feature of the situation had not escaped him. The English command could not be seen to deal lightly with such a matter, for fear of losing standing with their German allies. He hadn't thought consciously about the other side, but plainly the same must be true for the Germans.

'Yes. Would you have done – what you did – had there not been the prospect of a notorious trial and public execution?'

'Killed my lieutenant?' Von Namtzen would not accept any softening of reality. 'I do not know. Had the men both been German, it is possible that they would simply have been discharged from the army, perhaps imprisoned for a time, perhaps banished. I think there would have been no trial.'

'So it was my presence, in part, that led to this. You have my great regrets.' God only knew how great.

Von Namtzen turned his head then, and gave him a smile of surprising sweetness.

'I would not for one moment regret your presence, John, no matter what the circumstance.' He had never before used Grey's Christian name without his title, though Grey had often invited him to do so. He spoke it now with a touching shyness, as though not sure he was entitled to such familiarity.

Von Namtzen coughed, as though embarrassed by this declaration, and hastened to cover it.

'Of course, there is no saying what might be done on any occasion. On the one hand, we – the army, that is to say – do not tolerate such perversions. The penalties are severe. On the other' – he glanced at his missing sleeve, and one side of his mouth lifted – 'there is Friedrich.'

'Fried – what, the king?'

'Yes. You know the story?' von Namtzen asked.

'Which one?' Grey said dryly. 'Such a man is always the focus of tales – and I suppose some might even be true.'

Von Namtzen laughed at that.

'This one is true,' he assured Grey. 'My own father was present at the execution.'

'Execution?' Grey echoed, startled. 'Whose?'

'Friedrich's lover.' The Graf's momentary laughter had left him, but he smiled crookedly. 'When he was a young man, his father – the old king, you know? – obliged him to join the army, though he disliked it intensely. A horror of bloodshed. But he formed a deep attachment to another young soldier, and the two decided to flee the country together.'

'They were caught – of course,' Grey said, a sudden hollow opening behind his breastbone.

'Of course.' Stephan nodded. 'They were brought back, both charged with desertion and treason, and the old king had Friedrich's lover beheaded in the courtyard – Friedrich himself forced to watch from a balcony above. He fainted, my father said, even before the sword fell.'

Grey's own face felt suddenly cold, his jaw prickling with sweat. He swallowed hard, forcing down a sense of dizziness.

'There was some question,' von Namtzen continued, matter-of-fact, 'as to whether Friedrich might himself face the same fate, son or not. But in the end . . .'

'He bowed to the inevitable, and became not only a soldier, but a great soldier.'

Von Namtzen snorted.

'No, but he did – after spending a year in prison – agree to be married. He ignored his wife; he still does. And there are no children,' he added disapprovingly. 'But there she is.' He shrugged.

'His father gave him the chateau at Rheinsberg, and he spent many years there, up to his ears in musicians and actors, but then' – he shrugged again – 'the old king died.'

And Friedrich, suddenly aware that his inheritance consisted of several tasty chunks of disconnected and vulnerable land, most of them being eyed by the Habsburgs of Austria, had hastily become a soldier. Whereupon he had united his territories, stolen Silesia from the Austrians, and two years before, decided to invade Saxony for good measure, thus making enemies not only of the Austrians and Saxony, but of Russia, Sweden, *and* the French.

'And here we all are,' von Namtzen concluded.

'Not a gentleman given to half measures.'

'No, he is not. Nor is he a fool. Whatever the nature of his affections now, they remain private.' Stephan spoke rather grimly, then shook his head, like a dog flinging off water. 'Come, it grows soon dark.'

It *would* be dark soon; already, the air between the trees had thickened, the forest drawing in upon itself. The path before them was still visible, but as they plunged back into the trees, the ground under their feet seemed insubstantial, rocks and tussocks nearly invisible, but unexpectedly solid.

The effort of walking without stumbling kept them from conversation, leaving Grey to reflect on the story of the King of Prussia and his lover – and the irony that the latter had been executed not for crimes of the flesh or seduction of his prince, but for treason. While Captain Bates . . . He felt as though those sardonic eyes watched him from the forest, and hurried on, feeling darkness at his heels.

Nor was he the only one. He could sense von Namtzen's disquiet; see it, in the awkward shifting of his broad shoulders, tensed as though fearing some pursuit.

In a few moments, they reached the edge of the clearing in which the lodge stood, and emerged with a shared sense of relief into a soft haze of lavender, a pool of light still cupped between the forest's hands.

They paused for an instant, taking their bearings. Von Namtzen turned toward the lodge, but Grey stopped him with a hand upon his arm.

'Show me, Stephan,' he said suddenly, surprising them both.

Von Namtzen's face went blank.

'Deinen Arm,' Grey said, as though this were quite logical.

Stephan looked at him for a moment with no expression whatever, then away. Grey was already berating himself for clumsiness, but then Stephan's one hand reached for the pin that held the loose sleeve to the breast of his coat.

He shed the coat without difficulty, still not looking at Grey, but then paused, his hand on the white linen of his neckcloth.

'Hilf mir,' he said softly.

Grey stepped close, and reached behind von Namtzen's head with both his own hands, fumbling a little with the fastening. Stephan's skin was very warm, the neckcloth damp. It came loose suddenly and he dropped it on the ground.

'I would not make a good valet,' he said, trying to make a joke of it as he bent to pick the cloth up.

From the corner of his eye, he saw Stephan's throat, long and powerful, a reddish mark across it from the cloth. Saw him swallow, and knew quite suddenly what to do.

He took Stephan's shirt off gently, with no further fumblings. He was ready for the sight of the arm, not shocked, though the thought of the solid forearm, the kind, broad hand now gone, made him sad. The stump was clean, cut just above the elbow; the scars well-knitted, though still an angry red.

Stephan's muscles tensed instantly when Grey touched him, and Grey whistled softly through his teeth, as though Stephan were a nervous horse, making the German snort a little, the sound not quite a laugh. Grey ran a soothing hand down the slope of von Namtzen's shoulder, his thumb tracing the groove between the muscles of the upper arm.

Von Namtzen had the most beautiful skin, he thought. No more than a sprinkling of dark gold hairs across his breast. Poreless and smooth, with a dusk that drew both eye and hand.

You are like porcelain, he thought, but didn't say it. *And damned near as breakable, aren't you?*

He lifted the unresisting arm, and lightly kissed the end of the stump.

'*Schon gut,*' he said.

Saw Stephan's belly muscles spring out tight against the skin. The evening air was mild, but he could smell von Namtzen's sudden sweat, salt and musk, and his own body tightened, too, from scalp to knees. But this was not the time or place – nor the man. To allow Stephan to acknowledge his own desire now would destroy him – and to be the agent of such destruction would shatter Grey himself; he had no illusions regarding his own fragility.

There was one thing, perhaps, that he might give Stephan; it might not help – it hadn't helped Percy – but it was what he had.

'I love you, brother,' he said, straightening and looking Stephan in the eyes. 'So you will stop trying to kill yourself, *ja*?'

He picked up the shirt and rolled it up in his hands, so that it went neatly over von Namtzen's head. Helped Stephan to slide his arms into the sleeves, and bent for the coat.

'I think . . . you would be a very good valet.' Von Namtzen blurted it, then blushed so deeply that it was visible, even in the fading light. '*Entschuldigung!* I – I do not mean to insult you.'

'I think it a great compliment,' Grey assured him gravely. 'I am hungry – shall we go home to dinner now?'

Chapter 27

The Honorable Thing

Grey found himself steadier in mind upon his return from von Namtzen's lodge, and met all inquiries and expressions of sympathy with a remote, impeccable courtesy that kept the questioners – as well as his own feelings – at a safe remove. This technique, however, was ineffective with Hal.

It was several days after his return before he saw his brother, Hal having been with Duke Ferdinand. Hal came unannounced to his tent in the evening after supper, sitting down without invitation across the table from Grey, who was writing orders.

'Have you got any brandy?' Hal asked without preamble.

Grey reached beneath the table without comment and lifted the jug of very good brandy von Namtzen had sent with him – half empty now, but still plenty left.

Hal nodded thanks, lifted the jug in both hands and drank, then set it down, and shuddered slightly. He leaned his elbows on the table and put his face in his hands, rubbing slowly at the scalp beneath his wig. Finally, he looked up, his eyes bloodshot with travel and lined with a weariness that went far beyond mere bodily fatigue.

'Have you seen Wainwright since you came back?'

Grey shook his head, wordless. He knew where Percy was; a small country gaol in a nearby village. He had made the minimal inquiries necessary to assure that Percy was decently fed, and beyond that, had tried not to think of him. With a marked lack of success, but still, he tried.

'I suppose the news has spread,' he said. His own voice was hoarse with disuse; he hadn't spoken to anyone in hours, and he cleared his throat. 'Does the duke know?'

Hal grimaced, and took another drink. 'Everyone *knows*, though the matter hasn't been brought up officially as yet.'

'I suppose there will be a court-martial.'

'The general feeling among the high command is that it would be much better if there wasn't.'

He stared at Hal.

'What the devil do you mean by that?'

Hal rubbed a hand over his face.

'If he were a common soldier, it wouldn't matter,' he said, voice muffled. Then he took his hand away, shaking his head. 'Court-martial him and hang or imprison him and be done with it. But he's not. He's a bloody member of the family. It can't be done discreetly.'

Grey was beginning to have an unpleasant feeling under his breastbone.

'And what do they think *can* be done . . . discreetly? Try him and discharge him for some other reason?'

'No.' Hal's voice was colorless. 'That might be done if no one really knew what had happened. But the circumstances . . .' He gulped brandy, coughed, and kept coughing, going red in the face.

' "Unfortunate," ' he said hoarsely. 'That's what Brunswick kept saying, in that precise sort of way he has. "Most unfortunate." '

Ferdinand was more precariously placed than King Friedrich. Friedrich was absolute master of his own army; Ferdinand commanded a number of loosely allied contingents, and was answerable to a number of princes for the troops they had supplied him.

'Some of these princes are strict Lutherans, and inclined to a rather . . . rigid . . . view of such matters. Ferdinand feels that he can't risk alienating them; not for *our* sake,' he added, rather bitterly.

Grey stared down at the tabletop, rubbing the fingers of one hand lightly back and forth across the grain.

'What does he mean to do?' he asked. 'Execute Wainwright outright, without trial?'

'He'd love to,' Hal said, leaning back and sighing. 'Save that that would cause still more stir and scandal. And, of course,' he added, reaching for the brandy again, 'I informed him that I'd be obliged to pull our own troops out and make an official complaint to the king – or kings; ours *and* Friedrich

– should he try to treat a British soldier in that fashion.'

The knot under Grey's heart seemed to ease a little. The departure of Hal's regiment wouldn't destroy Ferdinand's army, but it would be a blow – and the resultant uproar might well cause fragmentation among his other allies.

'What do they – or you – propose to do, then?' he asked. 'Keep him locked up in hopes that he'll catch gaol fever and die, thus relieving you of awkwardness?' He'd spoken ironically, but Hal gave him an odd look, and coughed again.

Without speaking, he picked up the haversack he'd dropped by the table, and withdrew a pistol. It was an old one, of German manufacture.

'I want you to go and see him,' he said.

'What?' Grey said, disbelieving.

'Do you know what happened to... Wainwright's...' Hal searched for a word. '...accomplice?'

'Yes, I do. Von Namtzen told me. Are you seriously suggesting that I call upon Percy Wainwright and murder him in the gaol?'

'No. I'm *suggesting* that you call upon him, give him this, and... urge him to – to do the honorable thing. It would be best for everyone,' Hal added softly, looking down at the tabletop. 'Including him.'

Grey stood up violently, almost overturning the table, and went out of the tent. He felt that he might fly into pieces if he didn't move.

He walked blindly through the camp, down the main alley of tents. He was vaguely conscious of men looking at him – a few waved or called to him, but he didn't answer, and they fell back, looking after him with puzzled faces.

Best for everyone.

Best for everyone. Including him.

'Including him,' he whispered to himself. He reached the end of the alley, turned on his heel, and walked back. This time no one hailed him; only watched with fascination, as they might watch a gallows procession. He reached his own tent, pulled back the flap, and went in. Hal was still sitting at the table, the pistol and the jug of brandy in front of him.

He felt words like bits of gravel stuck in his throat, and chewed them fiercely, feeling them grit between his teeth.

You're *the goddamned head of the family!* You're *his colonel, his commander. And you're his bloody brother, too – as much as I am.*

He might have spit out any one of these things – or all of them. But he saw Hal's face. The bone-deep weariness in it, the strain of fighting – yet again – scandal and rumor. The everlasting, inescapable struggle to hold things together.

He said nothing. Only picked up the gun and went to put it in his own haversack.

You protect everyone, John, Percy's voice said, with sympathy. *I don't suppose you can help it.*

On his way back to the table, he opened the small

campaign chest that contained his utensils, and took the two pewter cups from their slots.

'Let us at least be civilized,' he said calmly, and set them on the table.

Percy was sitting on the wooden bench that served him as seat, bed, and table. He looked up when the door opened, but didn't move. His eyes fixed upon Grey's face, wary.

The small whitewashed room was clean enough, but the smell of it struck Grey like a blow. There was no window, and the air was close and damp, rank with the smell of unwashed flesh and sour linen. It had plainly been a storeroom; chains of braided onions and black loops of blood sausage still hung from the rafters, their smell battling the bitter stink of an iron night-soil bucket that stood in the corner, unlidded, unemptied. A protest at this small indignity rose to his lips, but he pressed them tight together and swallowed it, nodding to the guard. Given his errand, what did such things matter?

There were narrow slits beneath the eaves of the room, but the room itself lay in a shadow fractured by the moving leaves of the tree that overhung the building. Grey moved through the dim, shattered light, feeling that he moved underwater, every thought and motion slowed.

The door closed behind him. Footsteps went away and they were alone, in no danger of being overheard. There were noises in the distance: the shuffling of boots and the shout of distant orders in the square, the sounds of boisterous companionship from the tavern next door.

'Are you treated decently?' The words were dry, emotionless. He knew only too well what the attitude of guards toward a prisoner accused of sodomy was likely to be.

Percy glanced away, mouth twisting a little.

'I – yes.'

Grey set down the stool the guard had given him, and sat upon it. He'd envisioned this moment hundreds of times since Hal had given him the gun; sleepless, sweating, ill – to no avail. He could not find a single word with which to begin.

'I'm glad to see you, John,' Percy said, quietly.

'Don't be.'

Percy's eyes widened a little, but he made a game attempt to smile. They'd let him shave, Grey saw; his cheeks were smooth.

'I should always be glad to see you, no matter your errand. And from the look of you, I doubt it is pleasant.' He hesitated. 'Have you – will they try me here, do you know? Or send me back to England?'

'That – I don't know. I've—'

He gave up any thought of speaking. Instead, he took the gun from his pocket, handling it gingerly, as though it were a venomous serpent, and laid it on the bench. It was loaded and primed, requiring only to be cocked.

Percy sat for a moment staring at it, expressionless.

'They made you bring it?' he asked. 'The duke? Melton?'

Grey gave one brief nod, his throat too tight to speak. Percy's eyes searched his face, quick and dark.

'At least it wasn't your own notion,' he said. 'That's . . . a comfort.'

Then Percy rose abruptly and turned, putting out both hands as though to grasp the sill of a window that wasn't there. Hands flat against the white-washed brick, he lowered his head so that his forehead rested against the wall, his face invisible.

'I must say something to you,' he said, and his voice came low but clear, controlled. 'I have been waiting in hope of your coming, so that I might say it. You will think I tell you by way of excuse for actions for which there can be no excuse, but I can't help that. Only listen to me, I beg you.'

He stood waiting. Grey sat staring at the pistol, loaded and primed. He'd loaded it himself.

'Go on, then,' Grey said at last.

He saw Percy's back swell with his breath, and saw the naked lines of it beneath broadcloth and linen, slender, perfect.

'The first time I lay with a man, it was for money,' Percy said quietly. 'I was fourteen. We had had no food for two days – my mother and I. I was going through the alleyways, looking for anything that might be sold. A man found me there – Henry, he was called, I never knew his last name – a well-dressed man, rather stout. He told me he was a law clerk, and he may have been. He took me to his room, and when he had finished, he gave me three shillings. A fortune.' He spoke without irony.

'And so you . . . continued. With him?' Grey strove to keep his own voice colorless.

Percy's head rose from the bricks, and he turned round, dark eyes somber.

'Yes,' he said simply. 'Him, others. It made the difference between poverty and outright hunger. And I discovered that my own tastes . . . lay that way.' He gave Grey a direct look. 'It was not always for money.'

Grey felt something turn over inside him, and didn't know whether it was regret or relief.

'I . . . when I thought . . . that there might be something between us . . . I would not come to you at once; you noticed, I think?'

Oh, yes.

'There was a man – I will not give his name; it is not important – call him "Mr. A," perhaps. He was . . .'

'Your protector?' Grey gave the word an ugly intonation, and was pleased to see Percy's jaw clench.

'If you like,' Percy said tersely, and met his eyes directly. 'I would not come to you until I had broken with him. I did not wish there to be any . . . complication.'

'Indeed.'

'Michael – the man with whom you saw me . . .' He pronounced the name in the German way, Grey noticed: 'Meechayel.' 'I knew him. Before. We met in London, a year ago.'

'Money?' Grey asked brutally. 'Or . . . ?'

Percy took a deep breath and looked away.

'Or,' he said. He bit his lower lip. 'I told him I did not . . . that there was someone – I did not tell him your name,' he added quickly, looking up.

'Thank you for that,' Grey said. His lips felt stiff.

Percy swallowed, but did not look away again.

'He insisted. Once, he said, what harm? I would not. And then he said – it was not quite a threat, but clear enough – he said, what if there began to be talk? Among the German officers, among our – our own. About me.'

Clear enough, Grey thought bleakly. Was it the truth? Did it matter?

'I do not tell you by way of excuse,' Percy repeated, and stared at Grey, unblinking.

'Why, then?'

'Because I loved you,' Percy said, very softly. 'Since we began, I have not touched anyone else, or thought of it. I wished you to know that.'

And considering his history – as he told it – that was a considerable affirmation of affection, Grey thought cynically.

'You cannot say the same, can you?' Percy was still looking at him, his mouth tight.

He opened his own mouth to refute this, but then realized what Percy meant. He had not touched another, no; but there *was* another. And exactly

457

where was the boundary to be found, between the flesh and the heart? He shut his mouth.

'Do not tell me I have broken your heart. I know better.' Percy's face was pale, but hectic patches of red had begun to glow across his cheekbones – as though Grey had slapped him. He turned suddenly away, and began to strike the white wall with his fist, slowly, soundlessly.

'I know better,' he repeated, his voice low and bitter.

If it is your intent to place the fault for this disaster upon my shoulders – He swallowed the words, unspoken. He would neither defend himself nor engage in pointless recriminations.

'Perseverance,' Grey said, very softly. Percy halted abruptly. After a moment, he rubbed a hand over his face, once, twice, then swung round to face Grey.

'What?'

'What do you want of me?'

Percy looked at him for some moments, unspeaking. At last he shook his head, one side of his mouth turned up in what was not quite a smile.

'What I wanted, you couldn't give me, could you? Couldn't even lie about it, honorable bloody honest bastard that you are. Can you lie now? Can you tell me that you loved me?'

I could tell you, he thought. *And it would be true. But not true enough.* He did not know whether Percy spoke out of panic and anger – or whether from a calculated effort to evoke Grey's guilt, and thus his help. It didn't really matter.

The air in the small room hung thick, silent.

Percy made a small, contemptuous sound. Grey kept his eyes fixed on his hands.

'Is that what you want?' he asked at last, very quietly.

Percy rocked back a little, eyes narrowed.

'No,' he said slowly. 'No, I don't. It's late to talk of love, isn't it?'

'Very late.'

He could feel Percy's eyes upon him, gauging him. He lifted his head, and saw the look of a man about to roll dice for high stakes. It came to him, with a small, sudden shock, that he recognized that look because he was a gambler himself. He hadn't realized that before, but there was no time to contemplate the revelation.

'What I want,' Percy said, each word distinct, 'is my life.' He saw the uncertainty cross Grey's face with the possibilities that conjured – if it could be done; a sentence of imprisonment, transportation – and the considerations of what those possibilities might mean – not only to Percy, but to Hal, the regiment, the family . . .

'And my freedom.'

A feeling of sudden, senseless rage came over him, so strong that he pressed his fists into his thighs to keep from springing to his feet and striking Percy.

'For God's sake,' he said, voice harsh with the effort to keep it low. 'You do this – make such a frigging *mess* – why did you not tell me? I could have made sure *Meechayel* was no threat to you. For that matter, how can you have been so weak, so stupid, as to give in to a feeble threat like that? Unless you wished it, and took the excuse – no, don't say anything. Not a fucking word!' He struck his fist violently upon his knee.

'You do this,' he went on, voice trembling, 'you not only destroy yourself, you embroil us all—'

'All. You and your bloody brother and your goddamned family *honor,* you mean—'

'Yes, our goddamned family honor! *And* the honor of the regiment – of which you are a sworn officer, I remind you. How dare you utter the word "honor"? Yet you *do* dare – and presume further to demand that I not only perform some miracle to save your life, but to save you from all consequences of your folly?'

The pistol lay on the bench before him, loaded and primed, requiring only to be cocked. For one instant, he thought how simple it would be to pick it up, cock it, and shoot Percy between the eyes. No questions would be asked.

'I didn't say that.'

Percy's voice was choked. Grey couldn't look at Percy's face, but saw the long hands clench, unfold, reclench themselves. There was silence between them, the kind of silence that rings with unspoken words.

There were noises, somewhere in the building. Voices, laughter. How was it possible that normal life continued, anywhere? He heard Percy draw breath, heard it catch in his throat.

'You could not give me love, you said – but kindness and honor; those were yours to give,' Percy whispered. Grey looked up, and saw that the hectic flush had faded, the luminous skin gone pallid and chalky.

'There is no honor left to me.' His lips trembled; he pressed them tight for an instant. 'If – if there is any kindness left between us, John – I beg you. Save me.'

He couldn't. Could not bear to remember: not Percy warm in his bed, not Percy in the fetid cell – certainly not Percy in the attic room with Weber – could not think about the current situation, could not decide what to do, or even how to feel. Consequently, he went through the necessary motions of each day like an automaton, moving, speaking, even smiling as necessary, but aware all the time of the clockwork within, and his inability to stir beyond the constraints imposed upon him.

Beyond a terse inquiry as to whether Percy was housed and treated decently, Hal had not inquired as to the results of his visit – a glance at Grey upon his return had told of the failure of his mission. The old pistol was still in Grey's haversack.

The note arrived a week later. There was no direction upon it – a German private had delivered it – but Grey knew where it had come from.

He should throw it into the fire. Grimacing, he slid a thumb beneath the flap and broke the seal. There was no salutation; was that caution on Percy's part, he wondered, to avoid incriminating Grey if the letter should be intercepted – or simply that Percy no longer knew how to address him? The question evaporated from his mind as he read the opening.

I will leave you to imagine, if you will, what the writing of this letter costs me, for that ultimate cost is up to you. I have been in perturbation of mind for days, debating whether I shall write it, and now, having written, whether to send it. The end of my deliberations, though, is the point from which I began: that to speak may mean my life; not to speak may mean yours. If you are reading these words, you will know which I have chosen.

Grey rubbed a hand over his face, shook his head violently to clear it, and read the rest.

You know something of my history, including my relations with the gentleman I will call A. One day whilst I was in his house, another gentleman called upon him. I was sent upstairs, their business being private. Looking out upon the drive, I saw the visitor's coach, which was a very elegant equipage, plainly not hired, but minus armorial markings or crests. After a short time, the gentleman came out and was driven away. I saw nothing of him save a glimpse of his hat as he passed out from beneath the porte cochère, though I did hear him exchange some words in farewell with Mr. A.

Being sent for, I came down, whereupon A told me that his visitor had heard of your mother's marriage, and thus of my putative relations with your family, and wished to know whether I had met you or your brother, and when we might meet again. A had told his visitor of my luncheon with you and Melton, adding that I had invited you to Lady Jonas's salon. The visitor had given A a packet of money to give to me, and asked that in return, I should undertake to guide you to the edge of Hyde Park upon our departing the salon, and should leave you near the Grosvenor Gate, as he wished to have a message delivered to you there.

This sounding innocent enough, I did as he requested. As you did not mention the matter upon our next meeting, I supposed it either confidential or inconsequent, and thus did not ask you about it. I did not learn of your encounter with the two soldiers in the park until you told me of it later. I was shocked to hear of it, but did not perceive that the incident might be connected with Mr. A's visitor.

Then we were attacked in Seven Dials, and I realized that you were the specific target of it. This caused me to recall Mr. A's visitor and his errand, and consider whether both attacks might have been at his instigation. I could see no reason for such a thing, however, and thus held my peace, though resolving to keep close guard upon you.

You then told me the true story of your father's death, and later of the other odd events, such as the page of your father's journal discovered in your brother's office. I began to suspect at this point that the matters were connected, but I still could not see how. As the regiment was bound to depart within such a short time, though, it seemed you would be removed from harm.

I had, as I say, debated for some time whether to write to you regarding my knowledge. The matter became exigent early this week. I heard a voice in the corridor outside my cell, and believe that I recognized it as the voice of Mr. A's visitor. I could not attract the attention of a guard for some time. When finally I succeeded in speaking to one, I asked who the English stranger had been. The guard did not know, had not seen the man – but was persuaded for a consideration to make inquiries, and next day returned to tell me that the man was an army surgeon, come to make trial of a new experiment upon one of the prisoners who had suffered a grisly leg wound.

I cannot swear it is the same man, and if it is, I still do not know why he should wish you harm, though I must suppose that it has to do with your father's death. If it is connected in this manner, though, then there is every reason to suppose that you and your brother lie in mortal danger.

Believe me always your servant,
P. Wainwright (2nd Lieutenant)

Grey said something blasphemous under his breath, and threw the letter on the table.

Mysterious visitors and army surgeons – with no names. It was possible that Percy had not been able to discover the surgeon's name – if Mr. *A*'s visitor had been the same man, or if he even existed. It was also possible that the man did exist and Percy knew his name, but wished to force Grey to see him again in order to discover it. He made no mention in his letter of trading further information for the Greys' assistance, but the implication was clear enough.

'Are you all right, me lord?' Tom Byrd was squinting at him dubiously. 'You look what my mam calls bilious. Ought you to be bled, maybe?'

Grey felt distinctly bilious, but doubted that bleeding would help. On the other hand . . .

'Yes,' he said abruptly. 'Go and ask Dr. Protheroe if he might come as soon as convenient.'

Tom, unaccustomed to having Grey accept his medical suggestions, looked stunned for a moment, but then lighted up.

'Right away, me lord!' He hastily stuffed the shirt he had been mending back in the chest, and shrugged into his coat, but paused at the door to offer further advice.

'If you feel as though the blood might burst from your nose before the doctor comes, the thing to do is put a key at the back of your neck, me lord.'

'A key? What for?'

Tom shrugged.

'I don't know, but it's what my mam would do for a nosebleed.'

'I'll bear that in mind,' Grey said. 'Go!'

He stood in the middle of the tent after Tom's departure, wanting to do something violent, but was forestalled by the lack of anything breakable within reach save his shaving mirror, which he was loath to part with.

He wasn't sure how much of his anger was due to this further evidence of Percy's perfidy in keeping the information from him, and how much to the discoveries that Percy had made. There was no doubt that the blood was pounding through his head, though. He went so far as to feel his nose surreptitiously, but perceived no evidence that it was about to spurt blood.

'What are you doing?' Hal stood in the tent, flap in one hand, eyeing him in puzzlement.

'Nothing. Read that.' He thrust the letter at his brother.

Hal read it twice; Grey was grimly interested to see Hal's color rise and a vein begin to throb in his forehead.

'That little shit!' Hal flung the pages down. 'Does he know the surgeon's name?'

'I don't know. Possibly not. You can go and ask him if you like; I won't.'

Hal grunted, and glanced at the pages again.

'Do you think there's anything to it?'

'Oh, yes,' Grey said grimly. 'He might with-hold the name, but I see no reason for him to invent the story. What would be the profit to himself in that?'

Hal frowned, thinking.

'Only to cause us to come to him, I suppose – that he might appeal for our help directly, in hopes that a personal appeal would be more efficacious than a letter.'

'There's no help we can offer – is there?' Grey was not sure that he wished to know, if there was – but could not deny the small flicker of hope that rose in him with the question.

'Not much.' Hal rubbed a knuckle under his lip. 'If he is condemned, I think it might be possible to exert some influence in order to get his sentence commuted to imprisonment or transportation. *Might,* I say. I would try,' he added, with a brief glance at Grey. 'For his stepfather's sake.'

'If he is condemned,' Grey echoed. 'Do you honestly think there is any chance that he will not be?'

'Not the chance of a snowflake in hell,' Hal said bluntly. 'We must be prepared for – who's this?'

It was Tom, returning with Dr. Protheroe, the regimental surgeon, who put down his bag and glanced from Melton to Grey and back again.

'Ahh . . . your man here says you are bilious?' The question was put dubiously. Protheroe was small-boned, dark, and handsome; a skillful surgeon, but quite young, and rather in awe of Hal.

'Well, not precisely,' Grey began, with a glance at the letter on the desk, but Hal cut him swiftly off.

'Yes, my brother is feeling a trifle indisposed. Perhaps you would not mind examining him?' He gave Grey a minatory stare, forbidding him to contradict, and before he could think of some suitable excuse, Grey found himself seated on a stool, being obliged to put out his tongue, have the whites of his eyes peered at, his liver prodded, and answer various humiliating questions regarding the more intimate processes of his body.

Meanwhile, Hal engaged Protheroe in apparently careless conversation regarding his experience in Prussia, what he thought of the food, how the men did ... Grey glared at his brother over Protheroe's head, which was pressed to his chest, mouthing, 'Get *on* with it!' at him.

'Do you have much to do with your fellows?' Hal inquired at last, pleasantly. 'The other regimental surgeons?'

'Oh, yes.' Protheroe was fishing in his bag. Grey grimaced; he was about to be bled, he knew it. 'One or two of the German fellows are quite knowledgeable – and the duke has an Italian surgeon, who has the most marvelous instruments. He showed me them once – never seen anything like them!'

'Quite,' Hal said. He glanced again at the letter. 'How many English surgeons are there, do you know?'

Protheroe continued to rustle through his bag.

'Oh, five or six,' he said vaguely. 'Now, Lord John, I think—'

'Do you know their names?' Grey asked rudely. Protheroe blinked and Hal rolled his eyes in exasperation.

'Why, yes . . . of course. Simmonds – he's with the Fourteenth. I do believe, my lord, that leeches will be the best thing. Your man says you've been troubled by headache of late—'

'*That's* certainly true,' Grey said, eyeing the lidded jar the doctor had removed from his bag. 'But I really—'

'Simmonds,' Hal interrupted. 'Who else?'

'Oh.' Protheroe scratched reflectively at his jaw. 'Entwidge – good man, Entwidge,' he added magnanimously. 'Though a trifle young.' Protheroe could not be twenty-four himself, Grey thought.

'And there's Danner . . .' A twist of the lips dismissed Danner as a charlatan. 'Have you any milk to hand, my lord?'

'Just here, sir!' Tom, who had been hovering in obvious anticipation of this request, sprang forward, milk jug in hand. 'You'd best take your shirt off, me lord,' he said importantly to Grey. 'You won't want to go about smelling of sour milk, should any of it drip.'

'Indeed I won't,' Grey said, with a foul look at his brother, who appeared to be finding something funny in the situation. Resigned, he stripped off his shirt and allowed the medico to anoint the skin of his neck and temples generously with milk.

'The milk encourages them to bite with so much

469

more enthusiasm,' Protheroe explained, dabbing busily.

'I know,' Grey said through his teeth. He closed his eyes involuntarily as Protheroe scooped a dark blob out of his jar. The bite of a horseleech did not really hurt, he knew that. The creatures carried some element in their saliva that numbed the sensation. But the clammy, heavy feel of the thing against his skin revolted him, and the knowledge that the leech was slowly and pleasurably filling itself with his blood made him light-headed with disgust.

He *knew* it was harmless, even beneficial. His stomach, however, was ignorant of any sense of scientific detachment, and curled up in agitation.

Protheroe and Tom were arguing as to how many of the vile creatures might be the optimum, the doctor thinking a half dozen sufficient, but urged on by Tom, who was of the opinion that if half a spoon of something was good, three were better, when it came to medicine.

'That's quite enough, sir, I thank you.' Grey straightened himself on the stool, chin lifted to avoid any more contact than necessary with the leeches now festooned round his neck like a ruff, sucking away. A film of sweat came out on his brow, to be wiped away by the doctor, seeking a good roosting spot on his temple for another of the obnoxious things.

'That will do capitally,' Protheroe exclaimed in satisfaction, drawing back to study Grey as though he were some work of art. 'Excellent. Now, my lord, if you will just remain still while the leeches do their work, all will be well. I am sure you will obtain relief almost at once.'

Grey's only relief was the observation that Hal had gone green around the gills, and was clearly trying not to look in Grey's direction. That was some slight comfort, Grey thought. At least he himself couldn't *see* the bloody things.

'I'll go out with you, sir,' Hal said hurriedly, seeing Protheroe close up his bag and make ready to depart. Grey shot him an evil look, but Hal gestured briefly at the letter and went out in the doctor's wake.

Tom tenderly draped a towel about his shoulders: 'Lest as you might take a chill, me lord.' It was midday and sweltering, but Grey was too busy trying to ignore the morbid fancy that he was being quite drained of blood to register a protest.

'Fetch me some brandy, will you, Tom?'

Tom looked dubious.

'I think you oughtn't to drink brandy whilst being leeched, me lord. Might be as the little fellows would get squiffy and fall off afore they've quite done.'

'What an excellent idea. Get me brandy, Tom, and get a lot of it. Now.'

Tom's disposition to argue was interrupted by the reappearance of Hal, who looked at Grey, shuddered, and pulled the snuffbox containing his smelling salts from his pocket. Grey was touched at this evidence of solicitude for his distress, but uttered a cry of indignation at seeing Hal put the vial to his own nose.

'Give me that! I need it more than you do.'

'No, you don't.' Hal drew in a deep breath, choked, and went into a coughing fit. 'Protheroe remembered another surgeon's name,' he wheezed, eyes watering.

'What? Who?'

'Longstreet,' Hal said, coughed again, and handed over the salts. 'Arthur Longstreet. He's here with the Prussians.'

Grey pulled the cork and lifted the vial to his nose.

'Brandy, Tom,' he said briefly. 'Bring the damned bottle.'

Beyond the interesting scientific discovery that brandy did indeed appear to intoxicate leeches, the effect of Mr. Protheroe's visit was indecisive.

'With the Prussians,' Grey repeated, pulling on his shirt with a sense of profound relief. 'Where with the Prussians?'

'Protheroe didn't know,' Hal replied, bending over the table to peer at a leech, which was extending itself in an eccentric and voluptuous manner. 'He just happened to meet Longstreet a week ago, and saw that he was wearing a Prussian uniform. But he naturally didn't take any notice of which regiment. Do you think that one's dead?'

Grey prodded the insensible animal in question,

then gingerly picked it up betwixt his thumb and forefinger.

'I think it's just passed out.' He dropped it into the jar and wiped his fingers fastidiously on his breeches. 'It shouldn't be impossible to find him.'

'No,' Hal said thoughtfully. 'But we must be careful. If he does mean you – or me – harm, it wouldn't do to alert him to the fact that we know about him.'

'I should think that would be the best way of insuring that he doesn't attempt to do us harm.'

'Forewarned is forearmed, and I have every faith in your ability to defend yourself from a mere surgeon,' Hal said, with a rare smile. 'No, we don't want to alert him beforehand, because we want to talk to him. Privately.'

Chapter 28

❧

Hückelsmay

He had reproached Percy for reckless stupidity. At the same time, he was painfully aware that he had often been as reckless and stupid himself. He had been luckier, that was all. Once, no more than a few seconds had saved him from precisely the sort of disaster that had now befallen Percy. The memory of that instance was enough to bring him out in a cold sweat – all the colder for his exact knowledge now of what could so easily have happened.

The immediate shock and the hurt of betrayal had faded, leaving in their wake a sort of dull wretchedness. He kept this wrapped round himself like a sheet of canvas against a storm, knowing that to let it go was to suffer instead piercing gusts of sorrow and terror.

The army had moved on, leaving Percy in his cell with the sausages. Tonight, they camped near the village of Crefeld – 'crowfield,' it meant in English, a very literal place-name; the fields teemed with the black birds by day, and flocks of crows burst cawing from the furrowed fields as the army passed.

But the army had settled now, and night rose gently from the fields near Crefeld. The air was still, and the smoke of watch fires mingled with the natural haze that always hung above the fields; a dark mist seemed to rise slowly about his horse's hooves as he rode.

Grey passed from company to company as the summer night came slowly on, dismounting at each fire long enough to share a swallow of beer, a bite of bread or sausage as he talked with the captains, the lieutenants, the corporals. Passed through each camp, nodding, smiling, exchanging words with men he recognized, assessing mood, readiness, equipment with seeming casualness. Hearing with one ear the concerns and talk of his officers, the other listening to the sounds of the encroaching night. Waiting for any interruption in the cricket song of the gathering dark between camps, any note of alarm in the muffled talk and laughter of the troops settling to supper and their rest. Somewhere nearby was the enemy.

'A day's march still, I heard, before we catch the Frenchies up,' offered Tarleton, one of the two ensigns who always trailed him in the field, ready to relay messages, carry dispatches, execute orders, find food, and be generally available dogsbodies.

'Where'd you hear that?' Brett, the younger, asked with interest. 'From the Hessians, I mean, or one of ours?' He sounded excited; this was his first campaign, and he thirsted for battle.

'Uh . . . quartermaster's lieutenant,' Tarleton

confessed. 'He'd got it from one of the Germans, but didn't say who. Do you think he's right, though, sir?' he called to Grey. 'Are we getting close?'

Tarleton was perhaps eighteen, to Brett's fifteen, and affected great sophistication. His voice had broken late, though, and still had a tendency to crack in moments of stress. The word 'close' soared perilously upward, but Brett was wise enough not to laugh, and the fading light hid Grey's own smile.

'Yes, they'll be close,' he answered patiently. 'They have artillery; they'll find it slow going.' So, of course, did Ferdinand of Brunswick's Prussians and Hanoverians and their English allies; they'd been chasing the Comte de Clermont's army for the best part of a month, down the Rhine Valley.

This was rich farmland and the soil was fertile and damp – so damp, in fact, that when latrines were dug, the seep filled them halfway with water within a day. The English artillery crews were perched, grumbling, on the driest patch of land available, off to the west. Karolus lifted his head as they passed, neighing to the horses in the artillery park. Grey felt a sudden surge of interest pass through the stallion, his mane lifting and nostrils flaring as the damp, drifting air evidently brought him the scent of a mare.

'Not now, you randy sod,' Grey said, nudging him firmly with a bootheel and reining him round. Karolus made a disgruntled noise, but obeyed.

'Pining, is he, sir?' Tarleton asked, joking.

'Eh, balls full to bursting will get anyone in

trouble, won't they?' said Brett, endeavoring to sound worldly.

Grey raised a brow and thought he had better have a word with each ensign, privately, regarding the unwisdom of dealings with whores – not that such warnings would be heeded in the slightest. The battalion had been encamped in its present position since mid-morning; more than enough time for the ragtag collection of camp followers to catch them up. He stood briefly in his stirrups, looking toward the river, where the line of sturdy farmhouses stood, all their windows lighted like beacons.

There was no smudge of smoke on the horizon yet, though, to mark the arrival of the heavy wagons and the mule drovers, the untidy straggle of laundresses, cooks, foragers, children, and wives – official and less so – and the women whose ill fortune condemned them to eke out a living following an army. But they'd be there soon enough; it was an hour at least before full dark, and he'd wager his best boots that the camp followers would be solidly entrenched before moonrise.

The ground in this part of the Rhine Valley was flat as a flounder, though the hedgerows and woods between the fields grew high enough to obscure the view. From where he sat at present, he could just make out the spires of one, two . . . yes, three village churches, poking black into a sky the color of molten pewter.

The ensigns had continued their raillery, daring each other into still more lewdly suggestive remarks.

477

Half listening, Grey caught a phrase and jerked his head toward the ensigns. It was a movement of surprised reflex, more than an actual realization that they had been making a clumsily veiled reference to Percy Wainwright, but the effect was immediate.

There was a brief hiss from Tarleton, and Brett shut up sharp. He was sure they had meant no deliberate offense; neither of them knew Percy well, and likely had not recalled the family relationship between the disgraced lieutenant and Grey – until it was too late.

There was a constricted silence behind Grey. He ignored it for a moment, then reined up.

'Mr. Brett?' he called over one shoulder.

'Sir!'

'Go back to Captain Wilmot; I'd forgot to tell him to join Lord Melton and the duke at field headquarters after supper. The same message to each of the other captains. Then you are relieved.' It was unnecessary to tell the captains, since they would naturally come anyway – and riding back through the camps would occupy Brett for the next couple of hours and cause him to miss his own supper. It gave the young ensign an opportunity of escape, though, and he seized it gratefully, reining abruptly round with an 'Aye, sir!' and making off at the gallop.

'Mr. Tarleton.'

'Sir?'

Tarleton's voice cracked; Grey ignored it.

'Do you see that church spire?' He chose one at random, pointing. 'Go up it. Survey the countryside.'

'Aye, s— but, sir! It will be black dark before I reach it!'

'So it will,' Grey said pleasantly. 'I suppose you'll have to wait for the dawn, then, before you report back.'

'Ah ... yes, sir,' Tarleton said, crestfallen. 'Certainly, sir.'

'Excellent. And don't fall into the *Landwehr*, please.'

'No, sir. The ... er ... ?'

'The land dyke. Large double ditch, walled canal filled with water? We crossed it, earlier.'

'Oh, that. No, sir, I won't.'

Grey remained where he was, until Tarleton had disappeared in the direction of the distant church, then swung off Karolus. He welcomed the chance to be alone, if only for a bit.

Holding the reins in one hand, he bent his head on impulse, pressing his forehead against the horse's neck and closing his eyes, taking a little comfort in the stallion's solid warmth. Karolus turned his massive head and blew a generous blast of moist breath down Grey's neck, as an indication that he forgave Grey's earlier thwarting of his desires.

Grey jerked, and laughed a little.

'All right, then.' With an eye to the nearness of the invisible mare, he hobbled Karolus and left him to crop grass, while he himself sought the relief of a quiet piss.

There were no trees in this country, save the orchards near the farmhouses. He nearly chose a pile of stones that loomed in the twilight, realizing just in time that it was in fact one of the small shrines that littered the countryside like anthills, and switched his aim to a convenient bush.

Finished, he did up his flies and put a hand to his pocket, almost involuntarily. It was still there; he felt the crackle of paper.

The note had arrived during the afternoon; he had nearly ignored it, but recognizing Symington's sprawling fist on the direction, had opened it. Symington-like, it was brief, blunt, and to the point.

Custis is dead, it said, without salutation, adding as an afterthought, *Flux.* It was discreetly unsigned.

He supposed he should feel sorry – perhaps he would, later, when he might have both time and emotion to spare. As it was, he felt Custis's death to be nearly as significant to himself as it undoubtedly was to Custis.

Everyone *knew* what had happened at the *Gasthof.* The fact remained that only Grey, Custis, and Hauptmann had seen it. Michael Weber was dead, Captain Hauptmann gone to Bavaria. Now Custis was gone, too. Which left Grey as the sole eye-witness to the crime.

Hal, with his usual obsessive ruthlessness, had laid hands on every record he could find of courts-martial for the crime of sodomy – surprisingly few, considering just how widespread Grey happened to know that particular crime was in military circles. The conclusion there was obvious, and something Grey had also known for years; the military hierarchy had no appetite for that sort of scandal – save, of course, when it might cover something worse. But when a blind eye might be turned, it almost certainly would be.

By the same token, a military court was not eager to convict an officer of sodomy – save the officer was a nuisance for other reasons, as Otway and Bates had been. Thus, while a court-martial was not bound by the rules of evidence that constrained the barristers and judges, there was still a strong reluctance to accept anything short of an eyewitness's account.

And Grey was now the only eyewitness.

The evening was not cold in the slightest, but he shivered abruptly.

Could he stand before the court-martial, swear to tell the truth – and lie? With everyone – including the judges – completely aware that it *was* a lie?

It would be the ruin of his own career and repu-tation. Some might see such an act as misguided loyalty to family; many more would see it as an indication that Grey sympathized with Percy's inclinations – or shared them. Either way, rumors would follow him. Discharge from the army was inevitable, and with the odor of such scandal cling-ing to him, he could not hope to find any reception in English society – or even in the service of a foreign army.

And yet . . . it was Percy's life. *If there is any kindness left between us . . . I beg you. Save me.* Could he tell the truth and see Percy go to the gallows – or to prison or indentured servitude – and then simply return to his own life?

For an instant, he fantasized the possibility of securing Percy's freedom, whether by lies or bribery, then going abroad, the two of them together. He had money enough.

To live a pointless existence of idleness with a man whom he could not trust. No, it would not serve.

'Damn you, Perseverance,' he said softly. 'I wish I had never set eyes upon you.' He sighed, rubbing the palms of his hands over his closed eyelids.

And yet he did not mean that, he realized. He *did* feel that way about Jamie Fraser – but not Percy. And became aware, very much too late, that he did love Percy Wainwright. But . . . enough to try to save him, at the cost of his own honor, his own life, even though there could be nothing left between them?

And then there was Hal. He touched his pocket again, distracted. If Symington knew about Custis, so did Hal. His brother would be grimly calculating what this might mean – and doubtless arriving at the same conclusions. The notion that Grey would lie at the court-martial, though – he doubted that Hal would imagine that possibility.

He did not know how much Hal might know or suspect of his own inclinations; the matter had never been spoken of between them, and never would be. But if he were to declare his intent to perjure himself before the court-martial in order to save Percy's life – Hal would likely do anything to stop him, including shooting him. Not fatally, he supposed, with a wry smile at the thought; only sufficiently as to justify shutting him up somewhere under a doctor's care.

Still, that would not solve the problem; Percy would merely languish in prison until such time as Grey was recovered enough to testify. No, he decided, Hal's response would more likely be to knock Grey over the head, bundle him into a sack, and have him smuggled aboard a merchantman bound for China, after which he would declare Grey lost at sea, and . . .

He discovered that he was laughing helplessly at the thought, tears coming to his eyes.

'Christ, Hal, I wish you *would*,' he said aloud, and quite suddenly thought of Aberdeen, realizing for the first time just how desperately his brother loved him.

'Christ, Hal,' he whispered.

Rubbing a sleeve over his face, he drew a deep breath of the heavy air, and smelled flowers. Peering downward, he saw a heap of wilted flowers, white and yellow, fallen to the ground. His elbow had dislodged them as he brushed against the little shrine; he gathered them gently into a bunch and laid them neatly back on the ledge at the front of it.

It was too dark to see the carving on the plaque

within the shrine, but his exploring fingers made out a roman numeral – II, he thought it was. It must be one of the Stations of the Cross von Namtzen had told him of. People walked from one such shrine to the next as a sort of devotional pilgrimage, meditating on the events in Christ's life leading to His crucifixion.

There was, of course, a threat in Percy's power, and one Grey was only too aware of, though Percy had sufficient delicacy not to have mentioned it. Facing the gallows, Percy might decide to reveal his relationship with Grey. Grey did not think such an allegation could be proved; no one had ever seen them in a compromising situation – but under the circumstances, the accusation would be damaging enough.

This, of course, was not something he could discuss with Hal.

He was not religious, but was sufficiently familiar with Scripture as to have heard the story of Gethsemane. *Let this cup pass away.*

He looked across the fields toward Hückelsmay, and saw the watch fires burning – the stations on his own road to Calvary, he thought grimly. He'd like to know what Christ would have done in his position, that's all.

He was quartered with several other British officers in one of the large farmhouses near the canal, a place called Hückelsmay. Despite the aura of suppressed tension, the atmosphere in the house was welcoming, the air filled with the scent of fried potatoes and roast pork, warm with smoke and conviviality.

Grey forced himself to eat a little, mostly for Tom's sake, and then went to sit in a corner, where he could avoid having to talk to people.

He was near a window, tightly closed and shuttered for the night, but he felt the draft from it nonetheless, and heard the occasional grunt of sleeping pigs, perhaps disturbed by the rich smell of their erstwhile brother roasting. All the houses near the *Landwehr* were encircled by small ditches or moats. As well as providing defense for the houses, these moats provided easy access to water, and provided an excellent wallow for the pigs, who lay blissfully sunk in the mud of the ditch, handy when wanted.

He should go up and sleep, he supposed – but he had the feeling that sleep would not come easily tonight. Better to be where there were other people than thrashing to and fro in darkness, alone with his thoughts.

He became gradually aware of eyes upon him, and looking up, found himself the cynosure of a small girl who stood in front of him. She wore a neat apron, a cap, and an unexpected pair of spectacles, which magnified her eyes remarkably, thus intensifying her gaze. She wore a small frown, as though not quite sure what he was.

'*Bitte?*' he said, employing that useful German

word which effortlessly encompasses 'please,' 'thank you,' 'I beg your pardon,' and 'what do you want?' in a single term of politeness.

The little girl at once executed a bob, and peered at him with increased intentness.

'*Herr* Thomas says I may speak to you, *mein Herr*,' she announced.

'Does he? Well, then, I am sure you may,' he said gravely. 'What is your name, *Kleine*?'

'Agnes-Maria. *Herr* Thomas says you are a great lord.' Her frown deepened a little, and her tone held a certain dubious note, as though suspecting that she had been practiced upon.

'Ah . . . something of the sort,' Grey replied warily. 'Why?'

She produced an inkhorn, a quill, and a copy-book from the folds of her apron, set these on the table beside him, and opened the book to a blank page.

'I am to write down, you see, a page.' She sighed at the enormity of the prospect, and turned her huge blue eyes reproachfully upon him, as though this drudgery were somehow his fault. 'A page about some foreign country. But I do not remember what the schoolmaster said about France or Holland. *Herr* Thomas, though, says that you have been to *Schottland* and know everything about it. So, you see—' She flipped open the inkwell on the table and picked up her quill, very matter-of-fact. 'You can tell me what you know, and I will write.'

'How efficient,' he said, smiling despite himself.

'Very well. Let me think how to begin. . . . Perhaps we should say first where Scotland is? Yes, that seems right. "Scotland lies to the north of England."'

'It is cold there?' the girl inquired, writing carefully.

'Very cold. And it rains incessantly. Let me spell "incessantly" for you. . . .'

A pleasant half hour spent in Scotland with Agnes-Maria left him, if not calmer, at least distracted, and he went to bed and fell asleep, to dream of cold, high mountains and the smoke of a fire in the Carryarick Pass.

Chapter 29

Dawn of Battle

He woke suddenly from a place beyond dreams, Tarleton's excited face an inch from his own.

'Sir! We've found them! It's starting!'

It was. All around him, officers were rolling from their beds, pulling curling papers from their hair, cursing and stumbling barefooted, calling for servants, ale, and chamber pots.

Tom was already there, jerking Grey's nightshirt unceremoniously off over his head and pulling his shirt over it in almost the same motion.

'Where?' he demanded of Tarleton, his head popping out of the neck. He jerked the garment into place, Tom already stooping with his breeches.

'Behind the dyke thing, the Land-ware.' Tarleton was dancing on his toes with impatience. 'We saw them – me and another scout who was in the church spire. The sky started to get light and there they were, creeping along the back of the dyke like skulking cowards!' His face shone under a sprinkling of soft, fair whiskers.

'Well done, Mr. Tarleton.' Grey smiled, tucking his shirt into his breeches. 'Go and shave. Then fetch Mr. Brett, see to my horse, and eat something. Both of you eat something. I'll join you – ouch!' Tom's hands paused in their hurry to untangle the snag of hair his brush had just encountered. 'I'll join you at the stable. Go!' He made a shooing motion and Tarleton shot out of the room like a flushed hare.

'Speak of shaving, me lord . . .' Tom's deft hands set by the hairbrush, and reached for the pot of shaving soap, the badger-bristle brush stirring up the foam with a scent of lavender.

Sitting on the bed as Tom shaved him, briskly plaited his hair, and bound it up, Grey wondered where young Agnes-Maria was. Probably moving hastily behind the English lines with her family. If Clermont's main body was indeed skulking behind the *Landwehr,* the French artillery was very likely within range of Hückelsmay – and the French were no respecters of private property.

'Here, me lord.' Tom thrust a pistol into his hands, then bent to fasten his sword belt. 'It's not loaded yet. D'ye want your cartridge box, or will one of your boys take it?'

'I'll have it. Shot bag, powder . . .' He touched the items attached to his belt, checking, then thrust his arms back into the leather jerkin Tom was holding for him, the one he wore in lieu of the usual waistcoat on battlefields.

He was aware that some of the English junior officers considered this garment mildly contemptible, but then, relatively few of them had been shot at yet. Grey had, repeatedly. It wouldn't save him from close fire, but the fact was that most of the French muskets had a very short range, and thus a good many musket balls were near spent by the time they reached a target. You could see them, sometimes, sailing almost lazily through the air, like bumblebees.

Coat, epaulets, gorget, laced hat . . . roll. Tom, always prepared, had thrust a crusty German roll into his hand, thickly buttered. Grey crammed the last of it into his mouth, shook crumbs from his lapels, and washed it down with coffee – one of the other orderlies had brewed some over a spirit lamp, the smell of it bracing.

Tom was circling him, eyes narrowed in concentration, lest he miss some vital detail of appearance. His round freckled face was anxious, but he said nothing. Grey touched him gently on the shoulder, making him look up.

'Me lord?'

'Thank you, Tom. I'll go now.' The jumble had almost sorted itself out. Officers were thundering down the wooden staircase, shouting to one another, calling for their ensigns, and the air was filled with the scents of coffee, powder, heel black, hot hair, pipe clay, and a strong odor of fresh piss, both from the chamber pots and from the urine-soaked lumps of stale bread the orderlies used to bring up the shine on gold lace.

Tom swallowed, and stood awkwardly back.

'I'll have your supper for you, me lord.'

'Thank you,' Grey repeated, and turned to go. He'd reached the door when he heard Tom cry out behind him.

'Me lord! Your dagger!'

He slapped at his waist in reflex, and found the place empty. He whirled on his heel to find Tom there, dagger in hand. He took it with a nod of thanks, and turning, ran down the stairs, tucking the knife into its sheath as he went.

His heart was thumping. In part from the natural atmosphere of excitement that attends a looming battle, in part from the thought that he might have found himself on the field without his dagger. He'd carried it since he was sixteen, and would have felt unarmed without it, pistol and sword notwithstanding.

The fact that he'd forgotten it, he thought, was not a good sign, and he touched the wire-wrapped hilt in an attempt to reassure himself.

Outside, the pigs were still snoring, both river and ditch invisible in a shroud of mist so thick that Grey wondered how the lookouts had ever seen the French troops. The air was fresh, though, with a spattering rain that came and went, and the weather did nothing to allay the spirits of the men.

He rode slowly through the forming columns, Brett and Tarleton foaming with excitement behind him. He felt the same excitement pulse through his own limbs – felt it in waves, coming off the men as they hurtled into position, clanking and cursing.

How does it work? his father had written in his campaign journal, after Sheriffmuir. *How do emotions transmit themselves between men, with no gesture, no slightest word spoken? Whether it be confidence and joy, despair, or the fury of attack, there is no evidence of its spread. It is just suddenly there. What can be the mechanism of this instantaneous communication?* Grey didn't know, but he felt it.

'Hoy!' he shouted at the retreating back of a bare-headed soldier. 'Hoy, Andrews! Lose something?'

He unhooked the calvary saber he carried and leaned down, neatly catching up the battered tricorn on its point before the hat could be trampled. It clinked; Andrews, like many of the infantry, had crisscrossed the inside of his hat with iron strips, the better to turn a blow.

Nudging Karolus through the throng, Grey deposited the hat neatly on Andrews's startled head, provoking gales of laughter from the man's companions. Grey bowed nonchalantly, accepting their salutes, and making no effort to hide his own amusement. It was like wine, the air before a battle, and they were all drunk with anticipation.

They looked well, he thought with approval. Rough, by comparison to the burnished Prussians, but brimming with uncouth spirits and an open desire for the fight.

'Corporal Collet!' he bellowed, and thirty heads snapped round in his direction. The largest – and best – of the companies under his command, he had managed to keep Collet's company together for more than two years, drilled and brought on with such skill as essentially to act as a single entity. A sight to delight a commander's heart.

'Sir!' Collet barked, bounding up beside him.

'Take your company to the front, Corporal. Form on the left; you're the pivot. Wheel on Captain Wilmot's signal.'

'Sir, yes, sir!' Collet's seamed face beamed at the honor, and he bounded back to his men, barking orders. The men cheered, and went off at the trot, shoulder to shoulder, like a flock of particularly bloodthirsty sheep.

Noise. Complete confusion, but an orderly confusion. Corporals shouting their companies into order, lieutenants and captains roving to and fro on horseback, minding their divisions. And the hussars who served as messengers, darting swiftly through the throng like minnows through the slow-moving shoals of reddish fish.

A pig burst suddenly out of the shredding mist and galloped in panic through a distant company, causing whoops and shrieks. One of the German officers shot it, and a small band of harpies rushed through the forming ranks to fall upon it with their knives, making the soldiers step round them. Grey sighed, knowing he would at some point be presented with a bill for that pig.

German camp followers. These women – some prostitutes, some wives, and half of them vicious slatterns, regardless of legal status – clung like cockleburs to the army's arse, following closely even into battle, ready to loot and plunder at the slightest opportunity. God help anyone who fell in their path, Grey thought, watching the butchery.

The sound of bugling cut through the thick air, and Karolus flung back his head with a snort. Grey felt a sudden sharp pang; he would so much have wished to share this with Percy. But there was no time for regret. The army was on the move.

There was no question of stealth. Duke Ferdinand's combined forces numbered something in excess of thirty-two thousand troops, the French and Austrians forty-seven thousand. It was a straightforward matter, insofar as anything done by an army could be so described, of speed, force, tactics – and will.

A young hussar dashed up to Grey, brimming with excitement and self-importance, delivering a note.

Luck, it said.

Grey smiled and stuffed the note in his pocket. He had sent his own, identical note to Hal a few minutes before. It was their habit, when possible, to wish each other luck before a battle. He valued Hal's wishing him luck the more, because he knew Hal did not believe in it.

Duke Ferdinand's plan was novel, and daring: infantry to swing out and encompass the French left flank, the Prussian cavalry to press the advantage, artillery advancing into position to pin the divisions on the right. And the 46th to be in the van of the flanking maneuver.

He chose to carry a cavalry saber, rather than the customary officer's hanger, both because he liked the weight and because it was more visible. He raised it now and bellowed, 'Advance by company! Quick . . . March!'

Brett and Tarleton took up the cry, which spread to the sergeants and through the lines, and the columns began to move with amazing speed, churning the ground to black mud.

The fog drifted in patches over the marshy ground, but did not clear. In spite of the intermittent rain – repeated bellows of 'Keep your powder dry, God damn your eyes!' rang from every quarter of the field in various languages – it was not a cold day, and the men, while damp, were cheerful.

Near the *Landwehr*, he pulled Karolus a little to the side, watching his men stream by, listening to the noises becoming audible from the French and Austrian lines forming on the other side of the dyke. The *Landwehr* itself was a formidable barrier – two water-filled ditches, each some ten feet wide, with a massive central bank, fifteen feet in width, between them – but not a very wide one. A thick growth of trees and bushes edged the dyke here; he couldn't see the enemy through mist and leaves, but he could hear them easily – French, he thought.

Shouts, cheers, the distant creak of caisson wheels as artillery wheeled into position . . . then these were drowned in the boom of drums, as

Ferdinand's Prussian cavalry came within earshot on Grey's side of the *Landwehr*, led by their drum horse. Dragon-Riders, they called themselves, with that typical German inclination for drama. They looked it, though. Tall men all, straight in the saddle and beautiful in their glory, and his heart was stirred, despite himself.

Karolus was stirred, too; he jerked, snorted, and made as though to join them. He had once been a cavalry horse – loved drums and adored parades. Grey reined him in, but the stallion continued to dance and toss his head.

Karolus was stirring up the ensigns' horses, too, and Grey was not sure that Brett and Tarleton could keep their own mounts under control. Clicking his tongue, he pulled Karolus's head round, and rode a little way into the trees along the *Landwehr*, trailed by his ensigns.

He could still hear the cavalry drums, but the horses had quieted a little, with the others out of sight. Brett's horse bobbed his head, wanting to drink from the ditch, and Grey nodded at Brett to allow it.

'Not too much,' he said automatically, his attention divided between the sounds behind them and those to his left, where the other British regiments were massing to attack the French right flank. The double ditches of the *Landwehr* were full to the banks, swelled by the recent rains, and the water ran muddy and quick below him, grass trailing in the current.

'What's that?' he heard Brett say, startled, and

looked where his ensign was pointing. Several tall, pointed shapes were dimly visible among the trees on the other side of the dyke. He blinked, and made sense of what he was seeing just as one of the shapes flung back its arm and hurled something in his direction.

'Grenades!' he roared. 'Get clear, get clear!'

The first one struck a few feet to his right and exploded, sending pottery shards in all directions. Some struck Karolus, who shied violently, then bucked and reared as more grenades struck the bank between the ditches – bright flashes from the ones that went off, others rolling like fallen apples, smothered and harmless in the dirt, a few with live fuses hissing like snakes.

Grey grappled the reins in one hand, fumbling for his pistol. There was a sudden feeling of warmth down his face, the sting of blood running into one eye. He got the pistol and fired blind. There were bangs nearby and the smell of powder; Brett and Tarleton were firing, too.

A thunder of hooves; Brett's mount, riderless, fled past Grey. Where . . . ? He glanced round – there. Brett had been thrown, was rising from the ground, smeared with mud.

'Get back!' Grey shouted, pulling Karolus's head around. The grenadiers were pulling back, too, out of pistol range, but one lucky last throw landed a live one in the grass at Brett's feet, a blue-clay sphere, fuse sparking.

The boy stared at it, transfixed.

In sheer reflex, Grey spurred the horse and made for Brett, struck him glancing, and knocked him away. No time to think, to swerve – Karolus shifted suddenly, bunching under him, and jumped the ditch. Hit the bank with a jolt that jarred Grey's teeth, flexed once more and leapt the second ditch, skidding and floundering as he landed in wet grass, flinging his hapless rider up onto his neck.

A hand grabbed Grey's arm and wrenched him off the horse. He fell, struggling, throwing elbows and knees in all directions, tore loose and rolled, yelling, '*Lauf! Lauf!*'

A yelp from the man who had grabbed for Karolus's bridle, then the drumming of hooves as the horse galloped off into the mist. Grey had no time to worry about him; the grenadier who'd pulled him off was crouching, a wary look on his face and a dagger in his hand. Three or four more lurked behind him, wide-eyed with surprise.

'Surrender,' the grenadier said in French. 'You are my prisoner.'

Grey hadn't breath to spare in reply. He'd dropped his saber in the fall, but it lay on the ground, a few feet away. Gasping and swallowing, he gestured briefly to the grenadier for patience, walked over, and picked up the sword. Then he gulped air, swung it two-handed round his head, and, lunging forward, struck at the grenadier's neck with the fixed intent of removing his head. He halfway succeeded, and the shock of it nearly dislocated every bone in his arms.

The grenadier fell backward, the spurting blood from his neck failing to obscure the look of total astonishment on his face. Grey staggered, barely kept a grip on his sword, but knew that to lose it was to die on the spot.

Two of the grenadiers fell to their knees, trying to aid their stricken comrade. Another was backing away, mouth open beneath his mustache in horrified surprise. And the last, God damn him, was shrieking for help, meanwhile rummaging frantically in his bag. Grey began to back away, bloody saber at the ready.

Grenadiers weren't schooled in hand-to-hand combat; they didn't normally need to be. But there were plenty of troops nearby who were, and dozens of them would arrive in seconds. Grey dashed a sleeve across his face, trying to clear the blood from his eye. His scalp was stinging now; a shard from the first grenade must have struck him.

Meanwhile, the grenadier had drawn two more grenades from his bag, clay spheres each the size of an orange, filled with gunpowder. He carried a coil of hissing slow-match in a brass tube at his belt; the smoke from it wreathed his features, and he coughed, but didn't blink.

Black eyes fixed on Grey, he touched the fuses of the grenades to the slow-match, one and then the other. Sweat and blood were running down Grey's face, stinging his eyes.

Jesus. At six feet, he could scarcely miss. Grey saw the man's lips move, counting.

Grey turned and ran for his life. There was a roar of voices behind him, and the loud sharp *pop!* of an exploding grenade. Small objects pinged hard against his back and thighs, stung his legs but failed to penetrate the leather jerkin.

They were all after him now. He could hear the thump of feet and grunts of effort as they heaved their grenades. Terror lent wings to his feet, and he zigzagged frantically through the trees, the *flash-bang* of explosions shaking the bushes and driving rooks and blackbirds shrieking into the clouds above.

He skidded to a halt and nearly fell. Oh, Christ.

A company of French infantry turned surprised faces toward him, then, as comprehension dawned, several of them slung the muskets from their shoulders and began hastily to load. No way past them. Beyond them . . . beyond them lay rank upon rank upon rank of soldiers, a serried mass of blue and white.

A tremendous boom seemed to shake the trees, and a cannonball smashed through the brush on the far side of the dyke, no more than a hundred yards from where he stood. The battle had begun.

Lord John Grey sketched a gesture of salute toward the startled infantry, turned right, and amid a belated hail of musket balls and the occasional grenade, scrambled up the bank, and jumped into the *Landwehr*.

He couldn't swim. Not that it mattered. He was wearing more than a stone's weight of equipment, and he sank like a stone, bubbles gushing up through his clothes. Hit the muddy bottom. Bent his knees in panic and jumped, to rise no more than a foot or so. Sank back and felt his boots sink deep in the silt. He struggled blind in the murky water, tried frantically to shuck his coat, realized finally that he was still gripping his sword, and dropped it. His chest burned, swelling with the vain, irresistible desire to breathe.

He got the coat half off, and churned what breath there was in his lungs up and down the column of his throat, in hopes of extracting the last vestige of air from it. Scrabbled for the buckle of his belt, couldn't get it loose, went back to yanking at his coat. Could hold his precious breath no longer, and let it go in a blubbering, bubbling cloud of relief and regret.

He was still mindlessly trying to get the damned coat off. It was stuck, wrenched askew over his shoulders, and he thrashed about in suffocating frenzy, fighting the murk, the mud, the weight of the water, the coat, the heavy boots, his straining chest, his goddamn *cartridge box,* for Christ's bloody sake, whose strap had got round his neck and was going to strangle him before he drow— bloody *hell!*

Something struck his hand, hard. Panicked images of sharks, fish teeth, blood – he jerked back.

Idiot, he thought, with what faint vestige of sanity

remained in his darkening mind. *You're in a fucking ditch.*

And with that, reached out quite calmly and took hold of the thing his hand had struck. A tree root, curving out of the bank. Waved his other hand gently around, found a bloody tangle of roots – mats and strings and woody stems, a fucking plethora of roots. Pulled the cartridge box off over his head, dropped it, took a good grip, pulled one boot from the muck, and began to climb.

His face broke the surface in a rush of air so glorious that he didn't care whether that breath might be his last.

He clung like a snail for several minutes, limbs trembling and heart pounding from the struggle, just breathing. Then, as his mind cleared, he realized that he had come up beneath an over-hanging shelf of grassy earth. If any marksmen lingered on the bank above, it was no matter; he was invisible.

There was a lot of noise near at hand, but none of it directly overhead, and from what he could make out, none of it concerned with him. Orders were being shouted in French; the infantry company above was about to depart. He put his forehead against the cool mud of the bank and closed his eyes, waiting. Breathing.

He regretted the loss of his saber. The pistol was still in his belt, God knew how – but soaked and useless.

That left the dagger as his only usable weapon. Though given his position, he reflected, it probably didn't matter.

He was on the wrong side of the *Landwehr*, crouched under a bush, sodden and cold, with several thousand enemy soldiers a few dozen yards away. No, it didn't matter much.

Cautious peeping through the bushes, together with what he could hear, gave him a general notion of the shape of the battle. Most of the artillery was to his left – the French right flank. The cannon were firing sporadically from both sides, still estimating range. A good deal of noise in the distance to his right, and brief clouds of powder smoke rising white as volleys were fired. Not a lot; no real engagement there yet. The ruse had worked, then; Clermont had been taken by surprise. Drums in the distance, a brief tattoo. The cavalry was still moving.

So Ferdinand's troops were on their way around the left flank, as planned, the French and Austrians caught in confusion, trying to turn to meet the attack. That was where he *ought* to be, commanding his men, in the thick of it. He glanced above him at the opposite bank in frustration – empty. God knew what was happening. Brett and Tarleton must have rushed off at once to tell someone – who? he wondered. His blood ran cold at the thought of Ewart Symington taking his command. He could only hope that the two ensigns had got to his brother first.

He didn't bother worrying about what Hal would

do to him. If he survived long enough to see his brother again, he'd think about it then.

Three choices: sit here shivering and hope no one stumbled over him; walk out and surrender to the nearest French officer, if he managed to do that without being killed first; or try to make it to the end of the *Landwehr*, where he could cross the canal and rejoin his own troops.

Right. One choice. He hesitated for a moment, wondering whether to discard his sodden red coat, but in the end, kept it. Coatless, he'd likely be shot for a deserter by either side, and it was possible that someone on the English side would spot him and lend aid.

His scalp was tender and still oozing – his fingers came away red when he prodded it – but at least blood wasn't pouring down his face anymore. With a last reconnaissance, he left the shelter of his bush, crawling through the thin screen of foliage.

He wanted desperately to go right, to find his own men. But they were nearly a mile away by now, and already fighting, if all was well. To the left, it was no more than two hundred yards to the near end of the *Landwehr*, and from what he could hear, the fighting there was mostly artillery. Much safer for a single man, moving on foot; if he didn't get close enough to a French gun crew for them to shoot him with their pistols, the odds of being struck by a random cannonball were reasonably low.

All went well, bar minor alarms, until he came in sight of the footbridge that crossed the canal at the end of the *Landwehr*. A group of women was sitting on it, watching the battle with avid attention.

Camp followers by their dress, and speaking German – but he couldn't distinguish their accents as Prussian or Austrian, God damn it. If they were Prussian, they likely wouldn't molest a British officer. Austrian, though – he remembered that pig, and the women's sharp knives. Only a couple of hours since the pig had died; it seemed much longer.

He tightened his face into a forbidding glower, put a hand on his useless pistol, and walked toward the women. They fell silent, and five pairs of eyes fixed on him, sharp and bright with calculation. One of them smiled and curtsied to him – but her eyes never left him, and he felt the ripple of anticipation run through the others.

'*Guten Tag, mein Herr,*' she said. 'You have been swimming?'

They all cackled, in a show of bad teeth and worse breath.

He nodded coolly to them, but didn't speak.

'What are you doing here, English pig?' another asked in German, smiling so hard that her cheeks bunched. 'You are a coward, that you run from the fight?'

He stared blankly at her, nodded again. Two of them moved suddenly, as though to give him room to pass. Their hands were out of sight, buried in their skirts, and he could feel the excitement shivering in the air between them, a sort of fever that passed among them.

He smiled pleasantly at one as he passed, then took his hand off the pistol, bunched his fist, and punched her just under the jaw. The women all shrieked, save the one he'd hit, who simply fell backward over the low wall of the bridge. He ran, seeing from the corner of his eye the woman's skirt, belled like a flower, floating in the water.

Something went *thunk!* behind him, and he glanced back over his shoulder. A large piece of ordnance had struck the bridge dead center – half the bridge was gone, and so were most of the women. One was left, staring at him from the far side, the water rushing past beneath her feet, her eyes and mouth round with shock.

He ran for the gun that had destroyed the bridge, trusting that his uniform would keep him from being shot. His lungs were laboring, the wet clothes weighing him down, but at least he was near his own lines.

It was a small battery, three cannon, one of the gun crews English – he saw the distinctive blue of the uniforms. No one was shooting at him, but active guns on the French side were keeping them busy; a cannonball hurtled past him, low and deadly, before crashing through a small tree, leaving the butchered stump quivering.

He was stumbling, barely able to breathe, but near enough. Near enough. He staggered to a halt and bent over, hands on his knees as he gasped for air. Men were shouting nearby, the rhythmic bark of a Prussian commander punctuated by an English voice, shrill with passion, screaming. He wasn't sure whether the screams were directed at the enemy or the English gun crew, and looked to see.

The crew. Something had happened to demoralize them – a heavy ball dropped within ten feet of him, sinking into the earth, and his flesh shook with the impact. Their lieutenant was shrieking at them, trying to rally them. . . . Grey wiped a sleeve across his face, and turned to look back across the river. The woman on the shattered bridge was gone.

A voice spoke suddenly behind him in a tone of absolute amazement, and he turned toward the lieutenant who had been screaming an instant before.

A cannonball came skipping across the ground like a stone across a pond, struck a buried rock, hopped high, and smashed through the lieutenant's head, removing it.

Blood fountained from the still-standing body, spraying several feet into the air. Ropes of blood lashed Grey's face and chest, blinding him, shocking hot through his wet clothes. Gasping, he dashed a sleeve across his eyes, clearing them in time to see the lieutenant's body fall, arms thrown wide in boneless grace. The sword he had been holding rolled from his grasp, silver in the grass.

Grey seized it in reflex, and whirled on the gun crew, who had begun to edge away from the smoking cannon. The bombardier with the linstock was nearest; Grey fetched the man a blow across the side of the head with the flat of his blade that sent him reeling back across the gun's barrel, then bounded at the rammer, who stared at him as though seeing Satan sprung from hell, eyes white and terrified in a sooty face.

'Pick it up!' Grey roared, stabbing the sword at the ramrod that lay fallen on the grass. 'Do it, damn your eyes! You – back to your duty, God damn you – go back, I say!' One of the loaders had tried to slip past him. The man stopped, frozen, eyes rolling to and fro in panic, seeking escape.

Grey grabbed the man by the shoulder, pushed him half round, and kneed him in the buttocks, shouting. There was blood in his mouth; he choked and spat, kicked at the loader, who was fumbling halfheartedly at the pile of cartridges beneath a canvas sheet. The sponger had already fled; he could see the man's blue coat bobbing up and down as he ran.

Grey lunged in that direction by instinct, but realized that he could not pursue the deserter and turned instead ferociously on the remnant crew.

'Load!' he barked, and snatched the linstock from the bombardier, motioning the soldier to replace the man who had fled. Sponger and rammer fell to their work at once, with no more than a hasty glance at Grey, blood-soaked and vicious. The erstwhile bombardier was clumsy, but willing. Grey barked them through the maneuver, once, again, forcing them, guiding them, and then felt them begin to drop back into the accustomed rhythm of the work and pick up speed, gradually losing their terror in the encompassing labor of serving the gun.

His throat was raw. The wind whipped away half his words and what was left was barely intelligible – but he saw the crew respond to the lash of his voice, and kept shouting.

Cannon were firing close at hand but he couldn't tell whether they were friend or foe; clouds of black powder smoke rolled over them, obscuring everything.

His soaked clothes had gone cold again, and it was raining. He had taken the coil of smoking slow-match from the bombardier and tied it in its bag to his own belt. His fingers were stiff, clumsy; he had difficulty forcing the lighted fuse into the linstock, but forced himself to keep the rhythm, shouting orders in a voice that cracked like broken iron. Sponge. Vent. Load cartridge. Ram. Load wadding. Ram. Check vent. Powder. Fall back! And the hissing small flame at the end of the linstock coming down toward the touchhole, sure and graceful, with no sense at all that his own hand guided it.

That moment of suspended animation and the crash and buck of the gun. The first one left him deafened; he knew he was still shouting only because his throat hurt. He snatched a lump of damp wadding from the ground and hastily crammed some of it into his ears. It didn't help much.

The rain grew momentarily heavier, cutting through the smoke and taste of blood with a freshness that eased his aching chest. The powder, was it covered? Yes, yes, the powder monkey was still at his post, a scorched-looking boy wide-eyed with fright but holding the canvas tight over the powder kegs, against the pull of the wind.

'Sponge piece!' he shouted, and heard the word muffled inside his skull as though it came from some vast distance, far away. 'Load piece! Ram!'

He spared a moment to look before touching off the next shot – so far, he had been firing with not the slightest thought for attitude or effect – and forced himself not to blink as the gun went off with a jump like a live thing and the thunder that made you feel as though the ground shook, though in fact it was your own flesh shaking.

The shot soared high, came down a dozen yards short of a patch of French artillery – smoke sucked suddenly away by the wind, he saw the red of their uniforms and the belch of black smoke from the French gun's barrel. The shot came wide of his own position and he made a hasty calculation of wind, already shouting orders to adjust the trunnions, lower the barrel . . . one degree? Two?

Now he saw the milling blur of white, green, and blue, infantry massing behind the French cannon.

Dare he try for that interesting maneuver whereby a cannonball was fired deliberately low, with the intent of bouncing repeatedly through an enemy phalanx? There was a seething mass of French and Austrian uniforms beyond the gun, perfect. . . . He would think the ground too soft with damp, save that he'd just seen the same technique employed successfully upon it. He gritted his teeth, but could not help but glance at the fallen lieutenant, noticing only now that the body had fallen at the foot of one of the stones marking the Stations of the Cross. 'IX,' it said, but he had no time to try to make out the picture on it.

'Five!' he shouted, an eye on the moving French line, 'and one degree west!' The rammer at once jammed his rod in the barrel and the powder monkey ran to lend his strength, as the loaders jerked out the trunnions and put them in again, then threw themselves against the cannon's limber, turning the barrel just enough . . .

'Load!'

The rain came and went in gusty squalls; it had stopped for a moment and he wiped his face again on his sleeve, feeling some liquid – water, sweat, blood – drip down inside his coat from his queued hair.

'Fire!'

By God, it worked, and a cheer went up from his crew as they saw the ball hop murderously across the field, knocking Frenchmen down like ninepins as it went.

'Again, again!' he bellowed, striking his fist on the breech. The sponger was sponging like a maniac, not waiting for the order, and the loaders were already passing the next cartridge to the mouth.

'Down!' he shouted, and fell flat along with the crew as a shot in reply thudded into the ground six feet away. They rose up again, yelling like demons and shaking their fists. The French gun crew was hopping up and down like fleas, gleeful at the effect of their shot. Grey was obliged to bellow and slap one man across the back with the flat of his sword again to bring his own crew to their senses.

'Swivel! Swivel to bear on them! Hurry, damn you!'

Suddenly realizing their precarious position of opportunity and peril, his crew fell to like fiends, swinging the barrel to bear directly upon the French cannon. The French abruptly stopped cheering and began hastily to serve their own gun.

The French had the range already, were sure to beat them – Grey snatched the useless pistol from his belt and charged the French position, shrieking like a madman and waving both pistol and sword. The ground seemed to pitch and sway beneath his feet, a blur of grass and mud.

It was perhaps two hundred yards between the English and the French cannons. He was close enough to see the Frenchmen's mouths hanging open when their officer suddenly realized what Grey was about and groped madly for his own pistol. Grey promptly turned and ran like a hare back toward his own crew, leaping low bushes and zigzagging, seeking cover in the drifting rags of powder smoke. He couldn't tell whether the Frenchman was firing at him or no; the air cracked with random fire and the sound of bugles. Goddamned cavalry, he thought. Always in the bloody way—

'Duck!' came a faint cry, and he threw himself headlong in the sopping grass just as his own gun spoke near at hand. Without looking to see the possible effect of the shot, he scrambled up into a crouch and scuttled the rest of the way, arriving winded and wheezing to the cheers of his men.

'Once more,' he panted. 'Give it them again!'

The men were already at it; the linstock was thrust into his hand and he fumbled for the fuse, but his hand was shaking too badly to manage. The powder monkey seized the wobbling end of the slow-match and thrust it through the hole, slashing off the bit of fuse so hastily that the knife tip scratched Grey's hand, though he didn't feel it.

'Fall back!' he gasped, and lowered the hissing match to the touchhole.

There was an instant of breathless expectancy, and then the world disappeared in a blast of fire and darkness.

He woke to a sensation of drowning and gasped for air, then froze, gripped by a pain so intense that he actually *saw* it, as a physical entity separate from himself. A red thing, shot with black, pulsing and whirling like a pinwheel. Sharp – he felt his lungs bursting and had to breathe, would have screamed if he'd had any breath, the knife edge of the spinning thing slicing through his flesh like butter. It cut straight through his chest and pressed him to the ground with a crushing weight.

'Major! Major!'

Someone touched him, and he flung out a hand, blind, grappling for help, God, help, he couldn't *breathe* . . .

Something smaller than the pain pushed him, hard, and he was suddenly on his side, doubled up, coughing, jerking in agony with each involuntary cough, but *had* to, couldn't not, couldn't stop, and spikes of air stabbed his chest coming in, as though he'd breathed in a mass of drawing pins, went out in a blinding sheet of white-hot pain and black smoke.

'Major!'

'Oh, shit, oh, shit, oh, shit!' someone said nearby.

He was in complete agreement with this, but couldn't say so. He was still coughing, but not as much; saliva was running from his mouth, making runnels in the soot, and he seemed to be making a whimpering noise with each jerked breath.

Hands on him, he felt them, frantic thumps and grabs, pulling at his coat, his limbs. He made a frenzied noise of protest and felt bone ends grate – Christ, he *heard* them grate – and a mass of green and brown and blue and red spun past, and he realized dimly that his eyes were open.

He blinked, tears streaming, saw the black spikes of his clotted lashes and cold gray stone by his face.

Jesus Falls the Third Time, he thought. *Poor bastard.*

Someone was bellowing overhead, meaningless sounds. Cannon was thumping somewhere near; he felt the ground shake, felt his heart stop with each crash, and wished it would stop once and for all, it hurt so when it started again. . . .

'Jesus! Look at the blood of him! He'll never last!'

'His arm, let me bind his arm—'

'No use, no use, it's blown clean off!'

'It's not, I saw his fingers move, back off – back *off*, I said, God damn your eyes!'

The voices seemed to come through a fog of noise, something rushing, like a waterfall that filled his ears. He still felt the thump of the guns, but that, too, had faded somehow, seemed safely distant. The pain had drawn in upon itself, and sat sullen in his chest, glowing like a lump of metal flung from a blacksmith's forge, molten and heavy.

He hoped his heart would not come too close to it. He could see his heart, too, a pulsing dark-red thing, almost black by contrast with the brilliant crimson of the pain.

They were saying something now about the gun – were they fighting the gun? – but he couldn't focus on the words; they all rushed past, part of a waterfall, loud in his ears. Water . . . warm water. It was rushing over him, his clothes felt sodden, he could feel the trickle of it down his neck, over his ribs, the feel of wet cloth stuck to his belly.

'Oh, Jesus,' said a voice above, despairing. 'So much blood.'

He was in a room somewhere, filled with light. Wounded, he'd been wounded. By reflex, he grabbed for his balls. Their reassuring presence compensated in some measure for the rending pain that shot through his body with the movement, but it was still enough to make him gasp.

Something moved across the light, and someone bent over him.

'Me lord!' Tom Byrd's voice came loud in his ear, halfway between fright and hope. 'Quick, quick! Get the earl – he's awake!'

'Earl?' Grey croaked. 'What . . . Hal?'

'Your brother, aye. He'll be right here, me lord, don't you trouble yourself. D'ye want water, me lord?'

He wanted water somewhat more than heaven, earth, or the riches of the fabled East. He was dimly aware of someone arguing about whether he should be allowed to have any, but his precious Tom snarled like a badger and elbowed whoever it was away.

Cool pottery touched his mouth, and he gulped, half choking.

'Slow, me lord,' Tom said, moving the cup away, and put a hand behind his head to steady him. 'Slow as does it. That's it, now. Lap it like a dog, now, just a bit at a time.'

He lapped, urgent for more, trying to will the water into the parched tissues of his mouth and throat, tasting the faint silver of blood from a cracked lip. For a brief period of ecstasy, nothing existed save the bliss of drinking water. The cup was drawn away, though, and Tom lowered his head gently to the pillow, leaving him blinking at the ceiling, panting shallowly.

He'd ignored the pain in his chest and arm for the sake of water, but now realized that he could not draw a full breath. The left side of his body seemed encased in something solid, and he recalled quite suddenly hearing someone say that his arm had been blown off.

He jerked, trying to raise his head to look, and reached across his body with his right hand.

'Oh, Jesus!' Colored lights danced before his eyes and a cold sweat broke out on his body – but his left arm was there, thank God. It was still attached, though plainly not in good shape. He tried wiggling the fingers, which proved a mistake.

'Don't move, me lord!' Tom sounded alarmed. 'You mustn't. Doctor says as it could kill you, if you move!'

He didn't doubt it. The pain was back, grimly sitting on his chest, driving the breath out of him, trying patiently to stop his heart.

He lay still, eyes closed and teeth gritted, breathing in sips of air. He could smell pigs, ripe and near at hand. It must be one of the farmhouses near the may.

'Tom. What . . . happened?'

'They said the gun blew up, me lord. But the battle's won,' he added, though Grey didn't really care at the moment. 'Mr. Brett nearly drowned in the dyke, but Mr. Tarleton fished him out.'

There were other people in the room now, he

didn't know how many. Voices, murmuring gravely. Tom was babbling nonsense in his ear, in a patent attempt to keep him from hearing what was being said. He raised his right hand, but let it fall, too exhausted to try to shush Tom. Besides, he thought he didn't really want to hear what they were saying.

The voices stopped and went away. Tom fell silent, but stayed by him, dabbing sweat from his face and neck, now and then wetting his lips with water from the cup.

He could feel the fever starting. It was a sly thing, barely noticeable by contrast with the pain, but he was aware of it. He felt that he should fight, concentrate his mind to drive it back, but felt too tired to do anything but go on breathing, one short, shallow gasp at a time.

Perhaps he fell asleep, perhaps his attention only wandered. He was aware all at once that the voices were back, and Hal with them.

'All right, John?' Hal's hand took hold of his sound right arm, squeezing.

'No.'

The hand squeezed harder.

'You see, my lord?' Another voice came from his other side. He cracked one eye open, far enough to see an earnest cove with a long face and a stern mouth, this downturned in displeasure at Grey's state – or perhaps his existence. The name popped into his mind, sudden as if the face had acquired a label – Longstreet. Mr. Longstreet, army surgeon.

'Shit,' he said, and closed his eyes. Hal squeezed

him again, evidently thinking this remark a response to the pain.

Another of the voices loomed up at the foot of the bed, this one speaking German. Burly sort in a green uniform, jabbing his finger at Grey in a definite sort of way.

'. . . must amputate, as I said.'

He was barely lucid enough to hear this, and flapped the uninjured arm in a feeble attempt at defense.

'. . . rather die.' Hoarse and cracked, it didn't sound like his voice, and for a moment, he wondered who'd said that. Hal was scowling at him, though, attention momentarily diverted from the doctor.

The lining of his mouth stuck to his teeth, and he worked his tongue in a frantic effort to generate enough saliva to speak. His body convulsed in the effort and he reared up from the bed, fire roaring up the left side of his body.

'Don't . . . let 'em,' he said to his brother's swimming face, and fell back into darkness, hearing cries of alarm.

The next time he came round, it was to find himself bound to a bedstead. He checked hastily, but his left arm was still amongst those present. It had been splinted and wrapped in bandages and it hurt amazingly, much worse than the last time he'd been awake, but he wasn't inclined to complain.

He was mildly surprised to hear that the surgeons were all still arguing – in German, this time. One of them was insisting to Hal that it was futile, as 'he' – Grey himself, he supposed – was undoubtedly going to die. Another – Longstreet, he thought, though he also spoke in German – was insisting that Hal must leave the surgeons to their work.

'I'm not leaving,' Hal said, close by. 'And he isn't dying. Are you?' he inquired, seeing that Grey was awake.

'No.' Some kind soul had wetted his lips again; the word came out in a whisper, but it was audible.

'Good. Don't,' Hal advised him, then looked up. 'Byrd, go and guard the door. No one is to come in here until I say so. Do you understand?'

'Yes, me lord!' The hand on Grey's shoulder lifted and he heard Tom Byrd's boots hurrying across the floor, the opening and closing of the door.

It occurred to Grey, with complete calm and utter clarity, that it would be extremely convenient for a number of people – not least himself – if he were to die as a result of his injuries.

Percy? He felt no more than a dim ache at thought of Percy, but retained that odd clarity of thought. Most of all to Percy. Custis was dead. If he were to die, as well, there would be no one to testify at the court-martial, and such a charge could not be pressed without witnesses.

Would they let Percy go on that account? Probably so. His career would be finished, of course. But the army would vastly prefer to dismiss him quietly than to have the ballyhoo and scandal of a trial for sodomy.

520

'Do you suppose it was my fault, as he said?' he asked his father, who was standing beside the bed, looking down at him.

'I shouldn't think so.' His father rubbed an index finger beneath his nose, as he generally did when thinking. 'You didn't force him to do it.'

'But was he right, do you think? Did he only do it because I couldn't give him what he needed?'

The duke's brows drew together, baffled.

'No,' he said, shaking his head in reproof. 'Not logical. Every man chooses his own way. No one else can be responsible.'

'What's not logical?'

Grey blinked, to find Hal frowning down at him.

'What's not logical?' his brother repeated.

Grey tried to reply, but found the effort of speaking so great that he only closed his eyes.

'Right,' Hal went on. 'There are fragments of metal in your chest; they're going to remove them.' He hesitated, then his fingers closed gently over Grey's.

'I'm sorry, Johnny,' he said, low-voiced. 'I don't dare let them give you opium. It's going to hurt a lot.'

'Are . . . you under th-the im . . . pression that this is . . . news to me?'

The effort of speaking made his head swim and gave him a nearly irresistible urge to cough, but it lightened Hal's expression a bit, so was worth it.

'Good lad,' Hal whispered, and squeezed his hand briefly, letting go then in order to fumble something out of his pocket. This proved, when Grey could fix his wavering gaze on it, to be a limp bit of leather, looking as though the rats had been at it.

'It was Father's,' Hal said, tenderly inserting it between Grey's teeth. 'I found it amongst his old campaign things. Ancestral teeth marks and all,' he added, making an unconvincing attempt at a reassuring grin. 'Don't know for sure whose teeth they were, though.'

Grey munched the leather gingerly, just as pleased that its presence saved him the effort of further reply. The taste of it was oddly pleasant, and he had a brief memory of Gustav the dachshund, gnawing contentedly at his bit of beef hide.

The picture reminded him of other things, though – the last time he had seen von Namtzen and the bitter smell of the chrysanthemums, the still more bitter smell of Percy's sweat and the night-soil bucket – he turned his head violently, away from everything. And then there was a looming presence over him, and he shivered suddenly as the sheet was lifted away.

His attention was distracted by a snicking sound. He turned his head and saw Hal checking the priming on the pistol he had just cocked. Hal sat down on a stool, set the pistol on his knee, and gave Longstreet a look of cold boredom.

'Get on, then,' he said.

There was a sudden chill as the dressing on Grey's chest was lifted, and he heard the sharp-edged hiss of metal and the surgeon's deep, impatient sigh. Hal's fingers tightened, grasping his.

'Just hold on, Johnny,' Hal said in a steady voice. 'I won't let go.'

SECTION V

Redivivus

Chapter 30

A Specialist in Matters of the Heart

In early September, he returned to England, to Argus House. Once well enough to leave the field hospital at Crefeld, he had been sent to Stephan von Namtzen's hunting lodge, where he had spent the next two months slowly recuperating under the tender care of von Namtzen, Tom Byrd, and Gustav the dachshund, who came into his room each night, moaned until lifted onto the bed, and then settled down comfortingly – if heavily – on Grey's feet, lest his soul wander in the night.

Shortly after his return to England, Harry Quarry came to call, keeping up an easy flow of cordialities and regimental gossip that demanded little more of Grey than the occasional smile or nod in response.

'You're tired,' Quarry said abruptly. 'I'll go, let you rest a bit.'

Grey would have protested politely, but the truth was that he was close to collapse, chest and arm hurting badly. He made to stand up, to see Quarry out, but his friend waved him back. He paused at the door, though, hat in hand.

'Have you heard much from Melton? Since you've been back, I mean?'

'No. Why?' Grey's arm ached abominably; he could barely wait until Harry departed and he could have Tom put the sling back on.

'I thought he might have told you – but I suppose he didn't want to hamper your recovery.'

'Told me what?' The pain in his arm seemed suddenly less important.

'Two things. Arthur Longstreet's back in England; army surgeon – you know him?'

'Yes,' Grey said, and his hand went involuntarily to his chest, the left side of it crisscrossed with barely healed weals. Tom, seeing it, had remarked that he looked as though he'd been in a saber fight. 'What – did he say why Longstreet's here?' Why would Hal not have told him this?

'Invalided out,' Quarry replied promptly. 'Shot through the lungs at Zorndorf; in a bad way, I hear.'

'Ah. Too bad,' he said mechanically, but relaxed a little. Longstreet was no threat, then – if in fact he ever had been. Grey would like to go and talk to him, but doubtless Hal had assumed there was nothing urgent in the matter, and wanted to wait until he had returned from campaigning himself.

'Two things, you said.' He recovered himself abruptly. 'What was the second?'

Quarry gave him a look of profound sympathy, though his voice was gruff in reply.

'They've moved Wainwright back to England. The court-martial's not yet scheduled, but it will be, soon. Probably early October. I thought you should know,' Harry added, more gently.

It was warm in the room, but gooseflesh rose on Grey's arms.

'Thank you,' he said. 'Where . . . where is he now, do you know?'

Harry shrugged.

'Small country gaol in Devonshire,' he said. 'But they'll likely move him to Newgate for the trial.'

Grey wanted to ask the name of the town in Devonshire, but didn't. Better if he didn't know.

'Yes,' he said, and struggled to his feet to see Harry out. 'I – thank you, Harry.'

Quarry gave him a grimace that passed for a smile, and with a small flourish, donned his hat and left.

'You all right, me lord?' Tom, who had never been farther than six feet from his side since Crefeld, came in with the sling for his arm, examining Grey with a look of worry. 'Colonel Quarry's tired you out. You look pale, you do.'

'I daresay,' Grey said shortly. 'I haven't been outdoors in three weeks. Here,' he said, seized by sudden recklessness. 'I'm going for a walk. Put that on, and fetch my cloak, please, Tom.'

Tom opened his mouth to protest, but seeing the look on Grey's face, shut it and sighed.

'Very good, me lord,' he said, resigned.

'And don't follow me!'

'No indeed, me lord,' Tom said, fastening the sling with a little more force than strictly necessary.

'I'll just wait for the rag-and-bone man to bring you home, after he picks you up in the street, shall I?'

That made Grey smile, at least.

'I'll come home on my own two feet, Tom, I promise.'

'Pah,' said Tom.

'Did you say, "Pah"?' Grey inquired, incredulous.

'Certainly not, me lord.' He swung Grey's cloak round his shoulders. 'Enjoy your walk, me lord,' he said politely, and stamped out.

The impetus of this conversation was sufficient to carry Grey as far as the edge of Hyde Park, where he leaned against a railing, waiting for his breath to come back. The wounds in his chest had healed fairly well, but any exertion made him feel as though his lungs were still riddled with bits of hot metal, and might fill with blood at any moment.

Early October. A month. Maybe less. Concerned with his own survival, he had managed not to think about anything for a time. And Minnie, Olivia, and Tom had gone to great lengths to be sure he was not exposed to anything upsetting; if Hal *had* mentioned Percy in any of his letters, he was sure Minnie had carefully suppressed the news.

He drew a shallow breath, breathed deeper, alert for rattling sounds in his chest, but there were none. Well, then. He straightened, taking his weight off the supporting railing. His arm was throbbing, despite the sling, but he ignored it. He had no idea what awaited him in October – but he would, as he'd promised Tom, go to it on his own two feet.

Slowly, he began the journey round the park, the thought of Percy like iron fetters on his feet.

The christening of Cromwell Percival John Malcolm Stubbs took place a week later, within ten feet of his birthplace. Olivia, displaying the same streak of stubbornness – some called it perversity – that characterized the family, had insisted upon the child's name, and as her husband was not there to stop her, it was done.

'Do you mind?' she had said to Grey. 'I won't do it, if you do. Melton would disapprove very much, I'm sure – but he isn't here to forbid it.'

'Are you asking me as *de facto* head of the family?' he'd asked, smiling a little, in spite of the circumstances. She'd come to find him in the garden, where Tom forced him out to sit every afternoon, on the theory that it disturbed the household to know that he was still lying in his bed, staring at the ceiling.

'Of course not,' Olivia had said. 'I'm asking you because – well, because.'

He probably should have tried to stop her. It was a private christening, with just the family and a few close friends – but people *would* talk. Lucinda, Lady Joffrey, was the child's godmother; Sir Richard stiffened visibly when he heard the vicar pronounce the child's names and shot a sharp look at Grey.

Grey was proof against looks, though, and speech, as well. He walked in a protective blanket of soft gray fog that muffled everything and made him feel invisible.

Now and then, something unexpected would penetrate the fog, sharp and wounding as the bits of shrapnel left in his chest, which worked their way one by one to the surface. Last week, it had been Harry's visit. Today, it was the light.

It had been cloudy outside, but now the sun burst through, and a flood of colored light from a stained-glass window fell over the christening party in soft lozenges of red and blue and green.

The space at his side had been no more than an empty expanse of floor slates. Suddenly, it was an abyss.

He looked away, heart pounding and palms sweating, and saw Olivia looking at him, wearing an expression of concern. He nodded at her, forcing a smile, and she relaxed a little, her attention returning to the infant in Lucinda's arms.

He spoke the words of the baptismal vows automatically, not hearing them. The air shook around him with the echo of organ pipes and clashing swords, and sweat ran down his back.

Lucinda removed the child's lacy cap, and Cromwell Percival John Malcolm Stubbs's head protruded from the christening robes, round as a cantaloupe. Grey fought back an inappropriate urge to laugh, and in the same instant, felt the piercing pain of being unable to turn to Percy and see the same laughter in his eyes.

It wasn't even the right name. He'd thought of

telling Olivia that, but hadn't. It might not be the only secret Percy still possessed, but it was the only one Grey could keep for him.

The date for the court-martial had been set: 13th October, at eleven in the morning. If they hanged Percy – on Grey's testimony – ought he to insist they do it as 'Perseverance'?

Lucinda kicked him in the ankle, and he realized that everyone was looking at him.

'Say, "I do believe,"' Lucinda said under her breath.

'I do believe,' he said obediently.

'I baptize thee, Cromwell Percival John Malcolm, in the name of the Father . . .'

The splash of water came to him, distant as rain.

I should have told her it was 'Perseverance,' he thought, in sudden panic. *What if it's all that should be left of him?*

But it was too late. He closed his eyes, and felt the soft fog come to wrap its comfort round him once again, the gray of it tinged with the light of saints and martyrs.

You don't look well, John.' Lucinda Joffrey circled round him, looking thoughtfully over her fan at him.

'You surprise me, madam,' he said politely. 'I made sure that I appeared the very picture of health.'

She didn't reply to that feeble retort, but closed

the fan with a snap and tapped him in the chest with it. He flinched as though she had stabbed him with a brooch-pin.

'Not. Well.' She tapped him with each word, and he backed up sharply, to get away from her. The christening party was being held in the garden at Argus House, though, and his escape was prevented by the fishpond behind him.

'Look at him, Horry,' she ordered. 'What does he look like?'

'The Duchess of Kendal,' Horace Walpole replied promptly. 'When I last saw her, two days before her unlamented demise.'

'Thank you, Mr. Walpole,' Grey said, giving him a look.

'Not but that your lordship has much better *taste* than my lady Kendal.' Walpole gave him back the look. 'The color of your face, however, is not what I would choose myself, to complement the shade of your suit. It is not *quite* the complexion of one of my darlings' – he nodded toward a sherry decanter on a nearby table, in which he had brought several small goldfish from his house at Strawberry Hill, as a present for Minnie – 'but approaching that hue.'

'You must see a doctor, John,' Lucinda said, lowering the fan and giving him the benefit of her lovely eyes, set in open distress at his condition.

'I don't want a doctor.'

'There is a very good man of my acquaintance,' Walpole said, as though struck by inspiration. 'A specialist in weaknesses of the chest. I should be more than delighted to provide an introduction.'

'How kind of you, Horry! I am sure anyone you recommend must be a marvel.' Lucinda opened her fan in gratitude.

Grey, who was not so far gone as to be unable to spot gross conspiracy and very bad acting, rolled up his eyes.

'Give me the name,' he said, in apparent resignation. 'I shall write for an appointment.'

'Oh, no need,' Walpole said cheerfully. 'Dr. Humperdinck expresses the keenest interest in making your acquaintance. I'll send my coach for you, at three o'clock tomorrow.'

'And I,' Lucinda put in swiftly, fixing him with a gimlet eye, 'will be here to ensure that you get into it.'

'Short of drowning myself in the fishpond, I see there is no escape,' Grey said, with a sigh. 'All right.'

Lucinda looked flabbergasted, and then alarmed, at this sudden capitulation. In fact, he simply hadn't the strength to make more than a token resistance – nor, he discovered, did he really care. What did it matter?

'Mr. Walpole,' he said, nodding toward the table, 'I fear that my nephew Henry is about to drink your fish.'

In the excitement occasioned by the rescue and subsequent ceremonious installation of the fish in their new home, Grey was able to make an inconspicuous departure, and went to sit in the library.

He was still there, an unread play by Molière

open on his knee, when a shadow fell over him, and he looked up to see the Honorable Horace Walpole again. Walpole was a slight man, and much too frail in appearance to loom over anyone; he simply stood by Grey's chair.

'It is a terrible thing,' Walpole said quietly, all affectation gone.

'Yes.'

'I spoke with my brother.' That would be the Earl of Orford, Grey supposed; Walpole was the youngest son of the late prime minister, and had three brothers, but only the eldest had any influence – though a great deal less than his father had had.

'He cannot help before the trial, but . . . if' – Walpole hesitated, ever so briefly, having obviously made a split-second decision to substitute 'if' for 'when' – 'your . . .' A longer hesitation.

'My brother,' Grey said quietly.

'If he is condemned, the earl will make what recommendations he can toward clemency. And I do have . . . other friends at court, though my own influence is not great. I will do what I can. I promise you that, at least.'

Walpole was not at all handsome, having a receding chin and a high, rather flat brow, but he was possessed of intelligent dark eyes, usually alive with interest or mischief. Now they were quiet, and very kind.

Grey couldn't speak. It was a risk for Walpole to be connected in any way with such an affair. He lived quietly, and his own affairs never came to public notice, nor ever would. For him to sacrifice his discretion so far as to involve himself in what would be a notorious case was a remarkable gesture, and Grey was not a personal friend, though Walpole's father had of course been a close friend to the duke.

He doubted that Walpole knew or suspected anything regarding his own nature, let alone his relationship with Percy. Even if he did, he would never speak of it, no more than Grey would mention Thomas Gray, the poet who had been Walpole's lover for years.

He put up his hand, and gripped Walpole's for an instant in thanks. Walpole smiled, a sudden, charming smile.

'Do go and see Humperdinck,' he said. 'He will do you good, I am sure of it.'

He had felt the name 'Humperdinck' vaguely familiar, but had not at first recollected its associations, and was thus surprised to find himself face to face with the gentleman he had last seen in a state of prostration on the sofa at White's, half frozen and wig askew, suffering the effects of some seizure.

Dr. Humperdinck was now pink and healthy, showing only traces of his misadventure: a slight hesitation of speech, a drooping left eyelid, and a dragging left foot that caused him to walk with a stick. He laid this object aside and sat down in his consulting room, bidding Grey do likewise.

'Lord John Grey,' he said, looking his new patient over with thoughtful, clear blue eyes. 'I know you, do I not? But I cannot recall the occasion of our meeting. I hope you will pardon my lack of manners – I suffered an accident last winter, an apoplexy of sorts, and since have discovered that my memory is not what it once was.'

'I recall the occasion,' Grey said, smiling. 'It was on the pavement outside White's.'

The doctor blinked, astonished.

'Was it? You were present?'

'Yes, my brother and myself.'

The doctor seized his hand and wrung it.

'My dear sir! I am so happy to meet you again. Not only for the natural pleasure of the occasion, but because I *do* remember you! I had thought all memory of the evening of my accident quite gone – and here is a piece of it after all! Bless me, sir, you have given me hope that perhaps other memories may also return in time!'

'I'm sure I hope they will,' Grey said, smiling. The doctor's patent joy at remembering eased his own melancholy for a moment – though there were many things he would himself prefer to forget.

'You do not recall where you were going that night?' Grey asked curiously, taking off his coat and unfastening his shirt at the doctor's request. Humperdinck shook his head, fumbling in his pocket.

'No, I have not . . .' He straightened up, a small sharp instrument of some sort in his hand and a look of astonishment on his face.

'White's,' he whispered, as though to himself. Then his gaze sharpened, returning to Grey with renewed excitement.

'White's!' he cried, seizing Grey's hand once again and disregarding the presence of the instrument in his own hand.

'Ouch!'

'Oh, I do beg your pardon, sir, have I cut you? No, no, all is well, no more than a slight nick, a bandage will fix it. . . . They told me I had been found outside White's Chocolate House, of course, but hearing you speak the name, in your own voice – White's!' he exclaimed again in glee. 'I was going to White's!'

'But—' Grey caught himself in time from saying, 'But you are not a member there,' for if he had been, Holmes, the club's steward, would have recognized the doctor at once. 'Were you meeting someone there?' he asked, instead.

The doctor pursed his lips, thinking fiercely – but gave it up within a moment as a bad job.

'No,' he said regretfully, fishing a clean bandage from his drawer. 'I suppose that I must have been, but I have no recollection of it. But if so, surely the gentleman I was going to meet would have recognized me? Ah, well, I must just let it be; perhaps more memories will return to me of their own accord. Patience is a great virtue, after all,' he said philosophically.

Half an hour later, he had finished his examination, conducted with the most cordial and attentive questions, and returned to his earlier statement of principle.

'Patience, Lord John,' he said firmly. 'Patience is the best medicine, in almost all cases; I recommend it highly – though it is surprising how few people are able to take that particular medicine.'

He laughed jovially. 'They think that healing must come from blade or bottle – and sometimes it does, sometimes it does. But for the most part, I am convinced that the body heals itself. And the mind,' he added thoughtfully, with a sideways glance at Grey that made him wonder uncomfortably just how much of his own mind the doctor had perceived in the course of their conversation.

'So you do not feel that the remaining fragments are dangerous?' he asked, buttoning his shirt.

The doctor made a moue of professional equivocation.

'One can never say for certain about such things, Lord John – but I think not. I hope not. I believe the occasional pain you suffer is only the result of an irritation of the nerves – quite harmless. It should pass away, in time.'

'In time,' Grey muttered to himself, on the way back to Argus House. That was well enough, so far as his body was concerned. Being assured that he was likely not about to die had worked wonders; he felt no pain at all in either chest or arm. But as for his mind . . . there, time was growing very short indeed.

Chapter 31

Nota Bene

Grey found himself improved in spirits after his visit to Humperdinck, but still at loose ends. Not yet healed enough to return to his duties, and lacking any useful occupation, he drifted. He would set out for the Beefsteak, and find himself wandering round the edge of Hyde Park or suddenly among the shouts of costermongers in Covent Garden. He would sit down to read, and come to himself an hour later to find the fire burnt down to embers and the book on his knee, still open at the first page.

It was not melancholy. That abyss was still visible to him, but he resolutely looked away from it, back turned to its beckoning verge. This was something different; a sense of suspended animation, as though he was waiting for something without which he could not continue his life – and yet with no idea what that something might be, and no notion how to find it.

His daily correspondence these days was scanty; those friends who had expressed sympathy and extended invitations upon his return had been discouraged by his continued refusals, and while a few stubborn souls continued to call or write – Lucinda Joffrey, for one – they left him alone for the most part.

He therefore looked at the letter the butler laid beside his plate with a faint curiosity. It didn't bear an official seal, thank God, or have the look of anything pertaining to the regiment. If it had, he reflected, he should have been tempted to put it into the fire. He daily expected notification of Percy's court-martial – or his death – and feared to read either one.

As it was, he waited until the meal was finished, and took the letter with him out into the garden, where he finally opened it beneath a copper beech. It was from Dr. Humperdinck; he caught sight of the signature, and would have crumpled the letter in disgust, had he not also caught sight of the opening sentence.

I have remembered, it began simply.

Grey sat down slowly, letter in hand.

My dear Lord John –

I have remembered. Not everything, assuredly; there are still considerable lacunae in my recollection. But I recalled quite suddenly this morning the name of the man I was to meet at White's. It was Arthur Longstreet, and I have it firmly in my mind that I was called to a medical consultation with him.

My mind is unfortunately still a blank, though,

with regard to the matter he desired to consult me upon, and also to his occupation and address.

I think I have not met him, as I have no face to attach to this name, and thus must have been summoned by letter – though if that be the case, it is not among my correspondence.

Are you by chance acquainted with Mr. Longstreet? If so, I should be very much obliged if you would send me his direction, that I might write and explain matters. I hesitate to impose upon you, but since I have the impression that it was a medical matter, I did not wish to make inquiries at White's and thus perhaps expose Mr. Longstreet's privacies inadvertently. Of course, if you do not know the gentleman, I shall do that, but I dare to presume upon our acquaintance and your good nature to begin with.

> *With my greatest thanks, I remain*
> *Your obt. servant,*

Henryk van Humperdinck

Grey was still sitting under the copper beech when one of the footmen came out with a tea tray.

'My lord? Mrs. Stubbs says you will take some refreshment.' Grey was preoccupied, but not so much so as not to notice the firmly directive phrasing of this particular statement.

'Does she?' he said dryly. He picked up the cup and sniffed cautiously. Chamomile. He made a face and poured it into the perennial bed.

'Do thank my cousin for her kind solicitude, Joe.' He stood up, picked up one of the pastries, discovered it to be filled with raspberries, and put it back. Raspberries made him itch. He took a piece of bread and butter, instead.

'And then have the coach brought round, please. I have a call to make.'

Longstreet's house was a modest one. Men of means did not become army surgeons, and while Longstreet's cousin was evidently able to place twenty-thousand-pound wagers, Grey noted, the doctor's branch of the family must be significantly less wealthy.

He had never heard whether Longstreet was married. A middle-aged female servant admitted him, looking surprised, and pottered off in search of the doctor, leaving Grey in a small, neat parlor whose walls, shelves, and cases held the souvenirs of a man who had spent much of his life abroad: a set of German beer steins, a trio of French enameled snuffboxes, a series of case knives inlaid with elaborate marquetry, four grotesque masks, garishly decorated with paint and horsehair, whose origin he did not recognize. . . . Evidently, Longstreet liked matched sets.

Grey hoped this tendency implied a desire on the doctor's part for completeness.

A halting step and a wheezing breath announced the arrival of the artifacts' owner. Longstreet was diminished physically, Grey saw, but still himself. Normally lean, he was thinner now, the bones of face and wrist sharp as blades, and his skin gone a strange shade of gray that seemed faintly blue in the rainy light of the window. The doctor leaned heavily on a stick, and his housekeeper watched him with a certain tenseness of body that suggested he might fall, but she made no move to help him, though from her face she would have liked to.

The eyes, though, were unchanged: clear, a little angry, half amused. Not at all surprised.

'How are you, Lord John?' he asked.

'Well, I thank you.' Grey inclined his head. 'And I *do* thank you,' he added politely. 'I gather that you are in large part responsible for my survival.' *Whether you meant to be or not,* he thought.

Longstreet nodded, and eased himself down into an armchair, from the depths of which he surveyed Grey sardonically.

'You were . . . somewhat more fortunate than I.' He touched his laboring chest briefly. 'Bullet through . . . both lungs.'

'I regret to hear it,' Grey said, meaning it. Longstreet gestured toward the other chair, and he pulled it forward and sat down.

'Have you consulted Dr. Humperdinck regarding your condition?' he asked. It was as good an opening as any.

Longstreet raised one iron-gray brow.

'Humperdinck? Me? Why?'

'He is an expert in conditions of the chest, is he not?'

Longstreet stared at him for a moment, then began to wheeze in an alarming manner.

'Is . . . that what . . . they . . . told you?' he managed at last, and Grey realized that he was laughing. 'Who–whoever sent you to him?'

'Yes,' Grey said, becoming mildly irritated. 'He is not?'

Longstreet suffered a brief coughing fit, and clapped a handkerchief to his mouth, shaking his head.

'No,' he wheezed at last, and breathed heavily for a moment before continuing. 'He is a specialist in mental disorders, par-particularly those of a melancho-cholic disposition.' Longstreet looked him over, openly amused. 'Was he of . . . help?'

'Oddly enough, yes.' Grey kept any hint of an edge from his voice, suppressing a burst of annoyance at Lucinda Joffrey. 'He sent me to you.'

'He did?' The sharp gray eyes went suddenly wary. 'Why? He does not know me.'

'No?' Grey thought it politic not to describe Dr. Humperdinck's disordered memory – just yet. 'Then why did you summon him to meet you at White's, on the evening when I first met you there?'

His own mind had been momentarily disordered by the revelation of Humperdinck's specialty, but was now working again. In fact, his sense of reason had suddenly reasserted itself, after what seemed months of absence, and the sheer relief of being able to think logically again was like water in the desert.

Longstreet had pressed the handkerchief to his mouth again, and was coughing, but it was apparent to Grey that this was no more than a gambit to gain time in which to think – and he did not propose to allow such advantage.

'You did not – I am sure – seek his professional opinion with regard to yourself,' he said. 'So it was for someone else. Someone who would not or could not go to Humperdinck on his own account.' He watched Longstreet's face carefully, but saw no flash of wariness or satisfaction at the word 'his.' Good, so it was not a woman; he had thought it might be a wife or mistress, which would likely be no concern of his.

Longstreet had taken away the handkerchief from his face, and was watching Grey through narrowed eyes, plainly trying to think how much Dr. Humperdinck might have told him.

'A doctor's patients are entitled to confidentiality,' he said slowly. 'I am sure that Dr. Humperdinck would not reveal—'

'Dr. Humperdinck still experiences some effects of the apoplexy he suffered that night,' Grey put in quickly. 'Most of his memories have returned, but he is not entirely himself. Alas.'

He smiled faintly, hoping that he left the impression that Humperdinck's judgment and sense of professional ethics had suffered impairment. He regretted impugning the doctor's reputation, even by implication – but reason was a ruthless master, and reason told him there was something here.

Longstreet pursed his lips, frowning thoughtfully, but no longer at Grey. He was looking at something inside his own head, and appeared to be questioning it. Absently, he reached to the table, where an aged meerschaum pipe lay beside a humidor.

'The worst of it is that I cannot smoke anymore,' he remarked, running a thumb lovingly over the bowl, elegantly carved in the shape of a mermaid. Her pert breasts glowed golden, stroked for years. 'A pipe is good for thinking.'

'I must try it sometime,' Grey said dryly. 'The person for whom you desired Dr. Humperdinck's consultation—'

'Is dead.' The words came down like an ax, severing conversation. Neither man spoke for nearly a minute; Grey heard the faint half-hour chime of his watch in its pocket, but was content to wait.

Something had been loosed; he felt it, like the sense of a mouse creeping round the corners of a room, but had no notion what it might be. Longstreet's eyes were fixed on his pipe, his mouth pressed tight. He was making up his mind, Grey saw, and to speak too soon or to say the wrong thing might startle the mouse back into its hole. He waited, the sound of Longstreet's wheezing breath just audible above the sound of the fire.

'My cousin,' the doctor said at last. He raised his head and met Grey's eyes. 'George.' He spoke the name with a sense of affection, and regret.

'My condolences,' Grey said quietly. 'I had not heard that Lord Creemore had died.'

'Last week.' Longstreet rested the pipe upon his knee. *'Le Roi est mort; vive Le Roi.'*

'I beg your pardon?'

Longstreet smiled, irony uppermost.

'I am my cousin's heir. I am Lord Creemore now – for what good it may do me. Wha— wha—' He cleared his throat and drew a rattling breath, then coughed explosively, and shook his head.

'What do you think is more important, Lord John?' he said, more clearly. 'The life of a man, or the honor of his name when he is dead?'

Grey considered that. The question took him by surprise, but it had been meant seriously.

'For myself,' he said at last, 'I should say firstly, that it depends upon the man. And secondly, that a man whose life lacks honor surely has no claim upon it after death.'

'Ah. But I did not say the *man's* honor, necessarily. I said, "the honor of his name." That, I expect, strikes you more cogently?'

'His family's honor, you mean.' Yes, that blow struck home – as it was meant to. He kept his temper, though. 'I would value that, yes. But honor is not only what the world perceives it to be, sir – but what it is. And I repeat that a man cannot be separated from his honor.'

'No,' Longstreet said thoughtfully. 'I suppose that is true.' *And yet . . .* his face said, as plainly as words. Some disagreement struggled within him,

549

and Grey suddenly thought that he might know its nature.

'But of course,' he said, 'you are a physician. From your point of view, perhaps, to preserve life must be the greatest good, regardless of other considerations?'

Longstreet – Grey could not yet think of him as Lord Creemore – shot him a startled glance, but whether because Grey's shot had struck in the gold, or because it had missed the target entire, he couldn't tell.

The appearance of the housekeeper with tea gave them both a moment to regroup. The little house was damp, and there was a chill in the air despite the fire; Grey's left arm ached where it had been broken, and he was glad of the hot china in his hands and the smell of good Assam. Beyond the physical comfort of tea, the small rituals employed in drinking it eased the atmosphere between them by degrees.

'You were your cousin's physician, then?' Grey asked, as casually as he might have asked the doctor to pass the sugar bowl.

Longstreet had recovered his composure, and the heat of the tea lent a slight warmth to his gaunt cheeks. He nodded.

'Yes. And he did not die of the syphilis, nor of any other disgraceful disease, lest you be thinking that the point of my original question.'

Dementia and insanity were quite as disgraceful as – if not more so than – a venereal disease, but

Grey did not – yet – mention that. Most medical men of his acquaintance had no delicacy of feeling whatever, and Longstreet was an army surgeon – or had been – and was thus presumably hardened to the realities of even the most disgusting physical phenomena.

'What did he die of?' Grey asked bluntly.

'Dropsy,' Longstreet replied, with no hesitation whatever. Either it was the truth or he had had his answer prepared ahead of time. Grey thought it was likely the truth.

'Your cousin died childless, if you are his heir,' he observed. 'Is there much family, besides yourself?'

Longstreet shook his head, his eyes hooded against the steam from his cup.

'Only myself now,' he said quietly. 'The title dies with me.'

Grey didn't argue that Longstreet might still marry and have sons; he was no physician, but had seen his share of death. His own brush with it had perhaps made him morbidly sensitive to its presence; he could hear the sigh of Longstreet's damaged lungs, and see the blue shadow on his lips.

'So,' Grey said slowly, 'if it is the honor of your family name that concerns you . . .'

The doctor's lips twisted in a wry expression, not quite a smile.

'You think that if the name ceases, there is no need to guard its honor?'

'Will you guard it at the price of your own?' The

words came unbidden, surprising Grey nearly as much as Longstreet.

The doctor's mouth opened, working soundlessly. Then he picked up his tea and drank, hastily, as though to drown the words rising in his throat. His hands were shaking when he set the cup down; Grey heard the faint rattle of the china in its saucer.

'No,' Longstreet said hoarsely, and stopped to clear his throat. 'No,' he said more firmly. 'No, I won't. I cannot say what chance inspired Humperdinck to tell you, or how much he told you . . .' He shot Grey a sharp glance, but Grey wisely preserved silence.

Very likely, Humperdinck had known nothing, as he had no chance of speaking with Longstreet before the apoplexy struck him down. Only that there was something to know. But Longstreet might have told him something when making the original appointment; best if he thought Grey knew whatever there was to know.

'My cousin was a Jacobite,' Longstreet said abruptly.

Grey raised one brow, though his heart began to beat faster. 'Many people have been, and are. Unless you mean—'

'You know what I mean.' The wheezing note was still in Longstreet's voice, but the voice itself had grown stronger, and the doctor's gaze was steady. He had made up his mind.

The story, in its essence, was much as had been given out at the time of the Duke of Pardloe's death

– save, of course, that the nobleman who was the centerpiece of the English plot to assassinate the king was not the Duke of Pardloe but the Earl of Creemore.

'And you learned of this . . . when?'

'At the time.' Longstreet looked down, fingers restless on the mermaid's scaly tail. 'I . . . was invited to join them. I declined.'

'Not very safe,' Grey observed skeptically. 'For them *or* you.'

'Only my cousin knew. It was he who invited me; tried to persuade me of the – the *rightness* of their cause. He did believe that,' he added softly, still looking down as though his argument were addressed to the little mermaid. 'That James Stuart was rightfully king.'

'So his motives were quite without self-interest, were they?'

Longstreet looked up at that, eyes fierce.

'Are any man's?'

Grey shrugged, conceding the point. Longstreet in turn conceded another.

'Whatever George's motives, those of his fellow conspirators were most assuredly mixed. I didn't know them all – George wouldn't tell me their names until I became one of them. Reasonably enough.' He paused to cough a little.

'You didn't know them all – but you knew some?'

Longstreet nodded slowly, clearing his throat.

'The Marquis of Banbury. Catholic – his whole family was ferociously Catholic. When – when your father was killed, he fled to France. Died there a few years ago. Another man – I never knew his name; George only called him *A*.'

A for *Arbuthnot*? Grey wondered, with a dropping of the stomach.

'You knew this – but you said nothing?'

Longstreet leaned back a little in his chair, surveying Grey, and after a moment, shook his head.

'I asked you – did you value life more, or honor? I asked myself that. Many times. And at the time . . . I chose my cousin's life above my honor. Your father was already dead; I could not alter that. I should have denounced Creemore, I know. But I could not bring myself to do it.'

'After all,' Grey said, curling his fingers under the edge of his seat in order not to strike Longstreet, 'what harm could it do, to let my father's honor be destroyed and his family live in the belief that he had killed himself?'

He hadn't tried to keep his feelings out of his voice, and Longstreet recoiled a little, and turned his eyes away.

'I chose my cousin's life,' he said again, so softly that the words were barely audible. Then his head rose and his gaze turned sharply on Grey.

'What do you mean – the belief that he had killed himself? He did kill himself. Did-didn't he?' For the first time, a note of uncertainty had entered the doctor's voice.

'No, he bloody didn't,' Grey said. 'He was

murdered, and I intend to find out by whom.'

Longstreet's brow narrowed in concentration, and he stared deeply into Grey's eyes, as though making a diagnosis of some kind. He blinked once or twice, then stood abruptly, and without a word, left the room, leaning on his stick.

Grey sat, nonplussed, wondering whether to follow. But the man had not seemed ill, or particularly offended. He waited, wandering slowly round the room, examining the doctor's collection of curiosities.

Within a few moments, he heard the sound of the doctor's stick, and turned from the mantelpiece to see Longstreet enter the room, a familiar book in his hand. Bound in rough leather, its cover darkened and shiny in spots from much handling.

The doctor held it out to Grey, breathing heavily, and Grey snatched it from his hand, his heart in his throat.

'I thought . . . you might . . . want that.' Longstreet nodded at the book.

'I . . . yes.' Grey glanced at him, though he could scarcely take his eyes from the book. 'Where did you get this?'

Longstreet had sat down, his face tinged with blue, and was breathing so heavily that he could manage no more than a helpless gesture.

Grey stood up and rummaged in his coat for his flask, from which he poured a substantial amount of brandy into the dregs of Longstreet's tea. He held the cup to Longstreet's thin blue lips, seeing in memory the doctor's hands performing a similar office for the stricken Humperdinck, that snowy night at White's Club.

It took some time before Longstreet was able to reply, but finally he managed, 'It was among my cousin's things. I brought it away with me after he died.'

'But you knew he had it?' The journal page had been left in Hal's office before Lord Creemore's death – but from the sound of things, it seemed unlikely that the gout-crippled and dropsical Lord Creemore had crept unobserved into the regimental offices. Whereas Longstreet, in his uniform, would have passed easily without notice.

Longstreet nodded.

'He . . . showed it to me. When I pressed him. That is how I knew where to find it.'

'You've read it?' The rough leather of the cover seemed to burn against Grey's fingers, and the impulse to open the book, see his father's writing spring to life, was nearly overwhelming.

The man's breath was coming more easily now.

'I've read it.'

'Did he – my father – did he write anything regarding a Jacobite conspiracy?'

Longstreet nodded, taking another sip from his cup.

'Yes. He knew a bit, suspected a great deal more – but he was circumspect enough to refer to the principals in code. He called my cousin Banquo.' One side of the doctor's mouth turned up. 'There were three others referred to by name – Macbeth, Fleance, and Siward. I think Siward was a man named Arbuthnot – Victor Arbuthnot. I don't know the others.'

Grey felt the blood pulse in his fingertips, where they touched the journal.

'I said that I was obliged to choose between the truth and my cousin's life – and I chose George, for good or ill. That choice, however, did not absolve me of further responsibility in the matter. I have no interest in politics – one charlatan on the throne is as good as another, and if the Pope meddles, so does Friedrich of Prussia.'

His hand curled protectively around the little mermaid, and he glanced at Grey, his voice growing softer.

'But I did feel a responsibility to prevent further harm being done, if I could. If any one of those men had become convinced that your mother knew what your father knew, they might easily have killed her, rather than risk the possibility that she might expose them.'

His mother must have feared precisely that eventuality – as well as the certainty that Hal would take matters into his own hands, if he discovered the truth. And so she had taken what precautions she could: disguising his father's murder as suicide, sending her younger son to safety in Aberdeen, and leaving the country herself. And then had remained quiet for the next seventeen years – watching.

'*Does* she know?' Longstreet asked curiously. 'Who killed your father?'

'No. Had she known which man it was, she would have killed *him,* I assure you,' Grey said.

Longstreet looked startled at that.

'They do say women are amazing vindictive,' the doctor said reflectively.

'If you think she would keep silence, sir, you know nothing of women in general, or my mother in particular. But since she did not in fact know who the murderer was, she did keep silent. But then, that is why . . .' The words died in his throat, revelation dawning.

'That's why you sent a page of this' – he lifted the journal – 'to my brother, and another to my mother? Because of her impending marriage to General Stanley?'

Longstreet shook his head, the breath in his lungs sighing like wind in river willows.

'No – because my cousin was dying. It was clear to me that he was near death; almost beyond the reach . . . of law or man. The others . . . if they . . .'

Grey was losing patience.

'And why did you set the O'Higginses on me?'

Longstreet frowned.

'Who?'

'Two soldiers who attempted to waylay me in Hyde Park.' It occurred to him that Longstreet certainly knew the name of Percy's patron, Mr. *A.* The temptation to ask was enormous – but if he knew, the temptation to find the man would be greater still. And then what?

Longstreet had been struggling with his breath, as Grey struggled with his baser instincts.

'That – I did not intend that you should be h-harmed.'

'I wasn't,' Grey said shortly. 'Not on that occasion. But then I was attacked in an alley near Seven Dials; was that you, too?'

Longstreet nodded, a hand pressed to his chest.

'A warning. They – both times, they were meant only to knock you senseless, and to leave a th-third page of the journal in your pocket. I had not expected you to f-fight back.'

'Sorry about that.' Grey rubbed his left arm. He had left off the sling, and it was beginning to throb. 'What the devil was the point of this – this charade?'

Longstreet leaned back in his chair, sighing deeply.

'Justice,' he said softly. 'Call it a sop to my conscience. I chose my cousin, as I said. But it became clear to me some months ago that he was dying. Once he was beyond the reach of the law . . . I could tell the truth. But I dared not do it openly – not then.' A brief smile flitted across his face. 'I had something to lose, then.'

He had read the journal carefully, and selected three pages, all of them mentioning the name of Victor Arbuthnot.

'That was the only thing those pages had in

common.' To leave a page in Melton's office would arouse alarm; another sent to the countess would increase it; to leave the third with Grey, following a physical attack, would, he thought, insure that the pages were carefully studied – Arbuthnot's name would spring out of the comparison, and the Greys would go looking for him. And so far past the event, Arbuthnot would likely admit to the truth himself. If he did not . . . Longstreet would still have the option of revealing the truth in some other way.

'That actually worked,' Grey admitted, though his displeasure over the stratagem had not abated in the slightest. 'But Arbuthnot didn't know my father had been murdered, either.'

What matters more? Longstreet had asked him. *The life of a man, or the honor of his name when he is dead?* Both, Grey thought. Longstreet had chosen; Grey had no choice.

'Who in bloody *hell* killed my father?' he demanded in frustration.

Longstreet closed his eyes.

'I don't know.' The doctor had been growing visibly more exhausted as he spoke, needing to pause for breath at shorter intervals, coughing in short, harsh bursts that made Grey's own chest ache in sympathy. He flapped a limp hand toward the journal.

'You know . . . what I know.'

Grey sat for a moment, trying not to burst with the force of the questions that boiled in his brain. But Longstreet did not have the answers to most of them, and the one thing he did know – the name of Mr. *A* – Grey could not bring himself to ask.

He rose, clutching the journal, and one final question came to mind that Longstreet might be able to answer.

'My brother challenged Nathaniel Twelvetrees to a duel,' he said abruptly. 'Do you know why?'

Longstreet opened his eyes and looked up, faintly surprised.

'Don't you? Ah, I see not. I suppose Melton wouldn't refer to the matter. Twelvetrees had . . . seduced his wife.'

Grey felt as though Longstreet had suddenly punched him violently in the chest.

'His wife.' It came to him, with a sense of mingled horror and relief, that Longstreet did not mean Minnie, but Esmé, his brother's first wife – who had been French and beautiful. She died in childbirth – and the child with her. Had the child been Hal's? he wondered, appalled. He remembered Hal's tearing grief at her death, but had not understood the half of his brother's feelings. His own heart burned at the thought.

'Thank you,' he said, for lack of anything else to say to Longstreet, and turned to go. One final thought occurred to him.

'One last thing,' he said, turning back, curious. 'Would you have killed me? Had my brother not been there when you removed the shrapnel from my chest?'

Longstreet put back his head and surveyed Grey

carefully, his eyes alive with ironic intelligence, still bright in his drawn face. Slowly, he shook his head.

'Had I met you in a dark alley, perhaps. H-had we met in a duel, certainly.' He paused to breathe. 'But you came . . . to me as a patient.' He coughed again, and tapped his chest.

'Do no . . . harm,' he wheezed, and closed his eyes.

The housekeeper, who had been standing silently in the shadows of the hall, came in, not looking at Grey. She went to Longstreet, knelt beside him, and smoothed the hair from his face, her touch tender. Longstreet did not open his eyes, but put up a hand, slowly, and laid it over hers.

Grey had dismissed the coach, not knowing how long his interview might take. It would be easy enough to find a cab, but he chose to walk, scarcely knowing which path he took.

His mind was a stew of revelation, shock, conjecture – and frustration. Beneath it all was a substratum of grief – for his father, for his mother, for Hal. His own grief seemed inconsequent, and yet magnified by all he now knew of his family's past.

The pressure in his chest made it painful to breathe, but he didn't worry about the remaining shrapnel; only stopped now and then when his breath grew too short to continue. At length, he found himself on the shore of the Thames, where he found an overturned dory and sat on it, the journal tucked under his coat, watching the brown water swirl past, lapping up the shore as the tide came in.

He let his thoughts go, exhausted, and his mind emptied, little by little.

Spatters of rain passed over him, but toward sunset, the clouds overhead began to thin and drift apart.

A conclusion is simply the point at which you give up thinking. He gave up, and as he rose stiffly to his feet, found that a conclusion had indeed formed itself in his mind, much as a pearl forms inside an oyster.

He had been confessor to Longstreet. It was time he sought his own.

Chapter 32

The Path of Honor

'I did as you asked, Lord John,' Dunsany said, his voice lowered, as though someone might overhear – though they were quite alone in the library.

'As I – oh!' Grey recollected, belatedly, his request that James Fraser might be afforded the opportunity to write letters. 'I thank you, sir. Was there . . . any result from the experiment, do you know?'

Dunsany nodded, his narrow brow furrowed in concern.

'He did send a number of letters – ten in all, I believe. As you specified, I did not open them' – his expression indicated that he thought this a grave mistake – 'but I did take note of the directions upon them. Three were sent to a place in the Highlands, to a Mrs. Murray, two to Rome, and the remainder to France. I kept a list of the names. . . .' He fumbled with the drawer of his desk, but Grey stopped him with a gesture.

'I thank you, sir. Perhaps later. Did he receive any reply to these missives?'

'Yes, several.' Dunsany seemed expectant, but Grey only nodded, without asking for details.

The question of hidden Jacobites, which had once seemed so vital, was eclipsed. What had his mother said? *Let the past bury its dead.* It had to, he supposed; the present was all he could deal with.

He went on conversing with Dunsany, expressing interest in the affairs of Helwater, and later, listening to the county gossip of Lady Dunsany and Isobel, but without actually noticing any of it. He did see that relations seemed to have healed between Lord and Lady Dunsany; they sat close together at teatime, and their hands touched now and then over the bread and butter.

'How does your grandson fare?' Grey inquired at one point, hearing wailing overhead.

'Oh, wonderfully well,' Lord Dunsany assured him, beaming.

'He's teething, poor lad,' Lady Dunsany said, though not seeming distressed at her grandson's pain. 'He's such a comfort to us.'

'He has *six* teeth, Lord John!' Isobel told him, with the manner of one imparting vital and exciting intelligence.

'Indeed?' he said politely. 'I am staggered.'

He thought the meal would never end, but it did, and he was at last allowed to escape to his room. He did not stop there, though, but went quietly down the back stair and out. To the stable.

One of the other grooms was working in the paddock, but Grey sent him away with a brief sign.

He didn't care whether anyone thought his desire to speak to Jamie Fraser in private was peculiar – and the other grooms were accustomed to it, in any case.

Fraser was pitching hay into the mangers, and barely glanced at Grey when he entered the stable. 'I shall be finished in a moment,' he said. 'Ye wish to hear about the letters, I suppose.'

'No,' Grey said. 'Not that. Not now, in any case.'

Fraser glanced sharply at him, but at Grey's motion to continue, shrugged and went on with his task, returning when all the mangers were filled.

'Will you speak with me, as man to man?' Grey asked, without preamble.

Fraser looked startled, but considered for a moment, and nodded.

'I will,' he said warily, and it occurred to Grey that he thought Grey had come to speak of Geneva.

'It is a matter of my own affairs,' Grey said, 'not yours.'

'Indeed.' Fraser was still guarded, but the wariness in his eyes relaxed. 'What affairs are these, sir? And why me?'

'Why you.' Grey sighed, and sitting down on a stool, indicated that Fraser should do the same. 'Because, Mr. Fraser, you are an honest man, and I trust that you will give me an honest opinion. And because, God damn it, you are the only person in this world to whom I can speak frankly.'

Fraser's look of wariness returned, but he sat down, leaned his pitchfork against the wall, and said only, 'Speak, then.'

He had rehearsed the words a hundred times on the journey from London, rendering the tale as succinctly as possible. No need for details, and he gave none. No doorknobs.

'And that is my dilemma,' he ended. 'I am the only witness. Without my testimony, he will not be convicted, nor condemned. If I lie before the court-martial, that is the end of my own honor. If I do not – it will be the end of his life or freedom.'

To speak so openly was an overwhelming relief, and Grey remembered, with a pang, that the same feeling had come to him when he told Percy the story of his father's death. To talk in this way did more good than hours of thinking; laying out the pieces of the matter for Fraser made the choice clear in his own mind.

Fraser had listened closely throughout this recital, ruddy brows drawn in a slight frown. Now he looked at the ground, still frowning.

'This man is your brother, your kin,' he said finally. 'But kin by law, not blood. Have ye feeling for him, beyond the obligation of kin? Kindness? Love?' There was no marked emphasis on the last word; Grey thought Fraser meant only the love that existed within family.

Grey rose from his seat and strode restlessly up and down.

'Not love,' he said finally. 'And not kindness.' There was some of both left, yes, but in the end neither of these would compel him sufficiently.

'Will it be honor, then?' Fraser said quietly. He stood up, silhouetted by the lantern light.

'Yes,' Grey said. 'But what *is* the path of honor, here?'

Fraser shrugged slightly, and Grey saw the glint of his red hair, caught by a stray beam of light that struck down from a chink in the boards of the loft overhead.

'What is honor for me may not be honor for you, Major,' he said. 'For me – for us – our honor *is* our family. I could not see a close kinsman condemned, no matter his crime. Mind,' he added, lifting one brow, 'infamous crime would be dealt with. But by the man's chief, by his own kin – not by a court.'

Grey stood still, and let the jumbled pieces fall.

'I see,' he said slowly, and did. Grey understood now what Fraser meant by honor. In the end, it was simple, and the relief of reaching the decision overwhelmed his realization of the difficulties still to be faced.

'It is honor – but not the honor of my reputation. The end of it,' Grey said slowly, seeing it at last, 'is that I cannot in honor see him hanged for a crime whose guilt I share – and from whose consequences I am escaped by chance alone.'

Fraser stiffened slightly. 'A crime whose guilt ye share.' His voice was careful, realization – and distaste – clear in the words. He stopped, clearly not wishing to say more, but he could scarcely leave the matter there.

'This man. He is not only your stepbrother,

but . . . your . . .' He groped for a word. 'Your catamite?'

'He was my lover, yes.' The words should have been tinged with bitterness, but were not. Sadness, yes, but most of all, relief at the admission.

Fraser made a brief sound of contempt, though, and Grey turned upon him, reckless.

'You do not believe that men can love one another?'

'No,' Fraser said bluntly. 'I do not.' His mouth compressed for an instant, and then he added, as though honesty compelled him, 'Not in that fashion, at least. The love of brothers, of kin – aye, of course. Or of soldiers. We have – spoken of that.'

'Sparta? Yes.' Grey smiled without humor. They had fought the battle of Thermopylae one night, in his quarters at Ardsmuir Prison, using salt cellars, dice, and cuff buttons on a map scrawled with charcoal on the top of his desk. It had been one of their evenings of friendship.

'The love of Leonidas for his men, they for each other as warriors. Aye, that's real enough. But to – to . . . *use* a man in such fashion . . .' He made a gesture of repudiation.

'Think so, do you?' Grey's blood was already high; he felt it hot in his chest. 'You've read Plato, I know. And scholar that you are, I would suppose that you've heard of the Sacred Band of Thebes. Perhaps?'

Fraser's face went tight, and in spite of the dim light, Grey saw the color rise in him, as well.

'I have,' he said shortly.

'Lovers,' Grey said, realizing suddenly that he was gloriously angry. 'All soldiers. All lovers. Each man and his beloved. *Who would desert his beloved, or fail him in the hour of danger?*' He gave Fraser stare for stare. 'And what do you say to that, Mr. Fraser?'

The Scot's eyes had gone quite black.

'What I would say,' he said, counting out the words like coins, 'is that only men who lack the ability to possess a woman – or cowards who fear them – must resort to such feeble indecencies to relieve their lust. And to hear ye speak of honor in the same breath . . . Since ye ask, it curdles my wame. And what, my lord, d'ye say to *that*?'

'I say that I do not speak of the indecencies of lust – and if *you* wish to speak of such things, allow me to note that I have seen much grosser indecencies inflicted upon women by men, and so have you. We have both fought with armies. I said "love." And what do you think love is, then, that it is reserved only to men who are drawn to women?'

The color stood out in patches across Fraser's cheekbones.

'I have loved my wife beyond life itself, and know that love for a gift of God. Ye dare to say to me that the feelings of a – a – pervert who cannot deal with women as a man, but minces about and preys upon helpless boys – that this is *love*?'

'You accuse me of preying upon *boys*?' Grey's fingers curled, just short of his dagger hilt. 'I tell you, sir, were you armed, you would answer for that, here and now!'

Fraser inhaled through his nose, seeming to swell with it. 'Draw on me and be damned,' he said contemptuously. 'Armed or no, ye canna master me.'

'You think not? I tell you,' Grey said, and fought so hard to control the fury in his voice that it emerged as no more than a whisper, 'I tell you, sir – were I to take you to my bed – I could make you scream. And by God, I would do it.'

Later, he would try to recall what had happened then. Had he moved, reflex and training cutting through the fog of rage that blinded him? Or had Fraser moved, some shred of reason altering his aim in the same split second in which he swung his fist?

Hard as he tried, no answer came. He remembered nothing but the shock of impact as Fraser's fist struck the boards an inch from his head, and the sob of breath, hot on his face. There had been a sense of presence, of a body close to his, and the impression of some irresistible doom.

Then he was outside, gulping air as though he were drowning, staggering blind in the glare of the setting sun. He had no balance, no bearings; stumbled and put out a hand for anchor, grasped some piece of farm equipment.

His vision cleared, eyes watering – but he saw neither the paddock, the wagon whose wheel he grasped, nor the house and lawns beyond. What he saw was Fraser's face. When he had said that – what demon had given him that thought, those words? *I could make you scream.*

Oh, Christ, oh, Christ. Someone had.

A feeling welled up in him like the bursting of blood vessels deep within his belly. Liquid and terrible, it filled him within moments, swelling far beyond his power to contain it. He must vomit, or—

He ripped at his flies, gasping. A moment, two, of desperate fisting, and it all came out of him. Remorse and longing, rage and lust – and other things that he could put no name to under torture – all of it ran like quicksilver down his spine, between his legs, and erupted in gouts that drained him like a punctured wine sack.

His legs had no strength. He sank to his knees and knelt there, swaying, eyes closed. He knew nothing but the sense of a terrible relief.

In minutes – or hours – he became aware of the sun, a dark red blur in the blackness of his closed lids. A moment later, he realized that he was kneeling in the puddled dirt of the yard, forehead pressed to a wagon wheel, his breeches loose and his member still tightly clutched in his hand.

'Oh, Christ,' he said, very softly, to himself.

The door to the barn stood still ajar behind him, but there was no sound from the darkness within.

He would have left at once, save for the demands of courtesy. He sat through a final supper with the Dunsanys, replying automatically to their conversation without hearing a word, and went up afterward to tell Tom to pack.

Tom had already begun to do so, delicately alert to his employer's mood. He looked up from his folding when Grey opened the door, his face showing an alarm so pronounced that it penetrated the sense of numb isolation Grey had felt since the events of the afternoon.

'What is it, Tom?'

'Ah . . . it's nothing, me lord. Only I thought mebbe you were him again.'

'Him?'

'That big Scotchman, the groom they call Alex. He was just here.' Tom swallowed, manfully suppressing the remnants of what had plainly been a considerable shock.

'What, *here*?' A groom would never enter the house proper, unless summoned by Lord Dunsany to answer some serious charge of misconduct. Still less, Fraser; the household were terrified of him, and he had orders never to set foot further than the kitchen in which he took his meals.

'Yes, me lord. Only a few minutes ago. I didn't even hear the door open. Just looked up from me work and there he was. Didn't half give me a turn!'

'I daresay. What the devil did he say he wanted?' His only supposition was that Fraser had decided to kill him after all, and had come upon that errand. He wasn't sure he cared.

The Scotchman had said nothing, according to Tom. Merely appeared out of nowhere, stalked past him like a ghost, laid a bit of paper on the desk, and stalked out again, silent as he'd come.

'Just there, me lord.' Tom nodded at the desk, swallowing again. 'I didn't like to touch it.'

There was indeed a crumpled paper on the desk, a rough square torn from some larger sheet. Grey picked it up gingerly, as though it might explode.

It was a grubby bit of paper, translucent with oil in spots and pungent, clearly used originally to wrap fish. What had he used for ink, Grey wondered, and brushed a ginger thumb across the paper. The black smudged at once, and came off on his skin. Candleblack, mixed with water.

It was unsigned, and curt.

I believe your lordship to be in pursuit of a wild goose.

'Well, thank you very much for your opinion, Mr. Fraser!' he muttered, and crumpling the paper into a ball, crammed it in his pocket. 'Can you be ready to leave in the morning, Tom?'

'Oh, I can be ready in a quarter hour, me lord!' Tom assured him fervently, and Grey smiled, despite himself.

'The morning will do, I think.'

But he lay awake through the night, watching the early autumn moon rise above the stables, large and golden, growing small and pale as it rose among the stars, crossed over the house, and disappeared at last from view.

He had his answer, then – or one of them. Percy was not going to die, nor to live whatever remained of his life in prison, if Grey could prevent it. That much was decided. He was also decided that he himself could not lie before a court-martial. Not would not; could not. Therefore, he would find another way.

Precisely *how* he meant to accomplish this was not yet quite clear to him, but in the circumstances, he found his visit with Captain Bates at Newgate returning repeatedly to his mind – and in those memories, began to perceive the glimmerings of an idea. The fact that the idea was patently insane did not bother him particularly; he was a long way past worrying over such things as the state of his own mind.

While he considered the specifics of his emerging plan, though, he had another answer to deal with.

His first impulse, upon seeing Fraser's one-line note, had been to assume that this was mockery and dismissal. And, given the manner of their final meeting, was willing to accept it.

But that disastrous conversation could not be expunged from memory – not when it held the answer to his quandary regarding Percy. And whenever some echo of it came back to him, it bore with it Jamie Fraser's face. The anger – and the terrible nakedness of that last moment.

That note was not mockery. Fraser was more than capable of mocking him – did it routinely, in fact – but mockery could not disguise what he had seen in Fraser's face. Neither of them had wanted it, but neither could deny the honesty of what had passed between them.

He had fully expected that they would avoid each other entirely, allowing the memory of what had been said in the stable to fade, so that by the time he next returned to Helwater, it *might* be possible for them to speak civilly, both aware of but not acknowledging those moments of violent honesty. But Fraser hadn't avoided him – entirely. He quite understood why the man had chosen to leave a note, rather than speak to him; he himself couldn't have spoken to Fraser face to face, not so soon.

He had told Fraser that he valued his opinion as an honest man, and that was true. He knew no one more honest – often brutally so. Which drove him to the inescapable conclusion that Fraser had very likely given him what he asked for. He just didn't know what it bloody *meant*.

He couldn't return to Helwater; there was no time, even had he thought it would be productive. But he knew one other person who knew Jamie Fraser. And so he went to Boodle's for supper on a Thursday, knowing Harry Quarry would be there.

'I've found a ring, Harry,' Grey said without preamble, sitting down beside Quarry in the smoking room where his friend was enjoying a postprandial cigar. 'Like yours.'

'What, this?' Quarry glanced at his hand; he wore only one ring, a Masonic emblem.

'That one,' Grey said. 'I found one like it; I'd meant to ask if you knew whose it was.'

Quarry frowned; then his face cleared.

'Must be Symington's,' he said, with the air of a magician pulling colored scarves from his sleeve. 'He said he'd lost his – but that's months ago! D'you mean to say you've had it all this time?'

'I suppose so,' Grey said apologetically. 'I just found it in my pocket one day – must have picked it up accidentally.'

He put his hand into his pocket and, leaning over, emptied the contents onto the small table between their chairs.

'You are the most complete magpie, Grey,' Quarry said, poking gingerly through the detritus. 'I wonder you don't build nests. But no, of course, it's Melton who does that. What's that, for God's sake, a pritchel?'

'Part of one. I believe you may throw that away, Mr. Stevens.' Grey handed the broken bit of metal to the steward, who accepted it with the air of one handling a rare and precious object.

'What's this?' Harry had pulled out a smeared bit of paper, and was frowning at it, nose wrinkled. 'Smells a bit.'

'Oh, that. It—'

'I believe your lordship to be in pursuit of a wild goose,' Quarry read. He paused for a moment, then looked up at Grey. 'Where did you get this?'

'From one James Fraser, erstwhile Jacobite.' Something in Quarry's face made Grey lean forward. 'Does this actually mean something, Harry?'

Quarry blew out his cheeks a little, glancing round to see they were not overheard. Seeing this, Mr. Stevens retreated tactfully, leaving them alone.

'Fraser,' Quarry said at last. 'One James Fraser. Well, well.' Quarry had preceded Grey as governor of Ardsmuir Prison, and knew Jamie Fraser well – well enough to have kept him in irons. Quarry smoothed the edge of the paper, thinking.

'I suppose you were too young,' he said finally. 'And it wasn't a term one heard much during the Rising in '45. But there was – still is, I suppose – a certain amount of support for the Stuarts in Ireland. And for what the observation is worth, the younger Irish nobles who followed the Old Pretender – they called themselves "wild geese."' He glanced up, quizzical. 'Are you by any chance in search of an Irish Jacobite, Grey?'

Grey blinked, taken aback.

'To tell you the truth, Harry, I haven't the slightest idea,' he said. 'Perhaps I am.'

He plucked Symington's ring out of the mess and handed it to Quarry.

'Will you see Symington gets this back when he returns?'

'Certainly,' Quarry said, frowning at him. 'But why not give it to him yourself?'

'I don't know quite where I might be then, Harry. Perhaps in Ireland – chasing a wild goose.' Grey shoveled the rest of his rubbish back into his pocket and smiled at Quarry. 'Thank you, Harry. Enjoy your cigar.'

Chapter 33

Leaving Party

The district near St. Giles was known as the Rookery, and for good reason. Rooks could not be half so filthy, nor so noisy, as the poor Irish of London; the narrow lanes rang with curses, shrieks, and church bells, and Tom Byrd drove with one hand on the reins and the other on the pistol in his belt.

As the horse clopped into Banbridge Street, Grey leaned down from the wagon, a shilling in his hand. The glint of the metal drew a ragged boy from a doorway as though he were magnetized.

'Your honor?' The boy couldn't decide where to stare – at the coin, at Grey, or at the contents of the wagon.

'Rafe and Mick O'Higgins,' Grey said. 'You know them?'

'Everybody does.'

'Good. I've something that belongs to them. Can you take me to them?'

The boy's hand shot out for the coin, but he had decided where his attention properly lay; his gaze was rapt, riveted to the wagon.

'Aye, your honor. They'll be at Kitty O'Donnell's wake just now, I'd say. Near the end of O'Grady Street. But you'll not get by this way,' he added, tearing his attention briefly from the wagon. 'You'll need to back up and go round by Filley Lane, that's quickest.'

'You'll take us?' Grey had another coin ready, but the boy was up on the seat beside him before he could offer it, neck craned round to look at the automaton.

Grey had paused just on the edge of St. Giles, and there removed both the discreet canvas that had covered the object on the drive through London, and also the upper cabinet, so the brilliantly colored figurine was now clearly visible, riding like an emperor in the bed of the wagon, its arms moving stiffly and its trunk rotating to the occasional whir of clockwork.

Tom Byrd, who had the reins, gave their guide a narrow look and muttered something under his breath, but clucked to the horse and guided the equipage carefully through the refuse-choked streets. Grey and the guide were both obliged to get down every so often and move some object – crushed barrels, a heap of spoilt cabbage, and on one notable occasion, a recently deceased pig – out of the way, but the distance was not great, and within half an hour, they had reached their destination.

'In there?' Grey looked dubiously at the building, which gave every evidence of being about to collapse. Structural integrity quite aside, it looked like a place that no one concerned with his personal safety would enter. Soot black faces peeped from the alley, loungers on the street drew casually upright, hands in pockets, and the doorless entry yawned black and lightless as the doorway to hell.

Somewhere above, inside the house, a tin whistle played something whining and lugubrious.

Grey drew breath to ask whether the boy might go inside and fetch out the O'Higgins brothers, but the sound of a door opening came from somewhere inside, and a sudden draft whooshed out of the entrance, wafting a stench that caught in his throat and made him gag.

'Bloody hell!' Tom Byrd exclaimed. He snatched a kerchief from his sleeve and clapped it to his nose. 'What's *that*?'

'Something dead,' Grey said, trying not to breathe. 'Or someone. And a long time dead, at that.'

'Kitty O'Donnell,' their guide said, matter-of-fact. 'Told ye 'twas a wake, didn't I?'

'You did,' Grey agreed, and groped in his purse, breathing shallowly through his mouth. 'I believe it is customary to contribute something to the, er, refreshment of the attendees?'

To his surprise, the boy hesitated.

'Well, so it is, sir, to be sure. Only that . . . well, d'ye see, it's old Ma O'Donnell.'

'The dead woman?'

'No, her mother, it would be.'

It was indeed the custom to offer gin at least to the mourners who came to wake the dead, the boy explained, and sure, it was kindly taken if the mourners then might subscribe a few pennies toward the burial. But Kitty O'Donnell had been popular, and so many folk came and such a fine time was had in the singing and telling of tales that the gin was all drunk and more sent for, and by the end of it, all the subscription money had been spent, and not a penny left for the shroud.

'So she did it again,' the boy said, with a shrug.

'Did what – held *another* wake?'

'Aye, sir. Folk thought a great deal o' Kitty. And there were folk who'd not heard in time to come before, and so . . .' He glanced reluctantly toward the open doorway. Someone had shut the inner door, and the stink had decreased, though it was still noticeable, even over the multifarious odors of the Rookery.

'How long's that corpse been a-lying there, then?' Tom demanded through his handkerchief.

'Best part of two weeks,' the boy said. 'She's taken up six subscriptions, Old Ma has; stayed drunk as a captain's parrot the whole time. The folk what live downstairs are fed to the back teeth see' – he nodded toward the windowless building – 'but when they tried to complain, the mourners what hadn't had anything yet put them out. So Rose Behan – it's her what lives downstairs, with her six kids – she went to Rafe and Mick, to ask could they see about it. So I'm thinking, sir – not to discourage yer honor from a kindly thought – as might be ye should wait?'

'It might be that I should,' Grey murmured. 'How long—'

The inner door was flung open again with some violence – he heard the bang, and the miasma thickened, so dense a smell as to be nearly visible. There was a thumping noise, as some heavy body rolled downstairs, and the tin whistle ceased abruptly. Noises of argument and the trampling of feet, and a few moments later, an elderly man, much the worse for drink, emerged backward from the building, staggering and mumbling.

He clutched the ankles of a fat, blowzy woman, whom he was dragging, very slowly, over the threshold. The woman was either dead herself or simply dead drunk; it made little difference, so far as Grey could see. Her head bumped over the cobbles, matted gray hair straggling from her cap, and her tattered skirts were dragged up round her raddled thighs; the prospect so exposed was enough to make him avert his eyes, from respect for his own modesty, as much as hers.

This small procession was followed by one of the O'Higgins brothers, who poked his head out of the doorway, frowning.

'Now, then, Paulie, you take the auld bitch home to your wife, and see she don't come out again 'til poor Kitty's put away decent, will ye now?'

The old gent shook his head doubtfully, muttering toothlessly to himself, but continued his laborious progress, making his way down the lane, his companion's ample bottom scraping a wide furrow in the layers of dead leaves, dog turds, and bits of fireplace ash as they went.

'Should someone not assist him?' Grey inquired, watching this. 'She seems rather heavy.'

'Ah, no, God save ye, sir,' O'Higgins said, seeming to notice him for the first time. 'She ain't heavy; she's his sister.' The man's eye passed over the wagon and its content with elaborate casualness.

'And what might bring your honor to O'Grady Street, I wonder?'

Grey coughed, and put away his handkerchief.

'I have a proposition, Mr. O'Higgins, that may be to our mutual advantage. If there is a slightly more salubrious place where we could talk?'

With Tom left sitting in the wagon, pistol at the ready, Grey followed the O'Higginses to a squalid ordinary, where the force of their presences promptly cleared a small back room. Grey was interested to note this; evidently his assessment of the O'Higginses' influence in St. Giles had not been mistaken.

He still could not tell one from the other with any certainty, but supposed it didn't matter. Rafe was the elder; he supposed the one who was doing most of the talking must be he. Both of them listened avidly, though, making no more than token objections to his proposition.

'Jack Flynn's leaving party?' Rafe – he supposed it was Rafe – said, and laughed. 'Sure, and that will be the grand affair. Rumor has it that he left all his proceeds with his dolly, with orders to spend every farthing of it on drink.'

'There will be a great many people there, then, you think?' Jack Flynn was a notorious highwayman, due to be hanged at Tyburn in two days' time. Like many well-known thieves, he was expected to have a large 'leaving party' at Newgate, with dozens – sometimes hundreds – of friends and well-wishers flooding into the prison to bid him a proper farewell and see him in style to his execution.

'Oh, indeed,' Mick – if it was Mick – agreed, nodding. 'Be a tremenjous crowd; Flynn's well liked.'

'Excellent. And there would be no difficulty in taking your automaton in, to provide entertainment at the party? Perhaps with a few companions to help carry it? One of whom might be visibly the worse for drink?'

Four Irish eyes sparkled with the thought. A fortune-telling automaton would be the greatest and most profitable attraction, particularly at a highwayman's send-off.

'Nothing easier, sir,' they assured him with one voice.

Kitty O'Donnell's wake had in fact suggested a refinement to his original plan. To begin with, he had thought of using the automaton's cabinet, the clockwork removed and left behind in the prison. But if a body could be procured . . .

'It will need to be fresh, mind, and of roughly a similar appearance,' Grey said, a little dubiously. 'But I don't want you to kill anyone,' he added hastily.

'Not the slightest difficulty there, your honor,' one of the O'Higginses assured him. 'A quick word in the priest's ear, and we'll have what's needed. Father Jim knows every corpus what drops in the Rookery. And it's not as though we mean any disrespect to the corpus,' he added piously. 'It will get decent burial, won't it?'

'The best funeral money can buy,' Grey assured him. It would be an Anglican funeral, but he supposed that would be all right. It was far from unusual for prisoners to be found dead in Newgate. And neither Newgate officials nor the military, he thought, would be eager to raise questions: the former not wishing to admit they had lost a prisoner, the latter only too glad to be rid of a troublesome nuisance before trial and scandal overtook them.

The O'Higginses exchanged glances, shrugged, and seemed satisfied, though Rafe did offer one last caution.

'Your honor does realize, don't ye, that a felon what escapes prison and is caught is promptly hanged, no matter what it was he was jugged for in the first place?'

'Yes, Mr. O'Higgins. As are those found to have conspired in his escape. *All* those found to have so conspired.'

The guards would almost certainly realize the deception, but with a choice between raising a hue and cry, during which their own dereliction would become obvious, and quietly listing one Percival Wainwright as having died of gaol fever . . . Hal wasn't a betting man, but Grey was, and a long way past reckoning the odds regarding this particular endeavor.

A gap-toothed grin split the Irishman's stubbled face.

'Oh, well, then, sir. So long as we're clear. Will your honor come along to see the fun?'

'I—' He stopped dead. He had not thought of the possibility. He could. Unshaven, dressed in filthy homespun, in the midst of a gang of Irish roisterers, he could pass into the prison undetected. Could be one of those who transferred the body into Percy's cell, saw him change clothes with the corpse. One of those who, arms about his warm and living body, carried Percy out in the same guise of drunkenness, and saw him laid in the coffin in which, disguised as a deceased relative of the O'Higgins brothers, he would be carried to Ireland and Susannah Tomlinson, while the nameless corpse was hastily buried.

For an instant, the desire to see Percy one more

time, to touch him, blazed through his body like a liquid flame. He drew breath, and let the flame go out.

'Better not,' he said, with real regret, and handed over a small fat purse. 'Godspeed, Mr. O'Higgins.'

Chapter 34

Duchess of Pardloe

After the private – but well-appointed – funeral of Percival [sic] Wainwright, Grey found himself at loose ends. Not yet healed enough to return to duty, but too healthy to be confined to bed, he found himself at once depressed and restless, unable to settle to anything. The family, sympathetic but relieved, left him largely to himself.

On the morning of October 13, he stood in the back garden of his brother's house, moodily flipping bits of bread into the fishpond, and trying to feel grateful that he was not standing before a court-martial.

He became belatedly aware that Tom Byrd was standing beside him, and had been there for some time.

'What?' he said, depressed spirits making him abrupt.

'It's some of them Irish, me lord,' Tom said, his tone making it clear that he spoke for the household, and the household did not approve.

'Which Irish?'

'Tinkers, me lord. But they insist as how you

know them?' The rising inflection of this statement suggested the gross improbability of its being the truth.

'Oh, his honor's well-acquainted with us, sure.'

Tom jerked round at this, offended at discovering two ragged, unshaven presences just behind him, grinning.

'Tinkers, is it?' one of them said, nudging Tom Byrd with a familiar elbow as he passed. 'And who died and made you Pope, boyo?'

'Mr. O'Higgins. And Mr. O'Higgins.' Grey felt an unaccustomed and involuntary smile come to his face, despite his surprise. He had never expected to see them again.

'The same, your honor.' One – Rafe? – bowed respectfully. 'Begging your pardon, sir, for the slight overstayin' of our leave. We'd a few family matters of urgency to be settled. I'm sure your lordship's known the like.'

Grey noticed that Mick – if that *was* Mick – had a heavily bandaged arm, the bandage fairly fresh but stained with blood.

'An accident?' he inquired. The O'Higginses exchanged looks.

'Dog bite,' Mick said blandly, putting his injured hand in his pocket. 'But the anguish has passed, your honor. We come to report for duty, see, all fit.'

Meaning, Grey supposed, that Ireland was at present too hot to hold them, and they proposed to take refuge in the army. Again.

'Have you indeed?' he asked dryly.

'Aye, sir. Having safely delivered your message to the lady – which she give us a missive to hand to you upon our return.' The Irishman groped in his coat with his uninjured hand, but failed to find what he was looking for. 'You got it, Rafe?'

'O' course not, clumsy. You had it.'

'No, I never. Now I think, *you* had it last.'

'God damn yer eyes for a bloody liar, I didn't!'

Grey rolled his own eyes briefly and nodded to Tom, who reached into his pocket and, with a long-suffering air, produced a handful of coins.

The letter being now miraculously discovered, the O'Higginses gracefully accepted a further generous reward for their service – with many disclaimers of reluctance and unworthiness – and were dismissed to report to Captain Wilmot at the barracks. Grey was sure Wilmot would be overjoyed at their reappearance.

He sent Tom to be sure the O'Higginses actually departed the house, unaccompanied by silverware or valuable small objects, and, alone, took out the letter.

It was addressed simply, *Major John Grey*, in an unfamiliar hand, without additional direction. Despite himself, his heart beat faster, and he could not have sworn on the Bible whether it was dread or hope that made it do so.

He slid a thumb under the flap, noting that it had been sealed but the seal was missing; only a reddish smear from the wax remained. Only to be expected – though he was certain that if pressed on the matter, the O'Higginses would claim virtuously that the letter had been given them in that condition.

There were several pages; the first held a brief note:

> If you are reading this, Major, you have fulfilled both my requests, and you have my thanks. You do, I think, deserve something more, and here it is. Whether and how you make use of it is up to you; I shan't care anymore.
>
> Your most obt. servant,
Michael Bates, Captain, Horse Guards

His first emotion was relief, mingled with disappointment. Relief, however, was uppermost, followed quickly by curiosity.

He turned to the next page. The name of Bernard Adams leapt out of the paper, and Grey sank slowly into his chair as he read.

> I make this statement as a condemned man, knowing that I shall soon die, and speaking therefore the truth, as I swear upon my hope in God.
>
> I first met with Mr. Adams at a party at Lord Joffrey's house, upon the 8th of April last year. Mr. and Mrs. T were also there, and Mrs. T spent some time in conversation with me alone. Upon her retiring for a moment, Adams came up to me and said without preamble that she was a handsome woman, but no doubt expensive. If I cared to hear

of a way of making some money, I should call upon
him at his home upon the Tuesday next.

    My curiosity was roused, and so I did. Taking
me into his private library, he shocked me by
producing a sheaf of notes, signed by me in promise
of payment of various gambling debts, some very
large. He produced also certain correspondence,
written to me by Mrs. T, *and of a nature which*
made the relations between us more than clear.
These would have ruined both of us, if made public.

    I perceiving that Mr. Adams had me in an
invidious position, I inquired what use he might
have in mind to make of me.

The note then detailed Adams's enrollment of
Captain Bates in a scheme involving the abstraction
and transfer of a number of documents. The names
of Ffoulkes, Otway, and Jeffords were mentioned;
others were involved, Bates believed, but he did not
know their names. Ffoulkes had been drawn into
the conspiracy by the offer of money, Bates
believed; Otway and Jeffords by the threat of
exposure.

Bates had stolen various documents from several
offices in Whitehall; he was well known there and
his presence passed without remark. He had given
these documents to Adams, who, he presumed, was
collecting information from his other cat's-paws, as
well.

The attack upon Adams was a sham; the plan
had been for Bates to meet him privately by the

river near Lambeth, where Adams would pass over a small chest containing all the documents. A boat would be waiting. Bates would create the signs of a struggle, wound Adams slightly for the sake of conviction, and then go aboard the boat, which would carry him to France, where he would deliver these documents to Mrs. Ffoulkes's brother. The chest would contain not only the official documents but also the evidence of Bates's gambling debts, Mrs. Tomlinson's letters, and a sum of money. Once safely in France, he might destroy the former, send for Mrs. Tomlinson, and live in peace.

> *Adams had told me that Otway and Jeffords were to burgle his house for the look of the thing, then make themselves scarce, but that he would keep hold of the documents himself until they were given me. I learned later from Otway that Adams had men in hiding, who sprang upon him and Jeffords the moment they had entered the house. Meanwhile, he proceeded to our rendezvous, where other men of his employ were already waiting.*
>
> *These emerged as soon as I had done my part of wounding Mr. Adams slightly, scratching his arm with a knife as agreed upon, and seized me.*
>
> *I do not know what became of the documents themselves. Adams had with him a small chest, but this was knocked over in the struggle and proved to be empty. You will know what followed.*

The statement ended abruptly.

This was signed by Captain Michael Bates, his signature witnessed by the governor of Newgate, and – a final touch of Bates's sardonic humor – one Ezekial Poundstone, hangman.

Grey folded the sheets carefully together. It was a brief, clear statement, but possessed of a sufficiency of detail – names, dates, places – and the nature of some of the documents Bates had removed at Adams's behest.

He stood looking into the pond for some time, quite unaware of where he was or what he was looking at.

Plainly, Adams's plan had been to have Bates, Otway, and Jeffords blamed for the theft. He could not have expected what had actually happened – that the theft would be hushed up, the conspirators condemned for unnatural vice rather than theft and treason – these being, of course, quite natural vices.

What had been Ffoulkes's part in the matter? Presumably, to conduct the negotiations with France, using his wife's relatives as the go-between with Louis's spymasters. But when had Ffoulkes shot himself? It seemed so long ago, and Grey's memory of anything further back than yesterday was still undependable. He did recall one thing, though, and going hastily into the house entered the library and rummaged through the drawer into which he was inclined to decant miscellaneous papers, until he emerged with a smeared and worn-edged broadsheet, the faint smell of coffee still in its creases.

He hastily unfolded Bates's statement to check a date. No, Ffoulkes had shot himself a few days before the arrest of Bates, Otway, and Jeffords.

The theft would have been discovered very shortly; Adams could not delay in executing the part of his crime designed to shield himself from blame. But what of the other part? The delivery of the stolen material to France? With Ffoulkes dead, that pathway might be closed.

He folded the letter again, and thrust it into his pocket. These were all questions that could wait. The important thing was that he now had a tool that might be used to open up Bernard Adams like a keg of salt herring. Someone in authority would need to see this letter – but not just yet.

'Nordman!' he called, going to the hallway. 'Call the coach, please – I'm going out.'

Bernard Adams's house was not grand, but it was elegant; an Inigo Jones jewel, set in its own small private wood. Grey was not of a mind to admire the scenery, but did observe a small stone building, a little way from the house, whose ornaments showed it clearly to have been originally a Catholic chapel. Adams was not Catholic, though – could not have held such positions in the government as he had, if he were.

Not openly Catholic.

'An Irish Jacobite,' Grey murmured to himself, appalled. 'Jesus.' Positions in the government. Adams's rise to power had begun with his appointment as secretary to Robert Walpole – and Grey saw, as clearly as though the scene was taking place before him on the drive, the picture of the tall, ailing prime minister, leaning heavily on his secretary – his Irish secretary – coming down the path to visit the widow of the late Duke of Pardloe.

Clenching his jaw so hard that his teeth creaked, he bounded up the steps and pounded on the door.

'Sir?' The butler was an Irishman; so much was obvious from the one word.

'Your master. I wish to see him.'

'Ah. I'm sorry, sir, the master's gone out.'

Grey seized the man by one shoulder and thrust him backward, stepping into the house.

'Sir!'

'Where is he?'

The butler glanced wildly round for assistance, and looked as though he was about to shout for help.

'Tell me where he is, and I'll go. Otherwise . . . I shall be obliged to look for him.' Grey had worn his sword; he put a hand on the hilt.

The butler gasped.

'He – he has gone to meet the Duchess of Pardloe.'

'He – *what*?' Grey shook his head, convinced that he was hearing things, but the man repeated it, gaining confidence, as Grey seemed not about to run him through.

'The Duchess of Pardloe, sir. She sent a note this

morning – I was there when the master opened it, and, ah . . . happened to see.'

Grey nodded, narrowly keeping a grip on himself.

'Did you *happen* to see where the meeting was? And when?'

'In the Edgware Road, a house called "Morning Glory," four o'clock,' the butler blurted.

Without a word, Grey let go of his sword and left. He felt dazed and off balance, as though someone had suddenly pulled a carpet out from under him.

It couldn't be – but it couldn't *not* be. No one but his mother would use that title. And to use it to Adams was a direct challenge. It must be her. But how had she got back to London, and what in God's *name* did she think she was doing?

Gripped by fear, he ran down the drive toward the street where he had left his carriage waiting. Morning Glory. He knew the house; it was a small, elegant house belonging to the Walpole family. What . . . ?

'Edgware Road!' he shouted to the coachman, ducking inside. 'And hurry!'

Morning Glory looked deserted. The shutters were closed, the fountain in the front court dry, the court itself unswept, carpeted with dead leaves. It had the look of a house whose family had gone away to the country, leaving the furniture under sheets, the servants paid off.

Neither was there any sign of a coach, a horse, or

any living person. Grey mounted the stoop softly, and stood for a moment, listening. The place was still, save the cawing of rooks in the bare-limbed trees in the garden.

He took hold of the doorknob; it turned in his hand. Slowly letting out the breath he had been holding, he opened the door and stepped warily inside.

The furniture *was* under sheets, he saw. He paused, listening. No voices. No sound, save his own breathing. He knew the house, had been here now and then, at musicales – the present Earl of Orford's wife sang, or thought she could.

The doors off the foyer stood open – all but one. That one led, he thought, to the library. He put a hand on his sword hilt, but decided against drawing it. Adams was a slight man, and twenty years Grey's senior; he wouldn't need it.

He set his hand on the doorknob; it was white china, painted with roses, and a pang went through him at the cool slick touch of it on his hand, but there was no time now to think of such things. He eased the door gently open – and came face to face with the barrel of a pistol, pointed directly at him.

He flung himself to the side, seizing a chair, which he narrowly stopped himself from throwing at the person holding the gun.

'Jesus!' he said. He stood frozen for an instant, then, quivering in every limb, set the chair slowly down and collapsed onto it.

'What the devil are you doing here?' his mother demanded, lowering the pistol.

'I might ask you the same thing, madam.' His heart was pounding in his chest, sending small jolts of pain down his left arm with every beat, and he had broken out in a cold sweat.

'It is a private affair,' she said fiercely. 'Will you bloody leave?'

He paid no attention to her unaccustomed language.

'I will not. What were you intending? To shoot Mr. Adams on sight? Is that thing loaded?'

'Of course it is loaded,' she said in exasperation, 'and if I'd meant to shoot him on sight, you'd be dead at the moment. Will you go away!'

'No,' he said briefly, and rising, reached for the gun. 'Give me that.'

She took two steps back, holding the gun – which was not only loaded and primed, but cocked, he saw – protectively against her breast.

'John, I wish you to leave,' she said, as calmly as she could, though he saw the pulse beat fast in the hollow of her throat, and the slight shaking of her hands. 'You *must* go, and now. I will tell you everything, I swear it. But not *now*.'

'He isn't coming.' That much had dawned on him. It was nearly half past four – he had heard the bells strike, just before his arrival. If Adams had meant to come, he would be here. The fact that he was not . . .

She stared at him, uncomprehending.

'Adams,' he repeated. 'It *is* Bernard Adams who killed Father?'

Her face drained of all color, and she sat down, quite suddenly, on a sofa. Her eyes closed, as though she could not keep them open.

'What have you done, John?' she whispered. 'What do you know?'

He came and sat down beside her, removing the pistol from her hand, gone limp and unresisting.

'I know that Father was murdered,' he said gently. 'I've known since the morning you found him. I was there, hiding in the conservatory.'

Her eyes sprang open in shock, the same light blue as his own. He laid his free hand over hers, squeezing gently.

'When did you come back?' he asked. 'Does Sir George know?'

She shook her head blindly. 'I – three days ago. I told him I wanted to be in London for the marriage of a friend. He will come back himself in a month; he made no objection.'

'He will probably have objections, should he come back to find you dead or arrested.'

He breathed, feeling his heart begin to slow.

'You should have told us,' he said. 'Hal and me.'

'No.' She shook her head, closing her eyes again. 'No! He would never have let it rest. You know what Hal is like.'

'Yes, I do,' Grey said, smiling despite himself. 'He's just like you, Mother. And me.'

Trembling, she bent her head, and buried her face in her hands. A constant fine tremor was running through her, like the shifting of sand beneath one's feet as the tide goes out, *terra firma* melting away.

'I have lost a husband,' she said softly, to her feet. 'I would not lose my sons.' Lifting her head, she gave him a quick, desperate glance.

'Do you think I know nothing about men? About you and your brother in particular? Or about the general?'

'What do you mean?'

She made a small sound that might have been a laugh or a sob.

'Do you mean to tell me that I might have told you this – any of you – and expected you *not* to go straight out in pursuit of the matter, regardless of the threat?'

'Well, of course not.' He stared at her in incomprehension. 'What else could we do?'

She drew a trembling hand down her face, and turned to the wall, where an ornamental looking glass hung.

'Would it be better if I'd had daughters?' she asked the mirror, in apparent earnestness.

'No,' she answered herself. 'They'd only marry men, and there you are.'

She closed her eyes for a moment, plainly collecting herself, then opened them and turned to him, composed.

'If I'd known who it was,' she said firmly, 'I would have told Hal. At least,' she amended, 'I would have told him once I'd decided how best to deal with the matter. But I didn't know. And for him – or later, you – to go charging into danger, with no clear notion where the danger lay, nor how widespread the threat might be? No. No, I wasn't having that.'

'You may have a point,' he admitted reluctantly, and she gave a small snort.

'But you did find out.' It occurred to him, with a sense of awe, that she had never been reconciled to the duke's death – that she had been waiting, patiently watching, all this time, for an opportunity to discover and destroy the man who had killed him. 'How did you discover Mr. Adams's name?'

'I blackmailed Gilbert Rigby.'

Grey felt his mouth fall open, and swiftly closed it.

'What? How?'

The ghost of a smile crossed her lips.

'Captain Rigby – I suppose I must call him "Dr. Rigby" now – gambles. He always did, and I kept an eye upon him. I knew he had run through most of his family's fortune, when he sold the town house his father left him, last year. He's using some of the funds donated for the Foundling Hospital now. And so I asked Harry Quarry to make inquiries, very quietly – and to buy up his debts.' She reached toward a leather case that lay on the table beside the sofa, and flipped open the cover, to show a sheaf of papers. 'I showed him them, and told him I would expose him if he did not tell me who had killed Gerard.'

What had he told Dr. Longstreet? *Had she known*

which man it was, she would have killed him, I assure you.

Grey felt shock, but no particular surprise.

'And he did.'

'I think it was a relief to him,' she said, sounding faintly surprised. 'Gilbert is not a bad man, you know – only weak. He could not bring himself to tell the truth at the time; that would have cost him everything. But he was sincerely appalled at what had happened – he said that he did not know for certain that Bernard Adams had killed Gerry, and had managed to keep his conscience dormant all this time by telling himself that Gerry must have committed self-murder. But faced with the truth – and with those—' she cast a sardonic eye toward the leather case, 'he admitted it. He still has something to be lost, after all.'

'And you don't?' Grey asked, piqued at the thought of her planning to face Adams by herself.

She eyed him, one brow raised.

'A great deal to lose,' she said evenly. 'But I am a gambler, too – and I have a great deal of patience.'

He picked the pistol up, and carefully uncocked it.

'Did you calculate the odds of being caught?' he asked. 'Even if you could prove that Adams killed Father – and Gilbert Rigby's admission is far from proof – you'd very likely be hanged for murder. And what would Sir George think of that?'

She looked surprised.

'What? What do you think I am?'

'You don't want me to answer that, Mother.

What do you mean?'

'I mean I didn't intend to kill him,' she said indignantly. 'What good would that do? Beyond the minor gratification of revenge, what would I want with his miserable little life?' she added bitterly.

'No. I meant to make him confess the crime' – she nodded toward the table, and Grey saw that besides the leather case containing Rigby's debts, there was a portable writing desk, as well – 'and then let him go. He could leave the country if he liked; he would be exposed, he would lose everything that mattered to him – and I could give Gerry back his honor.'

Her voice trembled on the last word, and Grey brought her hand on impulse to his lips.

'I'll see it done,' he whispered. 'I swear it.'

Tears were running down her face, but she took a deep breath and held her voice steady.

'Where is he? Adams?'

'Running, I think.' He told her what Adams's butler had said. 'As he hasn't come, he probably supposes that you *do* have proof. And there's this—' He fumbled in his pocket, turning out the usual assortment of trifles, among which was Captain Bates's postmortem denunciation.

She read it in silence, then turned back to the first page and read it again.

'So he's gone,' she said flatly, laying the papers on her knee. 'Taken the money and fled to France. I frightened him, and he's gone.'

'He hasn't left the country yet,' Grey said, trying to sound encouraging. 'And even if he should escape – plainly he *has* lost his position, his reputation. And you did say you don't want his life.'

'I don't,' she said, between clenched teeth. 'But this' – she smacked the papers with the back of her hand, sending them to the floor – 'is useless to me. I don't care that the world knows Bernard Adams for a criminal and traitor – I want him to be known as my husband's murderer; I want your father's honor back!'

Grey bent to pick up the papers from the floor, and rising, tucked them back into his pocket.

'All right,' he said, and took a deep breath. 'I'll find him.'

He hesitated for a moment, looking at his mother. She sat upright, straight as a musket barrel – but she looked very small, and suddenly her age showed in her face.

'Will I see you . . . home?' he asked, not sure where her home might be. The house in Jermyn Street had been closed; should he take her to Minnie's house? His heart sank at thought of the hubbub *that* would cause.

'No,' she said, obviously having thought the same thing. 'I have a carriage; I'll go to the general's house. You go.'

'Yes.' But he didn't go, not at once. Thoughts, fears, suppositions, half-baked plans were whirling through his head. 'If you should need . . . help . . . if I am not nearby—'

'I'll call on Harry Quarry,' his mother said firmly. 'Go, John.'

'Yes. Yes, that—' A sudden thought struck him. 'Does Quarry know? Everything?'

'Certainly not. He would have told Hal at once.'

'Then how did you induce him to . . .' He nodded at the leather case. To his surprise, his mother smiled.

'More blackmail,' she admitted. 'Harry writes erotic verses – very elegant, really. I told him that if he didn't do what I asked, I'd tell everyone in the regiment. It was all quite easy,' she said, with a certain degree of complacence. 'It is *possible* to deal with men. You just have to know how.'

Grey was so flabbergasted at the revelation of Harry Quarry's identity as the Sub-Genius that he barely noticed where he was going, and in consequence had walked a good quarter mile before remembering that he had left a coach waiting in a side street near Morning Glory. He turned back, hurrying, trying to think where to start in pursuit of Bernard Adams.

He thought it very likely that his mother was right; Adams was bound for France. That being so, though – would he take ship from the nearest port? Grey could quite possibly catch him up, if that were the case; he had no more than an hour's start, perhaps two. But what if he meant to travel overland, take ship from a more distant port, to confuse pursuit?

Was he expecting pursuit, though? He was presumably acting on the supposition that the duchess had proof of his actions, but it would take more than a day or two for her to make that proof – had it existed – known to anyone who might take action.

And if he did *not* expect pursuit – but he had left his house abruptly, without pausing to pack any personal belongings. That argued precipitate flight . . .

Caught up in these musings, and half-running in his anxiety, Grey mistook the side street where he had left his coach, became convinced that the coachman had become tired of waiting and left, realized his mistake, and went back. By the time he found the coach, he had sweated through his shirt, his arm was throbbing, and his chest had begun to burn. He seized the door of the coach, swung it open, and stepped in, then halted, startled to find someone already sitting inside.

'Here's hoping I find your honor well,' one of the O'Higgins brothers said politely. 'The devil of a time ye've been about your business, and you'll pardon my sayin' so.'

Grey sank onto the squabs, wiping a sleeve across his sweating forehead.

'What are you doing here?'

'Waitin' on yourself, to be sure.' He leaned out the window and called up to the coachman, 'On, me boy. Where I told you, and be quick, now!'

'And where is that?' Grey was recovering his breath and his wits, and eyed O'Higgins warily.

'The regimental offices, to be sure,' the Irishman said. 'That's where he'll be.'

'He?'

O'Higgins rolled his eyes.

'Bernard Adams. A poor excuse for an Irishman, and him a wicked apostate, too,' he added piously, crossing himself.

Grey relapsed against the cushions, realization dawning.

'You read Bates's letter.'

'Well, we did, then,' O'Higgins agreed, without shame. 'Proper shockin', it was.'

'Not nearly as shocking as you think,' Grey said dryly, beginning to collect himself. 'Why do you think Adams is at the regimental offices? And come to that, how do *you* come to be here?'

'Oh, I follied your honor, when you left Adams's house,' the Irishman said, airily. 'My brother having gone after Mr. Adams, when *he* left, just afore you. Don't be fretting, sir, even if he's gone before we get there, Rafe will stick to him like a bur.'

'But why has he—'

'Well, the money, to be sure,' Mick said, as though this were obvious. 'He hid it in our fortune-teller's cabinet. And he's gone to your brother's office for to get it back – not realizin' that it's gone.' The Irishman grinned cheerfully. 'We thought the least we could do to show our gratitude to your honor was lead ye to him.'

Grey stared at him, barely noticing the tooth-rattling bump of the carriage over rough cobbles as they hurtled through the streets.

'You found it. The money.' Something else occurred to him. 'Was there anything else there – papers?'

'Oh, there were some moldy bits of trash wedged beneath the clockwork, to be sure; we burnt them,' O'Higgins said comfortably. 'As to having found any money, I couldn't say as to that, sir. But I will say that, havin' had the chance to think it over, Rafe and me decided that perhaps the army don't suit us after all. We'll be for going back to Ireland, once this business here is done.'

The coach rattled round another corner and pulled to a stop, horses blowing, at the corner of Cavendish Square. It was late in the day; the regimental offices would be deserted. Which was, of course, what Adams had waited for, Grey realized.

Tossing money up to the coachman, he turned toward the building, to see a slouching figure detach itself from a patch of evening shadow and come toward him.

'Is he inside, then?' Mick asked, and Rafe nodded.

'Just gone in, not five minutes ago.' He glanced at Grey, then up at the building's facade.

'No need to call the guard, I think,' he said. 'Should your honor care to deal with the matter man to man? We'll see he don't get out, Mick and me.' He lounged against the doorjamb, looking most unsoldierly, but thoroughly competent, with a hand on his shillelagh.

'I – yes,' Grey said abruptly. 'Thank you.'

The door was unlocked; he went in and stopped, listening. Sweat trickled down the back of his neck, and emptiness murmured in his ears.

All the doors in the ground-floor corridor were closed. Hal's office was upstairs. Almost by reflex, Grey drew his sword, the whisper of metal against the scabbard cold in the silence.

He made no effort to mute his own footsteps. It didn't matter if Adams heard him coming.

The corridor upstairs was empty, too, lit only by the fading light that came through the casement at the end. A sliver of light showed to the right, though; Hal's door was open.

What ought he to feel? he wondered, as he walked along the hall, bootheels steady as a heartbeat on the floor. He had felt too much, for too long. Now he felt nothing, save the need to continue.

Adams had heard him; he was standing by the desk, his sallow face tense. It relaxed as he recognized Grey, and put out a hand to the desk, to steady himself.

'Oh, Lord John,' he said. 'It's you. I was just looking for—'

'I know what you were looking for,' Grey interrupted. 'It doesn't matter.'

Adams's eyes turned wary on the instant.

'I fear you have mistaken me, sir,' he began, and Grey raised the point of his rapier and pressed it to the man's chest.

'No, I haven't.' His own voice came oddly to his ears, detached and calm. 'You killed my father, and I know it.'

The man's eyes went huge, but with panic, not surprise.

'What? You – but, but this is nonsense!' He backed away hastily, hands batting at the blade. 'Really, sir, I must protest! Who would tell you such a – such a taradiddle?'

'My mother,' Grey said.

Adams went white, pushed the blade aside, and ran. Taken by surprise, Grey went after him, to see him running full-tilt down the corridor – at the end of which stood the burly figure of Rafe O'Higgins, shillelagh at the ready.

Grey followed, fast, and Adams whirled, jerking at the knob of the nearest door, which was locked. Adams's face went tight as Grey approached, and he pressed himself back into the doorframe, hands against the wood.

'You can't kill me!' he said, voice shrill with fear. 'I'm not armed.'

'Neither was the cockroach I stamped on in my quarters last night.'

Adams stood his ground for an instant longer, but as Grey drew within lunging distance, his nerve broke and he dodged away, rushed back past Grey, running for his life.

There was nowhere for him to go. The corridor stretched ahead of him, a long dim tunnel, lit only by the rainy twilight of the tall window at the end—

a window that opened on thirty feet of empty space. Adams beat upon the locked doors as he passed, shrieking for help, but no one answered; the doors were locked. It was the stuff of nightmare, and Grey wondered briefly whether the nightmare was his, or Adams's.

He hadn't the strength to run himself, and there was no need. His chest pulsed with each heartbeat, and he could hear each single breath echo in his ears. He walked slowly down the corridor, placing one foot in front of the other. The hilt of the sword was slippery in his hand. He found himself drifting to one side or the other, so that his shoulder brushed the wall now and then.

The door just beyond Hal's office opened, and a curious head poked out. Mr. Beasley, Hal's clerk. Adams saw him and rushed toward him.

'Help! Help me! He's mad, he's going to kill me!'

Mr. Beasley pushed his spectacles up his nose, took one look at Grey, lurching drunkenly down the corridor with a sword in his hand, and popped into Hal's office like a mole into its hole. He slammed the door, but was not able to lock it before Adams threw his weight against it.

Both men fell into the office in a tangle of limbs, and Grey hurried as fast as he was able, arriving in time to see Mr. Beasley lurch to the desk, hampered by Adams, who was clawing at his leg. The elderly clerk, now missing both spectacles and wig, snatched a letter opener from the clutter, and with a look of profound indignation, stabbed Adams in the hand with it.

Adams bellowed with pain and let go, rolling up into a ball like a hedgehog. Mr. Beasley, the light of battle in his eye, picked up Volume III of *Histoire de la Dernière Guerre de Bohème* in both hands and brought it down on Adams's head with some force.

Grey braced himself with one hand on the door-jamb, his feeling of being caught in an inescapable dream intensifying.

'Leave him to me, Mr. Beasley,' he said gently, seeing the old man, gasping for breath, looking wildly about for a fresh weapon. Mr. Beasley blinked, squinting blindly at him, but then nodded, and without another word, backed out into the hall, dived into his clerk's hole, and shut the door.

'Get up,' Grey said to Adams, who was trying to crawl under Hal's desk. 'Get up, I said! Or I'll run this straight up your cowardly arse, I swear it.' He prodded Adams in the buttock with the tip of his rapier by way of illustration, causing the minister to yelp in fright and bang his head on the underside of the desk.

Moaning and groveling, Adams backed out, and at Grey's peremptory gesture, rose to his feet.

'Don't.' He swallowed visibly and wiped a hand across his mouth. 'I beg you, sir. Don't take my life. It would be the gravest mistake, I assure you.'

'I don't want your fucking life. I want my father's good name back.'

Sweat was running down Adams's face, and his

wig had slid back on his head, showing a thin bristle of grizzled hairs beneath.

'And how do you propose to accomplish that?' he said, the news that Grey didn't mean to kill him seeming to embolden him.

Grey stepped in close and fast, seizing the man's neckcloth in his free hand and twisting. Adams went red in the face and clawed at him, kicking. One kick landed painfully on his shin, but he disregarded it. The neckcloth popped before Adams's eyes did, though, and Adams sank to his knees, clutching histrionically at his neck.

Grey tossed down his sword, and drew the dagger from its sheath. He sank down on one knee, face to face with Adams, and gripping him by the shoulder, placed the point of the knife just below one eye. He was past threats; with a short, soft jab, he thrust the tip of the dagger into Adams's eye and turned it.

He let go, hearing the thunk of the dagger as it fell to the floor, Adams's shriek as a distant sound, muffled as though it were underwater. Everything swam about him and he closed his eyes against the dizziness.

He had to struggle to stand up; it felt as though two hundredweight of sandbags rested on his shoulders. But he managed, and stood swaying, waves of hot and cold washing over him, the muscles of his breast on fire, his left arm a dead weight by his side.

Adams was curled into himself, both hands clasped to his eye, making a high, thin moaning noise that Grey found very irritating. Small drops of blood spattered the confusion of papers on Hal's desk.

'My eye, my eye! You have blinded me!'

'You have one left with which to write your confession,' Grey said. He was very tired. But summoning some last vestige of strength, he raised his voice and shouted, 'Mr. Beasley! I want you!'

Chapter 35

'I Do Renounce Them'

Reginald Holmes, head steward of White's Chocolate House, was spending a peaceful late evening in going over the members' accounts in his office. He had just rung the bell for a waiter to bring him another whisky to facilitate this task when the sounds of an ungodly rumpus reached him from the public rooms below, shouts, cheers, and the noise of overturning furniture causing him to upset the ink.

'What's going on *now*, for God's sake?' he asked crossly, mopping at the puddle with his handkerchief as one of the waiters appeared in his doorway. 'Do these men never sleep? Bring me a cloth, Bob, will you?'

'Yes, sir.' The waiter bowed respectfully. 'The Duke of Pardloe has arrived, sir, with his brother. The duke's respects, sir, and he would like you to come and witness the settling of a wager in the book.'

'The Duke of—' Holmes stood up, forgetting the ink on his sleeve. 'And he wants to settle a wager?'

'Yes, sir. His Grace is *very* drunk, sir,' the waiter

added delicately. 'And he's brought a number of friends in a similar condition.'

'Yes, I hear.' Holmes stood for a moment, considering. Disjoint strains of 'For He's a Jolly Good Fellow' reached him through the floor. He took up his accounts ledger and his quill, and turned to the page headed *Earl of Melton*. Drawing a neat line through this, he amended the heading to *Duke of Pardloe*, and with a flourish, inserted beneath it a new item reading, *Breakages*.

The singers had now reached the second verse and some semblance of unity.

'We won't go home until mor-ning,
We won't go home until mor-ning,
We won't go home until mor-ning,
'Til day-light doth appear!'

'Fetch up a cask of the '21 Santo Domingo,' Mr. Holmes instructed the waiter, writing busily. 'I'll put it on His Grace's account.'

It was with an aching head and dark circles beneath his eyes, but impeccably attired in blue-striped silk and cambric ruffles, that Lord John Grey took his place by the baptismal font at St. James's Church next day and received several yards of white satin and Mechlin lace, within which he was assured was his goddaughter, Lady Dorothea Jacqueline Benedicta Grey. Minnie had toyed with the notion of naming her daughter Prudence or Chastity, but Grey had dissuaded her, on the grounds that it was unfair to burden a child with such an onerous presumption of virtue.

The general, newly returned from the Indies, and Lady Stanley were there, standing close together, her hand upon his arm in a picture of the nicest marital affection. Grey smiled at his mother, who smiled back – and then stepped forward in alarm as the child wriggled in its wrappings and Grey momentarily lost his grip.

Snatching her granddaughter from destruction, Benedicta settled the christening robes more securely, and with a look of some reservation, handed the child back to her son.

Minnie, on the far side of the font, eyed him severely, but was occupied in restraining her own three sons, all of them decently silent, but wriggling like small satin-clad worms. Hal, beside her, appeared to have fallen asleep on his feet.

Mr. Gainsborough, the portrait artist who had been commissioned to commemorate the christening, skulked in the shadows, motioning to his assistant and squinting back and forth from his sketching pad to the scene before him. He caught Grey's eye and motioned to him to lift his chin and turn toward the light.

Grey coughed politely and turned instead toward the priest, who was speaking to him.

'Dost thou renounce the devil and all his works, the vain pomp and glory of the world, with all covetous desire of the same, and the carnal desires of the flesh, so that thou wilt not follow, nor be led of them?'

'I do renounce them.' Minnie's sister, the child's godmother, stood beside him, and murmured the words with him.

'Dost thou believe in God the Father Almighty, Maker of heaven and earth? And in Jesus Christ, His only-begotten son, our Lord? And that He was conceived by the Holy Ghost; born of the Virgin Mary; that He suffered under Pontius Pilate; was crucified, dead, and buried; that He went down into hell and also did rise again . . .'

Grey looked down into the sleeping face of innocence, and swore. He did not know if he might believe. But for her, he would try.

Following the christening, the family rattled home by coach to the Grey manor on the edge of Hyde Park. The trees were in their autumn glory, their falling leaves borne on the wind, and bits of red and gold and brown flew up in showers from the wheels as they passed.

Minnie and her sister went up to return the baby to her nurse, but the boys demanded food, and shedding their pumps, satin coats, and linen neck-cloths with abandon, besieged their father for nourishment.

'I want almond biscuits, Papa!'

'No, apple 'n' raisin pie!'

'Treacle tart, treacle tart!' piped Henry, raising a general cheer.

'Yes, yes, yes, yes,' Hal said, trying in vain to quell the riot. He put a hand to his head, which seemed somewhat the worse for wear. 'Come along, Cook will find us something, I daresay.'

He ushered his troops firmly before him, but then paused and looked back at Grey, hand on the baize door to the kitchen passageway.

'Will you do us the honor to share a dish of treacle tart for breakfast, my lord?' he asked politely.

'With all my heart,' John said, and grinned exceedingly. 'Your Grace.'

He handed his cloak to the footman and made to follow them, but was stopped by a glimpse of his own name. The early post had been left on the silver salver by the door, and a letter addressed to Lord John Grey lay on top. Frowning, he picked it up. Who would send a letter to him here?

He broke the seal and unfolded two sheets. The first was a drawing; a sketch of the Roman Forum. He recognized the view, from the top of the Capitoline Hill. The message on the second sheet was brief, written in a clear, round hand.

The seagulls on the Tiber call all night, and call your name.
'Ave!' they cry.
'Ave.'

There was no signature, of course.

'*Ave,*' Grey said softly, '*atque vale, frater meus.*' Hail – and farewell. And touching the corner of the note to the candle flame, held it until his fingers began to scorch, then dropped it on the salver, where it flared and burnt to ash. He put aside the drawing – to remember.

AUTHOR'S NOTES

'**Hogg house.**' When Lord John reflects that surely Geneva's body does not lie 'in some hogg house or desolate shed,' he is not considering that her family might have left her in a pig-sty. A 'hogg house' was a storage building for dried peat.

Homophobia. I am greatly indebted both to Norton Rictor (*Mother Clap's Molly-House*) and to Byrne Fone (*Homophobia: A History*) for insight into the perception and treatment of homosexuals in the mid-eighteenth century. Quotes in this book regarding the social and legal prosecution of 'sodomites' are taken from *Homophobia,* and are actual quotes from the newspapers and other periodicals of the period.

Horace Walpole was one of the best-known letter-writers of the early- to mid-eighteenth century, and his collected correspondence is as valuable to a student of that period as Samuel Pepys's diaries are to an earlier one. Fourth son of the formidable Robert Walpole (First Earl of Orford, who more or less invented the office of prime minister, though he himself refused to use that title), Horace was not political himself, but had great insight – expressed with wit and irony – into the social, military, and political processes of his *milieu.*

Prejudice. Speaking of phobias . . . historical attitudes in England toward the Irish, Scottish, etc. are rendered as they were (interpreted through writings of the period), rather than as modern political correctness might desire (e.g., descriptions of the Irish gathering 'like fleas' and other opprobrious remarks are taken from primary sources of the period, as quoted in M. Dorothy George's *London Life in the Eighteenth Century* and Liza Picard's *Dr. Johnson's London*).

A Note on Scots/Scotch/Scottish

So far as I know (judging from published material from the period), everybody in the British Isles (including the Scots), used 'Scotch' to refer to the people (as well as the whisky) up until about 1950. At which point, the SNP (Scottish Nationalist Party) got their feet under them and started in.

I'm sure you've noticed that one of the first things a political action group representing a minority does is to respecify the name of said group as a means of asserting independence – i.e., 'negroes' became either 'black' or 'African American,' 'Indians' became 'Native Americans,' etc. By the same token, the Scotch became 'Scots.' (In all justice, 'Scots' as a term referring to the people was certainly in use for centuries prior to that; however, 'Scotch,' 'Scotchman,' etc. were also acceptable and widely used; post-SNP, this was seen as deeply offensive.)

Just to be confusing, 'Scots' is also the term used (both historically and in modern times) for the Scottish dialect – or language as the case may be (again, with the political activism). I asked a friend – a well-known linguist and the dean of the college of Arts and Letters at a prominent university – what the position was on Scots in linguistic circles: Dialect of English, or distinct language? She (an Englishwoman) looked round to be sure we were not overheard (we were at a cocktail party, surrounded by wealthy alumni, none of them either Scottish or linguists), lowered her voice, and said, 'Well, if you're Scottish, then of *course* it's a separate language – and if you aren't, then plainly it's not.'

Anyway, 'Scotch' and its derivatives ('Scotchman,' 'Scotchwoman') were used by everybody – including Scottish people (I have a book of popular jokes and comic routines done by Sir Harry Lauder – a popular Scottish comedian of the '40s and '50s, which uses 'Scotch' as a designation of people throughout) up 'til about the mid-twentieth century. You still see such references in novels published later than that, but by about 1970, 'Scot,' 'Scots,' and 'Scottish' had become pretty much *de rigueur,* and 'Scotch' was now strictly limited to whisky and 3M's™ brand of transparent tape. In the eighteenth century, though, 'Scotchman' was still common usage.

The Seven Years' War

I made a conscious decision not to provide detailed explanations, maps, etc., regarding the political, military, and geographical nuances of the Seven Years' War. While this was a complex and fascinating conflict – it was, in many ways, the first 'world war,' being fought on several continents and involving virtually all the countries of Europe and their colonies – this isn't actually a book *about* the Seven Years' War; it's a book about a soldier.

Lord John Grey, Major in His Majesty's army, is a career soldier. He doesn't ask whether a particular cause is worth his labor or his life; he fights because it's his duty and his calling. Therefore, other than indicating theaters of military operation, and brief references to important battles or events, I've focused on the details of an English officer's daily life, rather than on the larger issues of the war.

For those military buffs interested in the Seven Years' War, there are masses of material available – far too much to cite even summarily here. For those who would enjoy a quick overview, though, allow me to recommend Osprey Publishing's *The Seven Years' War*, by Daniel Marston, part of their Essential Histories series (ISBN 1-84176-191-5, Osprey Publishing Ltd., London, 2001).

British regiments

Owing to the way in which British army regiments were named – i.e., in a generally sequential numbering system – I was obliged to appropriate an existing regimental number of approximately the right vintage for the Duke of Pardloe's fictional regiment. The real 46th Regiment of Foot was the Duke of Cornwall's regiment, also known as 'Cornwall's Light Infantry' and 'The Red Feathers.'

Uniform notes

There was a great deal of variation in uniform during the Seven Years' War, owing to the great number and variety of political entities participating. For example: While most people are accustomed nowadays to thinking of the British as 'redcoats,' and thus to assuming that all British uniforms *were* red, in fact, they were not. Soldiers of the Royal Artillery during this period wore blue uniforms, while – confusingly enough – the French artillery wore red.

Lord John and the Hand of Devils

Diana Gabaldon

A must-have for any Gabaldon fan, Lord John Grey's shorter adventures are collected here for the first time.

Lord John and the Hellfire Club

In Lord John's first appearance outside of the Jamie and Claire novels, he witnesses the murder of a young diplomat in the street. Vowing to avenge the death, he sets off on a trail that leads from the notorious Hellfire Club to the sinister dark caves beneath Medmenham Abbey.

Lord John and the Succubus

Grey's assignment as liaison to a Hanoverian regiment in Germany finds him caught between two threats: the advancing French and Austrian army, and the menace of a mysterious 'night-hag' who spreads fear and death among the troops.

Lord John and the Haunted Soldier

When Lord John is called to answer a Royal Commission of Enquiry's questions regarding a cannon that exploded at the battle of Krefeld, accusations ensue. Soon he finds himself knee-deep in a morass of gunpowder, treason, and plot – haunted by a dead lieutenant, and followed by a man with no face.

Century · London